About the Author

Grace Octavia is a n ...
of New York Universi...
English at Georgia St...
Delta Sigma Theta Sor...
member of the Sigma...
Honour Society. The f... *...olling Out*
Urbanstyle Weekly, she li... ...lanta, GA. She enjoys
international travel, hiking, cooking, and being with her
girlfriends. She currently teaches writing at Spelman
College.

Kandy Shepherd swapped a fast-paced career as a
magazine editor for a life writing romance. She lives
on a small farm in the Blue Mountains near Sydney,
Australia, with her husband, daughter, and a menagerie
of animal friends. Kandy believes in love at first sight
and real-life romance – they worked for her! Kandy
loves to hear from her readers. Visit her website at:
kandyshepherd.com

RITA® Award-winning author **Leah Ashton** never
expected to write books. She grew up reading
everything – from pony books to cereal boxes at
breakfast. One day she discovered romance
novels – and one day, much later, wondered if she could
write one too. Leah now writes happy-ever-afters for
heroines who definitely don't need saving. When she's
not writing, Leah loves all day breakfast, rambling
conversations and laughing until she cries. She really
hates cucumber. And scary movies.

Romantic Escapes

Romantic Escapes:
Bali

GRACE OCTAVIA

KANDY SHEPHERD

LEAH ASHTON

MILLS & BOON

First Published in Great Britain 2022
by Mills & Boon, an imprint of HarperCollins*Publishers* Ltd,
1 London Bridge Street, London, SE1 9GF

www.harpercollins.co.uk

HarperCollins*Publishers*
1st Floor, Watermarque Building,
Ringsend Road, Dublin 4, Ireland

ROMANTIC ESCAPES: BALI
© 2022 Harlequin Enterprises ULC

Under the Bali Moon © 2016 Calaya Reid
Best Man and the Runaway Bride © 2018 Kandy Shepherd
Nine Month Countdown © 2014 Leah Ashton

ISBN: 978-0-263-30459-6

MIX
Paper from
responsible sources
FSC™ C007454

UNDER THE BALI MOON

GRACE OCTAVIA

To my first love, who helped me discover my first
true self and grow boundlessly from there.

Part I

Total Eclipse

Chapter 1

Attorney Zena Nefertiti Shaw looked like a million bucks in the courtroom that afternoon. She was wearing burgundy, thin-heeled suede pumps with matching straps and golden buckles at the ankles that made her feet arch downward with unmistakable femininity. A fitted merlot skirt paired with a dramatic black suit jacket that was gathered in pleats in the small of her back showed off her tiny waist and flat stomach. Her long black hair was pressed and hanging down her back with a subtle curl at the bottom. When Zena moved, her hair floated as if an invisible fan was blowing in her direction for dramatic allure.

In the courtroom in downtown Atlanta, Zena knew she looked good while delivering her closing argument.

"In closing, dear jury, what I want to ask all of you, each of you, is, what would you want if the one you love, the person who stood before man, his family and friends and your family and friends, the church and God in heaven and swore to always love you back, dishonored the innocence of your vows with the unspeakable behaviors Mr. Rayland has imposed upon my client's ever-delicate heart?" Zena posed, releasing the stare that had been locked upon the jury and turning to face Tanisha Rayland, her thirty-seven-year-old client who was at the center of a very ugly and controversial divorce from her bed-hopping R & B husband of twelve years.

Zena stood with her profile parallel to the jury as she gazed at Tanisha. She wanted them to see the connection she had with this woman. Wanted them to see what sympathy for this woman could look like. She folded her arms and exhaled long and deep and dramatically.

"As you all learned throughout these proceedings, and as this woman had to relive, Mrs. Rayland's college sweetheart slept with and impregnated the eighteen-year-old they hired to enter their home to care for their children. And that's only the worst part. *Maybe.* Because in twelve years of marriage, Mrs. Rayland can't recall one year when she wasn't sharing her husband's affections with another woman. Especially not after the fame came to him. Not after the singing career she helped him build took off. After the money started rolling in. Well, then she had to share him with three and four young women at a time."

A tear fell from Tanisha's left eye. She was a woman of striking beauty. Light skin with a red undertone that made her ethnicity unclear until she opened her mouth and the South Side of Chicago came out. Full, pouty lips. Long eyelashes. If it wasn't for the weight she'd put on after having five children—she'd confessed to Zena that she had the last three with hopes of keeping her husband at home and other women away from him—she might look like one of the video vixens with whom Mr. Rayland enjoyed his many indiscretions. And even with the weight, Zena thought Tanisha could easily find work as a full-figured model.

Zena exhaled again, adding hyperbole to Tanisha's tears. She turned back to the jury. As she rolled her eyes along her path, she got a glimpse of Mr. Rayland sitting beside his attorney on the other side of the courtroom. His head was hung low and twisting back and forth in embarrassment or disagreement, as if Zena had shone a light on his deepest, darkest secret. When the divorce proceedings had started, days ago, he'd arrived with

huge diamonds in his ears, a pernicious smile and
a Rolex on his wrist that seemed to connote this
would be a breeze; his wealth would prevail. He
was confident. He stated he would beat the entitlement case. But after days in the courtroom,
he didn't look so sure of this articulation. That
wicked smile was so yesterday. Also gone were
the diamond earrings. That Rolex was a ghost.
He was in his simplest form now. A man without
airs. Humbled.

Eyes on the jury, Zena added, "And the torment
didn't stop with the many affairs. Add in the drugs,
the weeks away from home, the year Mr. Rayland
was in jail and my client had to care for their five
children alone, and the lies." She pursed her lips.
Gave the jury time to recall these infractions she'd
been feeding them over the past few days. Time
to be disgusted with the images of Mr. Rayland
she'd so carefully painted. "The lies. Lie after lie."
She glanced back at Tanisha and her tears. "So, I
ask again, what would you want in return? What
should she want? Can we really place limitations
on what this woman deserves when all she wants
is enough support to care for her children in the
manner to which they've become accustomed, a
return on her investment in her husband and to
stay in the home where she's been living for the
last six years? Respectfully, in contrast with how
Mr. Rayland's attorneys have painted this woman's

request, this isn't about anger or being vindictive or asking for someone to support her. This is about justice. It's about making things right."

Amid grumbles from her opposition, Zena paused and straightened her suit jacket. She leaned against the jury box to appear more vulnerable, as if she was one of them sharing some secret. "Ladies and gentlemen of the jury, I implore you to return to this room with a righteous verdict. To do what's fair. What's just. Award Mrs. Tanisha Rayland twenty-five million dollars in entitlements as she dissolves ties from Mr. Rayland and her sad past with him. Release her, so she can move on. Do what you would want done. What she deserves."

Zena bowed deeply toward the jury, and she actually saw some heads nod back to her. One older woman who'd always smiled at her looked as if she was about to clap. Zena turned back to her seat and winked at her client as she walked toward her. When she sat and grabbed Tanisha's hand beneath the table to reassure her of their success, Zena's assistant and best friend, Malak, who was sitting in the front row, leaned forward smiling.

"This one is in the bag, Z!" Malak cheered in a low voice.

"I hope you're right," Zena whispered, eyeing Mr. Rayland's attorney, who was standing before the jury, ready to present his closing arguments before the jury would return to their room to vote.

Zena really did need to have this one in the bag. When Tanisha left her husband, he froze all of her accounts and she had little money to cover Zena's high hourly fee. Since news of the Raylands' pending divorce broke, the hungry media made a gossip sensation of Tanisha's life and split from the R & B crooner many saw as a stable and loving husband—at least that's how his team had been portraying him in all the gossip rags. Zena had to play offense and defense, creating a team for her client, which now included her firm's personal publicist, security staff member and photographer. This robbed her other cases of valuable time—and her bank account of precious dollars. Zena told herself this was the cost of maintaining her firm's reputation. All of this while praying a big payday would come when, as Malak predicted, "this one is in the bag."

"Don't worry," Zena said to Tanisha, but it was clear she was also trying to encourage herself. "Everything will be fine."

Luckily, Malak's psychic sensibilities were better than her jet-black-and-blond ombré weave.

After just twenty minutes of deliberating, the jury returned with a verdict that made a rich woman of Zena's client. She'd be able to pay Zena's fees and those of her associates and, more importantly, move on with her life.

Moving on for Zena, though, meant her usual posttrial trip to Margarita Town with Malak in tow. After debriefing Tanisha on their next steps and assuring her this was "really it—she'd won," Zena hopped into a Town Car waiting outside the courthouse and quietly thanked God for the magical mix of tequila and strawberry flavoring awaiting her arrival at Margarita Town. It would wash away all of her thoughts of Mr. Priest Rayland and his deplorable behavior.

"You shut that fool all the way down," Malak said later, sitting across from Zena at Margarita Town. Before her was a behemoth of a margarita glass, the size of a baby's head, filled to the rim with frothy blue ice chips and liquid. "I thought he was going to hop out of his chair and run across the room to start choking you at any moment." Malak laughed and held her hands up as if she had them wrapped around Zena's neck.

Behind her was the normal fare of a margarita bar. Nothing fancy. Nothing too nice. Soft red lights set aglow garage-sale rainbow ponchos, sombreros and dusty, half-clothed Lupita dolls tacked to the walls. No one was there for the decor, though. It was just a theme for the real prize that attracted professionals to Margarita Town's lop-sided high-top tables and sticky bar each night after work. The clientele included burned-out teachers, lawyers, doctors, publicists, business owners, even yoga teachers.

The red ice in Zena's significantly smaller margarita glass was nearly gone, and Zena was already feeling the soothing affects of the concoction, so she laughed more deeply than Malak had expected.

"Slow down, cowgirl," Malak teased. "You know you're a lightweight. I don't want to carry you out of here."

Malak and Zena had been best friends since high school. They were nothing alike, but since the first day they met when Zena had moved to Atlanta, Georgia, from Queens, New York, and chose a seat behind Malak in her first-period history class, they were together through most of life's laughs and hard times. That was why when Zena finished law school at Howard and returned to Atlanta to start her own practice, she called Malak, who only finished high school with a GED, and offered Malak a job as her assistant. Zena trusted Malak, and as a new attorney building a practice in the ever-cliquish legal field, she wanted someone by her side who would anticipate her moves, encourage her and keep her laughing. Malak was good at all of those things, but what made her most valuable to Zena, what she knew when she hired Malak, was that she was whip smart. While she'd made some poor choices, including getting pregnant by her boyfriend senior year of high school,

Malak was smarter than many of the cohorts Zena went up against during mock trials in law school. While Zena always made it a point to check in on her old friend and encourage her to go back to school, Malak wanted to try to make her family work and got married right out of high school. By the time she was twenty-five, she was divorced with two children. Zena vowed to return home to make sure Malak had a chance to really turn things around.

"No slowing down for me tonight. Actually, I think I'll have another," Zena said, signaling for the waitress to bring a second margarita. "I need to wash the memory of that sneaky, slithering snake out of my mind. We have new blood in the morning, and I don't want to stay up all night thinking about—" She stopped and looked off, forlorn.

"I know what you mean," Malak agreed pensively, flipping ombré tendrils over her shoulder. "He really did a number on her. A number on you, too."

"Me?" Zena smiled as if Malak had to be joking. "How did he do a number on me?"

"Um…" Malak nodded to the new margarita the waitress was sliding on the table before Zena.

Zena was no drinker. While she always indulged a little after they'd closed a case, too much alcohol almost always made her a bit emotional.

"Come on. I'm just celebrating. Of course, I

hated that toad, but it's not like I took anything he did personally. It's not like he did that mess to me."

"I couldn't tell," Malak pointed out. "Not the way you were carrying on these last few days—hell, since the case began. It was like you *had* to win. You had to beat him."

"Isn't that common? Why I have an unblemished record in the courtroom?" Zena's tone was snarky. Overly confident. But still comical. While she was just thirty-one, after six years in the courtroom as the sole attorney at Z. Shaw Law, she made a name for herself as a fearless and swift attorney. One of her first cases was a long shot. Her sorority sister from Bethune-Cookman had married a football pro who was smart enough to lock her into an ironclad prenup before making her his punching bag. The football wife came to Zena with no money and no way out of the dysfunctional marriage. While Zena had little experience and could barely pay her bills, she took on the case pro bono. There was something about the messy marriage that turned a knife in Zena's gut, and she spent day and night on the case. In the end, she found a loophole in the prenup and won a nice settlement for her client.

Of course, the case took over news headlines for weeks, making young Zena a new name to know in legal circles. Quickly, Z. Shaw became one of a few top firms in the city that represented high-

profile clients in divorce cases involving entitlement hearings where large sums of money were on
the table. Ninety-nine percent of her clients were
women seeking settlements from their cheating
and very wealthy husbands. These were cases with
obvious winners and losers. Bad boys who'd done
good girls wrong. Zena knew the right buttons to
push in the courtroom. She always got her ruling.

Zena's cell phone started rattling beside her
margarita on the table. She looked down. Zola
was on the screen.

"Oh, man, I don't even feel like talking to her
right now," Zena said, letting the phone vibrate.
"You know she only calls if she needs money—or
to borrow something."

"Maybe you should answer. She's been calling
all day," Malak said.

"All day?" Zena repeated, surprised and staring at Malak as if she'd somehow failed as an assistant. "Why didn't you tell me?"

Zena moved to answer the phone, but the ring-
ing had already stopped and was replaced with the
clatter of an incoming text message:

ZOLA: Z, call me back. I've been calling you all
day. I have news.

Zena looked at the screen and repeated "news"

aloud. "What the hell?" she added. "What kind of news could she have?"

Malak looked away nervously, but Zena didn't question her because she was busy getting up from her seat to return Zola's call.

"I'll be right back," Zena said, already out of the booth across from Malak. "Don't let anyone spike my drink."

"Sure won't, Boss Lady," Malak confirmed solidly.

The friends laughed, and Zena made her way through the joyous, drunken crowd of now-smiling professionals. Zena recognized a guy she'd met on a dating website standing by the bar with a beer in his hand. His white business shirt was unbuttoned to his chest; opposing ends of an open tie flanked each shoulder. Men and women who looked as if they must be his colleagues stood laughing at something he'd just said. When he saw Zena, he waved, but she turned her head, pressed her cold cell phone to her ear to pretend to be on a call and padded quickly toward the door.

Outside Margartia Town, Zena found a place on the curb beside a skinny and stylish East Indian couple smoking cigarettes and dialed Zola's number. Beneath the amber glow of an oversize blow-up margarita glass filled with plastic golden liquid, she pressed the phone to her ear again, crossed her arms and rolled her eyes at the couple in heightened disgust at their activity. While the early-summer afternoon heat had cleared with the sunset, it was still too hot and muggy outside in Georgia to withstand the stale, dry air of cigarette smoke. Just when Zena was about to mention the local ordinance banning smoking in the private dining zone, Zola answered.

"Zeeeennnaaaa!" Zola squealed into the phone so loudly Zena winced and pulled the receiver back from her ear. There was a brazen exuberance and cheeriness to Zola's voice. She sounded like a pre-game high school cheerleader, eager and enthusiastic, but decidedly so. Determinedly so. The voice was simply the calling card of everything else about the little sister on the other end of the phone. She was the metaphor of a smile. Anxiously happy. Not only was her glass always half-full, but it was also filled with sugary pink lemonade and she was all too excited to share with everyone else. But that was how she'd decided to be; how Zola made herself function.

As the sisters exchanged common salutations filled with updates and weather predictions, Zena relaxed in the comfort of her sister's arbitrary joyfulness. There was always something about the sweet spirit in Zola that calmed and loosened the uptight and upright spirit in Zena.

"I was actually surprised we won," Zena acknowledged on the tail end of a summary about her adventure in the courtroom closing Priest Rayland's case. "Of course, we had enough evidence stacked against that fool to make it impossible for the jury to rule in his favor, but you just never know these days. I used to expect the jury to rule based upon facts, but it's really all emotion. All feeling. You'll see." Zena inhaled deeply as the couple departed after taking their final puffs. "Enough about me. What's up with you? How's studying going for my future partner?" Zena's voice was wrapped in giddiness then.

Just two weeks ago, Zena was in Washington, DC, for Zola's law school graduation at Howard. Though Zola originally planned to move to New York City to pursue her dream of being a fashion critic after undergrad, with much prodding and planning and some strings pulled by Zena, Zola attended her big sister's law school alma mater, graduated with decent marks, and now it was just a matter of getting Zola to pass the Georgia Bar Exam before she'd be the newest addition to Z. Shaw Law, soon to be Z. and Z. Shaw Law.

"Um…it's going fine," Zola let out with a marked zip in her zeal. "Okay, I guess… It's cool—"

Zena cut in, ready to inspire, ready to employ the swift hand of big sister judgment that had already decided that Zola wasn't living up to her potential. She needed to let Zola know this slacking was dangerous. She needed to inspire Zola to do better. And this was the way things had always been between the sisters.

"You don't sound like it's 'cool.' Come on, Zola. Don't drop the ball now. You can do this. I'm paying your bills, so you don't have to work. All you have to do every day is study. You know how many people wish they had that privilege? I know I did."

Sounding diminished, Zola started, "I know. I know—but—"

Zena cut her off again, though. "Look, you're smart. You can do this. You have to focus. Focus and don't accept mediocrity. I keep telling you that."

"I know I *can* do it, Zena, but that's what I'm calling to talk to you about—I don't think I *want* to do it right now."

"What? What do you mean 'want'?" Zena's face contorted into something that looked like an angered question mark. She looked at the phone as if Zola could see her cold stare. As she had all of those times in the past, Zena felt she just needed to find the right words of encouragement to entice Zola to change her view. Should she be stern or sensitive? What would work best at such a crossroads just shy of eight weeks before the July Georgia Bar Exam?

"This isn't about your clock, Zola. It's not about whether now is the time for you. Now is the only time. You have to take the Bar. You have to take it this summer."

There was silence then—the kind that signifies that there's more information coming.

"Wait, didn't your text say you had news?" Zena recalled. "Is that what this is about? What's going on?" Images depicting a reel of disaster rolled through Zena's mind—Zola had already run off to New York to dance in hip-hop music videos; she'd used all the money Zena had been giving her for rent to pay for a secret drug habit; she hadn't even started studying; she was preg— "Are you preg—?"

Zola stopped her sister's stream of dark thoughts with a soft and mousy revelation: "Alton asked me to elope. That's what I've been trying to get out. That's why I've been calling you all day. We decided to just do it—to just get married. Now." Zola was referring to her recent status as the fiancée of Alton Douglass, her childhood sweetheart and long-term boyfriend, who'd just popped the question at Zola's graduation in DC. While Zena wasn't exactly hip to the idea of Alton and Zola getting married right when Zola was about to really start her career, as she watched her baby sister cry when Alton slid the stoneless silver ring he'd called "antique" onto Zola's finger, Zena was reconciled knowing that it would be at least one year before there was even a discussion about a wedding. By then, Zola would be back in Atlanta, have passed the Bar Exam and be a practicing attorney.

"Zena? Zena? You there?" Zola called after a long pause.

"Yes. I am." Zena's words were void of emotion but somehow also overly laden with something else.

"So?" Zola paused awkwardly. "What do you think? No big wedding. We're just going to do it. Get married and start living our lives. It's a smart decision—right?"

Though there was the common glee in Zola's tone, there was a stiffness there now, too—a covering used to veil her joy in some way. To protect it.

Zena could sense all of this.

Zena began pacing in small circles, subconsciously reaffirming the existence of her environment as she prepared to quiz Zola. She felt as if she was being sucked away. As if the smoking couple had returned and lit up new cigarettes to steal her air.

She looked back up at the oversize plastic margarita glass hovering over her. It was glowy and amber. Happy. This was her happy place.

She wished Malak was outside Margarita Town standing beside her to hear this. She'd put Zola on speaker and have her best friend there to share her disbelief, confirm this horrible mistake Zola was about to make. A mistake Zena would have to clean up. The thing was, Zena had been protecting her baby sister for so long, there was no way she would let anything like that happen. She loved Zola so much, and she'd gotten her so far. They were almost there—almost at the finish line.

"Well did you tell Mommy and Daddy? What did they say about this?" Zena asked.

"Daddy's too busy with whatever up in New York. And Mommy loves Alton, of course. Who doesn't love Alton?" The adoration in Zola's voice was so absolute Zena imagined that Alton must be standing right beside her, listening in and probably laughing at Zena's reaction. Maybe *Zena* was the one on speakerphone.

"Of course everyone loves Alton," Zena said with years of knowing and, yes, loving sweet and kind Alton, Zola's spiritual twin, laced in her words. While Zena, at fifteen, was nearly in love with the mere vision of Alton's older brother, Adan, Alton was actually like a little brother to Zena.

"All of this seems so sudden. Like, who's going to pay for all of this?"

"Really, Z? I can't believe you asked me that. I say I'm getting married and you ask who's paying?"

"It's a perfectly reasonable question. I've been supporting you, and Alton isn't exactly rolling in the dough."

"He's a singer. That's just how it goes when you're just starting out. But he is getting money for his songwriting. And he's about to sign a deal with a major label. We just have to hold out."

"Sure, 'hold out,'" Zena shot nastily, though she hadn't intended on sounding so awful.

"Z, I knew you wouldn't take this well—especially since I'm supposed to be preparing and everything. But I at least thought you'd be excited. Like happy for me," Zola said.

"I am happy for you. It's just—" Zena paused and looked at the inflated margarita glass again for inspiration. She needed to say the right thing, find the right words. She needed to support her sister. Be there for her sister. But how could she do that if she felt her sister was doing the wrong thing? Marriage? It wasn't the right time. How could she support that? Be there for that? Didn't support and being "there" for her sister mean telling the truth? Telling it like it is? Zena looked away from the margarita glass and let go of the idea of saying the right thing. She decided to say exactly what was on her mind. "What about your life... your future?" Zena let out, and she immediately hated every word she'd said. She sounded like their mother, like their grandmother.

"My *future*?" Zola laughed at this assertion in a way that Zena hated. The statement and tone reeked of "my big sister is crazy and cold. She doesn't get it." Zola took to using the tone whenever Zena said something with which Zola found fault or could easily deconstruct. "Z, listen, Alton is my future. Not being an attorney. That's just a job. I know how you feel about it—it's your life—but that's not how I see it."

Zola's last sentence grated against something in Zena.

"Don't do that. Don't go there." Suddenly, Zena felt incredibly lonely standing out there in front of Margarita Town. Cold. Bare. Though no breeze had passed, she shuddered and turned to peek through the front window of Margarita Town to find Malak's face. "I'm just trying to look out for you. You know? That's all I'm doing. That's all I've ever done."

"I know. And I love you for it. And I'm still taking the Bar Exam. Just not this year."

"What? Why not? It's scheduled for July—that's like eight weeks from now. You've been studying, right?"

"Well, that's kind of the other thing I wanted to tell you."

"What?"

"Alton is so excited about this whole thing—well, we both are—anyway, he really wants to do it right away. And I agree with him—I love him and I want to be his wife—sooner rather than later, of course," Zola clattered out as if she was explaining this all to herself. "He wants to elope—now."

Again, Zena felt herself drifting away. What was happening?

"So, we're getting married in two weeks," Zola went on, ignoring her sister's silence.

"Two? Two weeks? I thought you meant like six months—three at the very least. How are you going to get married in two weeks? And where are you going to get married in two weeks? That's like impossible. Any decent place has a waiting list of like nine months. And please don't tell me you two are going to the Justice of the Peace. And not Vegas!" Zena felt herself growing more aggravated, so she paused for a second before beginning again with less sharpness in her tone. "Listen, Zol, why are you doing this? Is there something you need to tell me? Are you pregnant?"

"I can't believe you just suggested that, but I already told you that I'm not pregnant. I'm just in love. And I'm not getting married in Vegas or at the courthouse. We're going to do it in Bali. We're getting married in Bali."

Zena could hear the smile return to Zola's face as she went on revealing her plan. The wedding would be a small seaside ceremony. No audience. Only two witnesses in attendance. Zola wanted Zena to be there as her maid of honor. The second witness would be the best man: Alton's older brother; Zena's old flame... Adan.

After more minutes of sibling emotional wrangling in the form of probing questions and slick statements, Zola was back in Margarita Town sitting across from Malak.

"You knew? You knew? All this time, you knew they were eloping and you didn't tell me?" Zena had shifted her interrogation to Malak, who sat there buzzing from her second big blue margarita and holding her hands in the air innocently.

"She just told me a few hours ago. Right before we went into the courtroom," she said. "I didn't exactly want to tell you before you were walking in to give your closing."

"But what about after? Why didn't you tell me after? Immediately after?"

"Because I wanted Zola to tell you herself. I wanted it to be a surprise. And don't you think you're kind of missing the point here? The point is that your little sister is getting married? It's great news. Right?" Malak smiled, though she knew the expression would not be returned.

"Not exactly. This is a big mistake for her right now. They aren't ready to get married. Yes, they're in love. But they don't have enough money. They're just banking on Alton getting this record deal. This is a recipe for disaster and you know it.

We're in the business of watching marriages fail. And what makes most marriages fail?"

"Money," Malak reluctantly mumbled.

"Exactly. When money is short, people start changing. They become horrible versions of themselves. And I'm not saying they'll always be poor. I'm not going to wish doom on Alton's career or anything, but being a performer has its ups and downs."

"Alton and Zola have been together forever. They'll be okay."

"They have no idea what they're in for. What's going to happen to them," Zola said to herself as if she hadn't heard anything Malak said. "I just can't sit back and watch Zola do this—mess everything up that we've worked so hard for."

Malak's best attempts to placate her friend turned to annoyance. "Why do you do that to Zola? Always act like she has no clue? Like she's stupid and can't make any decisions without you?" Malak paused and looked down into her drink. She exhaled and grimaced frankly, as if she was about to say something she might regret. "You know, maybe this isn't about the wedding—about Alton and Zena getting engaged. Maybe your reaction is about—you know—*him*. And the fact that he is going to be there in Bali."

Him and *he* needed no further explanation. The words bounced from Malak's mouth like a fireball and landed on the table before Zena. She wanted to pick it up and throw it across the room, get it away from her as soon as possible, but she was also afraid to touch it, afraid to hear it, to think it, to think of *him*.

"Don't bring *him* up," Zena scoffed, and she sounded like a little girl.

"I have to. Sorry, Z. But there's no way you haven't thought about him. His brother is marrying your little sister. That has to matter. Right? Everyone thought you guys would do it first. And now Zola and Alton are getting married and you two will be together for that. It's been so long. When was the last time you spoke to Ad—"

"Don't say his name," Zena cut in. "I don't want to hear it. And I don't want to talk about it. And I don't care about him. And I don't think about him. My opinion of this disaster of a wedding that's about to take place in two freaking weeks has nothing to do with Adan—" Zena tried to stop her diatribe before she got to the name that was flashing in her head, but out it came.

Malak was right. Zena had thought of Adan, of course. And while she'd done a grand but strategic job of avoiding him and all topics concerning him, when Alton proposed to Zola in DC, Zena knew she'd finally have to see Adan. But then she figured she had at least a year—one year to get her head together. She could even meet a wonderful,

well-traveled, well-read man, who was also funny
and down-to-earth and rich, and get married—at
least engaged—okay, at least committed. She'd
arrive at Zola and Alton's wedding to see Adan
and his NYC doctor wife and perfect children, and
Zena would have to show for her own life a successful law practice, bombshell body and hot judge
husband, with dimples—fiancé—okay, boyfriend.
But now everything had changed.

"Okay. I won't make you talk about Adan. If
you say you haven't thought of him and you don't
want to think of him, then we can move on to
something else," Malak agreed patronizingly, as
if she was some kind of barroom therapist. "We
can focus on what's really important. And that's
Zola's happiness. That girl loves you. She trusts
you. She adores you. She admires you. She needs
your support. Can you just support her?"

"I'll support the right decision. That's what I'll
support." Zena rolled her eyes and waved to a random waitress who was rushing past their table.
She asked her, "Can you have our waitress get
our check?"

"No problem, hon," the woman said, sounding
more cheerful than she actually looked. "I'll actually just get it for you."

"Thanks," Zena said as the thought of seeing
Adan again suddenly hit her. After so many years
of blocking painful memories, she wondered if her

heart was strong enough to deal with his actual presence. Zena quietly considered that maybe they would be distant, even mockingly cordial. She'd feel like she was meeting a stranger, a stranger who maybe just happened to look like someone she knew. Someone she'd known for a very long time. But Adan was no stranger. He was once Zena's everything. He was her past, what she'd hoped would become her future. But that was all gone now. And it was all because of him.

Chapter 2

The morning after drowning the news of Zola's pending Bali wedding in the murky brown liquid of so many shots of reposado tequila she could hardly leave Margarita Town on her feet, Zena awoke to a spinning headache that released her from her morning run. She rolled over in the bed, turning her back to the bedroom window where the late-morning sun was beaming into the room. She was too tired to be fully awake and ready to enter a new day after tossing around in bed through the twilight hours, endlessly replaying worries she had no control over. Problems she'd trained herself to forget, to get away from, but now, there they were right in front of her. While her nighttime thoughts began with Zola, the prickling concern beneath her sister's future was Zena's own past.

Malak's psychic ability—or good sense—had struck gold again at Margarita Town when she boldly shared that maybe much of Zena's consternation about Alton and Zola getting married wasn't about them finding love. It was about the love Zena had lost and never forgotten.

Zola wasn't the only sister to fall in love with a boy who lived up the street. She actually wasn't even the first.

Lying in bed that night, Zena's thoughts went back—way back to the time she was a teenager and met Adan Frederick Douglass. He was the first boy to steal her heart away. He was the first man to tear her heart into tiny smithereens. She'd spent too much of her life and good money in therapy trying to pull the pieces back together.

It all started with her parents' ruined marriage and a popped bicycle chain.

After her father's second affair with one of the cashiers at the Sutphin Boulevard Burger King where he was a manager, Zena's mother paid a few hundred to a pimply-faced attorney who promised "quick" divorces in advertisements on subway cars. The couple had no money, property or belongings to split up. Her mother knew there was no way her husband would petition the courts for custody or shared visitation rights for Zena and Zola, fifteen and nine at the time—he had limited funds and no place for his daughters to stay. Zena overheard her mother telling their neighbor who worked on Jamaica Avenue that she just wanted the marriage to be over and to get her girls out of Queens.

Hearing this hurt Zena beyond repair. While her parents' marriage was mostly rocky, as her father was unreliable and could never keep a long-term job to support them and often stepped out on her mother, Zena loved her father and just wished he'd do right. During their father-daughter walks around the neighborhood, he'd often promise just that. He explained that he didn't mean to hurt her mother and said something about New York's poor public school system that diagnosed his dyslexia too late. His reasoning became scrambled into a massive puzzle in Zena's head. All she wanted to hear about was how her parents and her family could stay together. But he had no solutions. No plans. "I'm broken, babygirl. I done failed ya'll," he'd said.

A week later, Zena was standing in a Greyhound bus line with her mother and sister at the Port Authority Bus Terminal in Manhattan. Everything they owned amounted to five boxes being slid into the cargo hold of a bus en route to Atlanta, Georgia. Speaking as if she was a grown woman who'd lived a life and had the necessary scars on her soul one would need to give another grown woman advice, Zena said in her gruff Jamaica, Queens-girl accent, "You didn't even give him a chance. He was trying and you didn't give him a chance. And I resent you for that." Zena thought she'd really said something. Standing in line at the Port Authority Bus Terminal, she crossed her slender teenage arms over her chest and awaited a defense she felt was impossible.

"Mothers don't have time to give people chances. You're my top priority. Not him. Not even me. I did this to save you and your sister from growing up and being stuck in a hole like me and your daddy. I did this so you could be happy," her mother said.

"Happy? In Georgia?" Zena laughed the way any Queens-born girl who'd been torn from her home to live in Georgia would. "You're making us move from our friends and school. We're losing everything, Mommy."

Zena's mother paused and responded with unmistakable passion in her voice. "You may feel like that now, but I'm giving you a real opportunity to have a better life."

* * *

Zena's bicycle chain had popped the morning she met Adan. Her mother had just gotten the rickety red ten-speed from the Salvation Army and unloaded it from the back of the dented 4Runner some cross-eyed deacon at their new church let her mother borrow. Zena was complaining about being locked up all day in the house looking after Zola and begged for a bicycle. While she'd complained about cobwebs on the frame and the cracking fake-leather seat when they spotted the ten-speed in the back of the secondhand store, once Zena got the thing home and kicked off from the curb, she tasted the kind of freedom every fifteen-year-old knew while riding a bicycle.

At first, she heeded her mother's instructions and only rode around the corner a few times, but then she became curious about her new surroundings and rode faster, standing up on the pedals as she pushed two and three miles from her front door. The houses got bigger and the cars nicer as she sped along. She noticed that the house she lived in with her mother and her sister was the smallest one in the entire neighborhood. She'd heard her mother mention on the phone to her grandmother that she'd gotten the rental for a quarter of the price through some pilot fair-housing project that would later be known as "Section 8 housing."

It was late summer, and the Georgia heat kept

most people indoors, but she saw some stray gag-
gles of teenagers entering cars and front doors and
wondered if any of them would be her classmates
when she started classes at her new high school in
a few weeks. Walking up flower-lined driveways
in bright colors and smiling, they all looked so solidly middle-class, so happy, so far away from the
armor-clad, stone-faced friends she knew back in
the New York projects. Right then, Zena decided
that she wasn't going to tell anyone at her new
school that she lived in the smallest house in the
neighborhood.

Soon, droplets of warm sweat escaped Zena's
underarms and wet her T-shirt. The precipitation
seemed to descend on her brow and draw every
ounce of energy from her body. Zena, going on
pure zeal, continued her tour, but she was pant-
ing like a thirsty dog and she began feeling as if
she'd been away from home for hours, though it
had only been twenty minutes since her departure.
This was her official introduction to the stifling
Georgia humidity that suffocated everything that
had the nerve to move before 7 p.m. in late July.
Zena would never forget that feeling, that day; it
was as if she'd fallen asleep in a sauna and awoke
in a pool of her own sweat.

Growing concerned after considering her wet
knuckles and steamy scalp, Zena decided to head

home, fearing her mother must be panicked because she'd been gone so long.

She'd been resting her bottom on the prickly cracked bicycle seat but decided to get up and floor it home.

When she rounded the curb onto her new street, catching a breeze that did little to cool her off, Zena noticed a family getting out of their car in the driveway on the side of a house that looked identical to the one she lived in just seven houses down. It was a mother and father with two boys. One of the boys looked her age. The other couldn't be much older than Zola.

While Zena was two houses away, the family stopped and looked at her as if she was an alien pushing a ten-speed up the street.

Zena's delicate fifteen-year-old self-esteem made her wonder if she was doing something wrong. Could they see the sweat stains at her underarms? Had the wind swept her hair all over her head and she looked like a parading Medusa? What were they looking at?

The little boy started waving, but Zena was too afraid to wave back, fearing she'd lose control of her bike and crash into one of the cars parked on the street. Instead, her bubbling anxiety under their watching eyes made her want to simply disappear, so Zena decided to race home, where she'd run into the house and never ever emerge again.

That was when the chain popped.

The pedal push that was supposed to send her somewhere quickly actually split the chain. There was a click and then the bike simply stopped moving. Zena's insistence on continuing her pedaling sent her and the bike, rather quickly and very dramatically, to the hot tar pavement, where she really hoped she would die.

"Lord, she done fainted," Zena heard a man's voice say, so she knew she hadn't actually died, which was a letdown.

"No, she didn't. I think she just fell," she heard a woman's voice say, and she knew it was the mother, who'd been standing by the car, because as she looked up from the ground, she could see the woman's coral espadrilles rushing toward her.

Soon, the family of four was gathered around Zena as if she was a fallen angel. Worry was on everyone's face. Everyone but the boy who looked her age. He was smiling. Almost laughing at the sight.

Zena was quiet, quieter than she'd ever been in life. She watched as the four fussed over her, trying to figure out what had gone wrong. The father discovered that it was the broken chain that sent her tumbling to the ground, but he kept saying something about the heat and that it was too hot for anyone to be riding a bicycle at 3 p.m. And didn't she know that? The mother tried to quiet him after sending the little boy into the house for water.

She asked, "Where are your parents, honey? You live around here?" Her voice was Southern sweet. She sounded as if she could get anything from anyone. Zena had never heard a woman sound quite like that. It made her instantly like the woman.

Zena was listening but not speaking so the mother made the father check for broken bones. He found none and announced that Zena was just in shock. Just afraid because she'd fallen from her bike and here they were hawking over her like police officers. The couple laughed in unison at their hovering in a way that Zena had never heard her parents connect. It was as if they were suddenly alone and had heard lines in a conversation no one else could hear. Then the father kissed the mother. He said, "That's the nurse in my baby. Always worried about somebody." They kissed again and giggled.

The boy who was about Zena's age, the one who'd been ready to laugh at her fall, was frowning then and rolling his eyes at his parents as if he'd seen this all before and it was making him sick. He turned to Zena and pointed his index finger into his open mouth toward his tonsils as if he was about to make himself vomit.

The little comical gesture introduced Zena to

the saying, "I have butterflies in my stomach," because some new feeling was literally tickling her insides, from her navel to her throat. At that very moment, the tough girl from Queens awakened into feelings she'd never known. It was as if those little butterflies fluttered their delicate wings at her insides all at once and sent some mellifluous whispers of what she'd later recognize as first love straight to her heart. She'd never even thought of looking at a boy the way she did at that moment. She wanted to know everything about him. To smell him. To touch his curly black hair. Kiss those full lips. And if she'd ever heard the word *imbibe*, she'd want that—to imbibe him. Drink him in. Soak him up. Absorb him so she could feel what she was feeling in her stomach again and again. But that would come later. Junior year in high school. In someone's basement after a football game. Right then, she just wanted to know one thing—his name.

And without Zena even asking, he acquiesced.

"I'm Adan," he said, struggling so hard to make his pubescent voice sound masculine as his parents came out of their love bubble and noticed the teenagers' quick connection.

"I'm Zena," was returned.

"She speaks," the father said, looking at the mother with a kind of adult knowing in his voice.

"Good to hear, honey," the mother said. "We're

the Douglasses. You've met Adan already. This is Mr. Roy." She pointed to the father and then to herself. "I'm Mrs. Pam. And that little hellion who never came out with the water is Adan's little brother, Alton. He's probably playing his Nintendo game."

After helping Zena to her feet and carrying her bicycle to the sidewalk as she reluctantly revealed that she lived up the street and had just moved to Georgia from New York with her mother and sister, Roy abruptly excused himself and his wife. Attempting to pull Pam toward the house, he winked at Adan and ordered him to fix the chain with the supplies in the garage. Pam ignored Roy's clear desire that Adan and Zena get better acquainted and asked about Zena's mother again. She wanted to make sure Zena got home okay.

"The girl just told you she lives up the street. I think they're renting the Jefferson's old house. That ain't far. She'll be fine, Pam!" Roy protested. "Let these young folks figure it out. Everything will work out fine." He winked at Adan again and pulled his wife up the walkway and into the house.

"They're so weird. Weird and embarrassing," Adan said when they were gone, and with every word he spoke, Zena felt those wondrous flutters all through her body again.

"My parents are divorced," Zena announced as if she'd been holding it in her stomach all that time and needed to let someone know. "My dad cheated. He's having a baby."

Adan hardly reacted. He just shrugged in his learned teenage boy way. Zena would soon recognize this as his cool routine. "My mom would kill my dad if he cheated. She told him that one night. I think he believes her."

Adan picked up the bicycle and began rolling it toward the garage.

Zena followed close behind, watching him walk, spying his muscular arms and calves. She kept thinking that he had to be the cutest boy she'd ever seen. But, then, she couldn't remember ever really seeing any other boys. Memories of the ones who'd chased her around her neighborhood in Queens had faded so quickly. Who were they? What were their names again?

"Your chain is mad rusty. Where'd you get this bike? The Salvation Army?" he asked jokingly once they were in the garage and out of the hot sun.

"Yes," Zena admitted, embarrassed, and then she wished she hadn't fessed up to it. She didn't want Adan to know she was poor. Then he wouldn't like her. Could he like her? Did he? Zena looked into Adan's eyes for signs of something. Anything.

"Really?" Adan seemed surprised by the news and the obvious fumble of his joke about the Salvation Army. His light brown cheeks turned ruddy, and suddenly Zena saw in his eyes reflections of the same feelings she felt in her stomach. He liked her. Maybe he did. She felt her own cheeks turning red then.

"That's cool anyway. The bike is a little rusty. It could use some cleaning. But it's a nice bike. A Huffy," Adan said, suddenly cutting his gaze away from Zena as if he was becoming more nervous.

"You think it's nice?"

"Yes. It is. I could help you fix it up if you like. We could spray paint it. Make it dope." Adan looked back at Zena and smiled.

Zena smiled back. She felt as if she'd been asked out on her first date. "That would be cool," she said.

"We could set it up here in the garage. Work on it. Like a project."

Zena had never heard a boy her age use that word before—*project*.

She nodded and helped Adan flip the bike over. Standing beside him, she didn't want to breathe. She didn't want a second more to pass. She wanted everything to stop so she could just be right there, right then with him. She was afraid she'd miss something. Forget something about that moment. But she never would.

He turned on an old, dusty radio that his father listened to sometimes when he worked on his car in the garage. Some Goodie Mob song was playing, and Zena revealed that she'd never heard of the group. Adan's eyes widened. He didn't believe her. He then went through the entire history of the Dungeon Family, a local rap consortium that Adan heralded as the best MCs in the world. Zena laughed and pointed out that the best MCs were Biggie, Nas and Jay Z. This debate would continue throughout their relationship. But at that moment, Adan controlled the dial on the radio, so he turned up Goodie Mob's "Black Ice." Loud and proud, he rapped along about waking up and touching the sky.

Zena watched, listened and laughed. Soon, just as she'd done with the boys back in NYC, she forgot all about the time. The sun went down and her mother came looking for her.

It took Adan three long, hot weeks to make Zena's old rusty bike the envy of the street. With his father's help, he spray painted the Huffy hot pink and electric blue, reupholstered the seat with purple fabric and Pam even added a bell that Zena's mother insisted on paying for. As the repairs went on and the summer came to a close, Zena learned more about the Douglasses and everything about Adan. He was so smart. He seemed so much older than her. Sometimes he reminded her of Mr. Roy in the way he was always joking and pretending he was keen on a secret. He was cool, too. Seldom overexcited or sad. He seemed to have feelings right down the middle at all times. He took care of his little brother. Listened to his mother. Followed his father's direction. This all comforted Zena. Made her open up to Adan about everything that had her out pedaling fast on that old red bike that day. Over those afternoons in the garage she told him all about her parents' divorce. Her empty feelings. Her fear. He always seemed to know just what to say. Just when to be silent. Just when to reach out to wipe her tears.

One evening, Zena's mother had to work a double shift at the airport, where she'd lucked up on a job at Delta Air Lines. Zena was stuck in the house taking care of Zola, though she'd promised Adan she'd meet him at the local roller-skating rink. She was too embarrassed to call his house to say why she couldn't go, so she decided to just let the moment pass and later lie and say she forgot. While this line of thinking sounded crazy to her now, back then, it was a perfectly rational decision made out of shame and humiliation that her family had such limited funds that she was basically her sister's primary caretaker while her mother plated flight meals at the airport. Zena had been spending so much time at the Douglasses, and she now envied the ease and reliability of Mr. Roy and Mrs. Pam's stable marriage and home. Adan never had to take care of Alton. There was always someone at home to look after them.

After watching too many music videos on BET, Zena told Zola that it was time to get ready for bed and ordered her little sister to go take a shower. Once Zola finished complaining about the shower and begged to watch more videos, Zena scolded her as if she was the mother, and Zola stomped out of the living room toward the bathroom.

"I don't hear the water," Zena hollered after a while, and then the sound of the water in the shower finally started. She reminded herself to bust into the bathroom in a few minutes to make sure Zola was really in the shower and not just looking at the water—her mother always did that.

Zena got up to turn off the television and there was a faint, soft knock at the front door.

On instinct, Zena looked around the room for her father's baseball bat, but then reminded herself that she was no longer in the projects and that bat was still in New York.

"Who is it?" Zena demanded forcefully, trying to make her voice sound louder, gruffer in case there was a dangerous criminal at the door.

"Adan."

An alarm sounded in Zena's heart. She was quickly frantic. Why was Adan at her front door? He'd been past her house. He'd walked her home on some nights when she'd been at his house until it was too dark for her to walk home alone. But he'd never rung the front door. He'd certainly never been inside. Did he want to come inside? Everything around Zena seemed to be in complete disarray. Messy. Too messy. Zola's stupid Oreo crumbs on the secondhand couch. Their dirty sneakers lined up beside the front door. Her mother's work clothes on the chair. Zena looked into the dining room. They didn't even have a set in there yet. No chairs. No table. Just a bright light and an empty room.

"Zena?" Adan called from outside as if he sensed that he'd been forgotten.

"Yes."

"You going to open the door?"

Zena exhaled and walked to the entrance, where she forced a casual smile before opening the door only a few inches.

Adan was standing on the steps with his hands in his pockets. He looked confused. Maybe sad.

"You okay?" he asked.

"Yeah. Why?" Zena said.

"Because you weren't at the skating rink. I figured something was wrong." Adan tried to peek into the house, but Zena shifted her head to block him.

"Oh, that," Zena said vaguely. "I forgot."

"Forgot? But you seemed so excited."

"I was but, you know how it is. I just got busy."

"Oh." Adan's face went from maybe confused and maybe sad to definitely hurt.

Zena's heart sank. She hated her world for making her say what she'd said. She didn't want to hurt Adan. She was saying what she was saying because she wanted him to like her. Well, she didn't want him to not like her because her family was struggling and her mother wasn't a nurse and had to work overtime and she had to take care of her baby sister.

"Adan—"

"Zena—"

The two teenagers said each other's names at the same time as they tried to stumble out their feelings.

"You first," Adan said.

"No, you first," Zena countered.

"I'll just say this," Adan started with his voice cracking from its usual cool. "It's fine if you don't want to hang out and, like, be friends. I know school is starting soon and you'll make other friends. Okay? I know that. But I want to be your friend. I like you and I want to be your friend." He looked into Zena's eyes. "I really like you."

"Like, I like you, too," Zena blurted out clumsily.

The words were innocent enough, but the intentions had deep meaning behind them. What the two of them knew was their relationship had strengthened and left so much heightened emotional residue that they both laughed to lighten the moment.

"Hey, can I come in for a little while?" Adan asked.

"In here?"

"Yes. Into your house."

"Ohh." Zena looked over her shoulder as if maybe there was a circus breaking out in the living room behind her. She turned back to Adan. "You sure?" she asked him.

"Yes. I'm sure."

"Look, Adan. We don't have anything. I don't have a Nintendo like you do. Our television is on the floor," Zena said.

"That's fine," Adan answered in his cool tone. "I'm not here to play Nintendo or watch television. I'm here to see you."

"Ohh," Zena repeated. She stepped back and let Adan in. He kept her company and left right before her mother was to be home from work. That became their nightly ritual when her mother worked doubles. They swore Zola to secrecy and bribed her with Twix candy bars.

Zena was sure all of this would change when school started and all of the best friends Adan had, who frequently stopped by the house, got his attention before her. While she hadn't met any of the girls in the neighborhood, she imagined they'd all be prettier than her and have nicer bikes and already know all of the lyrics to the popular songs Adan played incessantly.

None of Zena's fears came to pass. Adan was also in the first-period history class where Zena sat beside Malak. One day when the teacher was absent and the substitute was late, the bored students started playing Twenty Questions, and Adan was selected first to sit in the hot seat in the center of the classroom. The girls led the questioning, asking if Adan was a virgin—he was and he admitted it—and soon Malak, who'd started the game for this very reason, asked if Adan had a girlfriend.

"Yes. I think so," Adan revealed, and the heartbreak from the girls in the room was palpable.

Malak pushed further: "Does she go to this school?" Adan nodded. "Is she in this classroom?" Adan nodded. "Is she wearing a red sweatshirt?" Adan nodded. All eyes moved to the only girl in that classroom who was wearing a red sweatshirt— the new girl. Zena.

When hungover and weary Zena could no longer ignore the sun rising outside her bedroom window, she decided to force herself out of bed. She suffered through her shower and pampering routine and stumbled through her condo trying not to remember Adan's face when he admitted that he liked her that night at her house.

When Zena finally made it out her front door and to her car, she decided she needed to make a stop before heading into the office, so she called

Malak to inform her of her extended late arrival. While Malak sounded surprised, Zena could also hear in her voice enthusiasm at the idea of her boss being out of the office a little while longer.

"Everything okay?" Malak asked with concern about the issues they'd confronted the night before laced in her tone.

"I'm fine," Zena said with forced brightness before adding rather dutifully, "Just email Judge Jones's assistant to let him know I won't make our appointment. I'll stop by the courthouse a little later, and I hope to catch him if he has time. And make sure those files from the new Patel case are entered into the system. I'll need them when I get in."

Zena could hear the sarcasm in Malak's voice when she replied, "I've already entered those files, and I'll send the email right away." Malak paused before adding, "Zena, I'm here if you want to talk about—"

"That will be all," Zena said, cutting Malak off as if she was a stranger trying to find her place in some tragedy she didn't understand. She hung up and exhaled through her mouth before jumping in her car to head to her mother's house.

Lisa Shaw still lived in the same little brick house in West End, Atlanta, she'd found refuge in after her divorce and escape from New York.

After years of haggling with the West Coast land-
lord she'd never seen, Lisa purchased the modest
property and was so proud of her achievement she
went about the work of turning the little abode into
an oasis in an enclave that was decent when she'd
moved in with her family but declined through
years of home owner flight, Section 8 hustles,
weak property flips and foreclosures during the
recession. But, Lisa, just happy to have her own
land, held firm and refused to leave, even when
Zena offered to purchase her mother a more lofty
condo in town.

When Zena pulled into the driveway outside
her mother's ranch house, she scanned the well-
kept front garden packed with blooming perennials
like the bog lily, the yellow flag iris and cannas.
In the middle of the yard was a freshly painted
white swinging garden bench Lisa forbade Zena
and Zola or anyone else from ever sitting on. "That
thing is just for show," Lisa said ten years ago
when she had two day laborers she'd picked up
in front of the Home Depot come and install it.
"Got me a garden and a swing," Lisa said, standing beside Zena and Zola that afternoon when the
work was done. "Can you imagine that? A girl
from 40 Projects? Got her own garden and swing!"
She laughed and repeated her instructions: no one
could ever sit on that swing.

Zena was about to use her old key to unlock

the front door, but it was already swinging open. Standing there was Lisa with her right hand on the knob and a lit cigarette in her left hand.

"Babygirl, your ears must be itching," Lisa said. She craned her neck over the threshold and looked past Zena toward the street, scanning the right and left side of the sidewalk. As usual, she was wearing one of the dozen dashikis Zena and Zola had gotten her for Kwanzaa. Her long gray dreadlocks were up in a bun, and her glasses were set low on her nose. While she was fifty-three and had endured what most would call a hard life, Lisa's appearance belied that fact. Beneath the gray dreadlocks, thick spectacles and frumpy house dress, she hadn't aged a day since they'd gotten off the bus in Atlanta.

"Itching? Why do you say that?" Instinctively, Zena turned and looked out at the street with her mother.

"I had a little visitor a few minutes ago," Lisa answered mysteriously as she backed up from the door to let Zena into the house.

"Zola? So she told you?" Zena charged, ready to argue her points against everything she'd come to her mother's house to discuss. Beginning her plea, she led her mother into the kitchen beside the front door, where most discussions occurred.

"No. Not Zola." Lisa laughed in a way that left a clue for Zena.

"Who?"

"You know." Lisa took a seat at the kitchen table beside Zena and put out her cigarette. While she'd stood firm in most of her fights with Zena about her smoking, reminding her firstborn that she was grown and Zena could not control smoking or anything else about her, she seemed like she was in no mood to have that fight again.

"Who was it, Mommy?" Zena pushed, though it was clear she'd read right into the clue.

"You know," Lisa repeated more firmly and enticingly.

Zena rushed to the bay window above the kitchen table and peered through the half-open blinds, careful not to reveal her position. "What? Why was he here? When was he here?" she asked, struggling to look up the street as if she could actually see anything five houses down where Roy Douglass, Adan and Alton's father, now lived alone after Mrs. Pam had died of breast cancer New Years Day.

"The usual," Lisa said. "Pretending he was here to check on me, but really trying to get news about you. You know these Southern men—so charming and a little manipulative." Lisa laughed. "He looked good. I don't see how you missed him. I swear he left just a few minutes before I saw you pull into the driveway."

Some tall teenage boy came into view, walking in the street in front of the house, and Zena thought for a second maybe it was Adan, so she jumped back, afraid her cover was blown, but then the baggy pants and basketball jersey proved otherwise.

"Asked about me? You didn't tell him anything. Right?" Zena looked back at Lisa.

"Don't start worrying. Lord! I told him the usual—I don't know anything. You don't tell me anything. Wasn't hard to say since it's the truth." Lisa's gaze cut to Zena.

"Mommy, don't go there." Zena plopped back into her seat like a teenager. She felt exhausted by everything—her mother's comment, Zola and the wedding, the idea of Adan lurking outside. What did he want anyway? Why was he always visiting her mother? She looked back at the window. She didn't feel like herself. She knew she didn't look like herself. She remembered being in the courtroom just twenty-four hours earlier. She was winning. She was what she wanted to be. Who she wanted to be. But now she was back at home in that little house and arguing with her mother.

"Don't go where? Ain't nowhere for me to go. I'm just an aging old lady, sitting at home and minding my business. You and your little teenage love are the ones who came knocking on my door," Lisa retorted.

"Fine. I didn't come here to talk about that man

anyway," Zena said snidely. "I don't care what he wants or why he was here."

"You sure don't sound like it. I thought you'd be over Adan by now, but I guess I also know that's impossible." Lisa grinned.

"First, we broke up in freaking college and I'm completely over him. Second, you know I've asked you not to say his name."

"Adan!" Lisa slapped her own lips playfully to punish herself for the intentional slip.

Zena ignored her comical routine and went on with her list: "And third, I don't care! I don't care! I don't care! And finally, like I said, that's not why I came here to talk to you."

"Well then why did you come to bless me with your presence, Ms. Zena Nefertiti Shaw?" Lisa joked.

"It's Zola. Did she tell you what she's planning to do?"

"What—you mean the wedding?"

"Yes. About eloping. So, she did tell you? You told her she couldn't do it, right?"

"No. Why would I do that?" Lisa asked.

"Because, it's crazy." Zena stared at her mother. Behind Lisa on the wall was a framed print of one of her many Gordon Parks pictures that were in the center of most walls throughout the house. This one was of a black girl standing before a whites-only water fountain. All through Zena's childhood, the picture inspired her to become a lawyer and fight injustices. "And because she's supposed to be studying for the Bar, so she can be an attorney," Zena went on. "And because you're her mother and you should be at her wedding."

"Oh, I don't care about that. She can do whatever she wants to do. She's twenty-five. I keep telling ya'll that. I've lived my life. You can't live for me. Got to live for yourself," Lisa said with too much Zen.

"That's ridiculous. Who doesn't want to see their daughter get married?"

"Who said anything about not wanting to see it? All I'm saying is that Zola is young and she's a free spirit. You know that," Lisa said. "I want her to have whatever she wants. Besides, I get it. I'm single and I don't have the best track record with marriage. Your father is up in New York doing God knows what, and then with Pam just passing from breast cancer four months ago, I see why Alton isn't trying to put his father through a wedding right now. Maybe it's best they elope. They're happy. Let them have some fun. We can always throw them a reception later."

"But what about her life? Her career? She could be making a huge mistake. You know the Bar Exam is in like eight weeks! She's talking about waiting to take it next year."

"She should be talking about not taking it at all," Lisa said.

"Why would you say that? After all she's done?"

"That's your dream, Zena. Not Zola's." Lisa stood to pour herself the last remaining cup of coffee from her electronic carafe.

"It's her dream, too. She finished law school and now she's set for the Bar. She's going to be an attorney." Zena looked at her mother sipping her coffee and grinning at her. "What? If she's not a lawyer, what will she be? What could she be?"

"Who the hell knows. Maybe Alton's wife?" Lisa laughed.

"I can't deal with you right now!" Zena stood and reached for her purse.

"Oh, you're going to run off now that I don't agree with everything you're saying?" Lisa said.

"I'm not running. I'm just frustrated. It's like in the last twenty-four hours all of this crazy stuff is happening. And I came here hoping you'd talk some sense into Zola, but it's like, as usual, you're on her side."

"I'm on no one's side. I just want peace. And I'm hoping to make you see Zola's side."

"Zola's side?" Zena laughed sarcastically. "Let me see—Zola's side includes eloping to Bali when the Exam is right around the corner. Zola's side includes getting married just when she's about to begin her career. I know all about Zola's side,

Mommy. I thought you'd see my side just this once."

Four eyes rolled, and Zena whisked out of the house in a way that was too common for her mother to be moved. Before Zena was in her car, Lisa had lit a new cigarette and was searching the kitchen table for the television remote. *Maury Povich* would be on in twenty minutes.

Zena made an aggressive right turn out of her mother's driveway—a turn away from Adan's old house. Her thoughts concocted a scenario where Adan was standing in his parents' front yard waiting for her to drive by. What did he want to say? Why had he asked about her? She gripped the head of the steering wheel and looked out the rearview window. The car slowed as she searched, deciding where he wasn't, which cars weren't his, which shadows in the bushes couldn't be his. Her emotions bullied her into forcing all thoughts of him away, so she resolved to snap herself back to "normal," but before she could refocus a glance to the driver's side door, her thoughts took her back—way back—to a memory that had taken place in that very location she was passing—the corner of Sassafras Street and Blue Stone Road.

It was junior year of high school. Zena and Adan were walking home from school. The dented Nissan Maxima Adan's parents got him when he turned sixteen was in the shop again, and while his best friend, Hakeem, volunteered to drive them home, Zena wanted to walk. She never minded walking home, not with Adan anyway. They could talk, really talk, about things in the world, things nobody else ever talked about, not at their school anyway. The longer she'd been around Adan she was learning that this was something that separated him from anyone she knew—he could talk about anything and seemed to know everything. And not in an annoying way, either. He was humble and charming. One afternoon, the two were walking hand in hand debating the possibility of love at first sight, a new concept Zena had encountered in a romance novel she found in the library at school. Zena said no, true love wasn't possible, and was completely dominating the conversation for a long while as Adan listened quietly, nodding from time to time. "It's ridiculous. Impossible. You can't love someone after seeing them just one time. Like one time?" Zena posed. "Like looking at someone doesn't let you know who they really are. They could be a horrible person. A liar. A killer. Right?"

Adan nodded again in acknowledgment of Zena's comment. "You just don't know someone. Like sometimes, I don't think you ever really know anyone. But definitely not from first sight. You don't know them enough to love them," Zena went on.

"But…" Adan began slowly before pausing to

gather his ideas. "But, what if it is possible? Like if it does happen for some people?"

Zena looked at Adan as if he'd gone crazy. "What kinds of people?"

Adan shrugged. "I don't know. Just, some people. Like, maybe us."

Zena laughed at the idea. "Us? You and me? Love at first sight?" She laughed again, though something in her stomach flipped the way it had when they'd met when her bicycle chain popped.

"Yes, us."

Adan let go of Zena's hand and took a few steps ahead of her so he could turn and face her. "You don't think we were love at first sight? You're saying you didn't feel anything when you first saw me? Nothing?"

Zena stopped walking and bit the inside of her upper lip to stop herself from smiling. She had felt something when she first laid eyes on Adan. But "love"? Was it love? Zena looked up at the street signs: Sassafras Street and Blue Stone Road. She readjusted her purse on her shoulder—Adan was carrying both of their book bags. Looking up at the signs, she said, "I did feel something."

Adan reached out and caught ahold of one of her hands. "Me, too. I felt something, too," he admitted.

The hold Zena had on her upper lip failed, and

a huge smile was produced on her face, one that was so big, it almost hurt her cheeks.

"What? What's so funny?" Adan asked. Standing there in his Aeropostale sweatshirt and with his and Zena's fake matching Benetton knapsacks hanging from his back, Adan looked so nervous, as if he was starting a conversation he'd never wanted to have.

"Nothing. I'm not laughing. I'm just smiling. Smiling and wondering," Zena said.

"Wondering what?"

"I'm wondering if you're saying you love me. If we're in love," Zena said.

Just then everything went black. The sky first and then everything around Zena and Adan went to shadows as if night had come from nowhere. Adan grabbed Zena's hand—not as if he was scared, but just automatically, as if it had been his first instinct to hold on to her, to protect her. "What's happening?" she asked, spinning around. It was just three-fifteen in the afternoon but no one was outside in their neighborhood. Not one dog was barking. No cars were speeding by in the road blasting music. It was dark and quiet.

"I don't know," Adan answered, turning, too. At some point, while he was holding Zena's hand, the two were back-to-back surveying their surroundings. It was the year 2000, and cell phones hadn't become a thing yet. The only way they could get anyone's attention was to scream. But something told them not to. Something told them everything was fine. Adan looked up at the sky. That's when he saw it. The moon—right in broad daylight. "Look," was all he said.

And feeling his head tilted back behind her, Zena looked up, too. After staring for a while, Zena uttered, "It's beautiful. It's an eclipse."

Chins up, ear to ear, hands still clasped from behind, Zena and Adan stared at the moon as if it was their first time seeing it, as if it was a pearl pinned to the sun. Everything beneath the sky disappeared. They were floating astronauts, space twins, drifting in a celestial storm of miracles somewhere between Earth and the heavens.

At school the next day, Zena and Adan told their science teacher, Mr. Palabas, what happened to them the prior afternoon. He was one of those spunky, white, hip earth science teachers who spent far too much time at the school trying to get the students he taught to understand that science was interesting and applicable and cool. When they talked to Mr. Palabas, he acknowledged there hadn't been an eclipse—including the fact that he had not seen one. The rookie science teacher nodded along as Adan and Zena recalled their story before beginning to let them down gently. From the bookshelf behind his messy desk, he pulled a textbook that weighed more than a toddler and flipped through pages with recorded eclipse dates in the past and future predictions. There were no predictions for April 14, 2000. Without saying it, Mr. Palabas was implying a scientific reality: there had been no eclipse.

"So you don't believe us?" Zena asked as more kids started filing into the room for class to begin.

"I believe you two experienced an eclipse," Mr. Palabas answered.

"But was there an eclipse—an actual eclipse of the sun?" Adan asked.

"Not according to these books—not according to science. But that doesn't mean you didn't experience one. Maybe it was your eclipse. An eclipse just for you two," Mr. Palabas said, and Zena and Adan looked at each other.

After switching from her driving flats to her red-bottom pumps, Zena walked into the lobby of the Peachtree skyscraper, where she rented a small but extravagant space with floor-to-ceiling windows and complementary plush leather office furniture. She promised herself she wouldn't bring up the wedding or Zola or her mother and definitely not Adan as she got off the elevator on the tenth floor. But when she saw Malak sitting at her desk in the reception area, everything she'd been hoping to hold inside came up and out her mouth the way secrets and gossip force their way to the surface when best friends resume company.

Zena leaned into Malak's desk and just started.

"Can you believe he went to my mother's house looking for me again?" She paused but went on with no answer from Malak, who was in the middle of a conversation with the phone receiver to her ear. "I mean, what the hell? What do you want from me? Why are you looking for me? Just because our sister and brother are getting married doesn't mean we are suddenly besties and you can just roll up at my mother's house," Zena said as if she was suddenly talking to Adan, but then she switched back to Malak with, "Can you believe that? Can you believe that mess? Wait, girl. Are you on the phone? Never mind. Sorry."

Malak slid the phone onto her desk and looked up at Zena with little surprise. "I'm off now," Malak said. "And, yeah, I know he was looking for you."

Zena dropped her workbag to the floor. "How?"

"He came here," Malak revealed.

Zena looked around as if maybe he was still in her office hiding out. "Here?"

"Yes."

Zena reached over the desk and grabbed the sides of Malak's arms like she was a reluctant witness to some atrocity. "What? Are you kidding me? He was here? What did he want? Why was he here?" She shook her friend.

"Clearly, he was looking for you."

Malak raised her arms to break from Zena's hold. She was used to Zena losing all composure when these kinds of things happened. In fact, she'd already told herself that she wouldn't bring Adan's pop-in visit up, but since Zena had already opened that door, all promises of silence had been recanted. "Calm down, Z," she said. "He was just downtown and wanted to talk to you. I think it's about the wedding or something." Malak grinned. "He looked good, too. Smelled good. Had on one of those fancy suits. He obviously wanted to impress someone— and it wasn't me." She sucked her teeth playfully.

"I don't care how he looked. He isn't my man," Zena said defiantly as she slid into the seat before Malak's desk—a clear sign she wanted more information. "But what did he say? I need to know everything he said."

Malak went through Adan's visit second by second for her best friend—how he'd said, "Ze-ena"; how he looked crestfallen when Malak revealed that Zena hadn't showed up at the office just yet; that he said he was in town looking for a new office space; that he was bringing his practice to Georgia. He was tired of the New York hustle and wanted to be closer to his dad. Malak shared her condolences about his mother passing and he'd looked down at the floor. He changed the subject quickly, told her she didn't have to tell Zena he'd stopped by. He'd see Zena soon. He'd make sure he did this time.

Zena froze with her mouth open and heart beating wildly. "What?" she managed to get out. "He said that? Are you sure he said that—like exactly?"

"No, I'm crazy, I made it up. I made it all up," Malak teased but then added, "Of course, I didn't fabricate this story. Why would I do that? He said it. All of it."

"Why? Why would he say that? Why does he want to see me?" Zena asked.

"I have no answers—only information. Good information, though. But, like I said, it seemed like he wanted to talk about the wedding."

"The wedding? Why do we need to talk about that?"

"Again, I have no answers, but I'm guessing it's about you being the maid of honor and him being the best man," Malak said. "Maybe he wants to go half on a gift with you. Or maybe he doesn't want them to get married, either. Maybe he's just as pissed off about all of this as you are and needs to vent."

Zena pondered. "But, still, why talk to me about it? Not like I can stop it." She scowled as she recalled the last conversation with her sister. "I don't even want to think about this. And I sure don't want to talk about it with Adan. Shouldn't he go vent to someone else if he has an issue? Someone like his wife?"

While she'd been nodding along with all of her friend's commentary, the last question gave Malak pause. She looked at Zena like she'd misspoke. "His wife?" Malak repeated as if Zena knew something she didn't or maybe Zena was confused or just wrong. "What do you mean 'his wife'?"

"His wife!" Zena shot back solidly like there was no way Malak couldn't know exactly what she'd been talking about. "His wife! Adan's wife! That's who he should be talking to. Right?"

"Talking to his wife who?" Malak's furrowed brow confirmed further confusion.

"His wife! The woman he married. That doctor— the surgeon in New York," Zena said so confidently, she sounded like she was identifying the color of the sky.

"What wom—" Malak stopped herself and directly said to Zena, "He never married that chick. Adan's not married—not unless you know something I don't know."

"He married her. It was in the damn *New York Times*!"

"No—their engagement was in the *New York Times*. But not the wedding. They never got married."

Zena felt all the blood in her body leave her

extremities and flood her brain. Her heart quivered. Something behind her eyes turned red, and she felt like she could faint—if she didn't have to hold on to ask Malak more questions. She had to be certain she was hearing what she was hearing. What was she hearing? Adan not married? Not married? Not married three years ago and probably on his second child by now? Moved on from her and into his life, a suburban dad with a suburban wife and life that was comprised of elegant dinner parties in the Hamptons and Paris vacations? What? What the hell?

"But he was engaged and it was in the newspaper! He was supposed to marry her! Why didn't he? Why didn't you tell me?" Zena looked somewhere between bewildered and amazed.

"Tell you? I'm not even supposed to mention his name. Remember that? You forbid me from ever saying his name after that *Times* article came out," Malak said.

"But my mother? Zola? No one has said anything to me about it. Why didn't you tell me? Why didn't anyone tell me?"

"Z, you forbid all of us from saying anything about Adan."

"Who cares about me forbidding you? You never listen to me any other time. And I'd think you'd know this was big enough to tell me. You can't just have me walking around in the world thinking my ex-boyfriend is married and he isn't!"

"But you said you didn't care. Remember? You said you couldn't care less about anything he was doing. He was so far in your past you hardly remembered anything about him," Malak recalled, sharing the fake sentiments as dully as Zena had. "Plus, I figured you knew anyway. That you would get the information the way everyone else gets information about their ex." Malak picked up her phone, unlocked it and handed it to Zena with a blue screen flashing. "Facebook," she said, leading Zena to Adan's page.

"Single!" Zena read aloud on his profile. She clicked into his pictures and scrolled through. There he was, all brown and peering into her. He'd aged, grown into something more distinctive, distinguished like his father and his uncles. Had a short fade and expensive-looking spectacles. He looked like the kind of man who read the newspaper at a coffee shop every morning, as if maybe he was a professor or a UN ambassador. He was handsome. The perfect depiction of what he wanted to be. In one picture he was sitting on a couch reading a book. In another, he was standing a few feet left of the Leaning Tower of Pisa. Zena quickly wondered who'd taken the pictures.

"So, you're saying you've never looked at this

page?" Malak inquired, surprised by what she knew was the answer. "It's public. It's like...public."

"No. Why would I?" Zena asked.

"Because he's your ex. I look at all of my exes' pages on Facebook. I even look at my exes' exes' pages."

"I don't have time for that. I'm too busy with this." Zena looked around the office suggestively. "I can't worry myself with what's happening to Adan. I wasn't trying to get my feelings—" Zena stopped herself.

Malak completed her thought. "Hurt?" she offered.

"No—confused," Zena corrected her. "I didn't want to get *confused* by whatever *this* is." She flippantly flicked the phone back onto Malak's desk and jumped up to regain her composure.

"It's the truth—reality—you know, what you've been avoiding all these years," Malak said.

"Don't start!" Zena picked up her bag and started walking toward her office. "I'm not avoiding reality. I'm avoiding Adan. Totally different."

"Sure you're right," Malak said, unconvinced.

"Of course I'm right," Zena said. "Look, I'm done with this. I'm letting it roll off my back." She smiled obnoxiously and pretended to shake invisible feathers on her back. "I'm feeling great. I'm ready to get on with my day and move on from all of this nonsense. I'm going to my office to look over these Patel files, and then I'm heading over to the courthouse to try to catch Judge Jones. Can you email his assistant so they're expecting me?"

"About that meeting—"

"What?"

"Zola called. She's going to get fitted for a dress today, and she wanted you to go along with her. I think she wants you to pick out a dress, too, or something," Malak revealed.

"Today?" Zena looked down at her watch. "I can't do that today. What, she thinks because she decided to get married in like forty-eight hours I need to rush and change my whole schedule to be at her beck and call? No way. I am an important attorney, and I have things to do—none of which include picking out a wedding dress."

"Actually you don't have anything to do," Malak said nervously.

"Nothing? What do you mean, nothing?"

"I cleared your schedule."

"The hell? Why would you do that?"

"Because this is more important," Malak said, standing up to meet her best friend eye to eye. "Because you said you would at least try to support your sister. And because she needs you. And because I love her. And because I love you."

The sweet statements at the end softened the impact of Malak's actions.

"Please give me the strength to be a fence!"

Zena shouted in disgust before turning to her office. "I need a barrier to stop me from screaming at somebody this morning."

Chapter 3

Zola was standing on the sidewalk in front of the big shop window at Madame Lucille's Lace, one of the last black-owned couture bridal boutiques in Atlanta. On display in the window was an elegant, slender brown mannequin draped in crystal-lined lace and organza that swept the floor. A Mississippi transplant with a French name and fake French accent, Madame Lucille Archambeau was known for making dramatic, big-entry wedding gowns that piqued the interest of the city's new elite ladies who used their wedding day to make a statement about who they were and where they were going.

When Zena pulled into the parking lot at Lucille's, still rolling her eyes at the idea of participating in the dress selection and fitting, she noted how small and humble her baby sister looked standing before the bedecked mannequin. She was so lanky, so svelte, her frame seemed smaller than the mannequins. Zola was sporting her common puffy topknot, vintage pink bifocals, weathered white high-top Chuck Taylors and secondhand-store clothing. She was boho chic, pipsqueak cute, no frills and no Atlanta fly girl fashion. Just beautiful without trying to be. But fragile and small. Too delicate. So delicate, Zena almost felt bad for her standing there by herself. If she didn't know Zola, she'd wonder where her people were—where her friends were. If anyone cared a thing about her.

"You came!" Zola called to Zena when she spotted her walking toward the building from the parking lot. Zola had been thumbing through her phone; she looked as if she might have been calling Zena. She quickly stashed the phone into the hobo sack on her arm and embraced Zena. "I can't believe you came. Malak said she'd make you, but I can't believe she really did!"

Zena let Zola wrap her arms around her, but Zena kept her arms straight and at her sides. She could smell weed and some spicy perfume in Zola's hair. It reminded her of when Zola started smoking marijuana in high school. Zena had discovered her stash beneath the sink in the bathroom they shared between their bedrooms. Zena was home for spring break and needed to borrow one of Zola's tampons, but when she pulled out the box, a rather large Ziploc bag of marijuana fell to the floor.

"Malak can't make me do a damn thing," Zena said as Zola let her go at Lucille's.

"So you came on your own accord?" Zola grinned.

"I came, Zol. I just came. Okay?" Zena said flatly. "I'm saying, what more could you want from me? Just last night you told me about the wedding, and today you're picking out wedding dresses. It's a bit much—and a bit fast."

"Well, I have two weeks, and Madame Lucille was the only couture dressmaker who said she could have something ready."

"A rush order? Sounds expensive." Zena pointed out. "How are you paying for this?"

"No worries. It's a gift," Zola said grinning. "And you don't even have to worry about your dress, either. All covered."

"Well, I know it's not Mommy. And where is she? Isn't that how this is supposed to go? Like, your mother should be here, right?" Zena asked. There was no reason to add friends to that list. Zola never really had many friends. Growing up, Zola always complained that the girls in their neighborhood were too shallow or too mean. She preferred her books of poetry and her Alton.

Zola stepped back and looked up the street pensively. "I invited Mommy. But she claimed she had things to do in her garden and that I could do it myself. You know how she is. Ever since Daddy—" Zola stopped herself and looked back at Zena as if there was something she was about to say that both of them knew but neither really wanted to hear. She went on, leaving gaps where those words might be. "If she doesn't want to be here, I'm fine with that. I don't want to deal with her pessimism anyway. That's part of why Adan and I decided to elope. I can't deal with all of her negativity. *She* can't deal with all of her baggage."

While Zena's scowl hadn't dissipated, these words served as a bridge to her sister's emotional landscape and softened Zena's antagonism. She knew her mother's limitations too well, and although Zena always managed to live with them, to put them aside and continue to press forward, Zola saw her mother's shortcomings as short circuits in their own relationship. While Zena took Lisa's ever-swelling pain at her husband's betrayal as revelation of what came with loving someone, Zola internalized Lisa's disdain for their father as slight disdain for them, for her in particular.

Soon, Madame Lucille, a silver fox decked out in a black cashmere duster and thick black Dior lenses, came out of the dress shop chiding the sisters for loitering in front of her business and, worse, blocking the couture vision in the display window. When the sisters revealed that Zola was the bride, Madame Lucille snapped her fingers, and two perky assistants dressed in all black appeared from nowhere to whisk Zola into the empty shop, where they busied her with a bin of fabric swatches and photo albums.

One of the assistants took Zena's measurements. Madame Lucille reappeared with a sketch pad and began talking about Zena's bone structure, the length of her arms, the width of her ankles as she sketched what looked like a bunch of scribbling from Zena's perspective. After what felt like seconds, Madame Lucille exhaled as if she'd run a mile and dropped her pencil to the floor. Without conferring with Zena, who was leaning forward from the hold of the assistant with the measuring tape to get a peek at the dress sketch, Madame Lucille shared her work with Zola.

"I love it! I love it so much!" Zola squealed before looking at Zena. "Oh, my God! You're going to look fabulous."

Zena smiled and tried again to get a look at the sketch herself, but one step away from the assistant measuring her led to the woman mistakenly jabbing a straight pin into Zena's thigh.

"Ouch!" Zena hollered as Madame Lucille left the room with the sketch.

After Zola picked out a few bridal gowns from the look book, one of the assistants brought a stuffed rolling wardrobe into the showroom, and Zena sat on a plush cream parlor settee as Zola was tugged in and out of dresses that looked half-right and all wrong. Madame Lucille peeked over her glasses and gave adamant "no's," scolding her assistants as if they were the reason for the trouble finding something perfect for Zola.

Zena watched Zola's confusion in the scene and thought of what she had been doing this time of year when she was Zola's age. Along with some of her classmates from Howard, she'd locked herself up in a hotel room out by the airport and studied so long and so hard for the Bar Exam that when she closed her eyes, she could see the pages from her study guides burned into her pupils. While the room smelled stale and the delivery pizza got really old really fast, the dedication to passing the exam was addictive to Zena. The focus required that she leave thoughts of everything else, of everyone behind. She didn't have to worry. All she needed to do was focus. And soon that focus would pay off and fix everything that once worried her.

The only thing that kept threatening to splinter Zena's focus in that hotel room six years ago was the knowledge that somewhere in New York,

Adan was probably doing the same thing. Law school had been their dream together. On one of those long walks home from school, they decided they'd open a practice together. The name was to be something like Law: From A to Z, which Zena hated, but Adan's enthusiasm made it minimally appealing. They'd take on civil rights cases like Thurgood Marshall and Johnny Cochrane. The plan was to graduate from high school, go to Spelman and Morehouse, then they were off to Harvard Law. They would work part-time so they didn't rack up student-loan debt, return to Georgia to take the Bar and then Law: From A to Z would be born.

Adan made it all sound so simple in the love letters he passed to Zena in the hallway at school. But then Zena didn't get into Spelman, and Adan got a full scholarship to Morehouse. Resourceful, he changed the plan. He'd take the full Morehouse scholarship. Zena would go to Bethune-Cookman. They'd see each other on breaks and in four years meet up at Harvard. But then that didn't go as planned.

Adan got into Harvard, but Zena wasn't accepted, and while she'd gotten into some top-tier law schools, she loved her Historically Black College experience at Bethune-Cookman and how Howard's law alumni in Georgia began courting her when she'd been accepted. So after seven years together, lots of leaning on and dreaming, two weeks before college graduation, Adan showed up at Zena's off-campus apartment talking all philosophically about their relationship and love and what people have had to do to survive through the centuries.

Zena ignored most of this. She was used to Adan's speeches. His big ideas and pontificating. She sat at her kitchen table, eyeing her thick Howard acceptance folder and half listened as a girlfriend would. As Adan paced and talked about excellence and "keeping his eyes on the prize," she watched him and remembered the first day they met. How cute he was. That he stole her air. The butterflies. That night after the football game junior year in Jason Corbin's basement when she lost her virginity to Adan.

She remembered their long talks, talks just like this, where they figured things out, understood things, revealed their deepest secrets in whispers. Adan had been the only person she could talk to about her parents' divorce, how it felt to suddenly not have a father there every morning—how it felt to have him ripped from her life. What it was like to watch her mother waste entire weekends in bed, smoking and watching *Dallas* reruns. And even when Lisa managed to get up and out and meet someone, it would be weeks before she'd discover he was in a relationship or just emotionally unavailable. Soon, Zena watched as Lisa gave up and resolved to stay in bed, or as close to bed as possible.

Adan was the only person who would listen to this and drape his arm over her shoulders before kissing her cheek. That was when he was a boy, but standing there in her kitchen, Adan was a full-grown man. Maybe this meant all men weren't all bad and unreliable. And love was something she could trust. Not all marriages were like the ones she'd seen in New York, like her parents'. Some were good. Mrs. Pam and Mr. Roy were in love, always in love. For the first time, Zena wondered if she'd always be in love with Adan. If he'd be her husband and they'd be married.

But then she heard Adan say something.

"So we should just be friends," Zena remembered hearing Adan say that afternoon in her apartment, miles from Bethune-Cookman.

She watched the assistants stuff Zola into another horrible dress and remembered Adan standing there, his arms crossed, his eyes focused and serious. But he couldn't be serious. He couldn't. But he went on. "I'm going to be in Boston and you will be in DC. It won't be like Atlanta and Florida. You won't be home on weekends and I won't be able to stop everything to spend time with you. Look, we have to focus right now. We have to get this right, Z. We can't afford to lose."

Zena remembered feeling her chest grow warm

and looking at Adan as if he was slipping away and suddenly a million miles in the distance. "Lose what? Lose us?" Zena had asked, confused.

"No," Adan answered. "I mean lose sight of your dreams. Of where we are going and how that could benefit our people. We have to put that first, Z. We have to put that before ourselves. And who knows, maybe when we make it, we can get back together, but until then, I think it's over. I think we have to let this thing go."

Zola was standing in front of Zena, complaining about something. None of the dresses were working, and she was running out of options.

"What do you think I should do?" Zola asked in the middle of her lament, but Zena didn't know how to respond, as she hadn't been listening.

Zena took a sip from the bottle of Perrier one of the assistants had placed on the glass table beside the settee.

"She's getting annoyed," Zola said, pointing to Madame Lucille, who was pulling dresses from the racks and tossing them to the floor while admonishing her assistants in French for bringing them to the showroom. "I can't afford to mess this up. I don't have time to go somewhere else. But nothing is sticking. Nothing looks like me—you know? The dresses are too big and fluffy or too slender and elegant. I don't think I'm any of those things. I guess I don't know what I am."

Zola fell onto the settee beside Zena and leaned forward, resting her elbows on her knees.

"Maybe I'm in over my head. Maybe that's what this dress thing is about. Like, I'm rushing so nothing is working," she said helplessly.

Zena sighed audibly at her sister's inconsistencies. While the sudden sadness was new for free-spirited Zola, the flip-flopping wasn't. For the first time, Zena got the inkling that maybe the wedding didn't have to go down; that maybe there was something she could do to stop it. She could use Zola's indecisiveness to get her to see things the way Zena saw them; or at least get Zola to hold out long enough to pass the Exam and then have more options.

"You might be right." Zena fed the idea to Zola softly beneath Madame Lucille's fake French chattering with the assistants about what to put on the wardrobe next.

"You think so?" Zola asked, her eyes widening on Zena.

"I promised myself I wouldn't say anything else, since you've obviously made up your mind, but maybe this is a sign."

Heat from outside rushed toward the sisters, signaling that the shop door had opened. They turned to see a familiar figure walking toward them, but the harsh rays of the sun coming in from the display window splashed in over most of the features.

"Who is it? You can't come in here now! We have a private appointment!" Madame Lucille protested, walking toward the figure with her assistants behind her.

"I was invited," the person said, and Zola jumped to her feet.

"Mommy!" she yelped and ran to her mother for relief. "You came."

"Yes. Last minute, but I came," Lisa said, walking past Madame Lucille. She was wearing a sweat suit, a hot pink Wal-Mart jogger that she refused to give up though it was shrinking and losing shape. "I thought you girls needed me right now. Lord knows what would happen if I left you alone doing this."

Zola pulled Lisa to the settee as if she was joining a slumber party. Along the way, Madame Lucille greeted her as the mother of the bride and snapped for the assistants to bring her something to drink.

Zola pointed to all of the dresses she'd picked over, the ones she was sure she'd love and the ones she hated but tried anyway. She went into the speech she'd just given Zena about maybe making the wrong decision, but Lisa was obviously unmoved by her child's confusion. In the middle of Zena and Zola, Lisa looked around the shop and saw a mannequin toward the back in a thin rose-gold lace sheath that looked more like a cocktail dress than something a bride would say vows in.

"Try that one," Lisa said, pointing to the dress knowingly.

All eyes shifted to the back of the shop and then back to Lisa as if she was crazy.

"No, Madame! It's not enough," Madame Lucille argued, wagging her index finger at the simple design. "It doesn't have enough *gravitas*. It's not for the bride."

"Well, maybe not for all brides, but I think it may fit this one." Lisa slid her hand onto Zola's knee.

"Really? You really think so?" Zola kind of tilted her head toward the dress. It really was nice. Simple, but nice. Pretty and dainty. She stood and walked to the mannequin with her hands held out, set to grab hold of her mother's suggestion.

Minutes later, all in the shop would see that mother really does know best. Lisa's simple suggestion looked easy on Zola. When she stepped out of the dressing room in the rose-gold sheath, which looked whimsical, soft and romantic against Zola's mahogany skin, Madame Lucille covered her mouth as if she was about the cry.

"Magnifique! Magnifique!" Madame Lucille shouted. "It's perfect. Like it was made for you, *mademoiselle*! We can add some layering, a little fall from the shoulders. But I love it!"

"I know! I know!" Zola was back to her giddy self, nearly dancing her way to the fitting pedestal. "I love it, too!"

Zena watched her sister's glee as she floated by in rose gold. Zena always thought the talk about the moment the bride finding "her" dress and bringing everyone in the room to tears was a bunch of crap. It was just a dress. But in that moment, looking at Zola, she felt some of that sappiness. Lisa's selection made all the other dresses look silly. It was somehow an expression, an extension of Zola's beauty that pushed her into some new status of womanhood. It made Zena's thoughts toss through memories of Zola growing into her femininity: her first time wearing Zena's lip gloss, her first lace bra, Zena twisting Zola's hair up in a bun before her first high school dance.

As Zola posed for Lisa, Zena felt something like tears creeping up the backs of her eyes, but she held them back.

"You love it, Zena?" Zola asked.

"It's okay," Zena offered. "Nice."

It was a weak approval but enough for Zola, who turned and went back to smile at herself in the mirror behind the pedestal. The assistants went on pinning the dress to her thin frame for proper alterations and some personalized touches from the swatches Zola liked, and Madame Lucille assured

Zola she'd personally handle everything within the next three days.

After hearing this, when the fitting was done and everyone naturally gathered at the front of the shop, Zena inquired about the dress Madame Lucille quickly sketched on a pad for her.

"It's special," Zola said. "I wanted you to have something really special."

"But it's your wedding. Shouldn't you be in the special dress?" Zena asked.

"I know, but you've always been way more fabulous than me," Zola explained.

"Well, how much does it cost?" Zena asked Zola, remembering that Madame Lucille had promised to make and fix a dress in just days. "How much is all of this costing?"

"I already told you—don't worry about it," Zola said.

"It's taken care of," Madame Lucille said, and the tone of her voice made it clear that some astronomical fee she'd imposed had cleared someone's bank account.

"Taken care of? By whom?" Zena asked, looking to Lisa suspiciously, but she knew there was no way she could pay the thousands it was likely costing to cover these charges. "Who is paying?"

"Me."

A male voice shot into the small shop like a flock of seagulls suddenly taking flight. The door was wide-open as if it had always been that way, and in the frame stood a person, a being that brought a bounty of confusing sensations to Zena's body and mind. She was stimulated by the sight, excited, awakened, pulled to life the way anyone would feel seeing an old friend, but then she was angered and agitated, dragged through the past the way anyone would feel when that old friend was an ex-boyfriend.

"Adan!" Zola cheered, bulleting past Zena and jumping into Adan's arms, as if he was a big brother returned home from the war.

Lisa looked on, smiling, but Zena could feel her mother's eyes somehow focusing on her.

In fact, Zena felt as if everyone's eyes were on her at that moment—the assistants', Madame Lucille's, even God in heaven who'd stopped time so everyone in the shop could also hear her heart beating, her throat closing and her spinning thoughts: the shop suddenly smelled like the cologne Adan wore in college; his eyes were the same; his smile was so big. He looked happy. Why hadn't he gotten married? Why was he there? He was too handsome. How'd he get to be so handsome? He really wasn't married? There was no wedding band on his ring finger.

Zena pursed her lips tightly as if these thoughts were in danger of being spoken aloud. And though she'd relaxed a little and admitted that neither her mother nor Madame Lucille and her assistants were looking at her, there was no denying where Adan had set his eyes. They were on Zena.

"Z, I've been looking for you," he said really casually.

"Guess you found me," Zena replied, mocking his tone.

"The groom?" Madame Lucille asked, stepping between them and sort of grinning at Adan.

"No. I'm the best man." Adan shook Madame Lucille's hand. "I'm Adan Douglass. We actually spoke on the phone earlier."

Madame Lucille smiled. "Oh, yes. The financier. My favorite person in the room."

"That's me," Adan confirmed. "I just wanted to stop by to make sure everything was satisfactory with the payment."

"Everything is fine, Mr. Douglass," Madame Lucille said. "I just need your signature on a few things and we're all set."

Zena watched as Adan followed Madame Lucille to the register just a few feet away.

"He's paying for this?" Zena asked Zola.

"Yes. My wedding gift. Isn't that great?"

"No. It's not."

"Why?" Zola asked.

Zena watched Adan chatting and joking with Madame Lucille at the register as if he must be up to something sinister. "Because I don't want him paying for my dress. I can pay for my own dress. I can pay for your dress, too!"

Zola looked confused, but Lisa stood there glowering at Zena for her petty resistance.

"Really? But I thought you didn't want to pay for anything," Zola said.

"I never said that," Zena countered.

"Yes, you did," Zola argued.

"No, I didn't."

"Yes, you did!"

"No, I—"

"Girls!" Lisa jumped in just as Adan had made his way back to their circle, stuffing his credit card into his wallet.

The assistants had gone about their work in the shop, and Madame Lucille was on the telephone.

"All clear," Adan announced.

"That's wonderful," Lisa said. "And thank you so much for supporting Alton and Zola. I know how much they appreciate you."

"Of course. I've been watching those two fall in love since—" Adan paused. "I guess 1999 when you all moved to Atlanta."

"You remember the actual *year*?" Lisa asked, smiling with surprise.

"I'll never forget it," he replied before looking at Zena. "Changed everything."

Adan escorted the women out of the shop. Zena followed behind, watching everyone walk and lis-

tening to them talk with a frown on her face. She
scanned Adan's body. He was wearing loose-fitting
jeans and a fitted white T-shirt that showed off his
chest. His arms were muscular and smooth.

"So, what's going on with the case you were
telling me about—the one with the little boy from
Brooklyn who was abused by his foster parents?"
Zena heard her mother ask Adan. She squinted
and rolled her eyes at Lisa.

"We got him some help," Adan answered.

"Help? I don't care about that. Did you win? Did
you sue the state?" Lisa prodded.

Adan laughed and added, "We did, Mrs. Shaw.
I didn't want to put it like that, but we did. He's on
a long, tough road to recovery mentally, but finan-
cially, he's secure for the rest of his life."

"That's amazing. We need more good lawyers
out there like you, doing what you do. Every time
you call and tell me you've won a case, I cheer because I know you're on the right side of things,"
Lisa said.

Zena read into her mother's words and con-
cluded that Lisa and Adan chatted regularly. This
was news to Zena. It was also interesting that Lisa
knew what Adan was doing in his career. The last
she'd heard, he'd followed his dream of working in
civil rights but also took on some smaller pro bono
community cases. His firm was small but successful. He was in the headlines, but Zena struggled

not to catch any of them. Apparently, Lisa wasn't doing the same. She sounded as if Adan was her long-lost son.

"Thank you for saying that. I need to hear it every once in a while," Adan said to Lisa. "Things get hectic working in the community. I mean, it pays well in the heart, but it stresses the head and wallet." Adan looked at Zena. "I'm sure you understand, Zena."

Before Zena could respond, Lisa answered for her, saying, "Please, Zena works with rich people. Her clients are trying to add millions to their millions."

"Not true, Mommy," Zena said. "I take on some pro bono work, too."

"Really?" Zola looked at Zena as if this was a stretch.

Zena snapped back, "Yes, really."

"See, I knew you'd work with the people," Adan said, catching Zena's eye and locking in. "That was your dream. It was our dream. Remember?"

Zena didn't say anything. She was silent until the lull in the conversation was deafening.

Lisa announced that she had to get going. She was working the night shift at the airport. Adan volunteered to walk Lisa to her car, but she wouldn't have it.

Zena tried to follow Lisa and Zola into the parking lot without saying goodbye to Adan, but he stopped her.

"Zena, hey, can I talk to you for a second?" he asked.

The question split the air. All three of the women stopped. Zola and Lisa looked at Zena, anticipating her response with nervous excitement.

"Me?" Zena looked as if maybe she'd heard him incorrectly or maybe there was another Zena within a hundred-mile radius.

"Yeah. *You.*"

Zena looked at Adan discerningly, but she didn't respond.

After a few seconds of silence, Lisa said, "Of course you can, Adan," while reaching out for Zena. "But first, let me chat with her and Zola. I just need to make sure the girls are ready for our family dinner party."

"Dinner party?" Zola asked as Lisa pulled her and Zena to the side and forced them into a huddle.

"What dinner party, Mommy?" Zola repeated.

"Shut up, child. There ain't no damn dinner party," Lisa said bluntly. "I pulled you two here because I wanted to say something to you girls and I want to make sure I say it before I leave here. Now, I know I haven't been the best mother—the best role model. I never really got over your daddy cheating on me and that divorce. But I don't want you two to use that as a way to limit yourselves.

Love is a beautiful thing. And you can't be afraid of it. I haven't found anyone. But that doesn't mean you can't."

Lisa looked at Zola and said, "It doesn't mean you can't get married." Lisa looked at Zena and said, "And it doesn't mean you can't fall in love." She closed her eyes, and a tear rolled down each cheek. "I want you girls to support each other in love. To make sure you both find it. And keep it. And protect it. Even if I can't help you, I can tell you the truth." Lisa kissed Zola on the forehead, and then she went to kiss Zena, but before she did, she said sternly, "Don't mess this up. That man loves you."

"Mommy—" Zena started, but Lisa stopped her.

"No excuses! Just listen to me," Lisa ordered.

When Zola and Lisa left, Zena stood there facing the parking lot, watching them pull out in their cars, afraid to turn around to face Adan. She felt as if maybe he wasn't really there. Maybe this wasn't real. She'd imagined him walking into the shop. Imagined him walking out.

"I'm still here," Adan said as if he had been reading her mind. "Right over here." He waved jokingly.

At once, Zena felt Adan behind her. She could smell him. See his shadow above hers on the concrete. This only made it harder to turn around.

"You going to walk away or something?" Adan asked softly, and it might have been a joke but he sounded as if it was plausible.

Zena turned swiftly, ready for battle or confrontation. "No, Adan," she said. "I'm not going to walk away—not yet. So what did you want to talk about?"

"Are you free? Maybe we could go somewhere to get a drink."

"Why? What do you need to say to me over a drink that you can't say right here?" Zena asked harshly.

"Dang, girl," Adan said, responding to her gruffness. "I was just suggesting we go somewhere to get out of this heat. But I guess I do remember that you like being outside in the middle of the afternoon."

"Look, I don't have time for a drink. I need to get back to my office. I have work to do."

"I thought Malak said your day was clear," Adan said.

"Really? She told you that? I guess she's also the person who told you I'd be here."

"No. I didn't expect to see you here. I was just stopping by to make sure Zola was all right."

"Why? Why are you doing this? Why are you paying for her dress?" Zena asked.

"It's a gift. And why not?" Adan answered.

"Because." Zena slid her hand onto her hip and

furrowed her brow to bring the past into the discussion.

"Because we haven't spoken?" Adan asked.

"That's the understatement of the century."

"But this is about Alton and Zola. I want to support them. I thought we both should. That's why I want to talk to you—to find out where your head is on Bali and everything."

"Oh. That's what you wanted to talk to me about?" Zena asked. Just then, the heat had gotten to her. She felt sweat rolling down her back, her underarms moisten. The anxiety in her gut was bubbling up. She wanted to scream at Adan. Did he really think he was going to show up and just talk about Zola's wedding? Without talking about what he did? Without talking about how he left her apartment in Florida that day just two weeks before her graduation?

"Yes, I want to talk about the wedding," Adan confirmed. "What else would I want to talk to you about?"

Zena rolled her eyes.

"Look, what about the wedding? What do you want to talk about? That it's stupid? That these two have no grounds to get married? That they'll be divorced in two years? That you're wasting your money on this dress and God only knows why?" Zena listed. "Because if those aren't the key points of your conversation, I don't know what else there is for us to say to each other."

"Why shouldn't they get married?"

"Because we're a mess. Because we're not ready."

"We?"

"What?" Zena was confused.

"You said, 'we,'" Adan pointed out.

"I said *they*."

"Well, I disagree. I think they're ready. As a matter of fact, I was the one who told Alton to propose."

"You've got to be joking. You planted this seed?" Zena snarled.

"Yes. I think it will be good for Alton. Give him a little motivation. He loves Zola. He'll do anything for her—you know that. Maybe having a family will help him focus on his dreams," Adan explained.

"Focus? What about Zola's focus? What about her dreams? She's not ready for a family. She was just about to take the Bar. Do you know she's not taking it now? Not taking it because of this wedding?" Zena asked. "Wait! Was that your idea, too?"

"She can take it next year when they get settled," Adan said.

"She'll be pregnant by next year. And did you wait a year to take the Bar? No. You were focused.

Right, Adan?" Zena charged. "You kept your 'eyes on the prize.'"

"Where'd that come from?" Adan looked as if he hardly remembered saying that to Zena.

"It came from you. How could you possibly forget?" Tears gathering in her eyes, Zena turned and walked quickly to her car.

Chapter 4

A little after 6:00 p.m. and Zena was laying in the center of her bed, praying for sunset and sleep. She wanted nothing else to do with this day. Too many hours had been spent living in the past, and she'd convinced herself that the future would be better. Though she hadn't been to church in over a year, she was humming notes of Yolanda Adams's rendition of "This Too Shall Pass" while forcing her eyes closed and imagining her new day at sunrise. Then, she'd run five miles and meet the sun at the top of Stone Mountain. She'd get home in time to watch the news, answer all emails and voice mails, and indulge in her two-hour beautification regime before leaving the house in a perfectly tailored black suit that captured the correct ardor and acumen of her business style. She'd zip through traffic to work in her sparkling, freshly waxed Porsche—she would've stopped by the car wash on the way home from her run—to find her designated parking spot empty at the office. Malak would have anticipated her arrival and had all necessary files and information needed to have the perfect day stacked in a neat little pile ready for Zena's entry. There would be no Zola and Alton, no Mommy and no damn Adan. Everything would be back to normal, back to perfection in the morning—if only she could get there.

The bright sun outside her bedroom window sure wasn't helping. The loud rush-hour traffic buzzing past her building didn't help the situation. Neither was her praying and gospel singing. Not even the four shots of whiskey she'd downed like Kool-Aid. Nothing, in fact, was working. And the biggest setback of all: Zena's own heart. It just refused to cooperate. While her mind had the plot and plan to return to business as usual, her heart was a mess of business unfinished. And what was that? So many emotions she'd convinced herself to toss aside or bury deep down inside. So many complicated emotions she'd successfully hidden away that were now springing forth like those blooming perennials in her mother's garden. The worst thing about emotions springing forth from unfinished business of the heart was that the more Zena tried to take control, the stronger these emotions became, the louder they became, the freer, the wilder.

It was Adan's scent. How it had interrupted everything inside Lucille's Lace and had whispered something to Zena she couldn't understand or recall? And it wasn't his cologne or his aftershave. It was his real scent. The actual scent of him. The one she knew. The one she'd inhaled through so many nights and woken up to on so many mornings. It was his aura. His entire being collected in free aromatic notes set for olfactory seduction. And that was it. Straight seduction. After all these years, Adan had walked into Lucille's Lace and seduced her with his scent. How could she have been so stupid? Have fallen for this trick? It was a trick, right? Why hadn't she covered her nose? Held her breath? Pulled one of those gas masks soldiers wore in those World War II movies out of her purse and run for cover the moment Adan walked into the store?

But, no, it wasn't seduction. *Seduction* would mean she'd been *seduced*. That she'd fallen for the trick. That Zena wanted Adan. That Zena wanted anything from Adan. And she didn't. Right?

Zena denied response to this internal debate, but it reminded her of her first big blowup with Adan, the one that nearly tore them apart. The two were still head over heels and happily living in the land of puppy love. But, still, Zena had been feeling as if there was a change in her first real boyfriend. They'd been together five months and kept a pretty regular schedule: any waking moment when they weren't otherwise busy, they were with each other. Their relationship was equally a close friendship and a romance, and so hours together were heartwarming and sweet but also easy and comfortable. When she was with Adan, Zena felt as complete as she could possibly be. It was as if Adan was a part of her, a gateway into her conscious, her thoughts and feelings.

That was why when Adan canceled four hangout dates in a row, Zena became suspicious. Well, her feelings didn't begin with suspicion. First she was simply off put by his announcement that he wouldn't be able to take her to their normal Saturday-morning matinee movie when Zena's mother was home from work and she didn't have to watch Zola. They'd been going to see movies each Saturday morning for eight weeks, so it was different but not unimaginable that Adan wanted to miss one day. It gave Zena pause, but she kept it inside and stayed in bed that Saturday.

The next weekend, Adan canceled the movie date and backed out of the roller-skating rink with Zena and the rest of their friends from school. Zena went alone but felt so lonely without Adan, she sat quietly throughout most of the night and went home early. When Malak and her boyfriend dropped Zena off, she stopped at the top of the walkway to her house and looked down at Adan's house with sad eyes. Forlorn and a little curious, Zena thought to run to Adan's house and bang on the door, ordering that he tell her what was going on. After all, he didn't even have a reason for canceling all of these times. He kept saying he was tired or studying. But that was all. Zena decided against running down the street and cornering Adan. She didn't want to seem like some jealous and insecure girlfriend who couldn't ever leave her boyfriend alone even to study or sleep.

But then the last straw was a week before her sixteenth birthday. Everyone was heading to the Civic Center downtown to see Goodie Mob, Adan's all-time favorite group in the world. The day before the show, though, Adan announced that yet again, he couldn't go, because he had to study. Standing beside Adan's locker as he got his books together for his next class, Zena scoffed and turned to stomp away from Adan in disgust.

"Wait! What's wrong?" Adan asked, grabbing her arm to stop her.

"Study? Yeah, right. Study what? I'm in all of your classes, and we don't have any tests coming up."

Adan frowned as if Zena was being irrational,

and Zena hated that. "I don't only study for exams. I study to be intelligent," he said.

"Well, go right on ahead. You be intelligent," Zena snapped back.

"What?" Adan pushed.

"You love Goodie Mob! Why would you miss their concert?" Zena asked. "Look, are you seeing some other girl? Is that it? Do you want to break up?" The words from Zena's mouth released some emotional torrent inside of her. She didn't even know where it came from, but she started crying and shaking and saying things to Adan that she didn't even mean. Some other kids in the hallway started looking on, so Adan quickly pulled Zena into the classroom beside his locker.

The room was empty and dark. Zena walked over to the window and wrapped her arms around her waist. "Adan, I can take it now. If you want to break up now, I can take it."

Adan responded with, "What are you talking about?"

Zena turned to him, looking surprised that he wasn't following. "You keep canceling dates with me. You're not talking to me. You keep saying you're studying and sleeping. So, I'm thinking you just want to break up."

Adan still looked lost, even more confused. "No. Not at all. That's not it." He laughed a little, but quickly hid his chuckles. He walked over to

Zena beside the window. He opened her closed arms and smiled at her.

"What are you smiling about?" Zena asked.

"I'm smiling because this is funny. Because you think I want to break up with you and what I feel is the opposite," he said. "Zena, do you want to know why I've been canceling on you? Why I'm not going to the concert?" Zena nodded. Adan reached into his back pocket and pulled out his wallet. He handed it to Zena.

"What? What's this for?" she asked.

"I can show you better than I can tell you," Adan said. "Open my wallet and inside you will find $73.48. All the money I've saved for the last month."

Zena opened the wallet and counted the money. Adan knew the exact amount. "So? Why is that important?" she asked him.

"It's the money I've been saving to take you out someplace nice for your birthday. I asked my father for money, but he said it was important that I saved my own money to take you out. That's what a man should do. That's why we haven't been going to the movies and I couldn't go skating or to see Goodie Mob—because I want to take you out to a nice dinner for your birthday. Can't you see? I don't want to break up with you. I want to be with you. I love you."

Struggling to erase this sweet memory of the

first time Adan said he loved her, Zena was rolling around in her bed like a toddler in the middle of a tantrum. Soon, she gave up on sleep and reached for her cell phone. Thankfully, Adan's number was not in her phone book, because right then he would've gotten a confusing, whiskey-tinged earful about how he'd lied to her that day in the empty classroom.

Instead of phoning her ex with a drunken diatribe, naturally, Zena called her best friend.

"You told that man where I was?" Zena blurted out when Malak answered.

"Hum. I guess this means you saw Adan?" Malak posed the question coolly. "And judging from your voice, you've seen Jack Daniel's, too. I thought it would take you at least a week to turn to the bottle. But I see it's been what—like eight hours?— and you're already giving me Diana Ross in *Mahogany* over the phone. Do you need me to come over there?"

"No!" Zena protested, poking out her lip as if Malak could see it. But her protest wasn't quite convincing. She needed her best friend with her. She knew it and Malak knew it.

As if she'd heard the opposite, Malak replied, "Okay. I'll be there in like two hours. I need to get the kids and drop them at my mama's. And don't drink all the liquor, either. I want some."

Zena hung up and covered her face with the first

thing she could grasp—some lumpy red throw pillow she kept reminding herself to throw out. The simple satin square matched nothing in her stark taupe and ecru bedroom, and it mostly maintained its residency due to tradition and Zena's own forgetfulness. In fact, she'd actually forgotten where the little red pillow had come from in the first place, and that was part and parcel of her reluctance to toss it out. She remembered having the pillow on her bed at her first apartment in Daytona Beach. But she didn't remember how it had gotten there. Didn't ever remember buying it. Sometimes she imagined showing up to one of her Bethune-Cookman reunions and hearing one of her old roommates ask if anyone had the old red pillow her dead grandmother had made, or something like that. Zena would reveal that she still had the thing, and they would have a good hug before Zena produced the pillow and saved the day.

But right then as the lumpy satin pillow soaked up Zena's tears and anger, she knew this was all a figment of her imagination. As she pressed the pillow to her face, it pulled her thoughts back. That pillow didn't belong to any of her old roommates. No one's dead grandmother had made it with her bare hands. The little stupid pillow was a Kmart Bluelight Special Adan had picked out for Zena's first apartment two weeks before the start of sophomore year. He'd tossed it into her cart.

"Red? Why did you put that into the cart?" Zena stopped pushing the cart and reached to pull out the red pillow, but Adan grabbed her hand.

"Just get it. It'll look nice on your bed," Adan said.

"But my comforter is purple and tan." Zena pointed to the full-size bed-in-a-bag set in the cart. Beneath it, she had a purple lava lamp, a set of plastic purple hangers and a tan photo collage wall hanger, all decorations for Zena's bedroom in her first off-campus apartment she'd share with three other coeds.

"You need a pop of color, Z," Adan said confidently.

Zena grinned. "What do you mean 'a pop of color'? What do you know about that?"

"It's the style. All the girls at Spelman have one pop of color in their dorm rooms. Like pink and white with turquoise. Or red and black with yellow."

All summer after freshman year, Zena had to listen to Adan talking about how the Spelman girls across the street from Morehouse did this and that. How they wore their hair and what kind of music they were listening to. Adan would go on about his Spelman sister, Morenike, and her natural hair. That Morenike was going to study in Paris sophomore year and Zena should do the same thing. It would look good on her Harvard application.

"Red, black and yellow is disgusting, and how do you know what the dorm rooms at Spelman look like?" Zena asked suspiciously; she'd already decided that Adan was cheating on her and had fallen in love with Morenike.

"Because I've been in the dorm rooms at Spelman," Adan replied with not one marker of nervousness.

"Really? And what would you say if I said I'd been in the male dorms at Bethune-Cookman?" Zena pushed herself between Adan and the cart and put her hands on her hips to strengthen her inquisition.

"I'd say, 'I'm happy for you,'" Adan answered. "I'd ask what colors the guys in Daytona Beach are using to decorate their rooms."

Zena huffed and stomped to the back of the cart before tossing the red pillow back onto the shelf.

"Really? Don't do the jealous thing, Z. You're so much cooler when you're confident."

"I am confident, but I don't care how the girls at Spelman decorate their rooms, and I definitely don't want to hear about it or that you're all up in their rooms."

"Why not? The only reason you wouldn't want to hear it is if you think I'm cheating with one of them."

"Are you?"

"Hell no!"

"Then why are you always talking about them?"

"Because they're great girls—great women. And they're my friends. Why not? You want me to talk about dudes all the time?" Adan asked.

Zena said, "I want you to talk about me."

"About you? You want me to talk about you?" Adan smiled and walked toward Zena. He pushed the cart away and stood in front of her. "You know, it's funny that you complain about me talking about all those girls because all those girls complain about me talking about one girl."

"Who?"

"You," Adan revealed. "They complain because I'm always talking about how you have straight As. And how you got the Presidential Scholarship. And that you're the first in your family to go to college, but they'd never know it because you're taking junior-level classes and acing them all. And that you're so pretty. And while the girls at Spelman are cute, really cute, none of them are as beautiful as you. Not even close."

Zena was blushing and feeling stupid about arguing over the red pillow. She was about to apologize, but Adan stopped her.

"I'm not going anywhere," he said. "I know everyone keeps telling us this long-distance relationship thing doesn't work, but we're going to show them all. We're going to make it. We have a plan, and no girl at Spelman, not even my Spelman sister, is going to ruin that. I love you, Z."

The Bluelight Special red pillow made it back into the cart and through checkout. Adan was right. It added the perfect pop of color to the purple and tan Kmart bed-in-a-bag.

By the time Malak made her way to the apartment, Zena had cut the little red pillow into so many pieces it looked as if rose petals and cotton balls were scattered all over her bedroom floor. Zena was sitting on the floor in the middle of the mess, looking as if she was trying to figure something out.

"I see you finished the liquor," Malak said, looking at the empty bottle of Honey Jack on Zena's nightstand. "How many times do I need to tell you that you can't drink?"

Malak dropped her purse and jacket on the bed and went to gather her friend off the floor.

"Let's get you back into bed," Malak said, pulling up a reluctant Zena.

Zena groaned something that sounded as if it might be a cry or helpless whimper as she allowed her friend to move her body.

"How did you get in here?" she asked Malak.

"I'm your assistant. I have a key."

Zena nodded and slid into her normal place in

the bed. Malak hopped in beside her. She reached for her purse.

"I didn't know what you had, so I made this a BYOB party." She pulled out a bottle of Hennessy. "No sense in just one of us being drunk." She giggled and slid the bottle onto the nightstand so she could go to the kitchen to get one glass.

When she returned, Zena had already opened the bottle and was taking sips through tears.

"Oh, shit!" Malak climbed onto the bed and grabbed the bottle. "You're turning down epic breakdown lane right now! I'll go with you, but you have to let me catch up." Malak poured her glass, took a quick shot and poured more Hennessy before putting the bottle back into her bag and zipping it shut. She took a sip and lay back on the pillow adjacent to Zena.

The friends rested in silence for a while, letting the moment catch up to Zena's racing emotions and Malak's alcohol level.

"I was fine," Zena whispered. "Doing just fine. I was over him. I'd moved on."

"Chile, wasn't nothing fine about you. Yes, you were doing something that looked like moving on. But wasn't nothing fine."

"I'm a successful attorney. I make a good salary. I vacation in Tahiti. I have perfect credit. I own a horse," Zena listed, struggling so hard to sound sober.

"And you don't have a man. Not-a-one!" Malak countered. "When was the last time you had a man? I sure can't remember."

Zena tried to recall this information herself; it was hard, but after some seconds she resurrected a name: "Corey! That was my last boyfriend."

"The dude with the perm? The one everybody said was gay?"

"He didn't have a perm! He was half-Panamanian. And he wasn't gay."

"You can keep claiming that, but he was gay as hell. Evidenced by the fact that he didn't ever want to get into bed with you," Malak said laughing.

"He was a Christian man who was saving it for marriage." Zena felt herself smile a little.

"No, he was saving his down-low lifestyle for marriage. As soon as you two crossed that threshold and he got those papers, you wouldn't have seen an ounce of affection for the rest of your life! Next!"

"Well…" Zena tried to recall another ex, and this required so much thought she was frowning and furrowing her brow as if she was considering some complex mathematical equation. "What about Obinna?"

"That fine African doctor?" Malak recalled. "He was a good catch. What ever happened to him?"

"He wanted me to move to Nigeria with him."

"Hell no! They get you there and it's *Not Without My Daughter* starring Zena Nefertiti Shaw as Sally Field. Next!"

Zena started frowning and furrowing again, trying to find another name, but the struggle was too difficult.

"You know what—just let it go," Malak said, "because you've already proven my point—ever since your breakup with Adan all you do is date these men who aren't available to you, or you aren't available to them. It's like you're waiting on someone or something to happen. Like you're waiting on this perfect man to show up, but we both know he doesn't exist so maybe you're waiting on a specific perfect man to show up."

"I'm not waiting on anyone. Especially not Adan."

"Then why aren't you married? Why haven't you found anyone yet, Z?" Malak asked.

"I could ask you the same thing. Why aren't you married? Why haven't you found anyone?" Zena countered.

"Because I've been married and it didn't work out. Marriage is a gamble. My ex was way too controlling. But we aren't talking about me. We're talking about you, Zena, and your lack of an ability to find a mate."

"You say it like there's something wrong with me," Zena complained.

"Because there is," Malak said flatly.

"But you just said marriage is a gamble, so how is there something wrong with me if I'm not married? That's the same crap everyone says to successful, independent black women like me! Maybe there's nothing wrong with us. Maybe we're just smarter."

"Look, I don't know about all that stuff you done read in some *Essence* 'Single in the City' article, but I know you. I'm your girl and I've been studying you more than half my life. I know what's wrong with you and when something is wrong with you. And I know exactly how you must've felt when you saw Adan today at the dress shop. And I know it broke your heart."

Zena rolled over to snuggle in Malak's arms and let her tears fall.

"That's it, girl! Let it out! Let it all out!" Malak said, patting Zena on the back.

The sun had finally set and the room was dim. Blue lights twinkled from electronic devices. Some sad Sade song should've been playing on the radio.

"What happened that night you and Adan broke up in Daytona Beach?" Malak asked. "I always wanted to know, but you never said anything. You just said it was over with him, and then you left for law school. When you came back, you made me pinkie promise never to say his name again. So I didn't, but I always wanted to."

Zena looked at the pieces of the red satin pillow all over her bedroom floor. The breakup was two weeks before graduation. She was on her third apartment by then. She only had one roommate. The red pillow was still in tow. Adan was giving his philosophical "Eyes on the Prize" speech and had broken up with her before she even realized what was happening. Again, she remembered him saying, "So, we should just be friends" in that fake, nasal "Man of Morehouse" accent he'd picked up on the debate team.

Those words sent Zena into a rage that frightened both her and Adan.

She had jumped up from the kitchen table and started wailing at him, calling him names and sobbing so deeply she wouldn't be able to stop long after she'd pushed Adan out onto the street without his car keys or his bags or anything and refused to let him back in until he returned with police.

Zena had tried to forget but still remembered all the things she'd said to Adan before she kicked him out—that she always knew he'd do this to her; he was just a liar. He was just like her father. No good. She struggled to slap him, to scratch him, to punch him, but Adan just held Zena down and told her she'd get over this—that she'd be okay without him. That only further infuriated Zena and sent her to a place beyond rage—to pure sorrow, to a real mourning over all of the love Zena had lost in her life that made her knees weak and delivered her to the floor, where Adan knelt down and tried to understand as she wept.

When it seemed as if she was almost calm, Adan had asked what she wanted him to do. How he could make things right?

Zena had cried, "Marry me. Let's get married. Then we'll move to Boston together and you can finish law school and I'll just go to school for paralegal or something. I can be your secretary. Whatever. I don't care, as long as we're together. I don't want to lose you. I can't!"

Adan had stroked Zena's hair into place. "No, we can't," he said as earnestly as he could. "I can't let you do that."

Zena had asked, "Why? Why can't you?"

"Because I believe in you too much to do that to you. And that's why I'm doing this. That's why we're breaking up. If we stay together, you'll lose yourself. Lose your dreams. And you losing your dreams, well, that's not a part of my dream," Adan had replied.

Zena found the last strength left in her knees and arms to get up and push Adan out the door.

"Malak, I asked that man to marry me," Zena said, remembering the confused look on Adan's face when she'd said it. "And he said he couldn't do it because he wanted us to keep sight of our dreams that apparently didn't include each other."

"That's messed up, Z," Malak said.

"It's beyond messed up. And every time I remember it, all I can think is that he was the first man I ever trusted, the first one I loved, and look at what he did. Look how he handled it. And now here he is back in Atlanta talking about how he encouraged his brother to propose to my sister, saying it will be good for them. If that isn't freaking irony? He has no problem taking my sister's eyes *off* the prize, paying for our dresses and God knows what else."

"He bought her dress?"

Zena ignored this. She popped up and looked around the dark room through newly puffy eyes. She leaned over and flicked on her bedside lamp.

"You know, the more I think about it, the more this thing just doesn't make sense," she said.

"What?" Malak sat up slowly and went for a sip of her Hennessy.

"Why is he so game to support this wedding? Is it because his own marriage failed?"

"Well, technically he was never married, so his marriage couldn't fail," Malak explained.

"You know what I mean, Malak. Maybe this is about his marriage failing to even exist and me doing perfectly fine without him," Zena said, adding up details. "I'm saying I made it! I made something of myself. I handled my part of Law: From A to Z. My *own* agency Z. Shaw Law is blowing up, and he knows it. And he knows that I also managed to pull my little sister up and make something of her—something he's only halfway done with Alton, the wannabe neo-soul singer. So now he wants to bring me down."

Malak squinted as she tried to arrive at Zena's conclusions. "Nah. Sounds kinda crazy to me."

Zena jumped up from the bed with her thoughts racing to epiphany.

"I'm not going to let him do this," she announced.

"Do what?"

"Ruin what I've worked so hard for, so he can just placate his own male ego!"

"I don't know what any of that means," Malak confessed, rubbing her forehead.

"It means—I can't let this wedding happen. I can't let Adan win. Can't you see it, Malak? If those two get married, the same thing Adan was so afraid was going to happen to me will happen to Zola. She'll be living in Alton's shadow forever. She'll never live her dream."

"The dream you gave her?" Malak pointed out.

Zena rolled her eyes. She stood before her bedroom window watching traffic roll up Peachtree Road toward Buckhead.

Malak was behind her, saying something about

Zola being in love and Zena needing to support it no matter what, but Zena was already caught up in her thoughts and heard little of the speech.

"I'm not going to let him do this," Zena repeated. "I can't."

Part II

Under the Bali Moon

Chapter 5

Zena got Adan's telephone number from a thoroughly surprised Zola and called him to apologize for her behavior outside Lucille's Lace. She chuckled coyly and claimed she hoped he'd accept her apology for being so reckless with her words. Adan sounded just as surprised as Zola, but he accepted Zena's apology and matched it with one of his own. He hadn't meant to upset her or anyone else. He explained that he simply wanted to "do what is right for Alton and Zola."

Zena gushed at his greatness and agreed to do the same. She revealed that she was so happy Zola was marrying Alton. And she'd decided she was going to Bali. She had to be by her baby sister's side. "Really?" Adan asked.

"Of course! What? Do you think I would lie about something like that?"

Adan should've said, "yes," of course, because Zena was definitely lying. Zena's saccharine-laced approval of Adan's support of the wedding and her sudden decision to be there to play the loving and devoted big sister were a meticulously orchestrated oral camouflaging set to conceal what Zena really had going on.

At the top of a long list of things Zena knew about Zola were two important facts she'd forgotten in recent days:

Zola thrived on love and trust.

Zola especially thrived on love and trust from Zena.

There were times during their childhood when Zena and Zola were just simply attached at the hip. And not because they were sisters; it was because with everything going on around them—Daddy cheating and making more babies with more women; Mommy struggling just to feed them and keep a roof over their heads—Zena and Zola only had each other to depend on.

They couldn't go to their father with their problems—half the time they didn't even know where he lived. They couldn't go to their mother with their problems—sometimes when she got home from working doubles in the catering department at Delta Air Lines, her feet would be so swollen all she wanted to do was lie on the couch in absolute silence.

The girls went to each other then; they leaned on each other. First periods. First dances. First boyfriends. First broken hearts. They trusted each other through it all. And even when Zena outgrew this full dependence on Zola, the little sister kept her focus and leaned on the big sister. And she never really stopped. Zola loved and trusted Zena more than anyone in the world—Malak had been right about that.

Once, when Zola was four and they were still living in the projects in Queens, she claimed there was a ghost under the bed. Zena, ten years old and left alone to take care of her little sister, pretended she believed Zola and asked Zola to show her the ghost. They crept out of the bed and got down on their knees and peeled back the sheet hanging over the bed. Zola was so nervous, she kept her little eyes squinted in fear of actually seeing something scary. Zena told her to point out the ghost. Zola peeked. Zena begged to see the ghost. Zola opened one eye. Zena asked where the ghost was. Zola opened her second eye. Soon, Zola was looking wide-eyed at her fears. "See, no ghost," Zena said, smiling. "No ghost here. No ghost anywhere."

If Zena wanted Zola to see that getting married

was going to set her back and potentially ruin everything she'd worked so hard for, she couldn't keep throwing it all in Zola's face. She couldn't keep telling Zola everything that was going wrong. She had to let Zola see things for herself. She had to let Zola get out of the bed, get on her knees and peek under the bed to find her own ghosts. And just as she did when they were little, she had to be by Zola's side.

"Zollie Rollie Polie!" Zena was standing in the lobby of Hartsfield-Jackson Airport with one arm open and ready to receive a hug from her sister. A huge black luggage roller was at her feet.

"Zollie?" Zola laughed, hugging Zena. "You haven't called me that in like years." She had her own luggage roller at her feet. It was hot pink and bigger than Zena's, and the word *Bride* was stitched on the front pocket in white.

Two weeks had passed, and after successfully showering her sister in sugary speeches and all the comforts any bride could desire, including a small spa shower the day before the Bali departure, Zena was officially a maid of honor to-be.

She arrived at the airport with her game face hidden beneath black shades and a surprise behind her back.

"Come on, how could I forget your nickname?" Zena joked with Zola before revealing her surprise. "And how could I forget how you got that old nickname?"

In her right hand, Zena was balancing a huge box of Krispy Kreme doughnuts she'd picked up on the way to the airport.

"You remembered?" Zola laughed. "I can't believe you remembered!"

"How could I forget? Like the one thing you loved when we moved to Atlanta was these damn Krispy Kreme doughnuts. You loved them so much, you got a little gut, and me and Mommy started calling you—"

Zola cut in with "Zollie Rollie Polie!"

The sister's laughed together at the memory of Zola going completely insane every time she saw that dark orange Hot Now sign lit up when they passed the old Krispy Kreme window on Abernathy in the West End. One day, Lisa pulled over and bought Zola an entire dozen of the sticky and doughy sweets and told her to eat them all so she could get over her infatuation. It didn't work. Zola's love affair grew and grew, and soon, so did her stomach.

"I figured we could eat these before we board the plane, so we can get a little rest," Zena said.

"Rest? After we eat these doughnuts, we'll be bouncing off the walls!"

"Not once we get on the plane and have a little bit of that free wine!"

"The *free* international-flight wine!" Zola recalled, reaching for the doughnuts.

"Exactly."

Zola and Zena tore through six Krispy Kreme doughnuts apiece—a small victory for anyone familiar with the addictive brand. They rushed toward their flight, and once aboard they celebrated Zola's coming new life with so many wine toasts they were both asleep within an hour.

It was still a long fifteen hours in the air before their layover in Korea. Zola and Zena kept each other company by telling stories and making plans. There were baby names and shared vacations. There were decisions about what religion Zola would practice in her new home—if any. Would she and Alton become full vegans as they'd planned? Would they raise vegan babies? Zena grimaced at the thought of any child eating soy crumbles all their life.

While Zena wasn't exactly excited to chat with Zola about these things, the subjects kept her from bringing up one of the things she promised she'd leave on the back burner until she got everything sorted out with Zola—the real future Zena was going to make sure Zola actually lived. The one where she was an attorney.

When they boarded the plane from Korea to Indonesia, frequent naps and in-flight movies filled the lull in the conversation between Zena and Zola.

Once, Zena looked over at Zola sitting beside the window in the first-class seats Zena reserved for their daylong journey. She found Zola looking off into the clouds, smiling at nothing. She imagined Zola must've been thinking about Alton waiting for her in Bali, setting things up for their big day.

Right then, Zena felt an arresting solitude that caught her completely off guard. There was no love she could see in the clouds. No face staring back at her. No future to project. It was just her. And what did she have? Her business? Her success? Her money? She could take care of herself. She could buy anything she wanted. Go anywhere she dreamed. But she was alone. She was worse than alone—she was lonely.

A stewardess seemed to show up from nowhere with a glass of merlot. She was an Asian woman with beautiful full lips and a wide nose that reminded Zena of some of the Melanesian women she'd met during her last vacation to Vanuatu.

Similar to her other trips to parts of Asia and throughout the Pacific, Zena noticed that when she and Zora transferred flights in Korea, most everyone on the flight was Asian; however, the diversity in complexion and hair texture and facial features was wide-ranging and similar to differences she saw between white and black people in America.

"These long flights can get to you," the stewardess said, handing the full wineglass over to Zena.

"Thank you," Zena replied.

She took a few sips of wine and looked out into the dusky night with Zola.

Adan had asked to see her a few days before they left for Bali. Actually, Adan asked to see Zena a few times. He'd called randomly. Sometimes in the middle of the night. Sometimes text. Sometimes email. He was sounding like a friend. An old friend who wanted to catch up. "I just want to see how things are with you," he'd said once when Zena actually picked up the phone to hear one of his lunch proposals.

Zena was always too busy. She was pleasant, cheery sounding, but too busy to see Adan.

What was there to see? What was there to talk about? She couldn't live in a world where she talked about how "things are" with her without screaming about how things had been with her— about how things had been with them. And even still, she didn't want to scream about how things had been with her or them. What would be the point? Why open that door? Adan was the one who'd closed the door and walked away. She was left on the inside, and she'd made herself comfortable; she'd found her own pleasure. She wasn't ready to open up and let him back in.

The villa Alton and Zola rented for the week they'd be in Bali was less than an hour from the airport. Mahatma House was a sprawling five-bedroom architectural beauty set in the middle of a lush beachfront garden.

When Zena and Zola climbed out of the disheveled minivan charged with transporting them from the airport to the villa, both tongues were wagging. Everything was gorgeous. Everything was lovely. Everything was every hyperbolic adjective they could recall: *magnificent, wondrous, amazing*! But none of their words could capture what they really saw.

From the airport to the drop-off at Mahatma House, their first impression of the Southeast Asian paradise known as Bali was a racket of beauties that made a mess of their five senses. Streets filled with dogs and motorbikes carrying men, women and children, sometimes entire families all at once. Horns beeping. Lights flashing. Red and purple and yellow flags hanging. Outdoor restaurants roasting pigs on front-yard spits. The beach. Rolling waves, black sand. Someone playing hip-hop. Another person singing a Balinese love song. Pigskin popping over the fire. Flowers blooming. Women walking the roads dressed in elaborate saris and carrying bright floral offerings to the temple. Street signs pointing in every direction. The heat—stifling and arresting.

And they'd only been there an hour.

"Where have you brought me!" Zola hollered

when she spotted Alton strumming his guitar by the pool in the central atrium at Mahatma House.

He tossed the guitar to the ground as if he couldn't care if it broke or flew away and ran to his bride.

"It's beautiful—isn't it, baby?" he said, picking Zola up and spinning her around.

"More than I could've dreamed. So much more," she answered in his arms.

Alton's countenance had far surpassed his boyish oddities. While Zena often questioned his neo-soul singing skills, there was no doubt he looked like a neo-soul star. He had big, brown pouty eyes, natural muscles and a head of auburn dreads that looked more like wild coils. He was always singing or humming something sensual and went nowhere without his beloved acoustic guitar.

Surrounded by the waitstaff in the open-air living room overlooking the pool, Zena looked on awkwardly at Zola and Alton's romantic reuniting. She smiled with pursed lips and unconsciously crossed her arms so she didn't look as if she was expecting anyone to greet her with open arms.

"Uhhh, Mister Adan, he come now for you," one of the housekeepers said to Zena.

"No, no, no," Zena said, and nervously sputtered out, "He's not for me. He's my childhood friend. We aren't together. He's just a family friend. I don't like him or anything."

The housekeeper nodded at her, though it was obvious she wasn't following along with the elaborate explanation of why a thirty-something woman was standing alone in the lobby of one of the most romantic villas in one of the most romantic places in the world.

"You guys are here!" Zena heard.

She turned to see Adan descending a set of black polished-concrete stairs that led to one of the bedrooms in the main house, where she was standing.

"Yes, we are," she said.

Adan walked over to Zena and hugged her. Over his shoulder, Zena saw the housekeeper smiling at her knowingly.

"How were your travels?" Adan asked, releasing Zena a bit but not letting her out of his arms. He kind of rested them on her waist and leaned back to look at her.

"Safe?" Zena answered, stepping back to escape his embrace.

"Good to hear you were safe." Adan nodded.

The night moon brought a delicious Balinese feast spread out on a long wooden table overlooking the black sand beach at Mahatma House. Dressed in all white, as requested by the house concierge, Alton and Zola, Adan and Zena arrived at their welcoming dinner to drink in a cornucopia of traditional culinary delights. Prawns as big as the men's fists, nutty chicken satay right off the grill, sweet and spicy tempeh, and at the center of the table was the *babi guling*, a suckling pig that had been roasting in the yard most of the day.

The ocean breeze rolled up the strand, mixed with the food and tantalized all at the table.

"I hope they don't think we're going to eat all of this," Zola said, looking over the foreign delicacies. "Look at all of this meat! And is this a baby pig? Yuck!"

"Well, if you don't eat your portion, I'll gladly take it," Zena offered, sitting beside her. She'd seen Alton hungrily eyeing the porker since they'd sat at the table, and she remembered Zola pondering his going vegan with her on the plane.

"Now, that's what I'm talking about! Let's get our grub on!" Alton said before giving Zena a high five from the opposite side of the table where he was sitting beside Adan.

"So you're eating everything on the table—even the meat?" Zola pointed to the steamy *babi guling* with the traditional apple stuffed into its mouth.

"Darling, we're in paradise. I don't think vegan rules apply," Alton joked. "Besides, we're not Muslim. A little pig never hurt nobody."

"Not *that* little pig, anyway. I'm pretty sure it hasn't hurt anybody," Adan said, fixated on the baby pig as he rubbed his stomach. "What, you think that porker is like two weeks old?" He leaned over to Alton and laughed.

"I don't know, but I bet he tastes good!" Alton replied, and both of the house waiters standing guard beside the table chuckled but then went back to their serious on-duty stances.

"I can't believe what I'm hearing! You guys are totally gross!" Zola complained.

"Okay! Okay! Okay! I'm totally sorry for grossing you out, future baby sister," Adan said. He picked up a spoon and tapped at his glass, making a clatter. "Hear ye! Hear ye!" he began. "Now, if I may have your attention for a moment please. I need to make some announcements."

Zena had taken in all of Adan in his loose-fitting white linen Havana shirt and trousers. He and Alton had only gotten to Bali two days before she'd arrived with Zola, but both men already had sufficient tans. Adan's brown skin was a smooth pumpernickel now, and the white linen made his arms and face look like something to touch. She made sure to look away as he spoke. She spotted two dogs chasing waves a mile or so down the beach. No owner in sight, no people around at all; however, they still appeared to enjoy a kind of human fun on a beauteous evening between the black sky and black sand.

"First, I want to say I'm so happy we are all to-gether," Adan went on in her ear. "I'm so happy to share this amazing occasion with so many amazing—"

Zena looked out to the ocean as Adan continued his welcoming. There, she focused on one ship floating so far out she could only see its navigation lights meant to both confirm and reveal its location as it floated through the night.

"You know what? Let's stop this right now?" Zena curtly interrupted Adan.

Everyone looked at Zena nervously, as if they'd been waiting for her to say something out of line or do something outrageous.

"What? What is it, Zena? Everything okay?" Zola asked carefully as she reached over and placed a calming hand on Zena's knee.

"Yes, silly. I'm just saying—let's stop all this welcoming stuff," she said, adding more cheerfulness to her tone. "In fact, Adan shouldn't be the one welcoming us all here anyway."

"Who should be welcoming us, Zena?" Alton asked, and at that moment he sounded as though he fully expected the people from the local crazy house to show up to take Zena away in a straitjacket and human muzzle.

"You!" Zena said. "You two. The bride and groom should be opening the wedding weekend with a welcoming for their guests." Zena looked to Adan for support. "I'm guessing you and I have been to the same amount of weddings. Am I correct? Isn't that how it goes?"

"Yes," Adan confirmed.

"Oh," Zola uttered, as if none of that had occurred to her, though Zena knew she'd been to and even participated in a few of her line sisters' weddings. "So, that's cool." Zola looked at Alton, who appeared just as surprised and also speechless. "Well," she giggled girlishly. "I guess, we both say, 'Welcome?'"

Alton nodded as if his betrothed had really done something, and he cavalierly repeated, "Yeah. Welcome," before easing back in his seat comfortably.

Even Adan looked perturbed by this nonchalance.

"Come on! You guys have to do better than that," Zena pointed out. "You sound like teenagers. This is your wedding. The most adult thing you could do. You have to do better."

"It's not that we don't want to do better. We just don't know what to say," Zola complained.

"Okay! Okay! Well, in the interest of time, and so our lovely food doesn't go untouched for too much longer, I'll give a suggestion," Zena offered. "How about you two stand and welcome Adan and me here. And then share something special with us. Say…" Zena looked around and snapped her fingers as if she was trying to find a solution, but the truth was that she'd planned this—she'd al-

ready used her interrogation skills to come up with
the perfect prompts to cause contention between
Alton and Zola. "You could ummm… I have it…
You could tell your guests what you see in each
other. Why you believe your mate would make a
good husband or wife."

Adan nodded at the suggestion and looked at
Alton and Zola, who started getting up rather awkwardly like two teens about to give a speech before their classmates.

"Welc—" Zola tried, but Zena quickly stopped
her.

"No, Alton should start," Zena demanded. "He's
the man. The husband. He speaks for both of you…
now."

Adan nodded again, though he also looked as if
this might have been a quizzical detail for someone
like Zena, who only ever let him speak first when
she had nothing to say when they were children.

"Well, it's the twenty-first century, and I don't
see my soon-to-be wife as a second-class citizen,"
Alton said sarcastically. "She's my equal. My soul
mate. But I'll play along." He cleared his throat and
shook away his nervousness. "Welcome, everyone.
My lovely bride and I are so happy to have you
here this evening as we prepare for our nuptials.
I *believeith* it was the good *brotherith* Common
who *saidith*, 'It don't take all day to recognize sunshine,'" he went on in jest. "Well, I did recognize

that sunshine in this badass chick beside me, and I'm never letting her put me in the dark again."

Zena was staring at Alton and struggling to hide her frown of displeasure at the cute but out-of-place Common rap song quote. "And tell us, beyond being *sunshine*—because we all know that about Zola—what will make her a good wife?"

Alton bit his upper lip as he contemplated. A bright light from one of the tiki torches set up around the table sparkled behind him. Soon, he said, "She's a good person. She's nice. She's nice to me. And she's beautiful. And I love her."

Zola swooned and leaned into Alton. "So sweet," she said.

Zena smiled weakly and turned her attention to Zola. "And you—why do you believe Alton will make a good husband?"

Zola grinned at Alton, and she had to hold the grin for a long while because it took her twice as long as it had taken Alton to gather a response. So long, in fact, that one of the staffers beside the table seemed to lean in with anticipation.

Soon, Zola spoke to Alton as if they were alone. "Alton, you are comforting. You are so fine!" She smiled. "You are always sweet. You love me. You're a good man."

"Oh, babe!" Alton said.

One of the staff members wiped a loose tear-drop as Alton kissed Zola.

Clearly unimpressed, Zena started a slow clap until Alton and Zola stopped kissing, and she offered a well-intentioned smile.

"That's sweet," she said. "Very sweet. And so original. No at all what I expected. I've heard so many brides and grooms respond to that very question and they say things like, 'She's good with money and children and has good credit and is godly,' and 'He's stable and successful and intelligent and ambitious.' Those are the kinds of answers I'm used to hearing, but I think what you two said was sufficient. It was well-meaning. It was beautiful. Right, Adan?" Her tone was indicting and a little sarcastic, but not blatantly attacking. She didn't want to cause alarm.

Adan had clearly caught on to something, though, and was staring at Zena, trying to discover her point.

"Right, Zena. You're right," he concurred.

Bellies filled with so much rice and pork—even Zola had eaten her share—and everything else at the table, the foursome ambled to their rooms to shut it down for the night. Though they'd chatted about an evening stroll on the beach and even planned a midnight pool party, the days of travel, gross sensual demands of the new environment, good eating and the ocean breeze around them had everyone feeling completely exhausted or so thoroughly relaxed they could fall asleep at any moment.

While Zola, who announced that she didn't want to sleep with Alton so she could be "chaste" before the wedding, had her own room in the main house, she opted to share a bed with Zena in the flat she'd selected toward the back of the property. The simple architectural offering was elegant and mysterious. Four walls of cool black polished concrete came together to create a kind of human-sized cocoon made for perfect sleeping.

When Zena got out of the shower, she found Zola sitting on the edge of the king-size bed wrapped in a towel. Zola's hair was completely covered with leave-in conditioner. She'd split it into four sections and was busy twisting.

"What are you going to do with your hair for the wedding?" Zena asked. She was naked and standing before the vanity a few feet away from the bed. She'd discovered two mosquito bites on her arm and was dutifully applying Skin So Soft, a bite repellant and remedy Lisa had passed down to her daughters.

"I don't know. I was thinking you could corn-row it up into a goddess knot or something. Like how you used to do when I was younger."

"I don't think my braiding skills are wedding day worthy," Zena said.

"I don't think I have a choice."

"Ahhh. The black-woman travel dilemma," Zena confirmed, laughing. "No one to do your hair."

"Exactly."

"You never know. There must be one hairdresser in all of Bali who can do braids! Some of these people here have some coarse hair!"

"Yeah, I know."

"Plenty of folks look surprised to see us, though. It's like they've never seen black people, period."

"Alton said some guy at the airport asked to take a picture with him. Can you believe that?" Zola revealed. "Then after taking the picture, the man gave him a thumbs-up and said, 'Michael Jordan!'"

"Ahhh. The black-man travel dilemma," Zena confirmed, laughing again. "Everyone thinks you're an athlete."

Zola laughed, and then the sisters were silent as she finished her third braid.

Zena brushed her teeth and looked at her hairline. She'd plucked three gray hairs. While Lisa kept telling her not to pull them out, that the aggressive action would only invite more, she just couldn't stand the sight of the white hairs.

"You hear that?" Zola said, looking at the door.

"What?"

"Listen."

Zena stopped moving and listened, but she heard nothing.

"What?"

"It's crickets." Zola smiled. "Crickets!"

Then Zena could hear them, too. It was a simple buzzing that sounded like nothing until she tuned in, and then the crickets were chirping all around.

"Night crickets. Just like in Georgia," Zola observed whimsically. "It's beautiful. We're literally on the other side of the world but still at home."

Zena slid on her nightgown and headed toward her side of the bed.

"I've been thinking about what you said," Zola started, rather abruptly changing the subject. "About the things Alton and I should have said about one another when we listed what would make a good husband or wife."

"I didn't say you should've said anything. I said what you revealed was enough."

"I know. I know," Zola agreed. "But I mean like the other things were important, too. People don't like to say it, but they are."

Zena grinned internally and asked, "Like what? What things are important?" Then she tried to sound more nonchalant and less leading with, "I don't really recall everything I said. Remind me."

"You said other people have told you their fiancé/ fiancée was good with money or had good credit."

"Finances? So you meant to say Alton is *good* with finances?" Zena asked naively.

Zola rolled her eyes at Zena. "Stop joking. You know he has no real finances to be good with. Not now anyway."

Zena nodded.

"And when he does get money, we've been so broke for so long, we just spend it because we're both so frustrated," Zola added.

"That's life with an artist." Zena sat beside Zola and reached over to twist Zola's last plait.

"But will it work?" Zola asked. "You work with people going through divorces all the time. Does it work? Like if Alton doesn't make it. If he never gets his career together."

"I'm not here to do that, Zollie," Zena said. "I told you I'm just here to support you and Alton on your special day."

"Cut the crap. Just answer the question." Zola pulled away from Zena's hold on her hair and looked at her.

"Fine." Zena groaned as if Zola had really pulled her arm and none of this was planned. "There's no right or wrong answer here. But I can say in my practice—money is most commonly at the root of divorce. That and cheating."

Zola sighed.

"Look, low cash makes everything more difficult," Zena said.

"But plenty of people with lots of cash have issues, too," Zola pointed out. "You know that."

"Low cash is an issue that can hit anyone. A rich man can have low cash issues if his wife is trying to be in a new Bentley every month. It's nothing to have $50K in the bank if your mortgage alone is $10K. If the light bill is $1,500."

"Good point," Zola said. "You know, Alton is talking about getting a house for us."

"Really?" Zena looked shocked. "Where?"

"Mr. Roy wants to give us their old house. He's been lonely with Mrs. Pam gone, and he's moving back to his family farm in Valdosta."

"That's wonderful. What a gift for you two."

"Not really. I don't want to live in our old neighborhood. I want something nice. I want something new. I want to stay downtown."

"I could sell you guys my condo," Zena offered easily.

"You'd do that?"

"Of course. I only owe like a couple hundred thousand on the loan. How's Alton's credit?" She didn't bother to ask about Zola. Her credit was so bad, Zena was surprised Zola was deemed fit to sit for the Bar Exam.

"You owe that much? We can't afford that. How much do you pay each month for the mortgage?" Zola asked with her mouth open in surprise. "Wait! I don't think I want to know."

Zola gasped and fell back on her pillow in time to hear a rolling wave beat out the crickets.

"I have so much to think about," she declared, sounding deflated.

Zena turned off the lamp beside the bed before lying back on her pillow.

"Too late for all that," she said, openly smiling in the darkness. "No cold feet allowed on this trip. You're getting married."

Chapter 6

Zena felt so rejuvenated by the bedtime discussion with Zola that she woke up in time for sunrise, endured a five-mile jog through the homey village outside Mahatma House, showered, blew out her hair and still managed to be the first person at the breakfast table. She wore a loose-fitting yellow beach dress and slid a red hibiscus she'd plucked during her jog behind her right ear.

The house chef greeted Zena with a cup of green tea that seemed oddly comforting in the early heat that invaded the outdoor dining area. She slid a plate of sliced exotic fruit onto the table and took Zena's breakfast order.

After a while, Adan entered. He was wearing a pair of Hawaiian print blue-and-white swimming trunks and no shirt.

Zena glanced and looked away quickly. How odd was it that he wasn't wearing a shirt? How odd was it that he was there?

She counseled herself that perhaps she should've expected these two things: his presence, his nude and muscular chest.

Zena suddenly hated herself for getting to the breakfast table first. She also hated herself for not having a T-shirt for Adan in her bag.

"Morning, Z," Adan said, now standing beside Zena with his nude chest still wet from the pool.

He kissed her on the cheek and sat in the chair next to her as if he'd been doing this every morning of every day of the year.

The chef brought his green tea and took his breakfast order.

"You see Zola and Alton?" Zena asked. When she'd gotten to the room after her run, Zola wasn't in the bed. She assumed Zola slipped off to Alton's room.

"Yeah. They were arguing about something way too early this morning," Adan revealed.

"Really? About what?" Zena leaned toward Adan but then quickly masked her interest.

"No clue. I heard Zola shout 'condo' and 'credit,' and I pulled my pillow over my head."

Zena smirked and flexed her pinkie as she took the next sip from her tea.

"I also saw you running earlier. I was going to join you, but a brother is a little too slow these days." Adan rubbed his stomach playfully. Zena watched as his fingers grazed his perfect abs and held back from swooning. "All work and no working out makes Adan a fat man!"

Zena found herself laughing. Adan could be funny. He could be really funny sometimes.

"You're not fat," she said. "Not at all." Her voice let on that she'd gotten an eyeful of his body.

"Stop lying to me."

"I'm serious. You're in great shape."

"So, you think I'm sexy?" Adan teased as he moved his hands back behind his head and flexed.

"I never said anything about 'sexy.'" Zena rolled her eyes.

"Guess that's a no." Adan frowned and lowered his arms.

Laughing again, Zena realized then that she was having a conversation with Adan. She was in Bali, sitting at a table eating star fruit with her ex and having a civil conversation. And everything was okay.

"You're pushing it," Zena said sternly.

"Maybe I'm trying to push it."

Just in time, two plates of what the chef had called

"American Breakfast"—omelets, potatoes, bacon—were slid onto the table before Zena and Adan.

"No rice for you, either?" Adan asked.

"I don't get it. I can't eat rice for breakfast. Sue me!" Zena held up her hands.

"I agree. America wins this battle. All of Asia loses! I mean, rice for breakfast?"

"Do you think we should wait to eat with Alton and Zola?" Zena asked.

"Nah. They'll resurface when they want to. You know young'uns don't need breakfast," Adan joked. "And anyway, I'm glad to have you to myself—"

Zena cut Adan off with a sharp eye and a suspicious, "Why?"

Adan went on uneasily: "Because I wanted to go over today's exciting schedule with you and get some ideas from you about the wedding."

"Oh. I thought all these things would've been handled."

"Nah. I'm trying to be more fluid in my old age."

"Fluid?"

"Yeah. Look, I'm trying to figure out if the wedding should be in the little temple they have down the beach or just on the beach."

"Shouldn't that be up to Alton and Zola? Perhaps we can let them make that decision?"

"Good point. Well, do you want to read something during the ceremony? Like a poem?"

"Again, let's let them plan that," Zena said.

Adan looked surprised, as if Zena was driving a hard bargain. "I guess I just want things to be really nice for them."

"If they want things to be really nice, they're old enough to see it through. You've done enough. Hell, I've done enough. I'm just here to support them and have fun," Zena said. "Now, tell me about all the exciting things we have planned for today."

"I will. But first, I want you to answer a few things for me."

Zena didn't respond. In fact, she turned to look away from Adan. His words, his tone, made it clear that they were edging into a conversation she was avoiding.

"Why didn't you meet up with me in Atlanta?" Adan asked the back of Zena's head.

He waited a second, and when she didn't say anything, he added, "I really, really wanted to see you."

Zena exhaled and looked down at her food. "I was busy," she said softly.

"No one's that busy." Adan's voice was softer. He actually sounded hurt. "Like all day… I called you all day." He laughed uncomfortably.

Zena looked over at him. "Okay. Fine. I didn't want to see you. That's why I kept saying no."

"Why not?"

"Why does it matter?"

"It matters because I care," Adan said as Zena pretended to return to her eating. "I truly wanted to see you."

"For what? You said you wanted to meet about Alton and Zola and the wedding—well, I'm here and they're getting married. Everything is fine." Zena stuffed a forkful of scrambled egg into her mouth.

"What if I wanted more? What if I had other reasons for wanting to see you?"

His words made Zena so nervous that she felt her mind go blank. She kept stuffing her mouth with food. At some point, she stopped chewing and was just stuffing. She couldn't decipher what Adan was saying and had no idea how she could respond.

Adan didn't stop, though. His voice lowered and soft, he added, "What if I wanted to spend time with you. Like a date?"

Her mouth filled with food, Zena now knew what she wanted to say, but she couldn't. She wanted to curse and scream. To holler. A date? He had to be kidding. But eggs and bacon and fruit were in the way. Trying to struggle it all down her throat, Zena began to cough.

Adan leaned over to her and patted her back. "You okay? You okay?"

He slid his other hand onto Zena's arm to calm her. His touch sent charges through her body.

While she was choking on the food, Zena instinctively went into action, getting up and pushing Adan and his concerned face away from her.

Soon, the chef and the housekeeper were trying to help, too, but Zena held them all off with one finger pointed at Adan, demanding that he stay away. The red hibiscus had fallen from her ear as she stammered to clear the food from her throat.

Then, she felt arms weave around her waist and lift her from the floor. She tried to get free from the tightening hold, but it got tighter and tighter, forcing her stomach in and up.

Whoever was behind Zena started jerking her body up and down and telling her to breathe. In seconds, the food lodged in Zena's throat came barreling out to the floor and landed in a squishy splat.

"Uhhh!" was the collective sigh when they observed the regurgitated eggs and bacon and fruit.

The arms around Zena's waist let up, and she turned to see that it was Adan. Alton and Zola were standing next to him.

"You okay?" Zola asked.

"Yes. I'm fine," Zena said.

"Are you sure you're fine? You were choking," Adan pointed out, now looking at Zena incredulously as the chef and housekeeper, who were standing beside him, scrambled to get the vomit mess cleaned up.

"Yeah, I'm good." Zena narrowed her eyes on Adan. "Thanks."

"Guess my brother saved your life," Alton said with pride.

Zola exhaled. "I'm glad Adan was here for you. Look, we were coming to get you guys. The driver is here."

Adan scheduled Mahatma House's private chauffeur to show the foursome the best of beautiful Bali. So, through much of the morning and leading into the afternoon, Adan and Zena, Alton and Zola, sat in the back of the minivan, crisscrossing Bali's complex terrain as they visited popular and off-the-beaten-path attractions that covered massive mausoleums, dramatic sculptures, seedy swap meets and ancient rice fields that reminded them all of the roadside plantations throughout the deep South back home. While the heat outdoors might have initiated a "keep the kids indoors" weather advisory in Atlanta, crowds of Balinese workers, Australian expats, and tourists from throughout Asia and Europe packed the streets and sidewalks so tightly they seemed to contribute to the stifling conditions.

Loading in and out of the van, Zena tried most often to sit beside Zola, who had been rather quiet through most of the day. Zena could feel that something was bothering Zola, but she didn't want to force the issue and seem too concerned. Of course, she wanted to know what was going on, but she had her own issues to contend with. The word *date* had been bouncing around in her head since they left Mahatma House. More specifically, two words: *date* and *Adan*. They sounded like opposites in her thoughts, contrasting ideas that she didn't want to connect. Did Adan mean to say *date*? Was he serious? He certainly seemed serious. He did sound as if he meant it. But how could he? How could he want to date her? Why? Zena tried to pluck these questions from her thoughts, but every time she looked at Adan, or heard his voice throughout the day, they all came rushing in. And soon, *date* and *Adan* didn't sound so opposite at all. And Zena hated that.

At one of the many four-way stops where the minivan was caught in a traffic jam mosh pit of cars and mopeds and motorcycles and trucks and pedestrians and wild dogs, all seemingly going in every direction—both on- and off-road—Zena leaned into Zola and commented that even though Zola was a bad driver in Atlanta, she could be a great driver in Bali. This didn't even get a giggle out of Zola.

"Something wrong?" Zena asked.

"No. I'm just a little tired. I think the heat is getting to me," Zola confessed, and this sounded quite plausible.

They'd just left a monkey forest reserve where more than six hundred wild macaques had taken over a Hindu temple and become a real-life *Planet of the Apes* episode. While the wild and not-so-humble monkeys provided lots of laughs and camera ops, after an hour walking through the gardens, Zena and Zola had split a gallon of water in the parking lot as the foursome waited for the chauffeur to return.

Adan was sitting in the front seat beside the driver. "Well, I hope you're not too drained. We're about to hit these waves," he said, turning to face Zola and Zena. "Abdul tells me Padang Padang has the best surfing in Bali. Isn't that right, brother?" He nodded to the driver, a portly bald man with scaly dark skin that had clearly seen too many days on the beach.

"Yes, Mr. Adan. Exclusive beach in Bali. Best waves," he replied.

"Oh, I don't know. I haven't been surfing in a while, and I am kind of drained after all this sight-seeing," Zena complained, still parched and a little dazed herself. The heat here added a kind of malaise that was hypnotic.

"Really? You can't be serious. Little Miss West End Swim Community Center Champ 2000 and 2001 doesn't want to surf?" Adan pressured Zena as he grinned at her.

When Adan's mother realized Zena and Zola

couldn't swim, Mrs. Pam immediately took it upon herself to see that the girls attended the free swimming classes offered at the local community center. While Zola got the hang of it quickly and became an average swimmer, Zena excelled at the sport and became competitive, going to local and state swim meets, where she usually lost but delivered a strong effort to represent their community. When Zena got to Bethune-Cookman, her love of swimming transitioned to surfing the waves at Daytona Beach. She even joined a black women's surf club, the Soul Surfing Sisters, and Adan came down to Daytona to see a few of her team's exhibitions.

Adan went on, "You came all the way to Bali, to some of the best beaches in the world, and you're not going to hit the waves the first chance you get? Some things done changed, Soul Surfing Sister!"

Zena laughed at Adan's memory, and she felt herself blushing, so she cut her laugh short.

"Well, I'm game, bro," Alton said, giving Adan a high five for his idea. He was sitting in the middle row by himself. "My love can get a few pictures of me on the board. Caption reads: Dread in the Water!" He shook his wild auburn dreadlocks as Adan laughed.

Zola hadn't. "What do you mean, 'get a few pictures'?" she asked.

"You'll be on the beach, right?" Alton said, confused. "You don't surf."

"I *have* surfed," Zola argued.

"When?" Alton asked.

"In Cancun when I went for spring break with my sorors."

"Okay," Alton acknowledged carefully. Now he was clearly sensing Zola's tension. "But this isn't some small beach in South America. This is the big time. Real waves."

"She okay," Abdul said, cutting in with his broken English. "Padang Padang good waves."

"See. I can handle it," Zola said.

"You know it's not safe for you," Alton added, concerned. "Why are you doing this?"

"If you go surfing, I'm going surfing, too," Zola replied, crossing her arms over her breasts with some newfound energy surrounding her.

Alton and Adan looked at Zena for a response, but she shook her head. She certainly didn't want to be on Adan's side.

"Don't look at me," she said. "I'm not her mama."

"But you know she's not a good swimmer," Alton argued.

"No. I know she's not the best swimmer, but she's a good swimmer. She can surf like anyone else. She can do anything she puts her mind to," Zena added.

Zola looked over at Zena with a new awareness in her eyes.

"Well, ladies," Adan resolved, wisely turning

back around to face the road ahead, "I guess we're all surfing, then."

Alton sighed and stared at Zola. "I can't believe you. You're not ready," he said.

Zola reached over and slid her hand onto Zena's lap, where no one could see. Zena felt Zola's need for warmth and covered her sister's hand with her own.

Abdul was right. The surf point at Padang Padang was like nothing Zena had seen: white sand stretching for miles against rolling waves that hit the shore unbroken and rough. Walking the strand to the surf shop, she watched bummy and new and professional surfers look out at the tide with privilege and expectation at a new wave coming in seconds. The beach was packed with sunbathers, too. Families of tourists had set up camp with beach umbrellas and coolers filled with overpriced imported beer they'd purchased from street vendors.

Zena saw how someone could spend her life out here with the sun and wind and waves. This was someone's heaven.

In the dressing room at the surf shop, Zola was struggling to get into her wet suit. She stumbled about on the wet clay floor. There was no ceiling. The sun overhead felt like a heating lamp.

"Getting a little thick, huh? Maybe you need

a bigger size," Zena said. She was already in her suit, smiling and sitting on a bench as she watched Zola struggle.

"Maybe you need to kiss my thick ass," Zola joked before giving the suit one final tug to get the zipper up. She exhaled to let her stomach loose and turned to look at herself in the mirror. "There we go," she said. "All ready."

"Got that right. Let's go show these Douglass boys how it's done," Zena said, standing to leave the locker room.

"Hey, Z. You remember what you said in the van?"

"What?" Zena stopped to look at Zola.

"About me—about me being able to do whatever I put my mind to."

"Yes."

"Did you mean it?" Zola asked.

"Why are you asking me this? Of course I do. Don't I always say that to you?"

"No. Not the way you said it just now."

"Come on," Zena said. "I'm always telling you that I believe in you."

"Yeah, but most times it's when you're trying to give me a pep talk—like to do something you want me to do. Not what I want to do," Zola pointed out. "When it's something I want to do, you say I can't do it. Or it's stupid. So, I always figured maybe you didn't mean it."

"I mean it always," Zena said, seriously feeling the weight of the moment. "You're a bright and driven woman."

"Thanks for coming with me," Zola said for probably the tenth time, but this one time it sounded different. And then she also repeated, "I couldn't do this without you."

Zola linked arms with Zena and began pulling her to the shore, where Alton and Adan were waiting with their surfboards.

"Hey, can I ask you something?" Zena started, hanging back a bit.

"What's up?"

"Did—" She paused before saying "Adan," as if maybe she shouldn't be saying his name. "Did Adan like say anything about me?"

"Like what?"

"I don't know. Anything?"

Zola looked off to recall. "He did say something about wanting to see you, like when we were back in Atlanta. He said he was trying to hook up with you, but you kept saying you were busy."

"He said, 'hook up'?" Zena repeated.

"No." Zola chuckled. "That doesn't even sound like Adan."

"I'm serious. What did he say? Like, exactly?" Zena pushed, while trying so hard to sound uninvolved, but her words and demeanor belied her intentions.

"Just that he wanted to see you, I think. To get up with you. You know?"

"Did he use the word *date*?" Zena stared at Zola as if her response could solve so many issues in the world.

"I don't know. I don't think so." Zola scrunched up her face. "Maybe. He could've." Zola stopped pondering and looked at Zena. "Wait—why are you so concerned? You turned him down. Are you having second thoughts?"

"Hell no," Zena answered, hardly giving Zola time to finish her question. "I just wanted to know."

Once the foursome was in the water and surfing along the beach break waves, it was quite clear to Zena that Abdul was wrong about the skill required to surf Padang Padang. The water was aggressive and filled with barrels ahead—water tubes created by rolling waves.

One of the instructors at the surf shop came out and gave Zola a short lesson, one Alton tried to avoid but then jumped in on because he clearly needed it after being knocked off his board a few times.

While Zena strategically kept her eye on Zola, noting that she was doing rather well on the waves and holding steady on her board, she and Adan charged the clean waves toward the middle of the beach break. They raced out, paddling quickly on their stomachs to get in the lineup with the other experienced surfers. Sometimes, the waves came between them and Zena couldn't see Adan, but when they subsided, there he was looking over at her smiling every time. She could see his brown arms moving around beneath the crystal clear water. He lifted his hand and pointed ahead toward the ocean. There was a barrel coming right toward them.

They hustled to their feet. Zena found her balance more quickly than she expected. Right foot over left. Lean right. Lean left. Ride the wave. Breathe. Balance the water in her body with the sea. She couldn't move against the water. If she did, she'd lose her balance. Come crashing down in the middle of the barrel, her body going one way, the board going the other.

Then Zena found herself in the middle of the barrel, an aquatic house in icy baby blue and emerald green all around her. She was standing on her board, measuring her weight, redistributing, trying to stay in the water house, but then she let go. She wanted to see it. To stop trying to be in it—and just see it.

She looked at the water spinning around her. Though it felt as if time had stopped, it was moving so fast, and this would only be her home for a few seconds. It was a magical moment for any surfer. Through the wave she could see the ocean, the shore. She looked to her left, and on the other side of a clear door of water there was Adan, standing upright beside her on his surfboard. His hand was reaching toward her. She tried to reach back toward him, but then the wave closed up and the sea spit Zena out in a yawn.

She fell to her board and wrapped her legs around the body, a rogue move one of Zena's surf instructors taught her to stop the board from spinning out beneath her.

When the water subsided, Zena sat up and found the surfers on the beach cheering her on. Zola and Alton were waving, and Zola screamed, "That's my big sister!"

"You still have it," Adan said.

Zena turned, and he was sitting on his board beside her in the water that had turned peaceful and soft.

"I guess you have it, too," Zena said. "I saw you in the barrel."

"I wasn't in the barrel."

"You reached for me!"

"Zena, I didn't make it. I clucked out when I saw that barrel. I wiped out and recovered just in time to see you perform."

"But I saw you." Zena clearly recalled Adan in the water bubble beside her.

More waves came, and Zena and Adan practiced cross steps and cutbacks. They laughed at each other as they fell off their boards. Looked after each other when the big waves came rolling through. They were talking without talking. Communicating. And it felt old. Comfortable. Familiar.

Zena and Adan watched and cheered as Zola and Alton conquered the scrappers, short waves closer to the shore.

Though she was far away, Zena could see a determination in Zola's stance on the board. Zola leaned forward, balancing her weight on her right knee as she spread her arms wide into a T to hold her balance on a dying wave beneath her board.

"Z! Look ahead!" Adan called, and hearing some sense of urgency in his voice, Zena snapped around to see a large wave, a big surf, headed their way. "Up!" Adan shouted. "Up!"

Zena popped to her feet in time to take off on the curl of the wave and ride the crest.

"Cowabunga!" she heard one of the shaggy long-haired Australian surfers nearby holler as he made his way through the wave.

Then she heard, "Swell!"—a surfer call meaning there would be waves of the same size and speed following right behind the one she was riding.

Zena steadied her toes on the edge of the board,

found her balance and held her breath as the water caught the board and flipped her over.

She wanted to curse but there was no time. She was underwater. Sand kicked up from the floor and bubbles burst all around her. She could see other surfers and their boards seeking reconnection in the blue.

Zena found her board and tugged at her ankle leash to bring it to her.

"You okay?" Adan asked, out of breath when she came up.

"Yeah, that was a tough one! Total wipeout!" Zena replied through her own bated breath as she sat up on her board.

"You ain't kidding." Adan nodded to the mess of struggling surfers gasping for air and trying to get back into the lineup to await the next wave.

Suddenly, and for no reason, because Zena hadn't surfed in months since her last vacation to Hawaii and seldom ever thought it, a word came to mind that shot fear through her body—the deep. This was the deepest part of a wave, the part near its peak where surfers were most often thrown wildly from their boards and accidents, sometimes tragic accidents, occurred in seconds.

There was an eerie quiet then. A damning calm.

"Zola?" Zena called, turning toward the direction of the swell that had passed them and gone toward the shore, where Zola and Alton were practicing.

Zena spotted the surfing instructor and scanned the water for Zola's brown face. She found Alton, but he was staring out into the water blankly. She searched backward and forward between the shore and then the sea, and there was no Zola. "Zola?"

She could see Adan stand on his board and call out to Alton. She couldn't make out what he was saying because she was already paddling toward the empty space where she'd last seen her sister.

She heard the lifeguard's whistle blow and saw the instructor dive into the water.

A wild board popped up. But then no one followed.

"Zola!" Zena paddled faster, but she felt as if she wasn't going anywhere and maybe she was moving backward. She wanted to break from the surfboard and swim, but removing the ankle strap would take too long.

She saw Adan swim past, and every dark thought she could ever imagine crept into her brain, leaving a sinking suspicion that something horrible was happening. "No! No!"

By the time Zena made it to shore, the lifeguards were pulling Zola's limp body from the water.

Adan and Alton were racing behind them as they made their way to the sand, where a crowd had already gathered.

"My sister! My sister!" Zena screamed, and some surfer she didn't know helped her pull the ankle strap off before she was free from her surfboard and could run to Zola's side.

"Zola!" Zena pushed through the crowd of worried spectators and tried to get to Zola, but Adan stopped her.

"Wait!" he ordered Zena with his face as alarmed as hers. "Let them help her!"

There, on the sand, surrounded by lifeguards, lay a lifeless Zola. To Zena, Zola looked as if she was six years old, a child she was supposed to be looking after.

"Wake up, Zola! Wake up! Please!" Zena cried, trying to break away from Adan's hold as the crowd tightened.

One of the lifeguards straddled Zola and pressed heavily on her chest as another did mouth-to-mouth. Zena reached for Alton, who looked stunned, and grabbed his arm.

"You weren't watching her! Why weren't you watching her? You're so irresponsible!" she screamed at him.

"I was watching her! It just happened. She fell off her board when the big wave came. It wasn't my fault," he said. "Maybe if you would've told her to stay out of the water, this wouldn't have happened!"

Adan pulled them apart and said, "You two stop it! Zola is going to be fine."

As if Zola had heard Adan's command, water came sputtering out of her mouth. She gurgled and spat.

The crowd froze, and there was silence as they waited. This was a miracle in Bali.

Zola opened her eyes and looked around aimlessly. "Al-to," she made out. "Al…"

"I'm here!" Zena cried before she realized who Zola was calling for.

Alton pushed past Zena and went to Zola's side before she passed out again. "I'm here," he said.

The lifeguards rushed Zola to the infirmary at one of the hotels across the street from the beach. While everyone spoke English and seemed to be trying to help, Zena felt as if no one could understand her questions, and quickly this once-beautiful place had become a paradoxical hell of rushing and then waiting for word about Zola's condition.

Sitting outside of the one medical bed in the infirmary, where a petite nurse and off-duty vacationing doctor were meeting with Zola in private, Zena tried not to panic, but panic was all she felt.

"I don't understand why we can't just go to the hospital," Zena complained to Alton and Adan, who were standing before her and working to keep her in the seat so she wouldn't charge into the room to see Zola, as she'd done three times already.

"It's too far and it'll take too long for an ambulance to get here. Didn't you see that traffic out there?" Adan replied. "We went over this. And Zola's fine. She's already awake and talking to the doctor."

"But she could have internal bleeding, or something could be broken," Zena went on.

"*Zena*, she is fine!" Alton said.

"Well, you'd better hope she is, because if she's not—" Zena paused.

"What? What's that supposed to mean?" Alton asked.

"You know exactly what it means. What kind of husband are you going to be? You were supposed to be looking after her."

"She's not a child. I don't need to look after her. She's a grown woman," Alton argued. "And I was the one who told her not to get in the water. Or did you forget that?"

The nurse opened the door. Zena, Alton and Adan bum-rushed her, trying to get in to see Zola, but she announced that Zola was only ready to see one person and she'd requested Alton.

"But I'm blood. I'm next of kin here," Zena said, using her official courtroom tone with the nurse, who looked bored with Zena's comments and questions she'd endured since they'd rushed into the infirmary.

The nurse didn't respond. She signaled for Alton to follow her after letting the doctor out of the room.

"Ridiculous and unprofessional!" Zena complained, pivoting from the closed doors with her arms folded over her chest to demonstrate her discontent. "We should really just go to the hospital. Who knows if these people are even qualified to take care of Zola?"

"Zena, again, the hospital is too far, and the doctor said she's—" Adan was tired of comforting Zena's demands now, too. He stopped his repetitious response. "Look, why don't you do something? Like call your mother? Did you tell her what happened?"

"Call her for what? To tell her Zola fell off a surfboard and almost died?"

"She didn't almost die. She just slipped and got pulled in by the undercurrent. Scary, but not uncommon."

"You don't understand. If something happens to Zola, I'm the one who's responsible!" Zena cried, now hysterical. "I'm the one who's supposed to be watching her! I'm always the one watching!" Zena began to cry fresh, new tears that let on that this was about more than the sister sitting up doing just fine in the other room.

Adan pulled Zena into his arms and pressed her head to his chest. "It's all going to be fine," he said tenderly. "Don't worry. I'm here for you, baby."

Zena snapped back and pushed Adan away.

"Baby? I'm not your baby!" she hollered. "And you know what? Really, this is all on you! You!"

"Me?"

"Yes! You were the one who made this whole thing happen! We shouldn't even be here! Zola should be home in Atlanta studying for the Bar!"

"I thought you moved on from that, Zena."

"Moved on? From what? You clearly haven't moved on," Zena said. "And that's what this is all about."

"You don't know what you're talking about," Adan answered, walking away from Zena then, but she was right on his heels.

"How about I do. I know you're just doing this whole wedding thing because you're jealous!" Zena said.

"Jealous? Jealous of what?"

"Of me! And of Zola. That I was the one who made it, and now she was about to do the same. She was about to do what you couldn't do for Alton!"

"That's crazy. Look I'm excited about anything Zola does. She's like my little sister. She's like family."

"But she's *not* your family. We're not a couple. You blew that!"

"I know I did, and I'm so sorry. Don't you think that's haunted me every day since we broke up?"

The door cracked open again, and all words stopped as Adan and Zena rushed over for news.

"Is she okay?" Adan asked as Alton walked out.

"She's fine," Alton confirmed. He looked at Zena. "She wants to see you now."

Zena wiped her tears and walked into the room as if she expected to see Zola hooked up on life support and completely covered in a full-body cast.

Reality was the opposite.

The sun was shining through the window of what looked like a dorm room, and Zola was sitting up smiling as if she was just waking up and had never set foot on the beach.

"You have to be kidding me!" Zola joked, getting an eyeful of her sister's countenance. "You're crying? I thought I heard you out there hollering."

She reached for Zena and hugged her before moving over so Zena could sit on the bed.

"How are you feeling?" Zena asked.

"I'm fine. I just lost my step, and then I felt the water pulling me back. I panicked," Zola explained. "I probably shouldn't have been in that water anyway."

"You were fine. I saw you on the board. I was watching you. I really was," Zena pleaded.

"You didn't need to watch me, Z. What happened wasn't anyone's fault. It was a freak accident."

"No, it wasn't a freak accident. We shouldn't be here. Look, I've been trying to accept this wedding and support you, but I shouldn't have let you come here," Zena said. "And I don't know why Adan is supporting this, but it's a mistake. It's clearly a mistake. You shouldn't be getting married. And maybe this is just a sign."

Zola pursed her lips, and then her own tears began to fall.

"What? What's wrong?" Zena asked. "Is it something I said? Because I'm just telling the truth. I'm not trying to hurt you. It's for your own good—"

"No," Zola cut in. "It's not you. It's me. It's about what I haven't told you." She looked off at the sunlight coming through the window and exhaled. "There's a reason Alton was nervous about me getting on the surfboard. It was ridiculous that he thought it would have any impact, but I know why he was scared. He was just looking out for me."

"What are you talking about? Why was he scared?"

Zola looked at Zena.

"I had a miscarriage," Zola said, the sad words slipping out of her mouth just one per second.

"What? When?" Zena placed her hand on Zola's knee.

"A few days before graduation. I was just so stressed and worried about everything and I woke up one morning and…" She paused and looked into Zena's eyes. "I lost my baby."

"Did you know you were pregnant?"

"I suspected. But I didn't even have any time to take the test. I think I was scared to know. I was terrified to know, because it meant everything was about to change. Everything I wanted was gone," Zola said.

"That's not true. And why didn't you tell me? Why didn't you call me or something?" Zena asked.

"The last thing you said to me before you left DC my first year of law school was that I shouldn't get pregnant," Zola said. "And there I was—pregnant."

"You should've told me, Zola. I would've been there for you."

"The funny thing is when I was at the hospital and I realized there was no way Alton could get to me, the only other person I wanted to call was you, but I just couldn't. It would be like I was letting myself down by just saying it to you. So, I called the next best person."

"Mommy?"

"No, Z. I called Adan."

"What?"

"He actually left his job in New York and flew to DC. Six hours after I called, he was by my side."

Zena jumped up from the bed and began pacing.

"You should've called *me*," she protested.

"You're not listening."

"I *am* listening. And I'm telling you that you should've called *me* and not Adan!" Zena turned to Zola.

"No, *you're* not listening. I'm trying to tell you something."

"Tell me what?"

"Adan has always been there for me. He visited me in DC more than you. More than anyone else—other than Alton," Zola revealed. "And when it was clear I needed help, like more help just to get through graduation, he paid for me to go to therapy. He was at my graduation, too. He sat alone, though…because he knew you'd be upset if you knew he was there. But he said he couldn't stay away. He knew I needed him there."

Zola got off the bed and went to stand before Zena.

"That's what this wedding is about. Why Adan is supporting it. It has nothing to do with Alton. It's about me. About me getting better," Zola said.

"So you've been communicating with him all this time and not telling me?" Zena asked.

"We all have. Me. Mommy. Malak. We just

don't tell you because we know how you'll get. We know how you get about him," Zola said. "I mean, you didn't even go to Mrs. Pam's funeral because he'd be there. After all she did for us, you—"

"I couldn't!" Zena shouted, cutting Zola off.

"I know. And I understand. Going through this, I completely understand how hard it can be to move on sometimes," Zola said. "And maybe it's time for you to admit to yourself that you haven't."

"I have."

"Just give him a chance."

"I've moved on!"

"He deserves a chance."

"For what?"

"You guys were just kids then. He was making the best decision he could. He thought he was doing the right thing," Zola said. "And you know that."

"What he thought doesn't matter. What he did does."

"He still loves you, Z," Zola confessed.

"You don't know what you're talking about."

Zola smirked at Zena's uneasiness. "You asked if he mentioned wanting to take you on a date? I don't remember that. But I do remember what he told me about you—about how he feels about you."

"What?" Zena asked, and then she turned from her sister. "Never mind, I don't want to know."

"He said he loves you. He still loves you, and he'd do anything to be back with you. I hope you give him that chance."

Chapter 7

Zola stayed in Alton's bed that night.

In the minivan on the way back to Mahatma House, Zena had watched Zola and Alton comforting each other, Zola resting her head on Alton's shoulder, him kissing her forehead, and it was as if she was spying something new in them and really seeing their love for one another for the first time—their adult love for one another for the first time. They were no longer teens falling asleep on the phone together. They were grown folks whose love had been tested, been through some things, and there they were, still holding on to each other.

Dinner was endured in silence. No speeches.

No tactics. They ate and let the ocean breeze play its melody of life moving on.

Zena could hardly look at Adan across the dinner table.

And he hardly looked at her.

The news she had, the news he knew she'd been given at the infirmary, was about to change everything. It had to. How could it not?

After dinner, Zena stood in the mirror of her black cocoon remembering the laughs she'd had with Adan before Zola's accident. How something as simple as surfing in the Indian Ocean had become a kind of temporary peacekeeping activity between the two in a time of war. Adan hadn't seemed like an enemy then. He didn't seem allpowerful. Or all evil. He didn't want to hurt her. He was just a man with brown skin and a smile she knew well.

Zena remembered his reaching for her in the barrel. Her reaching back. Him saying he hadn't been there wrapped in water with her, and then the vision of him in the barrel being clearer than it was when it happened. Was he telling the truth about wiping out? Why would he lie? And if he wasn't there, what had she seen? Was she seeing what she wanted to see?

"I needed you! I needed you to be there for me!" Zena was standing face-to-face with Adan at the door of his villa at Mahatma House. When she felt these words boiling in her gut in the mirror, she'd run out of her room and across the property in her panties and a tank top to say this to him—to his face. "I needed you more than anything. More than some stupid degree and some stupid dream of being a lawyer. I needed you to stay with me."

"Zena, I know. And I'm sorry. I'm so sorry that I—"

"No! Wait! I'm not here for that. I'm not here for an apology. I'm here to tell you that I know now. I know that as much as I needed you, Adan, you couldn't be there for me," Zena said. "It wasn't your job to be there for me." Zena paused as she began to cry, feeling so much hurt she'd tried to keep hidden in her hate of Adan. "You're not my father. You can't make up for his failures. You had your own life to live."

"No. I didn't."

"What?"

"Look, why don't you come in and we can talk about this." Adan glanced down at Zena's nude legs. "I can give you some pants to put on."

"Oh, my God!" Zena was embarrassed by her lack of clothes and remembered her rush to Adan. She hadn't felt a thing—not one chill or breeze against her legs in the heat of the night. "What am I doing? Why am I here?" She tried to turn to leave, but Adan stopped her.

"No. Don't go. I understand." Adan pointed

down at his jeans and the flip-flops on his feet. "I was actually on my way to you. To talk to you." He grinned at her. "But I took some time to put on the proper attire."

Adan pulled Zena inside and gave her a pair of his jogging shorts.

They agreed to walk to the shore behind the villa, where they could talk.

There was a cool breeze there from the water, but it still did little to contend with the heat that was emanating from the sand that had been baking all day.

"I know I sounded like a complete jerk. I couldn't think of anything else to say, though," Adan said, recalling his explanation to Zena about why he was supporting Alton and Zola's wedding outside Madame Lucille's Lace weeks before.

Now that Zena understood his predicament with Zola, his flimsy and seemingly selfish excuse sounded plausible.

"I wanted to tell you to mind your business, but I know you too well for that," Adan said after he and Zena had a good laugh at her digging into him that day.

"I wasn't that bad," Zena said. "I was just looking out for my little sister." She looked at Adan and said with clear sincerity, "And I'm glad you looked out for her when she needed you. I can't imagine what she went through."

"I was thankful I could be there. You know? I meant what I said earlier—she's like my sister. I don't want to ever see her in pain. And she did take the miscarriage pretty hard. The only thing that seemed to give her hope was the idea of someday marrying Alton and actually having a baby."

"So, that's how you all came up with the wedding?"

Adan answered, "Felt like a step in the right direction. We all know where those two are headed. I don't think I've ever seen two people who love one another more than them."

There was an awkward pause and step as the word *love* settled between Adan and Zena. It was clear there was something more they needed to discuss that they just couldn't. This was where they were comfortable—talking about other people and their love, but not what they'd had. Maybe that would be too much or too forward. Maybe it would break something in the new connection they might be forging. Both wondered this in step and in silence, but then Adan just stopped walking and looked up at the moon with a certain fire that gave Zena hope he might break that silence. Remembering everything Zola had told her at the infirmary, she was ready to hear something then. She was ready to tell her truth. She wasn't over Adan. She hadn't ever gotten over him or how it ended. She turned to look at the moon, too.

"You remember that day?" Adan asked in a question with little detail, but still Zena knew his point of reference.

"The corner of Sassafras Street and Blue Stone Road," Zena announced.

"Someone else had to see it," Adan said, still transfixed on the glowy moon in Bali. "Never made sense to me that we were the only ones. I asked everyone, though. No one knew what I was talking about."

"A celestial event." Zena had been standing behind Adan in the sand, but she stepped beside him when she said this.

"An eclipse for two," Adan repeated their science teacher Mr. Palabas's explanation of their spectacular view of the sky's magic.

Zena didn't know what to say to that. She thought she could simply nod in agreement, but then that felt wrong, so she just stood there staring at the moon with Adan.

After a while, he said, "Zena, I've missed you. I've missed you so much that sometimes I felt like it was going to kill me. That's how bad it ached."

Zena heard Adan's breathing quicken as if he'd just dropped something heavy from his arms.

"I had to say that," he said, and then he took another deep breath. "I had to say it." He turned to Zena and looked at her profile.

"Don't!" Zena ordered when she felt he was

about to speak again. Tears were already streaming down to her chin. She didn't know what she was afraid of hearing, what she didn't want to hear. But with those words from Adan, she felt in her heart that same aching he was describing. She knew it well, too. The feeling of being apart. The feeling of being without him had been too much on too many days. And right then, recalling it all was like pouring salt on those injuries.

"I have to," Adan said. "I have to say it all. And I know you don't want me to respond to what you said earlier, but I have to. I have to tell you that I should've been there for you. Your heart was my responsibility. I knew you needed me. And I was a fool for leaving you."

"But we were just kids. You were right. We needed to go out into the world. And follow our dreams," Zena said with Adan's old words in her mouth.

"No. We were kids who were lucky enough to have found our dreams in each other. I know that now. I've spent my whole adult life paying for not seeing that. That's why I couldn't get married. I called it off because I realized I was just making up for not having you. I was just pretending that everything was great, but it never would be. Not if you weren't there."

Adan went to stand between Zena and her locked view on the moon.

She closed her eyes to avoid his presence.

"Look at me," he said softly.

Tears continued to escape from her closed eyes.

"No," Zena uttered.

"Look at me!" Adan began to wipe Zena's tears and slid his hand beneath her chin. "Please, just see me."

He lifted her head, and Zena slowly opened her eyes.

"I know I'm supposed to be cool. I know I'm supposed to have a more elaborate plan to win you back and pay off your pain, but I don't have that. All I have is the truth," Adan said. "Yes, I supported this wedding because I wanted to help Zola and Alton. But I knew there was no way Zola would do this without you. And I wanted to see you." Adan moved his hand to caress Zena's cheek. "And I wanted to see you so I could say these things to you."

"Why?" Zena asked.

"Because I want to be with you."

"Be with me? But we haven't been together in nine years. It's been so long. Too long."

"Stop it, Z. Stop it with that wall! Just stop," Adan said, and then he started crying, too. "I'm Adan! You can let it down. I'm here. I'm here. I'm here. And I love you. I love you so much."

Did Adan pull Zena to him for that kiss that followed these words? Or was Zena the one who pulled Adan to her lips? Neither would ever know or remember. But it happened. It was as if the space between them in the sand evaporated and their toes touched and then their lips connected and then there was a kiss.

Zena closed her eyes and felt Adan's arms wrapping around her, holding her up and steadying her against his body. She didn't want to let go of his lips. She didn't want to be released from his hold. But still, she wondered, *What is this? What is happening?*

She opened her eyes to see him, to confirm that this was him and look at Adan as he kissed her so passionately.

And he was there. Adan was before her with his eyes closed and joy written all over his face.

Twinkling or sparkling behind his right ear caught Zena's eye. She refocused and saw something that looked like fireworks, but then she knew it couldn't be, so she broke the lip-lock from Adan and ordered him to turn around.

"Look! Look!" she screamed, pointing at the shining clear black night.

As soon as Adan turned, in one second there was a flicker and pop, and two shooting stars raced across the sky.

"Did you see that? Did you see that?" Zena rushed out, still in shock at what she'd just seen.

"Yes! I did! I did! I think it was a shooting

star—two shooting stars!" Adan said with his voice half-confused or in awe.

"Oh, my God! I can't believe we just saw that!" Zena was ecstatic then and jumping in the sand. She turned to Adan and said with significant cadence, "We just saw that. We just saw that together. Right as we kissed."

Adan began to lower his head to kiss Zena again, but then he had a thought: "Wait!" he said, stopping himself right before Zena's anticipating lips. "I wonder if anyone else saw it!"

"Who cares? It was just for us," Zena said before pulling Adan's face down to hers and kissing him again.

Inside Adan's room, there were no strangers, no nervous energy, no pretense or discussion about what should or could happen.

With the sound of waves rolling in the distance and the moon peeking into the slightly slanted shutters, in the darkness of the villa, Adan slid off Zena's clothes and knelt down to study her body as if it was something he'd cherished but lost and then found again. He closed his eyes as he kissed her stomach and caressed the outsides of her thighs. Into her navel he spoke of love and never letting go again. Still on his knees, he wrapped his arms around her waist and rested his head over the top of her vagina. He held her and waited as if he was meditating or praying. He held Zena there in that position for so long she didn't want to move him. To say a thing. To ask a thing.

Soon, Zena began to cry again. She palmed the top of his head and said, "I forgive you and I missed you. And… I love you, too."

Chapter 8

Zola was sitting at the breakfast table, holding Alton's hand so tightly neither could eat their food. She looked as if nothing happened the day before and was so perky and cheerful no one wanted to bring it up. While it was another lazy, hot morning in Bali, it was her wedding day and all knew she should enjoy the bliss moments like this could bring without interruption.

Over postbreakfast green tea, as the foursome debated the event of the double shooting star, Zena watched Zola and thought of how different she seemed than any other bride on their wedding day, at least the ones Zena had seen. Most were rushing and running, rummaging and ruling over everything. Their grooms were hidden away; their world was an oiled machine of pomp and circumstance that had to go just as planned. This circus grew and evolved until it ended with the bride looking exhausted and tuned out, ready to escape to the refuge of a honeymoon hours away. But here was Zola sitting at the breakfast table in a thin turquoise sundress they'd purchased in the market downtown. Her hair was up in her topknot and she had two ridiculously large hibiscuses tucked behind each ear. She looked like some Bohemian garden nymph, completely relaxed and just happy. She was already on her honeymoon and neither bothered nor vexed about what lay ahead.

"Bruh, there's no such thing as a double shooting star!" Alton teased Adan. "It just doesn't make sense. The spontaneity behind the single scientific event of one star shooting across the sky—and while two people are watching—is just too rare for two to occur at once—and, again, while two people are watching."

"What, are you an astronomer now? You hardly graduated from Clark Atlanta, and now you sound like freaking Neil deGrasse Tyson," Adan said, and everyone laughed.

"I watch documentaries on Netflix. I know many things!" Alton followed up, and then the laughter grew at his response.

"Seriously, though, there were two shooting stars. I saw it, too," Zena confirmed. "It was so fast. But I saw it. I know I saw it."

By then, Zena and Adan had questioned most everyone at Mahatma House, including the security guard and the beautiful long-haired girl who showed up each morning to do the flower offering at the villa's traditional altar. They wanted to know if anyone had seen the shooting stars. No one had seen a thing. And two people, the chef and the woman who cleaned Adan's room, confirmed that they'd indeed been looking at the sky at that exact hour and hadn't witnessed anything out of the norm.

"Maybe you did—maybe you didn't," Zola said. "The real question is, why were both of you looking up at the sky at the same time after midnight? That's what I want to know." Zola grinned and looked from Adan to Zena. They were sitting beside one another and looking very cozy. They weren't touching, but their bodies were still leaning into each other with enough normalcy to reveal the tale from the night before.

Suddenly, they moved apart after hearing Zola's question. Both felt the need to clear their throats. They looked like teenagers who'd been caught kissing.

"What!" Zola's grin grew to a full smile.

"Did something happen?" Alton asked, intrigued by their behavior, too.

"We just talked," Adan answered with forced calm in his voice. He patted Zena on her back. "Just had a friendly chat on the beach."

Zola looked unconvinced and kept her big smile. "Friendly, huh? I bet it was. I bet it also describes why, when I came to Zena's room this morning to drop off her maid of honor dress, she wasn't there."

"Actually," Zena followed quickly, "I'd gone for an early-morning jog."

Zola came back with, "*Actually*, I tripped over your sneakers when I walked into the room. Soooo…"

Adan and Zena held in their laughter at being caught as Alton and Zola traded stares.

Zena worked hard to shift the conversation from the topic of her whereabouts the night before by asking Zola and Alton about their wedding plans. They revealed that they'd decided to take a short walk through the village to the hut of a local Balian Tenung, a diviner, who would bless them before their ceremony.

After breakfast, Zola followed Zena back to her villa to try on their dresses and have Zena braid her hair. The dresses had arrived that morning, and while Zola had already tried on her dress, Zena hadn't even seen her dress.

As soon as Zola closed the sliding door of the villa and turned around to Zena, she begged, "Tell me everything that happened! I want to know it all! Everything!"

"Nothing happened. It was just a walk," Zena said, knowing Zola was referring to the events with Adan.

"You know I'm not stupid, right? I may have nearly killed myself in the ocean yesterday, but I didn't incur any brain damage. I'm operating with all my cards in the deck!"

Zena plopped down on the bed and sighed helplessly, the way a woman does when she's resolved that she's in love.

"Everything happened," she said. *"Everything."*

"Oh, girl, this sounds too good!" Zola sat down beside Zena and leaned over for gossip. "I'll get to that second everything later, but give me the first everything now."

"You're a mess. Look, he just told me he loves me and that he wants to be with me."

"I know all that, Zena. That's not news. I'm asking for the goods. What did you say?"

"I…I," Zena stuttered to try to find her words to reveal what she'd said to Adan, but Zola stopped her.

"Tell me the truth. Even if you didn't tell him

the truth. Tell me the truth. Tell me what you wanted to say," the younger sister ordered wisely.

Zena looked at Zola as if she was the big sister.

"I said it. I admitted it." She paused and remembered standing before Adan. "I admitted that I was in love with him. And that I've missed him. And I've been so sad without him. All these years."

Zola's back stiffened, and she pulled Zena's head to her chest. She kissed her forehead and smiled. Both knew the weight of Zena's admission to Adan. This was an act of fearlessness from a brave woman, who mistakenly thought the most selfless thing she could do was keep Adan away, but the real fear to face was letting him back in. This was peeking under the bed to find ghosts.

As she set up to braid Zola's hair, Zena went on with her recall about the shooting stars, Adan's kiss and him picking her up to carry her all the way to his villa. Zola listened to all of this. "Ya'll are back in love," Zola proclaimed. "Finally back in love."

"Well, I don't know all of that. I don't know where this is going from here. If it's going anywhere. I'm just happy we got it off our chests. It was cathartic."

Zola laughed. "Right. You can say that to everyone else," she said. "You can believe it if you want. Just know that's not what Adan's thinking."

"What's he thinking?"

"He's already purchased a condo downtown—

three blocks from you. And he's moving to Atlanta as soon as we get back."

"But that couldn't have anything to do with me. He didn't know how I'd react to him. If anything would happen between us," Zena said.

"I don't think he cared. I think he intended to keep trying. See, Adan thinks I'm slow. I know what this wedding thing was about. He was looking out for me, but he was also trying to win you back."

When Zola got up to look at her braids in the mirror, Zena revealed that Adan admitted that the night before but added that she was sure Zola was his chief concern.

"Well, I guess we'd better get this show on the road, then," Zola said. She left the mirror and reached for the garment bag containing Zena's maid of honor dress hanging on a hook beside the bed. "I tried to get in here earlier so you could try this thing on. I hope it fits. We won't have time for changes."

"I'm sure it'll be fine. I think I've actually lost weight since Madame Lucille took my measurements at the shop," Zena joked.

"Yeah. Right! You wish!" Zola winked and unzipped the bag, revealing a sleek bumblebee-yellow, single-shoulder satin robe with a thin cream waist bodice. The stylish dress was a mix of vintage chic and sophistication that immediately stole a smile from Zena.

Zena was up on her feet walking to the dress with her hands over her mouth to exemplify her awe and excitement. "This is for me? For me?"

Zola pulled the bag from the hook and let it fall to the floor, fully displaying her dress selection for her sister. "Yes."

Zena didn't know if she should hug Zola or go for the dress, so she did both. She took the dress from the wall and pulled Zola into an embrace. "I love it. I really love it."

"I helped Madame Lucille design it. I wanted something really special for you."

"But it's too much. No? Like, it looks like something that could be for a bride." Zena let Zola go and inspected the dress by holding the hanger out. "It's just that beautiful."

Zola was looking at Zena look at the dress. With pride, she said, "A beautiful dress for my beautiful sister."

"Oh, thank you, Zollie."

"Seriously. I really wanted to design something amazing for you. Something to show how special you are to me," Zola explained. "This day isn't just about me and Alton. It's about you, too. About everything you've done for me—how you've been there for me. For us."

"Of course, I'm there for you. You're my baby sister," Zena said.

"It's more than that. You know it. You've been

more than a sister. You've been a mother. A father. You've been there for me when I had no one. And you've believed in me," Zola continued. "Last night, after the accident on the beach, that's all I kept thinking about—you believe in me. Sometimes more than I've believed in myself. You see things in me that no one else can see. And I know for sure in my life that it has made all the difference."

The dress fell over Zena's skin as if she'd grown into it, as if it was a part of her.

Zola went to the bathroom to finish looking over her appearance. There was a soft knock at the door. Zena thought it was the housekeeper, so she quickly opened it up only to find Adan standing there in a tan linen suit. Somehow, Zena felt Adan shouldn't be seeing her dress, so she covered her chest as if she was a bride and he was getting a peek.

"I'm sorry," Adan said, covering his eyes.

"Wait! Wait!" Zena laughed, realizing her error. "I'm tripping. I'm not the bride. You can clearly look at my dress." She laughed.

"Really?" Adan asked, still covering his eyes. "Are you sure?"

"Yes, silly." Zena smiled at Adan's playing. He looked handsome in his suit. Not too pretentious or formal. He was dapper but relaxed.

He lowered his hand and peeked at Zena. "I don't know. I don't want to get in trouble. You women and your wedding-day rules about people seeing your dress."

"Well, it's not my wedding day so you can see my dress."

"Well, I was just coming over here before things get started to make sure you're fine."

"I'm fine," Zena said. "Why wouldn't I be? Shouldn't I be?" She looked at Adan curiously, as if maybe he was seeing their evening exchange differently than she had. She hoped he hadn't.

"I'm just wondering if you feel like I feel." Adan grinned in a way that made him look fifteen years old again. Right then, Zena felt as if they were back in Georgia, back on their street, blushing at each other. "Look, I'm just excited." Adan looked at Zena. "That's the best way I can put it. I'm excited. I'm happy it happened. And, I guess, I came to say I hope you're happy, too."

Zena leaned into the door frame before Adan. "I am," she admitted.

"Great." Adan's smile grew as he stepped back from the door to return to Alton. "I'm happy to hear that, because this is all I've wanted for a long time."

The next knock at the door was Kadek, the villa manager. He arrived ready to escort the sisters to the front gate. Adan and Alton were waiting there to begin the short walk to the beach hut where the Balian Tenung would bless Alton and Zola before the wedding ceremony. He was carrying a huge parasol made of iridescent silks and gold piping. Curly sheer fabric dangled from each corner.

"You ready?" Zena asked, looking at Zola standing in front of the mirror, nervously adjusting the crown of wild shore flowers she'd collected to decorate the goddess braids Zena put in her hair. The rose-gold lace sheath Lisa had picked out for Zola at Lucille's Lace was simple yet ethereal.

"Guess I have to be," Zola said. "Let's do this."

Zola began to walk to the door, but Zena suddenly felt she needed to add some words, some weight to the moment before Zola went to say her vows.

"I didn't come here with the best of intentions," she said.

"What?"

"I thought I was coming here to stop you from marrying Alton. I thought I could use my relationship with you as leverage to keep you from saying, 'I do.' But now, with everything that's happened, I know I was wrong. I know I was just holding you back from getting what you really want. And I know it's just my job to make sure you get that."

Zola responded, "You were just trying to have my back. I can't be mad at you for that. I'm only happy you're in my corner right now."

The sisters hugged, and Zena gave Zola a big kiss on the cheek.

"I wish Mommy could see you in this dress," Zena said. "I really wish she could've been here."

"Me, too."

Zola pulled Zena out the door, and the two floated under the colorful celebratory parasol toward the front gate.

When Zola spotted Alton and Adan standing there, she ran ahead of Zena and Kadek, kicking up her dress so all could see her gold gladiator sandals. She ran so fast it was as if she hadn't seen Alton in days or weeks, months. Or maybe it was as if she'd never seen him before and had only known him in dreams and this was their first time laying eyes on one another.

And he ran toward her, also. Standing beside Adan in his matching tan linen suit with a blooming bright yellow allamanda in his lapel that matched Zena's dress, Alton dropped his guitar and ran to meet Zola halfway on the path to the gate. He picked her up and held her in the air as if she was light as a flower petal.

Pretending to fly, Zola spread her arms out and hollered, "I love you, Alton Douglass!"

"Come on now. You two aren't even married yet. Calm down with the drama!" Adan joked from behind Alton and Zola. He walked over to Zena and kissed her on the forehead before putting one arm around her shoulder.

"Thank you!" Zena jumped in. "Let's save all the mushy stuff until after the legal stuff."

Alton and Zola guffawed at the elder siblings' comments and got in line to walk to the beach. Alton picked up his guitar and set out in the back of the crowd, playing a simple and sweet melody he'd played on many nights to lull Zola to sleep.

Kadek led the party, carrying the parasol in the front as they paraded through the small, rude and rocky streets of the country town that was busy with afternoon business. Lean-to shop owners and smiling locals came out to see the party pass. Some offered their blessings and others came out to tie ornate ribbons to Zena's and Zola's waists, a symbolic blessing of good luck and prosperity. Small children wanted to shake Zola's hand. One woman stepped up for a picture with the bridal party. This part of the journey appeared foreign from any wedding celebration they'd ever seen, but it also felt natural and intimate. As if it was the way that love ought to be celebrated, in the community, without excessive flair, with much love beneath the sun.

When they entered the portion of the beach that led to the Balian Tenung's hut, Kadek lowered the parasol and pointed to a small temple that had been meticulously decorated with flowers and sitting statues by the Tenung's followers and visitors throughout the years. It looked like a whimsical beach cabin or fairy-tale hideout. Two burning torches demarked the entrance. A little closer to the shore, a wooden altar and gazebo was overrun with fresh-picked fragrant plumeria. The Catatan Sipil, civil registrar, Adan hired to officiate over Alton and Zola's vows stood awaiting the occasion of the nuptials beneath the gazebo.

"Before marriage, you see Nyoman inside. He ready for you," Kadek said, pointing to the hut. "You go together. He bless you. Good for marriage."

Inside the hut, the foursome found a short, plump man with a bald head and few teeth sitting in the lotus position on a torn wool mat. Draped in white muslin, he smiled politely, said a few words to welcome them and gestured for them to sit before him.

For seconds or minutes, he glanced at their eyes, moving from one to the next, peeking wisely and knowingly at something that made each of them feel awkward but lucky to be in Nyoman's presence. He didn't look like a wise man, though, not like the stereotypical truth teller most Western visitors expected to see sitting in the hut. Nyoman appeared cheerful yet studied. He might be a schoolteacher or a chef—judging from his stomach—if he wasn't sitting in that hut.

"You love—you all love each other," he said finally. "You together. Always stay together. Always."

He signaled for Adan and Zena to join hands.

"Oh, no, we're not the ones getting married," Zena said as softly as she could, so as not to disturb the quiet in the space. "They are." She pointed to Zola and Alton sitting beside her.

Nyoman looked down at his lap and waited.

"You here for marry," he said as the sounds and breeze of the rolling tide outside crashed into the doorway. He looked up at Adan and added, "You here for love her. You here for marry her." He pointed to Zena.

The words were a secret spoken aloud. There was an uncomfortable chuckle from the foursome, with Zena leading. But Nyoman did not budge. He did not smile.

"Your heart is without cover," he said then to Zena. "He cover your heart. He give heart to you safe." He reached over and patted the ground before Zena's and Adan's locked hands. "You together. You love."

"But—" Zena tried, but her desired interrogation was met with a firm eye from Nyoman. There would be no more questions.

He lifted his hand and turned to Alton with his guitar and Zola with her wildflowers in her hair. He smiled at them as if they were children frolicking in a meadow.

"Love of flower in garden," he said to them.

"Flower no open. Flower closed. No pluck. No time. Soon time. Soon time pluck flower."

Zena looked over at Zola to see her stare at Nyoman, drinking in his words.

Alton wrapped his arm over Zola's shoulders and kissed her cheek, but she never once looked away from Nyoman.

"Well, we're about to pluck it right now, right outside," Adan joked in an attempt to break the stare between Nyoman and Zola.

Nyoman smiled and then reached into one of the copper bowls of water and uncooked rice on the floor between them. He uttered foreign words and placed the water and rice on each person's forehead with his thumb.

Kadek appeared in the doorway to escort them to the gazebo for the nuptials.

As the caravan rose to depart, Zena noticed Zola lingering in the back, still looking at Nyoman sitting there in the lotus position with a satisfied smile on his face.

She caught Zola's arm. "Are you all right?" Zena asked.

"I'm fine." Zola looked at Zena, and in Zola's eyes, Zena found some state of serenity, of enlightenment.

The sisters clasped hands and sojourned up the twisting strip of sand heading toward the plumeria-draped gazebo, where the civil registrar presiding over the ceremony was standing beside Adan and Alton, who was strumming his song on the guitar to entice his bride down the aisle to him.

While the melody was the same, he'd changed the words for that special day:

Kiss me and I know your heart is pure.
Love me and I swear I'll give you more.
You are my love, my breath to carry me away.
   You are my life—my days will be the same.

Some of the villagers who'd followed the procession to the beach had formed a thin circle before the gazebo. They waved and threw fresh-picked flowers at Zola and Zena as they walked by.

As Zena escorted Zola, she looked ahead at Adan standing beside his little brother. He was smiling, but unlike everyone else, his eyes weren't on the bride; he was watching Zena. He was staring at her. His gaze was so focused, in fact, that Zena looked away. She felt that if she'd kept her eyes on him, she might walk straight to him, forget where she was and what she was supposed to be doing, and stand by his side.

When the women reached the men, Zena kissed Zola on the cheek and stepped to the side.

The registrar, a little man with seesaw shoulders, began to read through his legal proceedings, nodding to Zola and Alton to be sure both understood his shaky English.

He paused and announced that the couple wanted to state their own vows.

Alton spoke first: "Zola, I don't remember any part of my life without you. Or else, maybe, all the parts before you, were me trying to get to you. Trying to make you see me. And when you did, when you finally saw me, it was like my life began again. And I never want it to end. Zola, I vow to be your partner. I vow to be by your side. I vow to be in your corner. You don't have to look for me. You don't have to call my name. I vow to just be there."

Zola wiped tears from Alton's cheeks and then stood still so he could wipe hers.

The registrar turned to her.

The sea breeze took on an expectant howl as new seconds ticked past. There was waiting for something to happen, and then there was this— awkward lagging where there should have been words—words from Zola.

There was near-inaudible chatter from the onlookers. Zena smiled at them and nudged Zola in the back.

The registrar lacked any Westernized notion of sympathy for those in contemplation at such times, so he kept a stare on Zola's eyes, which were solemn and maybe mournful by then.

"Zola!" Zena nudged Zola again and called her name rather unceremoniously.

"Alton, I love you but—" Zola started, but then her voice cracked and she looked down at her feet.

Not knowing what was happening or what to do, Zena grabbed her elbow as if she was afraid Zola was about to topple over.

"It's okay," Alton said softly. "It's really okay, Z. We don't have to. It's okay."

"What? What's okay?" Zena said, pulling Zola's arm then. She looked past Alton at Adan for help, but he appeared just as confused as she felt.

"I can't," Zola whispered to her gold gladiator sandals, but her voice was clear and distinct enough for all around to hear the two condemning words one should never say at an altar.

"I know, baby. It's fine," Alton said, his voice supportive and encouraging.

Zola found some strength and looked up at Alton with more tears and different tears streaming down. Firmly, she said, "I can't do this."

The registrar had forgotten his provisional English and was speaking harsh words in his native Balinese.

"I understand," Alton said as Adan leaned over to him to say something in his ear.

"No wedding?" the registrar said to Zola.

Before Zola could answer, Zena said over her to the registrar, "Yes, wedding! Yes!"

In a rush, she grabbed Zola's hand and tugged her down the steps leading away from the gazebo to the beach.

With nowhere to go, she stopped maybe a quarter of a mile from Alton and Adan and with all eyes on her, she asked Zola what was going on.

"I can't do it. I don't want to get married right now," Zola said. "You heard Nyoman. It's not time."

"Who cares what that old man said? It's Alton. You love him," Zola argued.

"I do love him and I do want to marry him, but I don't think I want to do it now."

"But we're here. That's why we're all here, because you said you wanted to marry him *now*."

"I think I was doing it because I thought it was going to make me feel better about—" Zola looked off to the water; one of the wildflowers dropped from her crown and floated away in the breeze. "But it hasn't. And I don't think marrying Alton will make anything better. It'll just make everything different."

Zena reached out and touched her shoulder. "Did you tell him this?"

"We talked about it last night a little—well, a lot. He knows how I feel. But I said I'd still go through with it." Zola looked back at Zena. "I don't think I can. Not now."

"Zola, I hope nothing I said changed your mind.

I love Alton, and I know you two belong together," Zena said.

Zola replied, "No. It's not you—well, I guess it is, in a way.

"Oh, no! I'm sorry. I—"

"No. Listen. I'm not talking about you discouraging me. I'm talking about you encouraging me," Zola said. "Another thing Alton and I talked about last night is me taking the Bar Exam. I'm going to do it."

"What?" Zena pushed surprised.

"I was scared and I was worried and I know now that some of this wedding stuff was also about me putting that off. I can admit that. And I can also admit that you're right. It is time for me to take the test. You believing in me helped me believe in myself."

"So what are we going to do?" Zena spied the confused crowd. "You know I'll support you in whatever you want to do, but these people are expecting a wedding."

"You know…they can still see a wedding," Adan said, suddenly stepping into view. "They will see a wedding if you say yes to marrying me."

Adan reached for Zena's hand. With no hesitation, he got down on his left knee and asked her, "Zena Nefertiti Shaw, will you marry me?"

Zena felt something in her heart humble under

those words, something break away and wither. It was pain. It was gone.

"Yes," she said. "Yes!"

Seeing this, the crowd cheered. Adan stood and grabbed Zena's hand, racing back to the gazebo, with Zola close behind.

The crowd, which had now doubled in size, began to applaud their return.

"Wedding, yes?" the registrar posed to Zola once they made it to the altar.

"Yes!" Zola said, pulling Zena in front of herself. "But not me—her."

Zola looked at Alton and communicated the plans to him with no words.

"Wedding, yes?" the registrar looked at Adan and Zena, his new subjects, as if it made no difference to him who got married. They could even pull a pair from the crowd forward.

When Zena, who was looking at Adan, did not respond to the registrar's eye prodding, he looked at Adan and repeated, "Wedding, yes?"

"Wedding, yes!" Adan replied.

The registrar said over the clapping crowd, "Wedding, yes?"

"Yes! Wedding, yes!" Zena nodded. "Yes!"

Zena felt the way anyone does when they're next in line and plucked from a crowd to receive their heart's desire. As if luck had finally chosen her. And it felt so good. This was her wedding. Her wedding to Adan. Their wedding in Bali, on the beach, with people they loved, with people they'd never know. And it felt right.

Adan had taken both of Zena's hands.

"This is my dream. You are my dream," he said. "I let you go so many years ago. I pushed you away. But I was a boy then. Now I'm a man and I know it wasn't right. I know for sure I'm the luckiest man who ever lived if you say yes to be mine. And if you take me back, not a day will go by when it's not clear that I know that—that I'm lucky to have you. I'm never leaving again. I'm never turning away again. I'm here to stay."

Zena started her vows with the first thing that came to mind: "I shouldn't take you back!" she joked, and Alton and Zola laughed. "But I have to. I have to take you back because you're my love. You're the only man I've ever loved. That's something I've kept in secret from everyone, from you, from myself, for too long, but I'm not willing to live in secret with that anymore. I'm not willing to live without you anymore. So, Adan, I vow to hold on to you. To be open to you. To the experience of you now, as you are now. And I'm never turning away again. I'm here to stay."

"Do you take this woman to be your lawfully wedded wife?" the registrar asked Adan.

"I do."

The registrar turned to Zena and asked, "Do

you take this man to be your lawfully wedded husband?"

"I do," Zena replied, and Adan wiped his forehead nervously for a laugh from the crowd.

Adan pulled two gold bands out of his suit jacket. "I've been carrying these rings around for years. They remind me of the love I thought I lost, but now I've gotten a second chance.

Adan slid the band onto Zena's ring finger, and then she put the ring Adan had given her onto his ring finger.

They separated and looked into each other's eyes, feeling the weight of those rings on their fingers.

"I now pronounce you husband and wife," the registrar said. "And you may now kiss the bride."

Adan stepped close to Zena, pairing the tips of his shoes with hers.

"Can you believe this?" she said as he leaned down to her.

"Yes," he said.

Adan lifted Zena into the air and lowered her down to his lips.

And there, with the sun beaming behind them, Mr. and Mrs. Adan Frederick Douglass celebrated their first kiss as husband and wife.

* * * * *

BEST MAN AND THE
RUNAWAY BRIDE

KANDY SHEPHERD

In memory of my dear friend Patrick J Houston,
married to his soulmate, my friend Louise,
for more than forty years after proposing
to her on their second date.
Charismatic, big-hearted and very handsome,
he was truly a real-life romance hero.

CHAPTER ONE

WHERE WAS THE BRIDE? She should have been at the church
a half-hour ago. Max Conway paced back and forth on
the pavement in front of the historic sandstone building. As best man at the wedding, he'd been despatched
outside to report on the bride's arrival status. Again, he
glanced down at his watch. Traditionally a bride was
tardy but this much late was ridiculous. No wonder the
groom, standing inside all by himself at the altar, was
grim-faced and tapping his foot.

Organ music drifted out through the arched windows
of the church. The notes had a trill of desperation as
the organist started her wedding repertoire for the third
time. Anticipation levels inside would be rising as the
congregation waited—and waited.

Max checked the traffic app on his phone to see if
there were problems. All roads leading to the church in
Sydney's posh eastern suburbs were clear. The bridesmaids had arrived without any problem. *But still no
bride.* He was about to turn on his heel and go back
inside to give the glowering groom an update—a task
he didn't relish—when the bridal car approached. His
shoulders sagged with relief. *She was here.*

Through the tinted window of the luxury limousine

he could see a froth of white veil framing a lovely female face. Nikki Lucas. Max recognised her straight
away, though he'd only met her for the first time at the
rehearsal two nights before. Honey-blonde hair. Soft
brown eyes. Tall and slender. A truly beautiful bride.
Well worth the wait for the lucky groom.

At the rehearsal she'd greeted Max with a smile so
dazzling he'd been momentarily stunned. She'd been
warm and welcoming to her fiancé's best man—a total
stranger to her. If she'd realised who he was—who he
had once been—she'd been too well-mannered to mention it. The rehearsal had gone smoothly and he'd got the
impression Ms Lucas was efficient and organised. Not
the kind of woman to be so late for her own wedding.

The wealthy father of the bride sat next to her in the
back seat. Why hadn't he hurried his daughter along?
Max found such lack of punctuality unpardonable. What
was Ms Lucas's game? If this were his bride—not that
he had any intention of marrying any time soon—he
would be furious. The limo slowed to a halt. No doubt
he'd be greeted with a flurry of excuses. He would cut
her short, bustle her inside and get this tardy bride up
the aisle pronto.

He ran to the bride's door and yanked it open. 'You're
here,' he said through gritted teeth, swallowing the
where the hell have you been.

He didn't get so much as a smile in response. In fact
the errant bride looked downright hostile. Her face was
as pale as the layers of tulle that framed it, her mouth
set tight. She swung her long, elegant legs out of the car,
shook off the hand he offered her to help, and stood up
in a flurry of fluffy white skirts.

She gave no apologies, no explanations, no excuses.

Just a tersely spoken command. 'You have to get me out of here.'

Max stared at her. 'Get you up the aisle, you mean,' he said. 'You're late. There's a church full of guests waiting for you. Not to mention your groom.'

'Him.' She shook her head so vehemently her long veil whipped around her face. 'I'm not going to marry that man. I thought I could go through with it but I can't.'

By now her father had clambered out of the car to join them. The limo took off with a squeal of tyres, the driver muttering he was late for his next job.

'Think about this, sweetheart,' said the older man. He handed her the bouquet of white roses that she had left behind her on the car seat. 'You can't just walk out on your wedding.'

'Yes, I can. You can't talk me out of this, Dad. If you won't help me, Max here will.' She spat out his name as if it were a dirty word. 'It's the least he can do as best man to the creep who convinced me to marry him under false pretences.' She glared at Max through narrowed eyes. 'That is, unless you're just as much lying pond scum as he is.'

Max wasn't usually lost for words. But the insult came from nowhere. Where was the smiling charmer from the rehearsal? Behind the perfect make-up the bride was grim-faced and steely eyed. 'I don't consider myself to be pond scum,' Max said through gritted teeth. 'But my duty as best man is to get you into the church for your wedding.'

'There isn't going to be a wedding. Your duty as a decent human being is to help me get away from here. Now.' Her hands shook with agitation and she kept looking anxiously towards the church.

Max's first reaction was to back away from the bride. He wasn't good with crazy. This was something more than pre-wedding nerves. There was no trace of the joyous, vibrant woman he'd met at the rehearsal. But then her lush pink mouth trembled and her eyes clouded with something he couldn't quite place—fear, anxiety, disappointment? It made him swallow a retort. How well did he actually know the groom? He'd played tennis with him back in high school but had only reconnected with him just weeks before the wedding—had been surprised to be asked to be best man. The groom could well be pond scum these days for all he knew. But he'd made a commitment to be best man. That made him Team Groom.

The father took her arm. 'Now, Nikki, there's no need to—'

The bride turned on her father with a swirl of white skirts, glaring back at Max as she did so. 'I'm sorry, Dad,' she said, her voice unsteady. 'I can't do it.'

She indicated the church with a wave of a perfectly manicured hand. Her large diamond engagement ring flashed in the afternoon summer sunlight. 'Please tell everyone to party on without me. Don't let all that food and wine go to waste.' Her mouth curled. 'Maybe someone could have the fun of smashing Alan's lying, scheming face into the wedding cake—all three tiers of it.'

'Maybe not,' Max said, trying not to let a smile twitch at the corners of his mouth at the thought of the somewhat supercilious groom facedown in the frosting.

He made his voice calm and reassuring. 'I know you must be nervous.'

Pre-performance nerves. He knew all about them. There was nothing more nerve-wracking than stepping out onto the centre court at Wimbledon with the world watching him defend his title.

'Nervous?' Her cheeks flushed and her eyes glittered. 'I'm not nervous. I'm mad as hell.' She brandished the cascade of white roses as if it were a weapon. Max ducked. 'The wedding is cancelled.'

'Why?' At the rehearsal she'd seemed to be floating on a cloud of happiness. For one long, secret moment he had envied her groom his gorgeous, vivacious bride-to-be. Despite his success at the highest rank of his chosen sport, and all the female attention that came with it, at age thirty Max was still single.

'You want a reason?' She raised her perfectly shaped brows. 'How about four reasons? His two ex-wives and two children.'

Max frowned. 'You knew Alan was divorced.'

'Divorced *once*. With no children. He lied.' Her voice ended on a heart-rending whimper. 'One of the reasons I fell for him was that he told me he was longing for children. Like…like I was.' Her face seemed to crumple; all the poise Max had admired melted away to leave only wide-eyed bewilderment.

'How did you find out?' he asked.

'His first ex-wife called to warn me off Alan. Didn't want to see me get fooled and hurt by him like she had been. He called her a vindictive witch. Then the second ex-wife wife called to tell me about their three-year-old twin sons and how he'd deserted them. Oh, and warned me he was on the verge of bankruptcy now that he'd gone through all her money.'

Max gasped. The dad hissed. Nikki was a successful businesswoman. Being both beautiful and wealthy made her quite the catch—and vulnerable to a fortune hunter.

'You believed her?' said Max.

She shook her head. 'I trusted my fiancé. But I had her investigated. Definitive proof she was telling the truth came just as I waved off my bridesmaids and was about to get into the limo.' Her breath caught on a hitch, dangerously close to a sob. 'I can't marry a liar and a fraud.'

'Go in there and tell him that,' said Max.

'I couldn't bear the humiliation.' She looked up at him, her eyes pleading now. 'You know all about humiliation.'

Max grimaced. Of course he did. Evidence of his disastrous final game where he'd injured his elbow so badly still circulated on the Internet: the thrown racket, his writhing in pain on the grass court surface of Wimbledon. People had even made memes of it.

'Yes,' he said through gritted teeth, not appreciating the reminder.

'Please help me get away. I can't run down the street to hail a cab dressed like this.'

Tears glistened in her brown eyes, making them luminous. Max had a weakness for female tears. But he was also a man of his word. He was the best man. An honourable position with duties he took seriously. It would take more than tears to recruit him to Team Bride. As she looked up at him, a single teardrop rolled slowly down her cheek. He had to fight an impulse to wipe it gently away with his thumb. *She was another man's bride.* She sniffed and her voice quivered as she spoke. 'You say you're not pond scum, now prove it to me.'

Nikki held her breath as she looked up at Max Conway for his answer. She hadn't expected to find him standing guard outside the church, ready to corral her inside. In fact, she hardly knew the guy. Just was aware he was a celebrity athlete and had a well-publicised love life.

The first she'd known that her groom's best man was the world's golden boy of tennis—featured in countless 'sexiest men alive' media round-ups—was when she'd met him at the rehearsal. Just another of her former fiancé's secrets, she thought with a twist of bitterness.

She could read the struggle on Max's face—with his spiky light brown hair and blue eyes, he was every bit as handsome as his photos. Duty warred an obvious battle with gentlemanly instincts to help a bride in distress. The media did not consider him a gentleman. She didn't care. All she wanted was his help to get away. The clock was ticking. Her father had reluctantly gone to tell everyone that the bride would be a no-show. If she was going to escape, she'd have to do it now.

'Are you quite sure you want to do this?' Max said.

'Yes, yes, yes,' she said, unable to keep the impatience from her voice. At any moment Alan might come raging outside. She shuddered at the thought.

'There'll be no going back. It's Alan who'll be humiliated.'

'*Huh!* Finding out the truth about him from his ex-wives rates high in humiliation. Being foolish enough to have believed his lies even higher.'

She clutched Max by the sleeve of his dark best-man suit. Looked with trepidation across to the Gothic-style arched wooden doors that led to the interior of the church. People were beginning to spill out down the steps. Ahead of the pack was the wedding photographer, brandishing his camera aimed at her. Forget Max. She gathered up her skirts. Got ready to run. Risked a final glance up at him. 'Are you going to help me or not?'

'I don't like liars.'

'Is that a "yes"?'

In reply he took her by the arm. Through the sheer fabric of her sleeve she could feel the warmth and strength of his grip. 'My car is around the corner. We'll have to run.'

She started to run but only got a few steps before she stumbled. The combination of bumpy pavement, long skirts and high, skinny heels wasn't conducive to a speedy escape.

'Ditch the shoes,' he said tersely. She kicked them off. One after the other they flew into the air and landed side down on the pavement. 'And the flowers.' The white flowers landed near the white shoes with a flurry of petals, forming a tableau of lost dreams on the grey of the tarmac. She didn't look back.

They had rounded the corner from the church when she heard the first shout. More outraged bellow than civilised protest. She cringed at the anger in Alan's voice. Max's grip on her arm tightened as he hurried her along. 'We're not going fast enough,' he said.

She wished she could tear away her long skirts. 'I'm moving as fast as I—'

Her protest ended in a gasp as he effortlessly swept her up to cradle her in his arms. 'Hold on tight,' he said as he broke into a run—at twice her speed.

Max Conway was a tall, powerfully built man famed for the relentless power of his serve. Instinctively Nikki looped her arms around his neck and pressed herself close against a solid wall of muscle.

'You...you don't have to carry me,' she managed to choke out.

'I do,' he said. She noticed he wasn't the slightest bit out of breath even while running at full stride weighed down by the burden of a bride. 'That is, if you really want to escape from your groom.'

The edge to his voice made her stiffen in his arms. Did he think this was some kind of attention-seeking ruse? That she would let Alan catch her and lead her triumphantly back to the wedding? She went to retort but realised he didn't know her any better than she knew him. She would never behave like that. But he wasn't to know.

It seemed like only seconds before he stopped by a modest sedan parked by the kerb. Wouldn't a sports celebrity like Max Conway drive something flashier? Unless he wanted to stay under the radar for some reason. In this case, it would serve her well if Alan tried to follow her. Once in the traffic, this car would be anonymous.

Max put her down by the passenger door. The pavement was warm to her stockinged feet. She was in a wedding dress and no shoes. It made her feel vulnerable and aware of her predicament. For the first time she questioned the wisdom of begging a stranger to take her away. But there was something about Max's assured, take-charge attitude that made her feel she could trust him.

He unlocked the car with a fob on his key ring and held open her door. 'Jump in,' he said. 'And be quick.'

That was easier said than done with a voluminous full skirt to tuck in around her. With fumbling fingers, she'd just managed to fasten her seat belt when the car took off with a jolt and a screech of tyres. 'We've got company,' Max said by way of explanation.

Nikki glanced behind her to see what he meant. Heading towards the car was a red-faced Alan, followed closely by her sister, resplendent in her bridesmaid's dress, her sweet face screwed up in anguish. The wedding photographer followed—snapping gleefully away at the runaway bride. Nikki's heart started to race and she choked on her breath. For the first time, she realised the enormity of what she had done. How it would affect so many people other than herself. She hadn't even told her beloved sister.

But she'd make it up to them later. Far better to offend a few people than to chain herself in marriage to the wrong man. 'Step on it,' she urged Max.

It wasn't long before they'd reached her older style waterfront apartment in Double Bay. She'd bought it with her first big profits from her business.

Max pulled into the driveway. 'Have you got keys?'

'No need. The entry is security coded.'

She expected him to bundle her out into the courtyard and speed off. Instead, he got out of the car to come around and open the passenger door for her. She realised Alan had never done that. Not once. Why had she let herself be so swept off her feet by him?

'Ouch!' The gravelled courtyard was not kind to stockinged feet. She started to pick her way across it, wincing as she went.

'Allow me,' Max said. Before she could protest she was swept up into his arms again as he carried her across the courtyard to the front door.

'This is very chivalrous of you,' she said, flushing.

'Nothing is chivalrous about the best man running off with the bride,' he said with a wry twist to his mouth that didn't quite pass as a smile.

'But the bride is very grateful,' she said. 'More grateful than she can say.'

He continued to hold her as she coded in her password. Then kicked the door open and carried her inside. It was as if he were carrying her over the threshold like a *real* bride on her wedding night. The thought was way too disconcerting. She struggled to be put down. He immediately set her back on her feet. She fussed with her dress to cover her confusion.

'What now for you?' he asked.

'I intend to barricade myself in my apartment.'

'And then?'

'I have a plan.' She didn't really. The plan had been to spend the night with her new husband—she shuddered at even the thought of it—in a luxury city hotel then next day set off to a honeymoon in an even more expensive hotel in Dubai. Alan's choice. 'But I'm not going to tell you about it. Then you can truthfully tell people you don't know where I am.'

'You mean Alan?'

She nodded. 'I really and truly don't want him to find me. And I don't want to make things more awkward for you than I already have.'

'I get that,' he said.

'Just one more thing.' She tugged the diamond engagement ring—that she had worn with such optimism for the future—off her finger. 'Can you give this to him, please? I have no further use for it.'

'Like a best man's duty in reverse.'

He took the ring from her, his warm fingers brushing against hers as he did so. She snatched her hand back, not welcoming the tingle of awareness that shot through her. She'd been about to wed another man, for heaven's sake. How could she feel such a flutter of attraction to his best man? Especially a guy who had cheated on his tennis-player girlfriend—a woman as famous as he was—and been involved in a highly publicised paternity dispute.

An awkward silence fell between them. She shifted from one stockinged foot to another, not wanting to meet his gaze. 'Thank you for helping me,' she said finally. 'It was very good of you.'

'Good doesn't come into it. I'm not proud of myself for helping you run away. I went against my principles. I'm not convinced it was the right thing for you to do either. I seriously hope you don't regret it.'

The full impact of what she'd done might not hit her until Max left her alone in her apartment, surrounded by the disarray of her wedding preparations and honeymoon packing. But he didn't need to sound self-righteous about it. It wasn't for Max Conway to sit in judgement against her. Grateful though she was for his help.

Anger flooded through her. 'There's one more thing you don't know about your friend Alan. After his twins, he had a vasectomy so he couldn't have more children. The man who used to toss names for our future kids around with me. Spent hours discussing what colour eyes they might have. Was he ever going to tell me he was shooting blanks? Or let me go through fertility treatment when I didn't fall pregnant?'

'I have no words,' Max said, tight-lipped. No criticism of his friend, of course. Not when the famous tennis player himself had cheated and lied.

'I'll never regret walking out on that despicable excuse for a man. But letting my family and friends down?

Not doing due diligence on the man before I agreed to marry him? I suspect I'll always regret my lapse in judgement. I wouldn't have done a minor business deal without all the facts, yet I was prepared to commit my life to a person I didn't really know. I wanted that life so much…the husband and kids.'

'I can only wish you good luck in whatever you end up doing,' he said. Looking serious suited him and it struck her again how good-looking he was. No wonder the public was so fascinated by him.

'What I don't regret is putting my trust in you to help me,' she said. Max might be pond scum in his personal life and be friend to a cheating, lying fraud. But he had come through for her. That was all that counted.

On impulse she leaned up and kissed him on his smooth, tanned cheek. She was stunned by the sensation that shot through her at the contact, brief as it was. He didn't kiss her back. Why would he? She'd just run out on his friend. 'I won't say I'll return the favour for you some day because it's not the kind of favour you want to call on, is it?'

He half smiled at that and turned to leave. She watched him as he strode back to his car, broad-shouldered and athletic. Unless she glimpsed him on television, slamming a tennis ball at his opponent in some top-level tournament, she would never see Max Conway again.

CHAPTER TWO

Six months later

MAX HADN'T COME to the small Indonesian island of Nusa Lembongan for fun. On previous visits to nearby Bali he had stayed with friends in luxurious private villas the size of mansions, with all their needs and whims catered to by a team of attendants devoted purely to their comfort. Near the beach in fashionable Seminyak. Overlooking the sea on a cliff top in exclusive Uluwatu. High in the treetops of Ubud.

Not this time.

The last six months had been hell. Everything that could have gone wrong had gone wrong in both his professional and personal life. He had come to this small island, off the east coast of the main island of Bali, on his own. Not to party. But to make plans to reinvent himself.

Yesterday he had checked in to the Big Blue Bungalows, a small family-run hotel on the beach at Frangipani Bay on the south-west end of the island. He'd come with just a backpack and his laptop. The accommodation wasn't backpacker basic, nor was it the five-star luxury he was accustomed to. Built as a collection of traditional-style bungalows and small villas with thatched roofs, the hotel was comfortable without being overly luxurious—and not without its own rustic charm.

Lembongan was much quieter and less touristy than Bali, with more scooters and bicycles and few cars on the narrow streets. He hadn't been there twenty-four hours and he'd already cycled halfway around the island on a pushbike he'd borrowed from the hotel. The friend who'd recommended the island had warned Max he might get bored after a few days. Max doubted that. He just wanted to chill, far away from anyone who had expectations of him. He particularly wanted to escape media attention.

The thing he hated most about his life as a *celebrity sportsman*—he loathed that label—was media intrusion into his private life. Ever since he'd been thrust into the public eye the media had published exaggerated and erroneous versions of events in his private life. A lunch date with a colleague blown up into infidelity. Such fake news had led to a rift with his former girlfriend and, even worse, the inciting incident that had led to his disastrous accident.

His return to Sydney had been purposely under the radar. He'd agreed to be best man to Alan in a low-key, private wedding. Now it seemed Alan had wanted his wedding out of the public eye for his own underhand reasons. Surprisingly to Max, the groom had not traded on the best man's celebrity. It wasn't paparazzi that had taken all those photos. It was the wedding photographer who had fully capitalised on his luck in being in the right place at a scandalous time and sold the pictures everywhere.

As a result, Max's role in the 'runaway bride' story

that had so captivated Sydney had catapulted him head-first into a rabid feeding frenzy of press speculation. Right when he'd most needed his privacy. He shuddered at the memory of it. Especially the photos of him carrying another man's bride in his arms—accompanied by salacious headlines—that had featured on magazine covers all around the world.

Boring would do him just fine. Today, he anticipated the joys of anonymity.

He'd cycled from Frangipani Bay to the village of Jungut Batu, where the fast boat service brought people from Sanur on the mainland across the Badung Strait to Nusa Lembongan.

Max had taken the fast boat ride himself the day before. On arrival, he'd enjoyed a particularly tasty *nasi goreng* from one of the local *warungs*, small family run cafés, on the road that ran parallel to the beach. He fancied trying some other speciality from the menu for lunch, washed down with an Indonesian beer. This was the first time he'd travelled so simply, blending in with the backpackers, without agenda. Already he was enjoying the slower pace.

His talent for tennis had shown up when he was barely tall enough to handle a racket. For many years afterwards, school vacations had been devoted to training. There'd been no gap years or budget bus tours around Europe with friends his own age. Later, vacations had often been linked to promoting events managed by his corporate sponsors. And always there had been tennis. Even on a luxury vacation, he'd trained every day of the year. Training on Sundays and even Christmas Day, when his rivals didn't, had helped give him the edge.

As far as he knew, there was no tennis court on Nusa Lembongan.

Already he was starting to wind down. Felt the warmth of the sun, the sparkling of the endless aquamarine sea, even the spicy scents so different from his everyday life loosening the stranglehold concern for his after-sport career had on his thoughts. The people of this part of the world were known for their warmth and friendliness—their genuine smiles were also contributing to the gradual rebirth of his well-being.

Cycling in the tropical humidity of the day had made him hot; prickles of perspiration stung his forehead, made his T-shirt cling to his back. He decided to walk down one of the narrow alleys that led from the street to the beach to cool off, maybe even plunge into the water. His clothes would dry soon enough.

A nearby boat was offloading passengers, including backpackers and tourists from all over the world. Max paused to watch them. There was no dock. Boats were tethered to shore by mooring lines that ran up the beach. Passengers were helped off the back of the boat and had to wade through the shallow waters to dry land. As people disembarked, he heard excited exclamations in German, Dutch, French, Chinese as well as English spoken in a variety of accents. Fascinated, he gazed at the local women who got off the boat then walked away with heavy boxes of supplies balanced on the tops of their heads.

A young woman with a large backpack turned to thank the boat crew with a wide, sunny smile. Idly, he wondered where she was from, where she was going. She looked like a typical backpacker in loose, brightly patterned hippy pants pulled up to her knees in preparation for her paddle through the water, a gauzy white top and a woven straw hat jammed over wind-tangled blonde hair. As she waded through the aqua-coloured water to the sand, she turned to a fellow backpacker and laughed at something he said. Max froze. That laugh, her profile, seemed familiar.

For a moment he thought… But it couldn't be. Then she turned to face the beach and he caught sight of her face full on. *No.* Not *her.* Not here. The last woman he ever wanted to see again. He blamed her in large part for the hell his life in Sydney had become.

'Terima kasih.'

Nikki thanked the crew as she left the boat to wade the few metres onto the beach shore, cool waters lapping around her calves. She'd been to Sanur to pick up supplies from the pharmacy for her friend Maya. Mission accomplished and back on Lembongan, she turned her thoughts to work and the snorkelling trip she was guiding that afternoon, currents permitting. July with its excellent weather was one of the busiest months for tourism here, coinciding with school vacations in both northern and southern hemispheres.

The island didn't get as overrun as some of the more popular areas of the main island of Bali. But in this peak season there were both day trippers and new guests arriving all the time. Tourists from all around the world seeking a more off-the-beaten-track Bali experience came to Lembongan.

As she neared the shore, she became aware of a man's intense gaze on her. The guy standing on the beach was hot. Tall, broad-shouldered, hair bleached from the sun, a sexy scruff of beard growth. Blue shorts and a white

T-shirt showcased an athletic, muscular body. But she wasn't looking for masculine company. Not now. Maybe not ever. The experience with Alan had left her too shattered to imagine ever trusting another man again. She ignored the stranger.

But his gaze didn't drop. In fact it turned into a distinct glare. Was he some discontented dive-boat customer? Some of the tourists were determined to swim with the manta rays or *mola mola* fish, no matter the time of year or conditions on the day they took a tour. They didn't understand how unpredictable the sea currents could be here and would go away to vent their anger on Internet review sites. She'd prefer them to express their disappointment to her. How would she have forgotten a man as attractive as this?

But as she got closer she realised exactly who the man was. *Max Conway.*

Anger and frustration rose in her so bitter she could taste it. After six months surely Alan had given up trying to find her? Now it seemed he'd sicced his watchdog best man onto her.

She marched across the sand to confront him. There was no call for niceties. 'What the hell are you doing here?' she demanded.

His blue eyes were intense with dislike. 'I could ask the same of you.'

She didn't owe him any explanations. 'Did Alan send you to drag me back to Sydney? If so I—'

'No. Why would he? And why would you think I'd jump to his command if he did?'

'He hasn't stopped hunting for me.'

Max shrugged. 'That's nothing to do with me. I

haven't seen the guy since your wedding day.' His tone was so decisive, his gaze so direct, she believed him.

His hand went to his nose in a reflex action he didn't seem to know he was doing. She noticed it was slightly crooked. The slight flaw only made him look more handsome. *So it was true.*

'I believe Alan didn't take it kindly when you returned my engagement ring to him.' She felt bad about what had happened. All her fault for dragging the unwilling best man into her drama. Not that she regretted it for a moment. She still shuddered at the thought of how lucky she'd been to escape marriage to Alan.

'You heard right,' said Max. 'His response was to try to knock me out.'

She cringed. The photos of the best man and the groom brawling had been all over the press. The erroneous implication being they were fighting over her. The photographer she had hired for her wedding had cashed in big time. 'Did he break your nose when he punched you?' She found herself mirroring Max's action by touching her own perfectly intact nose.

'I've had worse injuries.' He smiled a not very pleasant smile. 'Trust me, he was hurting more than I was when I punched him back.'

Secretly, she was glad Alan had been hurt. After all he'd done to her, his ex-wives, and others she'd since found out had been damaged by his underhand behaviour, her former fiancé deserved more than a whack on the nose.

'But you were friends,' she said.

'I wouldn't go so far as to call it friendship,' he said. 'I met him at tennis camp when we were teenagers and we became mates of a kind. He wasn't good enough to make the grade competitively. When he stopped playing tennis we pretty much lost touch. Until recently. I was back in Australia after years of living abroad. He'd returned to Sydney after living in Melbourne for a long time. I was surprised when he asked me to be his best man, but he said his friends were in Melbourne.'

'By marriage number three—thwarted marriage number three, I mean—he might have run out of bestman options.' Nikki couldn't help the cynical edge to her voice.

He frowned. 'Perhaps.'

'I didn't mean that as an insult,' she said hastily. 'He was lucky to have you.'

He shrugged. 'I was the sucker who said yes.'

'So you weren't pond scum after all. Not that I ever really thought you were.' It was a small white lie. She'd thought him pond scum by association. But when he'd picked her up and run with her in his arms, Max had redeemed himself in her eyes. There was still his media reputation as a love cheat but that had nothing to do with her.

'No. But he proved to be particularly unpleasant.' Should she offer to pay for plastic surgery on his nose? Perhaps not. He might be insulted. Besides, she hadn't been the one to swing that punch.

She looked up at him. 'I'm sorry if—'

He caught her arm. 'Can we move somewhere more private? I don't want an audience.'

She followed him to a quieter part of the beach, taking care not to trip over the mooring ropes that snaked along the sand. Max stopped under the shade of a spikyleaved Pandanus tree. She slung off her backpack and placed it by her feet. A backpack was best for carrying shopping to keep her hands free when hopping on and off boats. 'I'm sorry for being confrontational,' she said. 'I associated you with Alan. Even though you were so kind about helping me.'

He nodded in acknowledgment of her apology. *He looked so good with that beard.* 'So why are you here if not to track me down for Alan?'

'Why does anyone come to tropical islands?' he said. 'But I don't want people to know I'm here on vacation. I'd appreciate it if you kept it quiet.'

'How long are you here for?' she asked. Most people only stayed a few days. There wasn't a lot to do if you weren't into surfing or snorkelling.

'Two weeks.'

Nikki didn't know whether to be concerned by his reply or not. Only her family and very closest friends knew where she'd fled to six months ago. She'd prefer to keep it that way.

He indicated her backpack. 'What about you? Are you here just for the day?' He didn't have to say *I hope so.* She could see it on his face, hear it in the tone of his voice.

'I live here.' There was no way she could conceal it.

'What?' She could take his alarm as an insult. But their last meeting hadn't exactly led to sunshine and moonbeams for him. The media had been ruthless in their pursuit of him after the scandal of the wedding. Determined to drum up a romance, at the very least an affair, between the runaway bride and the best man. She'd run all the way up here. He'd been left in Sydney to bear the brunt of the intrusive attention.

'Do you remember I said I had a plan?'

He nodded.

'Well, I didn't. I escaped up here the day after the wedding to stay with my Indonesian friend while I thought about what to do. She was a boarder at the girls' school I went to in Sydney. We've been great friends ever since. She'd come to Sydney for the wedding, one of my bridesmaids, and I went home with her. I knew she'd keep my whereabouts secret. What I didn't know was that she was pregnant and suffering severe morning sickness that went on and on. She and her husband run a hotel here. I stayed to help her. And I'm still here.'

He shrugged. 'The island is small. Just four kilometres long, I believe. But large enough so we can stay out of each other's way,' he said.

'True,' she said. 'I promise to keep your whereabouts secret if you do the same for me.'

'Done,' he said. His shoulders visibly relaxed. She hadn't realised how tense their chance meeting had made him. If it weren't for what she had dragged him into six months ago she might feel hurt by his aversion to her.

'Where are you staying?' she asked. 'So I'll know which resort to steer clear of.'

'The Big Blue Bungalows in Frangipani Bay,' he said.

Nikki's mouth went suddenly dry and her heart sank somewhere below sand level. She couldn't look at him. 'It…er…might be difficult for you to avoid me. That's the hotel run by my friend Maya and her husband, Kadek. Not only do I work there, I live there.'

CHAPTER THREE

EVER SINCE HE'D helped Nikki flee her wedding, Max had been haunted by dreams of the lovely runaway bride. Dreams, not nightmares.

The real-life nightmares had been played out in his waking hours with the photos of the best man and the runaway bride splashed all over the media, rabid with speculation about a relationship between them. *'Cheater Best Man'* was one of the most innocuous. His past dating history had also been dragged out and picked over—again and again. Would they ever leave him alone?

He was, in his own way, famous. The media had become interested in him when he was still a teenager and had snatched the glory of winning the Australian Open from a much older international player. Then he'd dated a rising female tennis star until their conflicting commitments and ambitions had ended it.

Though apparently, it wasn't a juicy enough story that he and Ellen didn't make it because of their careers clashing. In London, a reporter had used an intrusive lens to shoot him and a female friend having a quiet lunch together and blown it up into a 'Love Cheat' scandal. The resulting headlines had made it impossible for him and Ellen to retain any kind of friendship. She'd been convinced he'd cheated on her while they were still together. If he ever played against her in a doubles game it was always a 'grudge match', according to the press. His love life—or lack of it—was of continuing interest.

What he hadn't realised was that Nikki had a public profile too, as daughter of a wealthy property developer and in her own right as a successful entrepreneur. That had ramped the interest in them as an illicit 'couple' up to a higher level. Those few weeks after the wedding when they were hot news had been nightmarish.

His ongoing dreams of Nikki might not be nightmares but they were unsettling.

The dream always started at the same moment. He was back at the wedding rehearsal in the church on the Thursday night before her wedding. As best man, he was standing next to Alan near the altar. Nikki walked down the aisle, slowly and gracefully, just as she had that night. She was wearing the same short, sleeveless blue dress and silver sandals. Her hair was tied back off her face in a ponytail. She carried a bunch of fake flowers so she could practise handing it to her sister, the chief bridesmaid. All just as it had been.

What differed in the dream was that Nikki veered away towards *him* not Alan. Her smile, the loving anticipation in her eyes, was for him. *He* was the groom. As she neared him he held out both hands to her and drew her close with a possessive murmur. She looked up to him and raised her face for his kiss. He dipped his head to claim her mouth—

And that was when he always woke up. Confused. Yearning. Disconsolate. Until he shook himself into consciousness and a return to common sense.

The dream was all kinds of crazy. For one thing, he

had no interest in getting married. Not now when his injury had turned his life upside down. Not until his life was sorted. And not until he could be sure his marriage was for keeps. He'd seen the stresses the life of an elite sportsperson could place on a relationship. He wanted the for ever kind of happy marriage his parents had. That meant stability and certainty. Right now all his energies were single-mindedly focussed on his new post-tennis direction.

Besides, he wasn't interested in Nikki Lucas in that way. He *couldn't* be. She was attractive, yes. Not just in her looks but also her warm, engaging personality. If they'd met in other circumstances perhaps he would want to pursue that attraction. But she'd impulsively stood up her groom and left him standing at the altar. That showed a certain messiness of thought that alarmed him. Max had abandoned all the rules that had governed his life to aid and abet the runaway bride. And paid the price with his name all over the scandal sheets. *They'd both paid the price.* The only way he could deal with the adverse press was the knowledge that he had nothing to hide. He could truthfully plead he was innocent of any romantic intent towards Nikki. No affair. No ongoing relationship. *Just those cursed dreams.*

And yet here she was. Not the Nikki of his memory or his imagination. But just as lovely. Just as appealing. *Just as off-limits.* With the uncertain future that lay ahead of him, he needed to stay scandal free with no appearances in the press for the wrong reasons. His behaviour that day had been quite out of character for him. To get where he had in the ultra-competitive world of international tennis, he'd had to stay focussed. He planned. He strategised. He drove himself with iron self-discipline. He did not let his emotions get the better of him.

Now Nikki looked up at him, not with the loving gaze of his dream but eyes again narrowed with suspicion. 'How did I not know you were staying at Big Blue?' she asked. 'I help out at the check-in desk. I didn't see your name.'

'I'm checked in as Maxwell James. James is my second name. It's a privacy thing.'

Her feet were firmly planted in the sand. She looked as combative as someone could in billowing hippy pants with the light breeze blowing her hair around her face. He noticed she didn't wear any make-up. She didn't need it. 'Why the Big Blue? Why Lembongan island? Isn't it a remarkable coincidence that you should end up here?'

'That's all it is. A coincidence. I'd never heard of the island until recently. And my travel agent booked me into the hotel. It ticked all the boxes for what I wanted.'

Her brows drew together. 'You really didn't know I was staying there?'

'Absolutely not. I would have steered clear if I'd had any idea.'

Hurt flashed across her face at his words. Max mentally slammed his hand against his forehead. 'Please don't take offence. I didn't mean to be rude. But you must realise that after our time in the headlines, I wouldn't want to see you again. To risk all the media speculation starting up afresh. That was hell.'

She took a moment to reply. 'It must have been awful for you. Being up here, I escaped the worst of it. Though my unavailability for comment sent them into a frenzy. I stopped reading after someone claimed to have sighted

me with you hiding in a...in a love nest in Fiji.' She
flushed high on her cheekbones at the words *love nest*.
Max had to force himself not to conjure up images of
how it might play out if that were actually true.

He cleared his throat. 'Yeah. I stopped reading them
after a while too. Then, thankfully, the stories dwindled
away when the next big beat-up scandal took over. I
don't want to give them something new to gossip about.'

'Me neither,' she said fervently.

'I'll move to another hotel. Maybe you can recommend one.'

She shook her head. 'No need for that. Big Blue is
a great place to stay this end of the beach. My friends
only took it over not so long ago. They won't want anyone cancelling a two-week booking. I especially don't
want that to be because of me.'

Max didn't know how to talk about avoiding her
without sounding offensive. He remembered how he'd
felt—as if his heart were melting—at the sight of her
tears on the day of her wedding. He didn't want to upset
her, or feel any urge to comfort her. He didn't want any
kind of relationship with the woman who had thrust him
back into those hideous headlines. 'We'll have to steer
clear of each other.'

But she didn't sound offended—in fact it seemed
she wanted to avoid him as much as he wanted to avoid
her. 'We can do that. For one thing I'm part of the staff,
unofficially that is, and you're a guest. That means few
opportunities to mingle. What room are you in? One of
the *lumbung* on the beach?'

'*Lumbung?*'

'Over two levels, the traditional thatched roof, the
woven bamboo ceilings, the open bathroom.'

'No. I'm in one of the two larger new villa-style bungalows further back from the beach. Number two. I have my own lap pool. I thought it would be more private than facing the beach.'

'Oh,' she said, her blush deepening. 'That…well, that could be another problem. I'm staying in the adjoining villa.'

Not just on the same island. In adjacent rooms. Nikki lying in bed just a stone wall away from him. What kind of dreams might that inspire? He swallowed a curse. 'Imagine if the media got hold of that? They'd have a field day. I *must* move to another hotel.'

She put up her hand in a halt sign. 'No. Don't do that. I'll move to the staff quarters at the back of the resort. I can have a room there. It's pretty basic but—'

'I can't allow you to do that.'

She scowled. Which made her look cute rather than fierce. 'It's not a matter of you *allowing* me to do anything. It's only for two weeks. I'm not such a "spoiled Sydney princess" that I can't deal with it.'

Her voice wobbled on the words. So she'd read that offensive story too. It had been immensely unflattering about both of them. He'd felt outraged on her behalf. Had thought about contacting her to offer his commiserations. Had decided against it. He could not be linked to her again. Besides, no one had known where she was. *Now he did.*

'And after the two weeks? What then for you?' he asked.

'Back into my own room, I guess,' she said.

'I mean, what are you doing up here?'

'Helping my friend Maya. Making plans. You know I sold my business?'

'I saw that,' he said.

The night of the rehearsal, when he'd first met Nikki, he had looked her up and read about her success story. How her sister had a very sensitive skin and couldn't use any of the commercial products. How Nikki had developed a range of products that worked for her sister. How she hadn't sought conventional distribution but got in early with her online store, stocking first her own products then other brands. Word of mouth and canny marketing had made it a very profitable hit. Just days after the wedding debacle he'd been surprised to see she'd sold out to one of the huge international cosmetic conglomerates under the headline *'Runaway Bride Cashes In'*.

'Congratulations,' he said. 'Did you sell because of what happened with Alan?'

She shook her head. 'The sale was put in motion before the wedding I thought offloading my very demanding business would give me more time to devote to...' Her voice hitched. 'To family life.'

'I'm sorry,' he said, not sure what else he could say.

She shrugged. 'As it turned out the timing was right—after all I needed a sabbatical from work, some time to put myself together again. Everything had fallen apart. I... I wasn't coping very well with the aftermath.'

'Understandably,' he said carefully.

She raised her eyes to his. 'You know, I really thought I loved Alan. And that he loved me. I'm nearly thirty. I wanted to get married and start a family. It was devastating to find out the truth about him. How horribly he'd lied. That he wasn't at all the person I'd thought he was. I didn't run away from the wedding on a whim, you know.' She scuffed the sand with the toe of her sandals, averting her gaze.

'I know you didn't,' he said. She'd been too desperate for it to have been whim. When the media speculation had been at its fieriest, he had asked himself whether, if he had the time again, he would have aligned himself with Team Groom and refused to help her. He hadn't had to think long.

'Almost to the time I got to the church I thought I'd go through with it,' she said. 'That he'd change. That I'd be the one to make him change where other women had failed. Deep down I knew that wouldn't happen. My father came good when he went into the church to tell Alan and the guests. But in the car he wouldn't hear of helping me bolt. My behaviour would have reflected badly on him. Then I saw you and—'

'And the rest is history,' he said drily. 'I don't regret helping you. I'd do it all again.'

She looked up, her eyes widened in surprise. 'Despite the aftermath?'

'Yes,' he said.

There were two defining moments that had made him certain he'd done the right thing that day. The first was when she'd kissed him. A polite kiss of thanks. And yet for these few seconds her soft lips had been pressed against his cheek and he'd breathed in her scent he'd felt something he hadn't felt in a long time. An awareness. A stirring of excitement, more thrilling perhaps because it was forbidden. *Out of bounds.* He couldn't share that moment and the feelings it had aroused in him with her. But the second moment he could.

'When Alan went for me, there was a moment when his eyes went dead,' he said. 'All the charm and bonhomie gone, unable to mask a ruthless violence that I suspect was habitual. I was very glad I'd helped you escape marriage to the man.'

Nikki gasped and her hand went to her heart. 'You recognised that? His first ex-wife hinted at abuse on that first phone call. Then confirmed it afterwards when I sent her flowers in gratitude for the warning.'

He pushed away the unimaginable dreadful thought of Nikki suffering at the hands of her ex. Thank heaven he had been there for her. 'You had a lucky escape.'

'Yes,' she said. 'Thanks to the people who helped me.'

Max couldn't help but wonder what kind of woman would be so generous as to send flowers to the woman who had warned her off her ex-husband? She was some-thing, Nikki Lucas.

'Why didn't I recognise him for what he was?' she said. 'How could I have been so blind?'

'If it's any consolation I was taken in by him too. Why else would I agree to be best man to a guy I hardly knew? He was persuasive. Played on a long-ago friend-ship. The fact I was back in Sydney after a lengthy ab-sence and looking to establish a new circle of people.'

'Did you know I agreed to marry him after only a few months? He knew exactly how to play me,' she said with a bitter twist to her mouth. 'Made me believe that everything I wanted from life, he wanted too.'

What did Nikki want? Max realised how very little he actually knew about her. And how tempting it would be to find out more.

Nikki had not intended to confide in Max about The Abominable Alan, the nickname Maya had given her former fiancé. But it was a relief to discover that his best

man had been fooled by him as well. Alan had probably
had an ulterior motive in his dealings with Max, as he
had with her. Max was a very wealthy man. A multi-
millionaire. That fact had come up again and again in
the media stories about him. She wondered if Alan had
approached him to invest in some dodgy enterprise.

She didn't dare ask. Max had given her the impression of being contained—a private person, in spite of his
public persona as a love cheat. There were tennis players who threw tantrums, were known for bad behaviour. Not Max. He was renowned for being courteous
and well-mannered on the court, the smiling assassin
with his killer serve. That first night at the rehearsal,
once she'd got over the shock that her groom's best man
was a tennis superstar, she'd found him surprisingly
reserved. She'd done her best to make him feel comfortable in a room full of people who were strangers to
him. Not that it had been a hardship. Not only was Max
heart-stoppingly handsome in that strong, athletic way,
he'd also made her laugh with his wry comments about
wedding procedure. She'd liked him. A lot.

It was ironic, she thought now, that her groom had
turned out to be a stranger to her while the unknown
best man had done her a favour. But even one moment
of her brainpower directed towards Alan was a moment
too many. Seeing Max here had brought back feelings
that she'd believed six months away from her old life
had insulated her against. The discovery of Alan's per-
fidy, the shattering of her happy-ever-after illusion had
left her broken. Her time on the island had helped the
healing process. She didn't want the plaster ripped off
old wounds. Or any controversy about her and Max

stirred up again. They each had much to gain by staying out of each other's way.

'You know we really shouldn't be standing here chit-chatting,' she said. 'I doubt anyone on this beach would recognise me. But you could be a different matter. I know your hair is longer and you're growing a beard—which by the way looks really good and suits you—but you're famous in a way I'm not. It would only take one fan to spot you and—'

'Disaster,' he said, taking a step back from her.

'May I suggest you wear a hat as a kind of disguise?' she said. 'You'll need to wear one anyway for the heat. The weather gets really steamy here.'

'It gets so hot on the uncovered courts at the Australian Open that players have hallucinated and collapsed during a game,' he said.

'But not you?' she said with a challenging tilt of her head.

'Not me,' he said. A smile tugged at the corners of his mouth.

'You laugh at the heat?'

In response she had the full impact of the slow, lazy grin he was famed for. Her heart beat a little tattoo of awareness. *He* was hot.

'I wouldn't say that. But I grew up in the central west of New South Wales where the summers are blazing. When I wasn't playing tennis I was helping my dad on the family farm.'

She'd like to ask him about that too. *'Boy from the bush made good'* was a popular description of him. She would have to content herself with looking him up on the Internet rather than engaging in the kind of first-date conversation she could never have with him.

'It's a different kind of heat here. It took me a while to get acclimatised.' Though the temperature seemed to rise just standing near him.

'I'll take your advice and buy a hat,' he said.

She bit her tongue to stop herself from offering to help him choose a style that suited him. *Not a good idea.*

Instead she gave impersonal advice. 'There are a few shops selling hats up on the main street. Well, it's the only street, really.'

'I saw a place that seemed to sell everything including hats near the *warung* where I plan to have lunch.'

'You're having lunch here? I was going to have lunch in the village as well. I like to have a change from eating in Frangipani Bay.'

They fell suddenly, awkwardly silent. Nikki looked up into his blue, blue eyes. She was aware of the gentle swishing of the water on the sand. People from the boats calling to each other in Indonesian. Laughter that would soon turn to squeals from the tourists decked out in orange life jackets climbing aboard the banana float that would be towed out to sea at speed by a small boat.

The words hung unspoken between them. *Why not have lunch together?*

When she finally spoke she knew her words were tumbling over each other too fast. 'Obviously that plan is out the window. I'll go straight back to Big Blue and grab a bite there. But I have a favourite café here. Excellent food. You must try it. I'll tell you the name.'

He frowned. 'Why should you miss your lunch? You go to your café. If my *warung* is too close, I'll find another one. I'm sure it's not the only one serving *nasi goreng.*'

Again the nervous giggle. *What was wrong with her?*

'It most certainly wouldn't be the only one. *Nasi goreng* and *mie goreng* are probably the most commonly served meals on the island.'

'What's the difference?' he asked.

'*Nasi goreng* is a spicy fried rice served with vegetables and maybe prawns or chicken and usually an egg. But then you know that as you've already tried it. *Mie goreng* is fried noodles made in a similar way. I actually prefer it.'

'Do you speak Indonesian?'

'A little. Quite a lot, actually. Maya taught me when we were at school. I'm much better at it than I was when I first arrived.' *Well, that was stating the obvious.* 'There are differences in Balinese and Lembongan, of course. You won't need to worry. Everyone dealing with visitors speaks English. They learn it in school.'

If Max thought she was gabbling he didn't show it. Again that slow, lazy smile. 'That's useful to know. I wish—'

'You wish what?'

Time seemed to stop as he looked down into her face. 'You could be my guide to all things Lembongan,' he said slowly.

A dangerous thrill of anticipation shot through her. She would like that very much. 'But that can't be,' she said, stamping down firmly on that feeling.

'I know,' he said, regret underscoring his words.

'We both know we can't spend time together. Not if we don't want to risk ending up sharing headlines again. I don't think I could deal with a new onslaught of that kind of attention.'

'If we had met under different circumstances, if we

were different people, perhaps—' She felt her heartbeat trip up a gear. *What was he saying?*

'Perhaps?'

'It would be a different story,' he said abruptly. Nikki wasn't sure that was what he had intended to end his *perhaps* with but there was little point in pursuing it. It was enough to know that the spark of interest wasn't completely one-sided. Not that she could do anything about it.

'So how should we handle this, Maxwell James? Pretend we don't know each other?'

'That could work,' he said.

'We'll make it work,' she said. 'We'll have to take Maya and Kadek into our confidence. She was there on the church steps. She saw it all.'

His eyes narrowed. 'Can you trust her?'

'Absolutely without question,' she said. She took a deep breath, took a step back from him. 'We need to start as we mean to continue. You go your way and I go mine. Strangers who happened to chat with each other on the beach about the difference between fried rice and fried noodles.'

'Yes,' he said. Was that regret shadowing his eyes? Or just the reflection of her own feelings?

'How did you get here to the village?' she asked.

'I rode one of the hotel's mountain bikes.'

'That was brave of you. The roads in some places are more potholes than surface and there doesn't seem to be much in the way of road rules.'

'I noticed,' he said in the understated way she was beginning to appreciate. 'You?'

'The hotel truck will come to pick me up when I'm ready.'

'The troop carrier?'

She smiled. 'That's one way of describing the taxis here.'

Transport on the island comprised mainly open-backed trucks where the passengers sat facing each other on parallel benches in the back. No seat belts. No safety rules like back home. It had taken some getting used to. But the drivers were considerate and courteous. And now Nikki never gave the fact she could be risking her life every time she climbed on board a second thought. That was how you lived here and there was a certain freedom to it that she liked. There were different risks and perils back in Sydney.

She reached down to pick up her backpack from where it rested on the sand. Max leaned down at the same time. 'Let me carry that for you.' Their hands brushed just for a moment as he reached for the strap but long enough for that same electric feeling that had tingled through her when he'd carried her over the threshold. She snatched her backpack back to her.

'That's very chivalrous of you. Again. But to see you carrying my bag might kind of give the game away, mightn't it?'

'I get that,' he said. 'But it goes against the grain to let you lift that heavy pack.'

'Must be your rural upbringing,' she said. It was part of the Max Conway mythology that he'd started playing tennis on a rundown community court in a tiny town in the central west of New South Wales.

'There's that. But I grew up seeing my father treat my mother well. He would have done that wherever we lived.'

'How refreshing,' she said, unable to suppress the

note of bitterness from her voice. She seemed to have spent a good deal of her twenty-nine years around men for whom treating women well was not a priority. Like her father—now divorced from wife number three. Like her cheating high-school boyfriend with whom she'd wasted way too many years in a roller coaster of a relationship. And then there was Abominable Alan.

'It's not always appreciated,' he said. Nikki remembered that as part of the 'best man betrayal' frenzy, one of the big women's magazines had run an interview with Max's hometown girlfriend who had nursed a grudge against him. Just another in a line of 'love cheat' stories about him.

'Trust me, I would appreciate it,' she said with rather too much fervour. 'But I've been looking after myself for a long time and am quite okay about carrying my own backpack.'

She picked up the bag and heaved it onto her back. It would have been crass to shrug off his help with getting the straps in place across her back. Even if she did have to grit her teeth against the pleasurable warmth of his touch through the fine cotton fabric of her top.

'Feel okay?' he asked as he adjusted the strap.

'Fine,' she said as nonchalantly as she could manage with the sensation of his fingers so close to her skin. *It wasn't the balance of the backpack that felt fine but his touch.* 'It's not very heavy, anyway.'

She straightened her shoulders. 'Now you need to go your way and I need to go mine. You head off up the alley through those two shops. It will take you onto the street. The café I like is to the right, so you turn to the left. About six shops down there's a great little *warung* serving Balinese food.'

'Hey, that's the place I was heading for with the great *nasi goreng*. Seems you know what pleases me.'

'Just a lucky guess,' she said, flustered by his tone, not wanting to meet his gaze.

'If I see you on the street, I ignore you, right?' he said. 'No hard feelings?'

'No hard feelings,' she said. 'I'll do the same.'

She watched him as he strode away. His back view was as impressive as his front—broad shoulders tapering to a tight butt, lean muscular legs. He was a spectacular athlete on court, leaping and twisting high in the air to connect with the ball in an incredible reach. Not that she'd ever taken much notice before their encounter at her wedding. But in her down time here on the island, she'd discovered there were many online videos of Max Conway's greatest sporting achievements to enjoy.

As he headed towards the street, she realised she wasn't the only one admiring his good looks and athletic grace. A group of attractive girls watched him too, through narrowed, speculative eyes. For a heart-stopping moment Nikki thought they recognised him. But no. They just thought he was hot.

So, heaven help her, did she.

CHAPTER FOUR

LATER THAT AFTERNOON, Max sat out by the lap pool under the shade of a frangipani tree in the small, private court-yard outside his room. He was trying to concentrate on a proposal from his agent for a new role—something very different that had potential to be either an exciting new direction or a monumental sell-out. But the words on the screen blurred before his eyes.

There was no reason he should feel so distracted. This place was a private paradise. His one-bedroom suite was spacious and comfortable, traditional with its thatched peaked roof and woven bamboo ceiling, modern in its stylishly appointed open-air shower and air-conditioning.

The courtyard was surrounded by high stone walls and planted with a profusion of lush, tropical plants. The pool was long enough to swim laps, the water cool and sparkling. It was quiet, with just the occasional cooing of doves and echoes of distant laughter coming from somewhere else in the resort to break the silence. The place had everything he'd wanted for his vacation. Seclusion. Privacy. Time alone with his thoughts.

Trouble was his thoughts were no longer his own. *Nikki Lucas.* Since their encounter earlier in the day she had been flitting in and out of his mind, getting in the way of everything else, tripping up his concentration.

As if the recurring dream weren't bad enough, now he was haunted by the image of her on the beach, laughing up at him, the turquoise sea behind her, green glints in her warm brown eyes, her gauzy shirt clinging to her curves. She had agreed so readily to stay out of his way. As wary, it seemed, as he was about adverse publicity. It was refreshing that she wasn't grasping after him.

He was used to women who, when it came to him, had an agenda. He was wealthy. Wealthier even, thanks to canny investments, than many people suspected. Reasonably good-looking. And, until the elbow incident, at the top of his game. That brought with it a lot of female attention. Not all of it the right type. At first he'd been dazzled by the attention—what red-blooded young man wouldn't be? But he'd soon learned he wasn't a bed-hopping kind of guy. He wanted more, a real relationship, a partnership, but his dedication to his career made that something for the future. Along the way, he'd been burned by women with no interest in him as himself, as just Max, but instead only as a celebrity sports star and what they could get from him.

Even his high-school girlfriend, Lisa, had proved herself to be not immune to the lure of his bank account. From the get-go he'd made it clear he could not commit to her. That his career, with its arduous training schedules and constant travel, came first and would for a long time. He'd broken up with her when he'd moved away for good.

But he'd held happy memories of her and in a moment of nostalgia had hooked up with her on a whirlwind visit to his parents. Only later to be hit by news she'd had a baby and a demand for child support. If it had been true, he would have totally stepped up to his responsibilities. But a DNA test had proved he was not the father. How the episode had leaked to the press he had no idea. But the speculation had not been pleasant. Though how they'd made *him* out to be the 'love cheat' in that case had been beyond him.

Perhaps Lisa's resentment of him had been behind her recent hostile interview where she'd claimed he was selfish, without scruples, and exactly the kind of man who would run away with his friend's bride just because he could. He shuddered at the memory of it—her words, untrue though they were, had hurt. No wonder he was wary, didn't easily place his trust in women. No wonder he hated the intrusion of the media.

But Nikki seemed different. After all, she'd already got what she'd wanted from him—help to escape from her wedding. He had done so and moved on. She needn't have any further role in his life. Avoiding her should be easy.

He forced his attention back to the screen. All of his adult years had been devoted to tennis—and a good deal of his young years as well. His tennis career had meant a tight schedule where every minute of every twenty-four hours was arranged and accounted for. Others had laughed to discover that he practised even on Christmas Day—but he'd felt the joke was on the people who didn't train at his level of intensity. It gave him the edge.

But deciding on a new direction that would satisfy his need to excel was not proving to be straightforward. It wasn't that he needed the money. He need never work again if he didn't want to. But he wanted a purpose, something to drive him forward, a focus. Sitting still had never been his thing. By the time he'd spent two weeks here he was determined to have made a final decision.

Just minutes later, he was surprised by the chiming of the wind chimes hanging by the gate that acted as a doorbell. He hadn't ordered room service. And it was too early for the bed to be turned down.

He opened the ornately carved wooden doors at the entrance to the courtyard. Nikki stood at the threshold. She was carrying a circular wooden tray of snack-sized foods wrapped in banana leaves and an array of sliced fruit, which she held out in front of her like an offering. Max was too surprised to do anything but stare.

She was dressed in the hotel staff uniform of a batik patterned sarong in shades of blue and a hip-length white lacy blouse, finished with a wide blue sash around her trim waist. Her hair was pulled tightly back from her face in a small bun into which was tucked a spray of delicate white flowers. The effect was both charming and quietly alluring. While modest, the outfit discreetly outlined her shape making no secret of the swell of her breasts, the curve of her hips. *She was beautiful.*

But what was she doing there? 'Nikki! I thought we'd agreed not to—'

She gave a quick, furtive glance over her shoulder. From where he stood it didn't seem that anyone was observing them. 'May I come in?' She sidled through the gate and pushed it shut behind her with her hip. 'Indonesian afternoon tea,' she explained. 'Delivering it made a good excuse for me to visit your room.'

Bemused, he took the tray from her, inhaled the delicious spicy aromas that wafted upwards. The food was enticing, it had been a while since lunch, but his thoughts were firmly on Nikki. He placed the tray on the nearby outdoor table.

'I'm sorry but it turns out I can't move into the staff quarters,' she said. 'Maya has assigned the room to a new housekeeper. The rest of the resort is completely booked out. That means—'

'You're still next door.' Why was there elation mingled with his dismay?

'I'm afraid so. My first thought was I could move out for the duration of your stay, perhaps to the mainland. But Maya begged me not to. It's their busiest time. The baby is very young. She needs me.'

'Then there's no choice but for me to move out to the mainland. That would solve any proximity problem.' *He would never see her again.*

Her eyes widened in alarm. 'Please don't do that. Sooner or later the news will get out that you booked in here. Hopefully long after there could be any connection to me. But for a celebrity like you to cancel his stay would be bad publicity for Big Blue. Kadek's family is in the hotel business. This place was run down and badly managed when they bought it. Kadek is a second son. It's his chance to prove himself by making a success of it. His and Maya's.'

Max gave himself time to think. 'Is it such a big deal to be in next-door villas? After all, there are no connecting doors.'

Her eyes brightened. 'Keep to our own side of those high stone walls and there shouldn't be a problem.'

He knew she was as worried about them being seen together as he was. Yet she was prepared to risk it for her friend. Her loyalty to Maya was appealing. Besides, what she said made sense. He looked around him. The high walls, the frangipani trees, the screen of large-leaved foliage acted like barricades against the outside world. Then he looked back to her. 'It's so secluded and private, right now no one would know we were here alone together.'

As if every throbbing cell in her body weren't aware of that. Of her proximity to one of the hottest ever sports stars in the world. Nikki knew the media interest in the scandalous runaway bride and the best man wasn't because of her but because of public fascination with *him*.

She could quite see why. Max was wearing only a pair of black swim shorts. He must recently have been in the pool. His hair was slicked dark and drops of water glistened on his broad shoulders, the super defined muscles of his chest and arms, his flat belly. Nikki had to force her gaze away. It was a real effort to maintain a conversation with him. She'd had to hand him the afternoon tea tray as she'd feared she might drop it because of hands that were suddenly shaky. Now she concentrated on three creamy frangipani blossoms that were floating on the surface of the pool. *Eyes off the best man.*

'You're right.' She forced her voice to sound normal. 'If we're careful, there's no need for either of us to move out of our accommodation.'

'That's done, then. You stay on your side of the wall and I'll stay on mine. But while you're here...' His eyes strayed to the tray of snacks on the table. 'That's like no afternoon tea I've ever seen. I suspect those intriguing parcels would go very well with a cold beer. Join me?'

Nikki glanced down at her watch. She was scheduled to help out on the desk but not just yet. 'Do you think it's wise for me to stay?'

He shrugged those magnificent broad, very naked shoulders. 'Probably not. But you're here, it's private and you're dressed as staff. I think we'd be safe.'

She pushed aside the promptings of her better judgement. 'I'll pass on the beer as I'm due soon at the reception desk. But a cold mineral water would be welcome.'

He headed inside the sliding glass door to the bar fridge. Nikki felt light-headed at the sight of him. She flushed and had to hold onto the back of a chair to steady herself. Could a man have a better rear view? At the beach, she'd thought he'd looked good in his shorts and T-shirt. But with those impressive muscles flexing under suntanned skin and damp swim shorts moulding the best butt she'd ever seen, her appreciation level shot off the scale.

Sadly, when he returned with the bottle of water and a glass, he'd put on a T-shirt. Covering up that chest was a crime. Inwardly, she sighed. Perhaps it was for the best. She couldn't allow herself to fancy Max Conway. She couldn't trust herself to fancy any man. Not after the monumental error of judgement she'd made with Alan. Come to think of it, she'd never been a good judge of men. Seeing in them what she wanted to see, not the reality that they were after no-strings fun or access to her money. Perhaps both. Leaving her with her heart broken and wondering where she'd gone wrong. Feeling like a fool.

'You look flushed,' he said. *If only he knew!*

'Er, yes. It is very hot today.'

'Sit down in the shade and have a cool drink,' he said.

Nikki took the cane chair he offered, one of four set around an outdoor table under the shade of a sweetly scented frangipani tree. She had the exact same furniture in her villa. But no outrageously handsome man solicitously pouring her a drink. 'Thank you,' she said. 'Just what I needed.'

He was just what she needed.

She pushed the errant thought from her mind. For six months she had been without a man's company. Wasn't sure she ever wanted to link her life with a man again. *Needs*, though. That was a different matter. The presence of Max Conway, all six feet two of him, sitting just knee-nudging distance apart was reminding her that her body had needs even if her heart had been put on hold.

She edged her chair a less distracting distance away from him, making the excuse of moving it further into the shade.

Max pushed the wooden tray closer to her. 'What am I looking at here? Samosa? Spring rolls?'

'Spring rolls are called *lumpia* here and those fried pastries are like Indian samosas. There's also *ayam sisit*, which is a shredded chicken dish, and a selection of spicy savoury fritters. For something sweet there's *dadar gulung*, a yummy coconut pancake, fried banana, then fresh pineapple and papaya.'

'You choose first,' he said. 'Be quick. I could probably demolish the whole tray in two minutes.'

She laughed. 'I guess a sportsman would eat a lot.'

Again she was treated to that big, lazy smile. 'I've had to watch every bite I eat for so long. Followed strict dietary guidelines for optimum performance. Had a nutritionist rapping me on the knuckles if I strayed. Now I'm eating what I want. I have a big appetite and love good food.'

Another of those disconcerting shivers of awareness travelled down her spine. Nikki refused to speculate about his other appetites. She really shouldn't be here alone with him. Thank heaven he'd put on that T-shirt, though it really didn't do much to disguise the strength and power of his awesome body.

She wasn't very hungry so she nibbled on a spicy vegetable samosa then a piece of papaya with a squeeze of lime juice. As Max reached out for his third snack, she noticed a small scar on his elbow, white against his tan. 'How is your elbow now? Is it fully healed?'

He stopped with a *lumpia* halfway to his mouth, put it back down on its banana-leaf wrapping. All trace of humour fled from his face and the air seemed to chill around him. 'Why do you ask?' he said, eyes narrowed.

Had she said the wrong thing? Didn't the whole world know he had injured his elbow in a spectacular manner? 'I was thinking—not that I think much about you, of course I don't—that this is summer in the Northern Hemisphere and the tennis season and you—'

'Should be competing?' His expression was bleak and Nikki wished she'd never raised the subject.

'Well, yes,' she said. 'I'm sorry I brought it up.'

'Don't be sorry. It's a valid question. One that more people than you have been asking. I can't avoid answering it any longer.' He sighed, a great heaving of manly shoulders that made her want to reach out and comfort him. But even a reassuring hand on his arm wouldn't be appropriate. Not when they couldn't even be friends because of the scandal that linked them—the fear of it erupting again when she was healing from her emotional wounds. 'Fact is, the elbow is healed. But not well enough to take the stress of competitive tennis.'

'Oh,' she said, not sure what else to say. She couldn't say she was sorry again. 'I'm sad to hear that.'

'The injury was serious. Tendons torn. Bone fractured. From the get-go, the doctors weren't optimistic that I'd ever get the strength back in it. But I refused to give into that diagnosis. I spent a year in intense rehab at a facility in California. I had orthodox treatments by the top practitioners in their field. Unorthodox treatments that seemed to have more hope than science behind them. I was willing to try anything.'

The anguish in his voice gave her no hope for optimism on his behalf. 'But nothing worked?'

'For everyday use, thankfully my arm is good. But not for elite tennis. If I can't play at the top of my form I don't want to play at all. No exhibition matches. No charity matches. There's been no announcement yet, but I'm retiring. That's another reason I'm staying out of the spotlight.'

There was a depth of sadness to his words that struck at Nikki's heart. 'I can't begin to imagine how difficult this is for you.' There was a fine line between sympathy and pity and she didn't want to cross it.

He shrugged but his voice was strained when he spoke. 'I'm not the first athlete it's happened to and I won't be the last. The constant risk of injury is something we live with. Every elite sportsperson has to move on at some time or another.'

'But you weren't ready.'

'At twenty-eight I was nearing the peak of my game.' Regret tinged with bitterness underscored his voice.

'With a serve speed of over one hundred and fifty-five miles an hour?'

'That's right,' he said.

She paused. 'I'm trying to see a silver lining here, but is it a good thing that you got out at your peak?'

'*If* that was indeed my peak. I felt I had further to go. Now I'll never know what I could have achieved.'

The depth of sadness and regret in his voice tore at her heart. She had to try and cheer him up. Without giving into the temptation to give him a hug. 'How many people come nowhere near what you achieved? In any field, not just tennis. You can be really proud of your amazing career.'

His mouth had turned down and she saw the effort he made to force it into the semblance of a smile. 'That's what my dad says. He's always been my number one cheerleader. My mum too. I've spent a lot of time with them over the last months, coming to terms with it.'

But no significant other to discuss his future with? *Not that it would matter to her.*

'So,' she said, not sure how far to go with her questions. 'What will you do?'

He shrugged those impressive shoulders. 'I've never done anything but played tennis. I started a university degree but it was impossible to continue with my sporting commitments. I never really thought beyond tennis. I'm in the same boat as many sports people who didn't plan beyond the next game.'

Only not all of them were multimillionaires. 'Someone as talented and well known as you must have options coming at you from all sides,' she said.

'There are offers on the table. That's one reason I came here. To consider them. And it's another reason I can't get caught up in any further scandal. The role I favour most is with a company with very conservative owners.'

At the pointed reminder, she wiggled uncomfortably

in her chair. 'And here's potential scandal, sitting right next to you eating your papaya.'

She was relieved to see some of the tension lift from his face and the return of that engaging smile. 'If you put it that way,' he said.

'Seriously though,' she said. 'I feel for you. It wasn't easy for me to sell my business. I started it from nothing. So much slog went into it. It was my baby.' Though at the time she'd been happy to trade it for a fat cheque and the prospect of a real baby in her arms. 'I thought I might feel rudderless without it.'

'Do you?'

'Surprisingly, no. Since I've been up here I'm dreaming up new ideas.' Now with no prospect of a family anywhere in the near future—if ever—she needed a new business baby to keep her occupied.

She'd put her cosmetics business before everything, social life, dating. According to her sister, Kaylie, she had done that as much to prove herself to her father as to help Kaylie with her skin allergies.

But Nikki had never really wanted to hear that. Her relationship with her father was fraught at the best of times. Deep down she didn't know if she could ever forgive him for the death of her mother. She had died just a few days after Nikki's twenty-first birthday of a fast-acting form of breast cancer. Nikki and her sister were convinced their mum had died of a broken heart. She'd never got over the discovery of her husband's infidelity with a much younger woman on his sales team, the subsequent divorce and her father's hasty remarriage. But Nikki had no intention of discussing that aspect of her life with Max.

'Did Alan know you were planning to sell your business?' Max's face tightened and she realised there really was no love lost there. The groom had shown his true colours to the best man. Along with his fist.

'Yes. He pressed me to sell. In hindsight, I think that's the only reason he proposed—the prospect of sharing in the bounty.'

Max frowned. 'Surely you don't believe that was the only reason?'

'Looking at what he turned out to be, I can only conclude he was marrying me for my money. His anger when I ran away from him was more about loss of a potential windfall rather than of his bride.'

She knew she had failed to keep the hurt from her voice. In spite of what a jerk her former fiancé had been, in spite of her full knowledge of her lucky escape, that fact still chipped away at her self-esteem. How could she ever again trust her judgement of a man's character?

Max leaned over towards her. He frowned. 'You can't be serious. You're smart, beautiful, kind—what man wouldn't thank his lucky stars you'd want him in your life?'

His gaze drilled into hers for a moment too long. 'Uh, theoretically speaking, of course,' he said, leaning back into his chair.

'Of course,' she echoed, dropping her eyes, unable to stop her spirits from lifting. *He thought she was beautiful.* 'Thank you for those kind words.' It was amazing how soothing they were.

'True words,' he said. 'Every one of them.'

She glanced down at her watch. 'I'd love to hear more. But duty calls from the reception desk.'

But she made no move to get up from her chair, reluctant to go. This kind of chat with Max wasn't likely to happen again and she was enjoying his company. Not because he was a famous tennis star sharing his doubts and hopes for the future but because she felt relaxed in his company. *She liked him.*

But she shouldn't. *Like, love, lust.* All were off the agenda for her. She no longer trusted herself to know the difference. She wasn't ready to think about men. Not for a long time. If ever.

Max indicated the tray. 'Have some more fruit before you go. Or take that last samosa.'

'You have it,' she said. 'I really do have to go.' Not just because duty called but also because it was disconcerting to be so close to him sharing food and conversation. *Enjoying it too much.*

Max reached for the samosa. As he picked it up, the fried pastry cracked to reveal the filling. Nikki jumped up from her chair. 'Max. Be careful. Don't—'

Too late. He bit into the pastry with gusto, then stilled, spluttered, swore, and threw the remaining half on the table. What was left of a big, mean green chilli pepper protruded from the pastry. Max's face flushed red as he pushed away from the table and stumbled up, clutching his mouth. 'Chilli. Burning. Agony.' He repeated the same swear word six times in a row.

He went to grab her bottle of mineral water. Nikki stopped him with her hand on his wrist. 'No. Water will make it worse. Milk. I'll get some.' She ran into his room to retrieve from the refrigerator the milk provided for coffee and tea. She didn't waste time pouring it in a glass but thrust the ceramic jug at him. 'Swill the milk around your mouth. It will help neutralise the burn.'

'Thanks,' he choked out as he gulped down the milk.

She handed him a piece of pineapple. 'Try this, too. The acid in the fruit helps with the heat.'

He followed instructions. She didn't try to engage him in conversation. Eventually a smile struggled through his obvious discomfort. 'I didn't know you were a nurse, Miss Scandal in Waiting.'

She was so concerned that she hadn't warned him about how hot some of the local food could be that she barely smiled her acknowledgment of his teasing comment. 'I got caught out by the heat in the chillies when I first arrived here. I know how much it burns.' She grimaced at the memory of her first encounter with those particular chillies. 'The one you just ate had seeds and the pith and they give lots of extra heat.'

Max went to wipe his mouth. 'Don't touch!' Again she stayed his hand with hers, her fingers resting on his wrist. She noticed his pulse accelerated, no doubt from effect of the chilli on his system. 'Let the milk and the acid of the pineapple do their work. The pain will ease.'

He rolled his eyes. 'I come up here for some peace and quiet and get burned. Max Conway, unbeaten champion, felled by a chilli.'

'I saw it too late to warn you. I should have thought—'

'After all those years of never eating anything that might upset my stomach before a tournament and I bite into *that*. I didn't know they grew chillies that hot.'

'I feel so bad about it. I wish I'd taken you up on the offer to eat it instead of—'

Before she could finish her words, Max started to laugh. His blue eyes were lit with humour, his laugh was deep and rumbling and utterly infectious. After a startled pause, Nikki started to laugh too, so hard she bent over from her waist. Her laugh ended in splutters but when she looked up at him again he widened his eyes and it set them both off again.

Somehow during the laughter her hand on his arm had become her hand in his hand and she was standing close to him. Now his fingers moved to hold her hand firm. 'If you feel so bad about it, why not share the burn?' he said.

Then his lips were on hers. Briefly. Fleetingly. Her lips tingled and her heart raced at the contact. 'Do you feel it?' he murmured against her mouth. Shaken, she pulled away. Not from the slight buzz of the chilli on her lips. But from the other sensations coursing through her. Awareness. Excitement. The dizzying impact of his closeness.

'I feel it,' she said shakily, all laughter dissipated by the heat of that sizzling kiss. Heat that had not been generated by anything as straightforward as the chemical compound *capsaicinoid* that lurked in the chilli.

He wasn't laughing either. 'So did I,' he said, his voice unsteady. She wasn't talking about the chilli. Was he?

This was too much. The empathy she'd felt when he'd told her about his injury. The pleasure in his company. The flare of awareness at that fleeting touch of his mouth, not intended as a kiss, she felt sure, but as a sort of meaningless game. She found him too attractive to be playing with this kind of emotional fire. She had to stay away from him. Not just because of the need to avoid any kind of publicity and the risk of further scandal. But for the sake of preserving her own hard-won composure.

She pulled her hand away from his. 'I have to go,' she said and fled. The last thing she wanted while she healed from the deep emotional wounds caused by her encounter with a liar and a fraud was any kind of involvement with a well-publicised love cheat.

CHAPTER FIVE

MAX HADN'T BEEN anywhere near Nikki for a day. To be precise, it had been two long nights and an entire day. A few times he'd seen her in the distance. Once walking head to head in deep discussion with a beautiful young Indonesian woman he assumed was Maya. Another when she was alone and rushing along the wooden pathways that connected the various areas of the resort.

But her eyes hadn't made contact with his. Either she hadn't seen him or she'd pretended not to see him. He couldn't feel offended because it was what they had agreed. She might very well be angry with him. He had not kept to his side of the bargain with that impulsive kiss. *Feel my chilli burn.* He cringed at the thought of it. Of all the stupid moves in the book he had to pick that one. With a woman who had made it very clear she had no interest in him. Who was, anyway, out of bounds. *He had to keep it that way.*

The resort was proving more than big enough for two people intent on avoiding each other. Not so the proximity of their rooms. Despite those high stone walls, he was aware of her presence in the villa next door. The odd snatch of music. The gentle splash-splash of someone swimming in her lap pool. Did she swim in a bikini? Or nothing at all? The courtyard was secluded enough for the latter. Then there was the shower—open to the sky, and paved with smooth pebbles. In the still of the early morning, he'd heard the splash of water coming from what he thought must be her bathroom and driven himself crazy with imagining her in there as she showered, soaping her lithe body, holding her face up to the water as if for a kiss.

That he heard evidence of Nikki being in residence so close by had nothing to do with the fact he'd pushed the outdoor tables and chairs nearer to the common wall. That was just to take advantage of the shade as he worked through the despatches from his manager. Or the moonlight as he drank a solitary beer by his pool.

Then there was that darn dream.

He'd had it again last night. The same but different. This time his lips actually brushed hers before he woke, seething with the same mixed emotions the dream always aroused. It didn't take much thought to link the progression of the dream to that real-time kiss they'd shared. That impulsive ill-thought-out move had generated heat that had nothing to do with the chilli and everything to do with Nikki's sweet laughter, the scent of flowers in her hair, her slender warm body close to his. The realisation that not only did he find her very attractive—a given since the moment he'd met her on the eve of her wedding to another man—but also he found her so easy to talk to.

He wasn't a guy who easily shared confidences and yet he'd found himself opening up to her. In truth, he hadn't enjoyed a woman's company as much for a very long time. But he was also a man who did not let his life run on impulse. This time on the island was scheduled for serious career planning. Not distraction by a woman. Especially one who, if he was seen with her, could drive his name back into those hideous headlines. The kiss had been a bad idea. *It couldn't happen again.*

Because of all those very serious reasons, he found it difficult to admit to himself that it was driving him crazy not being able to see her. Even though it made utter sense not to. Just because he enjoyed her company didn't make the fact that further scandal, if he were to be linked to her, could be any less disastrous. The directorship he'd been offered was with a very conservative company. People could speculate all they liked about his role in the 'runaway bride' scandal but the truth was he had had no relationship with the bride. To appear ethical, he had to keep it that way.

As he stood beneath his own outdoor shower, he reflected that so far his time on Lembongan was working out as he'd intended. He was getting all the privacy he needed. All the quiet time to reflect. But he was on edge, restless. *Since when had private become lonely?*

After a lifetime of extreme activity he was already going a little stir crazy. He was used to his life being timetabled to the max. In years past, he'd had so little chance to relax he didn't really know how to do it. The word had never been part of his lexicon. He wasn't dealing well with 'civilian' life after the regimented life his tennis career had demanded. No wonder he was spending too much time thinking about Nikki. It might be an idea to return to a timetable allocating time for exercise, eating, time at the computer, sleeping.

As a start, he'd booked a snorkelling trip for this morning. He'd told the guy at the desk yesterday afternoon he wasn't interested in being one of a boatload of

tourists. The guy had suggested he engage a small traditional fishing boat, known as a *jukung*, manned by a
fisherman who knew the local tides and currents. He'd
also need to hire a guide.

Max had refused a guide until it had been gently
pointed out that the currents were notoriously unpredictable around the island and could be very dangerous. That local knowledge was required to find the reefs
with the best coral and tropical fish. And that, for safety
reasons, the hotel could never recommend that a guest
snorkel alone. Reluctantly Max had agreed.

He had always enjoyed the water. He'd grown up
swimming in creeks and billabongs in the country town
where he grew up. The annual family vacation had involved the long trek to the coast, usually Sydney but
sometimes Queensland and the Great Barrier Reef.
Until the family vacation had no longer included him
because he'd been playing tennis. He now realised how
narrow the focus of his life had become—the process
starting when he was scarcely out of his teens.

At school, he'd been encouraged to compete in the
pool but tennis had already taken a hold of him and
his competitive efforts had been directed there. Later,
swimming had been relegated to part of his training regime. Backstroke and freestyle helped build muscular
endurance and strengthened the upper body and shoulders, which powered his serve.

In recent years there hadn't been much chance to
swim for pleasure. Let alone snorkel at leisure in warm,
tropical waters.

He'd bought himself some fins, a mask and snorkel
in a small dive shop not far from the hotel. No need for
a wetsuit in these warm waters. He ate the breakfast

he'd had delivered to the room and headed down to the bay for an early start. He felt truly excited for the first time since he'd been on the island. Except for when he'd given beautiful Nikki that red-hot-chilli kiss. But that was a very different kind of excitement.

As he walked down to the bay through the hotel's lush, tropical gardens, Max marvelled at the colour of the sea glistening in every shade of aquamarine interspersed with darker blues. At nine a.m. the sun was already hot, burning down from a blue sky. He was glad he'd worn the hat Nikki had suggested he buy.

His spirits lifted even further when he saw the small traditional outrigger fishing boat, powered by an outboard motor, moored near the beach. It was painted bright yellow and red. He thought it looked like a water spider floating on the calm turquoise surface of the bay. As he made his way down the sand, the boatman waved him over with a cheerful greeting.

The guide seemed to be already in the boat, with his back to Max, wearing a black top and leaning over to rummage under the seat in the front of the boat. The boat was small, no more than five metres long by his estimation, and Max wondered if there would be enough room for him and two other men.

But as Max neared the boat the guide turned. Not a man but Nikki, wearing a black swim shirt over a red swimsuit, pulling out a life jacket from where it had been stored under the wide slat that formed a seat. She looked ready to call a greeting but her eyes widened in alarm and she dropped the life jacket when she saw him.

'What are you doing here?' she said at the same time he spoke.

'What are you doing on my boat?' he said.

'Your boat? It's not your boat. It's booked for…' She straightened up to face him, her eyes narrowed. 'You must be James.'

'*Mister* James,' he said.

'The desk told me I was guiding for a man named James.' The drawing together of her eyebrows said *I didn't expect it to be you.*

Max was aware they had an audience of the boatman and the people already basking in the sun on the beach. They had an agreement to act in public as though they didn't know each other. 'And you are?' he said.

She cleared her throat. Obviously not a natural-born liar or used to pretence. 'Nikki,' she choked out. 'Your snorkelling guide.'

He decided to give her an 'out'. 'Pleased to meet you, Nikki,' he said. 'But I don't need a guide. I'm a strong swimmer and I've snorkelled before.'

She shook her head. 'You have to have a guide. These beautiful waters can be deceptively dangerous to people who don't know them. Wild, spinning undercurrents can come from nowhere. You cannot go out alone.' She indicated the boatman. 'Wayan grew up around here. He knows how to read the waters, be aware of changes in weather. If he thought it wasn't safe, we wouldn't be going out today. But he stays on the boat. You need someone with you in the water.'

'And that would be you.' He tried to keep the sudden surge of pleasure at the thought out of his voice.

'Yes. But I can try and find someone else for you if you'd rather not go with me as your guide.' Now she was giving him an out.

'That won't be necessary…Nikki,' he said. 'If I'm going to have a guide I'm happy for it to be you.'

Happier than he should be considering their agreement to stay out of each other's way, considering the awkwardness he felt that the last time they'd met he'd kissed her and she'd turned and run from him.

He couldn't tell whether she was glad or annoyed that he hadn't chosen to have another guide. She nodded. 'I'm a certified dive instructor and though I'm not a local I have extensive experience of diving and snorkelling here. Between me and Wayan, you'll be in good hands.'

Max thought about that. 'I surrender myself to your hands,' he said. She flushed high on her cheekbones and glared at him. 'And Wayan's hands, of course,' he added.

'With pleasure, Mr James,' she said coolly.

Max put his waterproof bag containing his snorkelling gear and a bottle of water onto the boat, then stepped over the outrigger to climb on board. With his added weight, the boat rocked from side to side. Nikki put her hand on his arm to steady him. He didn't really need it—good balance was a skill that served a tennis player well—but he left it there because he liked it.

She took the opportunity to lean in towards him to whisper, 'How did this happen?' Today she smelled of salt and fresh air and the lemongrass shampoo provided in their bathrooms.

'I have no idea,' he replied in a hushed undertone. 'I inquired about snorkelling at the desk at Big Blue and the guy suggested hiring Wayan's boat. He also stressed the unpredictable currents and insisted he book me a guide. He didn't say who it would be and I didn't ask.'

'He wasn't to know we knew each other, or how. Only Maya and Kadek know we're acquainted.'

He didn't want to get off that boat. 'Perhaps it's not such a big deal. No one is likely to see us out at sea. And a mask and snorkel would be a good disguise.'

'We still need to be careful,' she cautioned. 'There are quite a lot of people on the beach. There will be other boats out there too, though you make a good point about the mask.'

'It's agreed we'll be careful,' he said, tugging his hat down further over his face.

Nikki pulled away from him, as far as she could in the very confined space of the narrow boat. 'So, let's enjoy our time snorkelling,' she said out loud, speaking as impersonally as if she were, indeed, a total stranger to him. 'I'll need to get you a larger life jacket.' She reached back under the seat and handed him an orange life jacket. Then strapped herself into a smaller one. She spoke a few words to Wayan in Indonesian and within minutes the boat headed out of Frangipani Bay.

Max sat next to her on the wooden bench that spanned the boat. It was just wide enough so they could sit without touching, even with their torsos bulked up by the life jackets. She didn't talk, just looked straight ahead, calm, unconcerned. But she betrayed herself by the way she nervously twisted the strap of her life jacket.

Max looked straight ahead too. 'I…uh…must apologise about the incident with the chilli.' He couldn't bring himself to say the word 'kiss' to her.

'I'm sorry I didn't prevent it.' Did she mean the kiss? 'I mean, sorry I didn't warn you to be careful of the food until you got used to it.'

'I didn't mean that. I'm sorry that I—'

'Played that trick on me about the burn?' She still

looked straight ahead, her voice pitched higher than usual, as if it took an effort for her to control it. 'Don't worry about that. It was funny. Something my sister and I might have played on each other when we were young. You have a younger brother, don't you? Perhaps you and your brother did something similar. Though maybe not. Boys wouldn't ki— Do that.'

'No. They wouldn't. My brother and I were more for rough and tumble games. The farm was our playground.' No surprise when his brother had grown up wanting nothing more than to take over the family farm. As his father had taken over from his father, Max's grandfather.

So the kiss would be ignored? She obviously hadn't felt what he'd felt when he'd held her close. To her it had been a silly game of no consequence. 'No need for any further apologies, then,' he said. 'On either side.'

'Okay,' she said. Finally she turned to him. He drank in the sight of her face, make-up free, cheeks flushed pink, utterly lovely. How had he thought her eyes were plain brown? Those green flecks seemed to make them appear a different colour each time he saw her. Or maybe that was because he was looking more closely. 'I did enjoy the laughter though,' she said with, he thought, a touch of wistfulness.

'As did I,' he said.

She smiled.

'So we're good, then?' he asked, relieved. He'd felt uncomfortable with her initial chilliness.

'All good. Now hold on, the water gets choppy once we get out past the reef that surrounds the island and onto the open sea.'

The ride did become bumpy with water spurting over

them as the boat increased speed. 'This is fun,' he said, exhilarated by the splash of the spray, the thump as the boat rode the crest of the wave then slapped back onto the water. He gave up holding onto his hat and squashed it under the bench. Nikki had tied her hair back off her face but a few stray wisps waved wildly around her head in the wind.

'Better than a fairground ride,' she said, laughing.

Her laughter. It was warm and melodic and engaging. More than anything, he thought, that was what had prompted the chilli kiss. There was something very sensual about shared laughter with a beautiful woman. With *this* beautiful woman.

'Where is this wild ride taking us?' he asked.

'That depends,' she said.

'On what?'

'How competent you are in the water. You may be a champion top-ranking tennis player but I have only your word as to how safe a swimmer you are.'

'I think you can take my word on that.' Max couldn't help but feel affronted. He wasn't used to having his athletic prowess questioned.

'As your guide, I have to make my own judgement on that.' This time when she turned to look at him there was a spark of mischief lighting those extraordinary eyes.

'So you like having me in your power?' he said. Over the sound of the outboard motor and the swishing of the water, he doubted Wayan could hear what they were saying so felt free to skip the pretence they were strangers.

'Whatever made you think that?' she said with what looked suspiciously like a smirk hovering around her mouth.

'Just a thought,' he said, unable to stop an answering smile. Or to prevent thoughts of what it might be like to be in her power in a more intimate way.

'Seriously, I'd be remiss in my duty if I let you just dive in without knowing if you can stay afloat. You'd be surprised how many people tell me they can swim when they really can't. But I haven't lost a snorkeller yet.'

'That's reassuring,' he said with as good grace as he could muster. She was only doing her job—though how she'd ended up in a job like this was beyond his comprehension. From all reports she had been a supercharged CEO of her own company, with a business degree to boot.

'We're heading for the mangroves at the other end of the island,' she said. 'You know the island is only four kilometres long, right?'

'I cycled down to the mangrove forest yesterday,' he said.

He'd taken a boat ride through the quiet, dark waterways under the overhanging mangrove trees and passed the exposed roots that reached into the clear water. It had had an eerie peacefulness. Sitting by himself as the boatman had punted them along, again he had been struck by his aloneness.

The driven life of a professional tennis player had been followed by the rigid regime of rehabilitation. He'd been so determined to prove the doctors wrong and restore his career it had left room for nothing else—not even a flirtation with a cute physical therapist who had made her interest obvious. Looking back, he saw all the activity had masked the essential emptiness of his life.

Yet his solution was more control—timetables, schedules, goals set out and achieved. Control over himself, control over his time, control of the people he'd gathered around him to ensure he was the best he could be. One goal attained, another to reach for, no room in his life for someone to share it with him.

'Don't leave it too long to get hitched, son,' his father had said on his last visit. 'We don't want to be doddery old grandparents.' But marriage and a family of his own were still on hold as he determined a new future. He had loved Ellen, his tennis player girlfriend, but it hadn't been enough to keep them together when it had come to conflicts in their tournament and training schedules. When they'd broken up he'd played the worst tennis of his career—a fact noted by the sports media.

'We're heading for Mangrove Point,' said Nikki. 'The spot on the reef where we're taking you has a gentle current and is a great introduction to snorkelling off Nusa Lembongan.'

'And then?'

'If I think you can handle it, we'll take you to Crystal Bay around on the larger island of Nusa Penida.'

'So, baby steps first,' he said.

'If you put it that way.'

Max went to protest that he didn't need babying but he swallowed the words. Actually he didn't really care where they went. He was back in Nikki's very enjoyable company and out here on a small boat on a big sea they were about as private as they could be.

'How did you end up acting as a guide?' he asked.

'I lived in Manly on the northern beaches until I was a teenager and never far from a beach after that. I loved the sea—swimming, surfing, snorkelling. When I was old enough I learned to scuba dive. The first thing I did when I got here was dive the reef and I totally fell in love with the place.'

'Swimming on the reef is one thing. Taking people out as a guide is another.'

She shrugged. 'It's temporary, isn't it? Like a vacation job really.'

'That makes sense,' he said.

'I was too distraught the first few days I got here to do much but go out snorkelling or curl up in my room. Either activity meant I didn't have to talk to people. That eventually passed and I began to take note of what was happening here.'

'You mean with your friends' venture?'

She nodded. 'I could see Maya and Kadek had done an amazing job renovating and rejuvenating the hotel. They built the wonderful villas we're staying in to extend the range of accommodation. But there were a few areas where they could generate more revenue. Guests wanted to snorkel or dive or take a trip around the island. They'd just refer them to the existing businesses. My friends were too flat out with getting the buildings up to scratch to cut deals with operators and book them through the hotel, or even keep good boatmen and guides on retainer. I thought maybe they could build up to having their own dive shop attached to the hotel one day, buy their own boats.'

'Ever the business person,' he said. *'Sydney's energetic entrepreneur, Nikki Lucas'* was a common label applied to her in the media.

'My father says it's in the blood.' She smiled. 'I'm not so sure about that but if I see a way to make money—honestly, that is—I want to chase it. Luckily, Kadek didn't think I was interfering and welcomed my advice—not that he didn't have plenty of good advice from his own hotelier family, of course.'

'Has it all worked out?'

'So far, really well. They organised things in their own way, keeping staff and family on board. I'm happy to fill in as a guide when required.' She gestured around her to the glorious water sparkling and dancing in the morning sun, the large volcano over on Bali, Mount Agung mysteriously shrouded in cloud in the distance on the mainland. 'How could you possibly call this work?'

She looked up at him, her face shining with enthusiasm and a kind of joy that warmed Max. He wished he could have more quiet time with her. He'd like to bounce some of the ideas he'd had for his future off her. He'd like to— *No.*

Sitting so close to her, her curves accentuated by the tight stretch fabric of her swim shirt, her slender, bare legs so tantalisingly close to his, he couldn't let his thoughts stray to kissing her—properly this time— holding her, making love to her. Not when they were so scandalously linked they couldn't afford to be caught together. Not when he had nothing to offer her in the way of a relationship. Nikki was so obviously not a no-strings-fling kind of woman. And that was all he had to offer at this time of his life, retired from tennis and determined to focus on the transition from the man he used to be to the man he wanted to be now.

Not that she'd shown any such interest in return.

'Not work at all,' he said. 'Unless you find I can't swim and you have to save me from drowning and give me the kiss of life and—'

She raised her eyebrows, but a smile danced around her lips. 'Really? I can see where this is going and I—'

At that moment, Wayan shouted something from behind them. The wind caught the boatman's words and Max couldn't make out what he'd said.

But then Nikki pointed past the starboard side of the boat. 'Dolphins!'

All attention was then on the small pod of frolicking dolphins just a few metres away from the boat. And he never did get to hear where Nikki's thoughts on giving him the kiss of life—any kiss—were going.

CHAPTER SIX

NIKKI KNEW IT was probably a waste of breath to suggest that Max keep on his life jacket for his first foray into the water at Mangrove Point. But she felt obligated to do so.

'No. Flat out *no*,' he said. Then scowled in masculine outrage. 'I'm an Aussie, Nikki. We swim. You know that. I was swimming in the creek at the farm when I was three.' About the same time he'd first picked up a tennis racket, she remembered reading.

'I know,' she said. 'But some people freak out when it comes to swimming in deep water in the open sea.' And more people than she would have imagined—even Australians—either couldn't swim well enough to handle themselves in the sea or couldn't swim at all.

'That isn't going to be me,' he said emphatically as he took off the life jacket and tucked it under the bench. He pulled his white T-shirt up over his head, leaving that magnificent chest bare, just touching distance away from her. She caught her breath, mesmerised by the play of his muscles beneath his smooth, tanned skin even as he made the simplest movement. Like reaching into his kit bag to pull out his snorkelling equipment. *The guy was built.*

'Look, I can even put on my mask without any help, snorkel too.' He proceeded to put on his mask with great exaggeration and a running commentary that made her laugh.

'I concede you're a master at putting on your mask,' she said. A smile tugged at the corner of her mouth as she pulled her own mask over her head and secured it in place over her eyes and nose.

'While you, however, need help with yours,' he said, with a distinct note of triumph. 'You have some of your hair caught up in it. That will stop your mask from getting a good seal and salt water will leak into your eyes.'

'I was going to fix that,' she said in protest.

Too late.

He reached out to tuck the errant lock away from her forehead where it had tangled near the straps. 'Ouch,' she said.

But it didn't hurt. In fact she had to close her eyes at the pleasure of his touch, his fingers firm and gentle as he proceeded to straighten and adjust the strap.

How could something as mundane as helping a fellow swimmer with her mask turn into a caress? Did she imagine that his fingers lingered a touch longer than necessary, brushed across her cheek tantalisingly near her mouth? Did it thrill her because she'd been so long without a man's touch? Or was it because it was *his* touch?

Sadly, she thought it had everything to do with Max and how attractive she found him. What red-blooded woman wouldn't swoon at this gorgeous man's slightest touch? She was no more immune than the fans who'd voted him to first place in those 'sexiest man alive' polls. Only she was fortunate enough to be in close proximity to him.

For a moment—for a long, fervent moment—she wished they'd met some other way so they'd be free to pursue at the least a friendship. But even that, if detected by the media, could draw the kind of attention neither of them could bear to endure again.

'Th…thank you,' she stuttered.

'My pleasure,' he said.

How crazy, here they were both wearing masks that covered half their faces and smiling at each other. It would be comical if she weren't finding being so close to him so disconcerting. She needed to plunge into that water to cool off. Pronto.

But first she took Max through some common hand signals used in diving, to communicate both with each other in the water and with Wayan watching from the boat. When she suggested they keep each other near as they swam, Max didn't argue with her. She went to put on her snorkel. And hesitated.

There was something inherently unattractive about the effect of a snorkel on a person's mouth, she thought, as she held it in her hand. Inserting the mouthpiece so you could breathe easily pushed your lips into an extreme pout that she found a tad grotesque. She was reluctant to put hers on in front of Max. A silly vanity, she knew. Ridiculous, really, as it had never bothered her before.

Max had no such inhibitions. His snorkel was on in seconds. He grinned as well as he could around the mouthpiece and didn't look odd at all. Fact was, he was so good-looking it didn't matter. And he was so confident he wouldn't care anyway. She couldn't help a grin in return as she slipped in her own mouthpiece. He gave her the 'okay' signal.

From the side of the boat, she slid into the water and watched Max do the same. She needn't have wasted any worry about his swimming ability. It was immediately apparent he was as competent and confident in the water as she was. As he struck out away from the boat, facedown in the water, she followed him.

As soon as her head was under the water she was lost to any other thought save the wonder of exploring the underwater world that revealed itself to her. Vibrantly coloured fish darted through the coral, the sun filtered through the clear blue water in shafts right down to the floor of the sea, illuminating a waving sea plant, exposing tiny cobalt-blue fish camouflaged against brilliant blue coral. The feel of the water sliding over her skin.

She turned to see Max gliding through the water beside her, arms by his sides to reduce drag, just the kick of his long fins to propel himself forward. Yes, he'd snorkelled before, there could be no doubt about that. She swam alongside him and could see his pleasure in the water, his head turning to follow the path of a shoal of blue-and-yellow-striped angel fish, as he swam in an easy, well-paced rhythm.

Nikki suspected Max was a natural athlete. No doubt good at any sport he tried. Among the best in the world at the one he had chosen to excel at. Who knew what he might still achieve?

As she watched him, he dived down and swam deeper propelled by strokes of his muscular arms, the strength of his powerful torso. He stayed under, holding his breath longer than she could have imagined anyone could—but then as an athlete in peak condition he must have an amazing lung capacity.

On land, he seemed strong and athletic with an insouciant physical presence. His confidence underwater added a further element of gracefulness to his athleticism. His perfectly proportioned body was as streamlined as if he were himself a magnificent sea creature, riding the current rather than fighting it. To her, watching from above, it seemed he belonged there as much as the coloured coral and the sea plants waving gently in the water, the schools of brilliantly coloured reef fish darting in and out of the underwater landscape. He turned and twisted with, she thought, the sheer joy of his physicality.

As she watched him, Nikki felt torn by a yearning to be part of whatever it was he was experiencing. To be with him. She couldn't put a name on what she felt. It ached but it wasn't anything sexual. Or was it? As she watched him glide through the turquoise depths of the sea, the realisation hit her with full force. She flushed, even with the coolness of the water on her face. Yes, she admired him. But not in a dispassionate way. *She wanted him.*

During the time she'd avoided him, her growing desire had pushed insistently against her defences. Defences she'd rapidly put up when he'd held her in his arms as he'd helped her flee from her wedding—and she'd liked it. Liked it too much. That was what all that tingling had been about. Sheer sensual awareness of the best man. She'd taken it for nerves, relief, even embarrassment at the situation she'd got herself into.

The more she'd fought it, the more that desire had pushed to be acknowledged as she'd tried to ignore his presence at the resort. Tried to forget the feelings that had surged through her at his brief, unforgettable kiss. Even pretended she hadn't seen him when he'd crossed her path. When in fact she'd thought of little else but him. Had even found herself on her side of the common wall between their villas alert for sounds of his presence. She'd spent rather too long wondering if he swam in his lap pool in the black swim shorts he currently wore or nothing at all.

Now that dammed-up desire burst through, shattering her defences and leaving her vulnerable to him, to her awakened needs. She would have to make every effort to mask it. Nothing had changed. They still couldn't be seen to be in any way linked to that old scandal if they didn't want to be splashed all over the media again in such an unpleasant way. How foolish she'd been to even contemplate a friendship between them. Being platonic friends with Max wouldn't cut it for her. Not when she hungered for the physical.

He'd been under the water for so long she realised she was holding her own breath as she watched him. How long had it been, he swimming, she lost in admiration and newly acknowledged desire? She dived down to join him.

As she reached him, he pointed down to a brilliant blue starfish for her to admire then turned. They powered up to the surface together, emerged from the water at the same moment. Blew the water from their snorkels in plumes. He looked around to find her. Even through his mask she could see his exhilaration, the eagerness to share his underwater experience with her. She'd felt the same when she'd first snorkelled here. Her heart skipped a beat at the sight of him; she knew how difficult it would be to pretend indifference to this man. How much fun it had been for her to swim with him, like-minded, matched in their skills. How much more she wanted.

Now, she swam up beside him, removed her mouthpiece so she could talk to him, treading water. He did the same. His hair was slicked flat to his head, dark with water, his eyes bluer than the bluest patch of the sea. She was treated to his most dazzling smile yet.

'Wow,' he said. 'Just wow!'

Wow! Yep. That was exactly her reaction when she saw Max's half-naked body emerging from the water like some gorgeous mythical merman from his enchanted underwater kingdom. *Just wow.*

She had to swallow hard to make her voice sound normal. 'I'm so glad you enjoyed it,' she said, genuinely pleased at his reaction. One of the things she liked about helping out as a guide was introducing people to these beautiful waters and the marine spectacle that lay beneath the serene aquamarine surface.

'Thank you for bringing me here,' he said. 'It was brilliant. Better than any expectation.'

She forced her voice to sound how a swimming guide should sound, impartial yet encouraging. She the guide, he the client. 'Crystal Bay is even better,' she said. 'Deeper water, more coral, more fish, more colour.'

'So I'm being allowed to move up to the next grade?' he said, with just a touch of sarcasm.

'If you put it that way,' she said. 'Obviously, you're a really good swimmer and experienced at snorkelling. But you understand why I had to see for myself. Safety is paramount.'

'I understand,' he said. 'At the time I felt insulted by your refusal to believe me but—'

'Insulted? I didn't mean—'

'I know.' The smile dimmed. 'I guess I might have to get used to people questioning my skills at anything but tennis.'

She frowned. 'I'm sure that's not going to happen.'

'It will. It has. Taking a new turn in life is never straightforward.'

'No, it's not,' she said, thinking of the way her own life had gone since she'd made that fatal decision in the car on the way to her wedding. How she couldn't stay hiding on this island for ever. How maybe one day she might trust a guy enough to consider a relationship. But not now. And certainly not with a man she'd have to share with thousands of adoring fans who hung posters of him in their bedrooms. A man trumpeted in the media as a love cheat. Much as she might want him. 'But I'm sure with your skills and contacts, you will be successful in whatever you choose to do. I... I'll watch your new career with interest.' *From a distance.*

'I'll keep you posted,' he said politely. But she suspected he didn't mean it. How likely would it be that their very different paths in life would cross again after his two weeks on the island were up?

She looked across to the boat. 'Wayan has put the ladder down so we can easily get back on board. Crystal Bay is quite a way away. We have to go around Nusa Ceningan, which is even smaller than Lembongan, then around to the east coast of Nusa Penida, which is the largest of these three islands. *Nusa* means island, by the way.'

'How did I not know about this fabulous place?' he asked as he effortlessly pulled himself up out of the water and onto the boat.

She averted her eyes from the sight of his gorgeous, near-naked back view. *Eyes off the best man,* she had to remind herself yet again.

Max didn't feel much like talking in the boat on the way back from Crystal Bay. The water there had been everything Nikki had promised. More. As he'd swum in that underwater paradise he had realised for the first time since the accident he had felt happy, relaxed, and living in the present rather than angsting about the past or worrying about the future.

He'd enjoyed a non-competitive sport, swimming with Nikki for fun, not seeing her as a rival he had to beat at all costs. To crush his opponent had been his mindset for so long he'd found it difficult to switch out of it enough to enjoy a sport for sport's sake. That had been his only motivation during the gruelling year of full-time rehab. To focus both physically and mentally on getting back in shape so he could win again. The pressure had been so intense the knowledge that he wouldn't compete again had led to an immense letdown. Followed by an immediate drive to find a new direction in life that didn't hang on numbers on a scoreboard.

But today he'd forgotten all that. Thanks to Nikki.

Nikki was relaxed, easy-going, non-judgemental. He had soon realised she wasn't a particular fan of tennis, or of him as a tennis player—and he was okay with that. More than okay. She knew of him, but he suspected he hadn't really been much on her radar until he'd turned up as best man for her groom at her wedding. He felt he didn't have to prove anything to her, to be someone he was no longer.

Today they'd slipped into an easy companionship, swimming together, marvelling at the same beauty of the underwater world that revealed itself to them. In sync. Obviously, she was a kindred spirit in the water. And out of it? He had an overwhelming urge to find out.

Now she turned to him. 'Have you done any scuba-diving?'

He shook his head. 'Not interested. I don't want to be fussed with all that equipment. I'll stick with snorkelling where I'm in control.'

'I can see that point of view,' she said. 'However, there are deeper waters around these islands I'm sure you'd love that can best be appreciated by diving. The island is a good place to learn.'

'That rather depends on who my teacher would be,' he said. His eyes caught hers in an unspoken question.

She met his gaze full on, unblinking. 'I can recommend a good dive school.' There wasn't a trace of flirtation in his snorkelling guide's voice. She apparently had no interest in him as anything other than an inconvenient client foisted upon her by a misunderstanding. A happy misunderstanding from his point of view. Obviously not from hers.

'I'll keep that in mind,' he said, determined not to reveal any trace of disappointment. 'In the meantime I want to snorkel as much as I can while I'm here. Can I hire Wayan and his boat to be on standby for every day of my stay? I'd pay the full day fee, of course, whether I use him or not.'

Her eyebrows rose. 'No one has ever asked that before. But I guess it could be arranged. We'll have to ask Wayan.'

'What about my guide?'

She stilled. For a long moment she looked back at him. He was so intent on her face as he waited for her reply he was barely aware of the constant spray, the rhythmic slap of the water on the hull as the boat navigated the rougher waters of the open sea on the way back to Frangipani Bay.

'I'm not for hire, nor can you keep me on retainer. I might go out on the water with you if it suits my schedule. If not I can arrange for a different guide.' There was a distinct chill to her voice that had nothing to do with wind cooling them in their wet swimwear.

'I don't for one moment think you're for hire. I don't know what your arrangement is with your friends who run the hotel. But today has been…special for me. I doubt it would have been that special with another guide.'

'Thank you. I really enjoyed it too. You were great to swim with.'

She hadn't given him any indication that she felt anything at all for him beyond that. Except, perhaps, annoyance that he was on the island at all. Even further annoyance that he had crashed *Mr James's* boat trip. But she was too professional to show it.

He leaned a little closer. Not that he thought Wayan could hear him but it was important his words weren't snatched away by the breeze. 'Nikki. I enjoy your company. I like you.'

She flushed and dropped her gaze, seeming to fixate on her discarded swim fins on the floor of the boat. 'I…er… I like you too.' The flutter of her lashes, the slight stutter made her words sound like a major admission. Max was surprised at the relief he felt. But he could almost see the cogs in her brain wondering where this was leading.

He considered his words. 'This vacation is shaping up to be the best I've had in a long time.'

She looked up. 'That's really good to hear. Maya and Kadek will think so too.'

He shook his head impatiently. 'I don't mean that. Well, yes, I do. The resort is great. The island is wonderful. But what I'm trying to say is that today is all thanks to you. And I want to spend more time with you.'

Her eyebrows raised in alarm. 'But we agreed—'

'Yes, we did. But out here, on this boat, in this water, the media and all the scandal seems so far away. It's like we're operating on a different clock with different rules for the way time passes.'

'Jam karet,' she said. '"Rubber time", they call it here.'

'There's a name for it? *Jam karet.*' He rolled the unfamiliar words around on his tongue. Thought about what it meant to someone who had always been ruled by timetables, obsessed with punctuality. Could there be a different way for him? 'That's not a concept that would fit my old life. But here... I get it. Yeah, I like it.'

'Me too. Although I was so strung out when I first got here it took me a while to get my head around a different attitude. Now, I hope I'll take some of that relaxed feel back with me when I return to frantic Sydney.'

'What about we relax our attitude here? Out on the water, actually *in* the water, no one has recognised me—or you. I haven't seen a flicker of recognition from anyone, tourist or local.'

She assessed him through narrowed eyes. 'I think it's the beard. Even in the days you've been here it's grown. You look different. Maybe not to one of your rabid fans, but to a casual observer.' She shrugged. 'As for me, blonde Australian women are a dime a dozen in Bali.'

As she sat next to him, her damp hair a wild tangle, the imprint of her mask still around her eyes and nose, her cheeks reddened by windburn, he had never seen a more attractive woman. 'Women like you are not a dime a dozen *anywhere*, let me reassure you of that.'

That won him a self-deprecating smile. 'Thank you, it's very sweet of you to say so. But *you* being seen here, or *me* being seen isn't a problem. It's if we're seen *together* that there could be trouble.'

'The longer I'm here, the less I'm believing it,' he said thoughtfully. 'This island is hardly party central. Not a place where paparazzi are popping out of the undergrowth.'

'Perhaps not,' she said slowly.

'Maybe it's a good place to spend time with a person you like.'

'I guess it could be,' she said, not sounding very convinced.

He angled himself closer to her, injected a note of urgency into his voice. 'I'd like to spend some time with you, Nikki. More snorkelling, tomorrow perhaps. Maybe lunch today.' He glanced down at his waterproof watch. 'I'm grateful for those nuts and snacks you brought on board with you. But right now I'm starving.'

She sighed and he could see her conflicting thoughts play across her face. 'During those weeks after the wedding I felt ill every time I opened my laptop. The things that were said about me, about you. I wish there wasn't so much at stake if we were to be discovered enjoying each other's company by the media. No matter how innocent it might actually be.'

Innocent. Was that the right description for his feelings towards Nikki? They certainly weren't platonic. In fact, they were growing less innocent each minute he spent in her company. He wanted more time with her, more opportunities to get to know her.

Max wasn't used to giving into impulse or emotion. The times he had let his feelings rule had led him into trouble. The worst had been his reaction to the unprofessional opponent who had been taunting him both on and off court in an effort to break his concentration. He'd escalated from the professional to the personal. The final insult had been a snide comment about the doubt over the paternity of his former girlfriend's child. During that all-important game his sudden surge of anger in reaction to the guy's smirk had made him forget tactics, forget self-control and smash the guy with everything he had—resulting in the injury that had ended his career.

But there was something implacable about this impulse to be with Nikki. Something that urged him not to hold back for fear of possible consequence. That his time here with her was limited and the opportunity to act on that impulse might never come again.

Back there in the water with her he'd felt something he didn't think he'd ever felt before. Not just appreciation of her beautiful body, gliding through the water with effortless grace. Of her spirit, her beautiful smile. There'd been a harmony between them, as if he and she together were meant to be. Now he felt compelled to grab the chance to see if she felt in any way the same.

He found himself urging her to a course of action when only days before he'd been pressing for the opposite. 'If we're discreet. If we're careful. If we both wear hats and sunglasses—like everyone does here anyway—I'm happy to risk a lunch together. Maybe down at the mangrove end of the island. It seems quieter there.'

'I know a wonderful family-run restaurant there,' she said. 'Small, rustic but the food is incomparable.'

'Sounds perfect,' he said. 'Count me in.'

But the tone of her voice led him to believe there could be a 'however' coming and he wasn't wrong.

'However it's a risk,' she said. 'And not one I'm ready to take.'

Something made him wonder if she was referring to something altogether different from the risk of exposure by the media. There was something in her eyes he couldn't read. Wariness? Fear? Surely not fear of *him*?

His spirits plummeted. He hadn't realised how much he was counting on her saying yes. But as he started to plan his next strategy for winning her over, he realised she hadn't stopped speaking.

'But I'll think about it,' she said slowly, weighing out the words. 'I need some time.'

Despite the urge to want to ask her every five minutes if she'd thought about it yet, he and Nikki spent the rest of the boat trip back to Frangipani Bay in silence. He gave her the space she'd asked for. He knew it was a big ask. A turnaround. There was still risk they might be discovered, that his worst nightmare of press intrusion might rear up again. But there was a greater risk of future regret. He had ten days left on this island in near proximity to Nikki. After that it was highly likely he would never see her again.

By the time the boat headed into Frangipani Bay she still hadn't said a word—yea or nay. But he held his tongue. Until they had to slip back into the pretence that they hadn't known each other before this day.

As Wayan anchored the boat in the shallow waters. Max took off his life jacket and handed it to Nikki.

'I need to stay on board the boat,' she said. 'Tidy the life jacket, talk with Wayan.'

'Have you thought about what I said?' He realised he was holding his breath for her answer.

She paused, then slowly nodded. 'Your time on the island is short. I… I think I might regret it if I don't take the opportunity to…to get to know you a little better.'

He let out his breath in a whoop of relief, stopped short of punching the air. 'Yes! Lunch. Now. Nikki, I—'

She put up her hand to stop him. 'Not lunch. But I have a thought for dinner tonight. Don't make any other plans.'

'Right,' he said. Having got her this far, he wasn't going to argue.

'You might get a call from Maya. If so, just do as she suggests.'

He made a mock salute. 'Yes, ma'am.'

She laughed. 'Now, Mr James, I suggest you thank your boatman and your guide for a great day's snorkelling and get off the boat.'

His instinct was to hug her. But common sense told him that would not be the right move. She had met him more than halfway. The next move had to come from her. He thanked both Wayan and Nikki, jammed on his hat, put on his sunglasses, picked up his kit bag of snorkelling equipment and got off the boat. He waded through the water and onto the beach without looking back.

CHAPTER SEVEN

LATER THAT AFTERNOON, Max did indeed get a call from
Nikki's friend Maya. She apologised for not having
made contact earlier and invited him to come to her
house at the back of the resort complex for six p.m. to
meet her and her husband Kadek.

Max was intrigued. Was this an invitation to have
dinner with them and Nikki? If so, he had mixed feelings. Yes, it was one way of seeing her again safe from
the public gaze. But he would so much rather see her
one to one. No chaperones. Just him and her. Alone and
getting to know her better. Anticipation shivered up his
spine. When had he last felt this way about spending
time with a woman? Not just a woman. *This* woman.

The friend who had warned him that he might get
bored in Nusa Lembongan could not have been further
from the mark. Max hadn't experienced a moment's
boredom since he had seen Nikki step off that boat and
back into his life.

He arrived at Maya's house promptly at six. Although
finding himself seduced by the concept of *jam karet*, he
wasn't yet won over. Punctuality was deeply ingrained
in him. The house sat in its own garden behind the last
row of bungalows. He entered through traditionally

carved wooden gates into a stone courtyard complete with lush greenery, a water feature and eye-catching Indonesian artefacts.

A petite, lovely dark-haired woman in an elegant, traditionally inspired top and wrap skirt in a batik print greeted him with a welcoming smile. 'Hi, I'm Maya. So pleased you could come.' She introduced him to her husband, Kadek, tall, handsome in a high-collared white shirt over a boldly patterned sarong type garment. In this kind of heat, Max thought, a sarong would be a good idea. He'd always dressed conservatively, never knowing when a photo of him might be snapped by paparazzi. He must ask Kadek about the best type for a Westerner to wear.

'I've been looking forward to meeting you both,' Max said sincerely. Maya had obviously been a true friend to Nikki; that predisposed him to like her.

'We've kind of met before,' Maya said. 'I was one of Nikki's bridesmaids but I couldn't make it to the rehearsal so you might not recognise me.' She spoke perfect English with a distinct Australian accent.

Max narrowed his eyes as he thought. 'I think I remember seeing you getting out of the car with the other bridesmaids at the church. But I was watching out for the bride.' Already the bride had been running late and he'd been edgy.

'You did a great job on rescuing Nikki from that dreadful man. Her friends thank you for that.'

'Uh, yes,' he said, uncertain as to where this was going. *Where was Nikki?*

Maya laughed. 'You're probably wondering what you're doing here. Come on through.'

She and Kadek led Max through to an open living

area with a polished stone floor scattered with bright rugs and traditional Balinese wooden carved furniture. But it was the carved wooden settee, piled with colourful cushions, that drew Max's attention.

Nikki sat in the centre, cradling a tiny, dark-haired baby. She looked up to greet him and her eyes were still warm with a doting kind of love that had obviously been directed at the baby. 'You're here,' she said. She got up, baby still in her arms. 'Meet Putu, Maya and Kadek's firstborn son.'

Max was reeling at the sight of Nikki looking so at home with a baby in her arms. But as she took careful steps towards him he began to think he was hallucinating. She was wearing the same blue dress as at the rehearsal, as in his recurring dream. Her hair was pulled back the same, only now it was fixed with a spray of white flowers. She was wearing the same silver sandals. And her eyes had that dreamy look of love that was so disconcerting in his dreams. Though the love was for the baby, not for Dream Max. 'Nikki,' he managed to get out of a suddenly choked throat. Why did he feel as if he'd been aced?

'Isn't he cute?' she asked, in a doting tone of voice that did not completely disguise an undertone of yearning.

Max cleared his throat. 'Uh, yes. Very cute.'

He hoped she wouldn't ask him to hold the baby. He wasn't used to babies. Didn't know how to handle them. What to do with them. It had to be admitted—babies scared him. In more ways than one. Their unpredictable digestive systems scared him; their propensity to scream blue murder if placed in his arms scared him; but what scared him most of all was the effect an unplanned pregnancy could have on a guy's life. His brief legal battle with his former girlfriend had shown him that. Her baby had not been his, but before that had been proven by DNA he'd thought a lot about how he could do the right thing and maintain a relationship with the child.

But little Putu was cute, very cute, with fine black hair and merry dark eyes. 'He's a great little guy. You must be very proud,' he said to Kadek.

'We are,' said Kadek, the warmth in his eyes speaking to the truth of his words.

In fact, each of the other three people in the room were united in looking adoringly at the baby, eyes glazed with fondness. Secure in Nikki's arms, little Putu chortled with glee at the attention, waving his tiny hands about. Until suddenly he stilled and his face went very red and strained. A symptom, Max suspected, of something alarming happening in that baby digestive system. At one end or the other.

To Max's intense relief, Maya expertly swept the baby from Nikki. 'I'll see to him and be back as soon as I can,' she said.

Kadek made small talk and offered drinks from a tray on the carved wooden coffee table. 'Nikki tells me you enjoyed your snorkelling trip today,' he said.

'Very much so. I can't wait to get out there again,' Max said. But he was finding it difficult to concentrate on what the other man was saying. It was as if everything and everyone were out of focus, the spotlight shining only on Dream Nikki.

'I've seen you in that dress before,' he said, not attempting to hide his admiration. In fact, he remembered almost to the very minute when he'd first seen her wearing it.

The tall woman in the blue dress had caught his eye when he'd got to the church for the rehearsal. She'd been laughing at something an older lady was saying. He'd been struck not so much by how she looked—though he'd thought her very attractive—but what could only be described as her aura of warmth and vivacity. Not that he believed in actual coloured auras that psychic people claimed to see surrounding a person. In fact he didn't believe in anything supernatural of any kind. But there had been something about that girl in the blue dress that had drawn him so his gaze had kept returning to her again and again. He well remembered the intense stab of disappointment he'd felt when he'd discovered she was the bride, about to marry his recently rediscovered 'friend'.

'When did you—?' She answered the question herself. 'The rehearsal. I was wearing it that night, wasn't I? It was so hot.'

She was so hot. And he'd seen her many times in the dress since then in his dreams. He certainly had no intention of telling Nikki that. She'd think he was crazy and run screaming. He wouldn't blame her. Maybe he *was* a tad crazy when it came to her.

How sane was it to suggest they see each other alone when he knew what the outcome could be if they were discovered together by the media? His civil break-up with Ellen had degenerated into enmity thanks to the media casting him so unfairly in the role of love cheat. A reputation further cemented by the 'runaway bride' episode. If the press caught them together again his totally unwarranted reputation as a sleaze would endure. Yet seeing her here, he wanted to be with her more than ever.

'It's a lovely dress,' he said lamely. 'You look, uh, lovely.' What was the matter with him? He was usually not short of a reply, of banter and repartee to keep a social conversation going.

'Thank you,' she said. 'I'm glad you were able to come tonight.'

'How could I not?' he said. Nothing could have stopped him from accepting Maya's invitation.

'If you're willing to take a risk of being seen out together, I can help out Maya and Kadek at the same time. That's what you're here to talk about.'

Just then Maya swept back into the room. 'Putu is in bed and now we can return to adult conversation.' She turned to Nikki. 'You were explaining the plan to Max?'

'I'd just started,' Nikki said. 'Max, you know Maya and Kadek are working hard on making Big Blue an even better resort than it is already. They've made a lot of improvements.'

'But more to come,' said Maya.

'We want to make our restaurant a destination in its own right, not just somewhere for guests to have meals,' said Kadek.

The Big Blue restaurant was in a rotunda-type building right on the beach. Max hadn't eaten there yet—he'd had room service when he'd actually been at the hotel for meal time. Including, of course, the memorable afternoon tea. The food had been consistently good.

Nikki continued. 'Maya asked me to visit some of the island restaurants to check out their new menus.'

'To see if there was anything we could be doing better,' said Maya.

'Maya and I were going to go out together tonight to one of the good restaurants not far from here,' Nikki said.

'Even though there are risks in that,' Maya said. 'I might be recognised as a rival hotelier.'

Nikki directed her words to Max. 'You, however, would not.'

'What better front than a couple enjoying a nice dinner for two?' said Maya.

'While surreptitiously photographing the menu,' said Nikki.

'And taking photos of the plated meals supposedly for social media but really to show to our chefs,' said Maya.

'You mean me? Me and Nikki?' asked Max, bemused.

He looked to Kadek. Kadek threw up his hands. 'This is something the girls cooked up.'

'We would be like the secret shoppers they send into stores to check the service,' said Nikki. 'Only we'd also get a really good dinner.'

Her eyes pleaded with him to say yes. Max thought he would do anything she asked of him. 'Sign me up. I'm in.'

'Wonderful,' said Nikki. She and Maya gave each other a high five. Max couldn't help wondering what was more appealing to her, the dinner or his company. He'd take his chance on making sure the pleasure of his company won out.

Maya tucked her hand into the crook of Kadek's elbow and looked up at him lovingly. 'Good. I get to have a quiet night in with my husband.' Kadek put his other hand over his wife's and looked down at her with equal affection. Max felt a stab of something uncomfortably like envy.

What would it be like to have the kind of loving security that Maya and Kadek so obviously shared? As his parents did, even after all their years together? The closest he'd come to the kind of partnership he held as the ideal was with Ellen. But it had never developed past initial high hopes. He wondered if they'd both known deep down that the relationship had no future—that it would always come second to their careers. The breakup had hurt at the time, hurt more when she'd quickly moved on to date and ultimately marry the physiotherapist who travelled with her on tour.

Kadek stepped forward. 'If you're ready to go now, I will drive you both in the truck to the restaurant.'

Max frowned. 'Won't it look suspicious to have us arrive in the truck with a Big Blue logo on the side?'

Nikki shook her head. 'Not at all. It's common to drop off guests to other destinations. The restaurant would send its own truck to get us if we booked it. But we thought that would be drawing too much attention to us.'

Us. He and Nikki having dinner together. No matter the pretext, he was going to enjoy it. 'Okay. Let's do it,' he said.

The Big Blue truck was like the others on the island, open at the back and sides with just a canopy over the top that offered little protection from rain. Luckily the sky was clear. Nikki accepted Max's offer of help to climb in from the rear. Not because she needed it but because, in spite of her resolve to ignore her attraction to him, she couldn't resist the opportunity to enjoy the

sensation of his hand on her arm. Even that light, casual touch sent shimmers of awareness through her. It
was doubly intoxicating as she now recognised those
shimmers for what they were—the stirrings of desire.

Once in the truck, she settled herself on one of the
narrow, padded benches that formed the seating. She
slanted her legs neatly to the side, aware that her dress
easily rode up to expose rather too much bare leg.

'Be warned, there's not much padding on these seats,'
she said to Max as he swung himself aboard. She was
tempted to offer him a hand up but decided that might
be just too obvious. With his athletic build it was very
apparent he didn't need help.

'I'm tough,' he said, as he sat next to her at a polite
distance.

Tough in body and, she suspected, tough in spirit.
He must be to have got where he was in his sport. To be
one of the top-ranked tennis players in the world. It was
a mind-boggling achievement and she could only imagine the perseverance it had taken him to get there. For
the umpteenth time she wished she could get to know
him better. Tonight might give her that opportunity.

Kadek was a careful driver, but the roads were narrow with unexpected ruts, and tourists riding motor
scooters two or three abreast. They were not long out of
the hotel when the truck swerved and Nikki was swung
hard against Max. 'Sorry,' she said in that ridiculous
way she did when apologising for something for which
she wasn't responsible.

He looked down into her face with the slow, lazy
grin that made her melt. 'I'm not sorry at all,' he said,
his voice low and husky.

They'd been thrown together so closely their thighs

were touching. It would be crass to move away. To tug down her skirt from where it had, predictably, ridden up. As if she found his nearness distasteful—which was far, far from the truth. Nikki let her shoulders relax and leaned against him. She realised how long it had been since she'd been as close to a man. But she gave no thought to other men. Just this one. *Max.* She breathed in the scent of him: lemongrass, a hint of cologne, healthy, fit male. Heady. Intoxicating. Dangerously close to arousing.

He made no attempt to move away either. In fact he wedged his legs closer, which kept her from sliding in her seat but also brought them kissing-distance close. 'Where are we headed?' he asked. Did he mean something deeper by that than a question about the truck's direction? *Don't overthink things,* she told herself.

She took a deep breath to steady her racing pulse. Tried to speak normally. Even so, her words came out rather too quickly. 'The restaurant is right on the beach near the most western point of the island. We're passing through the village now. Those beautiful buildings are the temples where families worship. Over there is the elementary school.'

'So you're as good a local area tourist guide as you are a snorkelling guide,' he said, teasing.

'I do my best to excel,' she replied in the same tone.

She spoke with mock modesty but it was true. Nikki did try to excel at whatever she did. Which was why it was a constant nagging undercurrent to her life that, while she'd succeeded in business, done well with investments, had long-time close friends, she didn't seem to have what it took to succeed in a relationship with a man. Here she was staring thirty smack in the face with nothing but failure—spectacular, public failure in the case of Alan—behind her. No wonder she was terrified of trying again, of ever letting herself trust.

'Is the restaurant far?' Max asked.

'Just a few more hair-raising twists and turns. We should be just in time to catch the sunset.' She was about to say the sunset was very romantic but decided against it. This wasn't a date. They were on an information-gathering mission.

Kadek stopped the truck a short distance from the restaurant. Nikki called a 'thank you' to him then went to get off the back of the truck. Max jumped down first. 'I'm here if you need help,' he said.

'Of course I don't need help,' she said as she prepared to jump. 'I've done this lots of times and—oh!' She stumbled a little on the uneven ground and landed heavily against him.

'Whoa,' he said as he caught her and steadied her with his hands on her upper arms.

'Th…thank you,' she stuttered.

'You okay?' He looked down into her face.

'Fine,' she said. And feeling finer every second he kept his hands on her arms. His tennis-player calluses felt pleasingly rough against her sensitised bare skin, his fingers strong and firm.

When she didn't move away he pulled her closer, so close she could sense the hammering of his heart, breathe in the exciting maleness of his scent, thrill at the warm strength of his body. She slid her arms around his waist and looked up at him, feeling nervous, excited, uncertain, on the brink of something unexpected. His eyes seemed a deeper shade of blue in the waning light and the intensity of his expression made her breath come short. For a very long moment their gazes locked in what seemed a series of unspoken questions with only one answer. *Yes*.

She was only vaguely aware of Kadek driving away. The world had shrunk to her and Max. Her lips parted in anticipation and she murmured her pleasure when he kissed her. His mouth was firm and warm against hers, his beard surprisingly soft against her skin. She tilted her head so she could more easily kiss him back.

'Is this because we're pretending to be a couple,' she murmured against his mouth.

'No, it's because I want to kiss you,' he said.

'I want to kiss you too.' She licked along the seam of his mouth with the tip of her tongue. 'No chilli this time. You're naturally hot.'

'You think so?'

'Oh, yes.' She wound her arms around his neck and pulled him to her, deepening the kiss. What had started as tender very quickly escalated into something intense, demanding, passionate, so all-consuming all she could think about was Max and the heat they were generating. Desire burned through her. She pressed her body to his as lips and tongues became more demanding.

This. Him. Max. *She wanted him.*

She didn't know how much longer they would have stood there in the middle of the narrow lane kissing, oblivious to their surroundings, if another truck hadn't driven up to deposit visitors to the restaurant. At the sound of its blaring horn, she came plummeting back to reality. Reluctantly she pulled away, immediately had to hold onto Max's arm to steady herself on legs that had turned to jelly. She blinked with bewilderment.

'What happened?' She choked out the words.

Max looked equally shaken. He took in a deep, shuddering breath. 'The inevitable,' he said.

Nikki didn't have to ask what he meant. No matter how she'd tried to deny it, they'd been heading towards this.

'The…the question is where do we go from here?' She knew her voice sounded strained and uncertain.

Max reached out and gently smoothed the strands of her hair that had come loose back off her face. She stood very still, briefly closed her eyes at the pleasure of his touch on her skin. 'Wherever it leads us,' he said.

Could she do that? Could she risk it? The thought was terrifying.

The people from the bus rushed towards them. She and Max stood aside to let them past. 'They're hurrying so they don't miss the sunset,' she explained. 'We should do the same. We need to go.' She went to turn away.

He put a finger under her chin, tilted her face upwards so she was forced to look at him. 'Regretting it already?'

'No. Yes. I… I don't know.'

He released her but then took her hand in his. 'I'm not usually an impulsive person. But I feel compelled to follow where this is taking us—wherever it might be.'

'I'm not sure. I—' She could be impulsive, had used her quick decision-making to her benefit in the past. But feeling like this, about him, was scaring her. *She wanted him too much.*

'We don't have to think any further than tonight,' he said as he looked down into her eyes. 'Just tonight, Nikki. One night.'

CHAPTER EIGHT

THE RESTAURANT SAT by itself on the edge of a small, sandy beach lashed by fierce surf. People at the front tables could wiggle their toes in the sand. To the left were limestone cliffs where wild waves rolled in at all angles and crashed onto the cliff walls. The sunset was glorious, an enormous glowing red orb casting a fiery pathway onto the sea as it slowly sank into the horizon.

Nikki knew the sunsets on this coastline were reputed to be among the most splendid in the world. But she scarcely noticed nature's splendid display. She only had eyes for Max. His face seemed infinitely more interesting. Equally nature's masterpiece. Quite the best-looking man she had ever met. *And hers for tonight.* A thrill of pleasure and anticipation shimmied through her.

She was seated next to him at a table discreetly set towards the back of the restaurant. While the ones at the very front overlooking the beach caught the best view, the people seated there were also on display. Nikki's choice of table was as private as it could be in the well-patronised, fashionable restaurant. It was just as well no one was looking at them for several reasons, not least of which was that she was entranced by Max and he seemed equally entranced by her.

So much for having to pretend to be interested in each other as she and Maya had planned. The waitress had to ask them twice if they were ready to order—neither she nor Max had even noticed she was there. Such bumbling spies they'd turned out to be. More interested in each other than in analysing the menu and service in the interests of Big Blue. She would have to do better on the spying front. But not just yet. Being with him had suddenly become the overwhelming interest in her world. She kept reliving that unexpected kiss. *Wanting more.*

Max was holding her hand under the table. In fact he'd scarcely let go of it since they'd kissed outside the restaurant. 'How are we going to eat when our meals arrive?' she murmured.

'One-handed?' he suggested. 'You with your right and me with my left.'

She laughed. 'I guess it's possible.'

He leaned closer to her. 'I don't want to let go of you. I have to keep touching you to reassure myself you're still here with me.' There was an undertone of surprise to his words that she totally related to. This thing between them had flared up so quickly. *And could burn out as quickly,* she reminded herself. It wasn't something she could place any trust in.

She entwined her fingers with his even closer. 'I feel the same,' she said, her voice a little wobbly with wonder.

'I have to pinch myself that you actually said that.' He lowered his voice. 'You know, I didn't think you were interested in me at all.'

'I couldn't allow myself to be. Not when we'd been

so singed by the scandal I dragged you into. Not when I'd been the bride and you the best man.'

'But now we're two people without ties and—'

'Are you? Without ties, I mean,' she said. 'I wondered. After all, I'm talking to the guy voted sexiest man alive.' How could he be single?

He groaned. 'Don't remind me of that stupid title. I'll never live it down. You should hear what my father and brother have to say about it. There's nothing like the ribbing of two blokes from the bush to keep a guy from getting a swelled head. Though I think my mother was secretly tickled. But in answer to your question, there's no one. Hasn't been for a long time.'

Nikki realised she'd been holding her breath for his answer. She let it out on a silent sigh of relief. 'I see,' was all she managed to say.

'After the accident I was totally focussed on getting fit enough to play again. Obsessed. There was no room for the distraction of dating. What about you?'

'No one. I… I think I'd have to know a guy for ten years before I'd trust him enough to date.' Her comment was meant to be light-hearted but she couldn't help a note of bitterness from slipping through.

His brows raised. 'Really? Ten years?'

She nodded. 'The thing with Alan was that bad. To find out someone I'd believed in had lied to me about something so fundamental caused serious damage.'

Max's other hand went to his nose, once again, the slightly crooked bend showing in the evening light, as evidence of his encounter with Alan's fist. 'Bad for you too,' she said. 'If it's any consolation I think the new-shape nose suits you. It adds a touch of edginess. Make you look even…even more handsome.' She was going to say *sexier* but thought better of it. Not when she was clueless about where this was going. *But she had tonight.*

'I'll take that as a compliment,' he said.

'Please do,' she said. She would like to kiss that nose if she got the chance. Oh, yes, she'd like to kiss him, taste him, explore him. Now that she'd had her first taste of intimacy with Max she wanted more.

The waitress brought drinks, an aptly named sunset cocktail for her, a local beer for him. Still Max didn't let go of her hand and she didn't free it. Instead he demonstrated how well he could pour a beer using his left hand. Picking up her glass with her right was hardly an achievement as she was strictly right-handed. But it was fun. *He* was fun.

'Did you ever see me play tennis on television?' he asked after the waitress left.

'Yes,' she said, wondering where he was going with this. 'I enjoy watching the tennis. And it would have been difficult to avoid seeing you, reading about you. The entire country was behind you when you kept winning those big tournaments. And of course you were so hot you turned a lot of besotted young women onto tennis.'

'The more fans, the better. Good for the game.' It would be false modesty if he tried to deny his celebrity status. She was glad he didn't. 'So when did you first see me?' he asked.

'I think it might have been when you first won Wimbledon.'

'Men's singles. I was twenty-two.'

'I was twenty-one. Finishing uni and starting my own business.' Still with Ray, the high-school boyfriend, thinking they were headed for marriage when he'd been cheating on her for six months with the woman he eventually left her for. Ray, her first big fail when it came to men.

Max let go her hand, made a show of counting on his fingers. 'By my calculation, you've known me eight years.'

'What?' His statement was so audacious, she had to laugh. 'You have got to be kidding me.'

'I could be.' He shrugged. 'Or I could be seriously suggesting you take that first time you watched me on television as our introduction. Eight years ago. Two more years to go before you could trust me.'

'There's something seriously flawed in your logic.' She tried to sound serious but couldn't help laughter infusing her voice.

'Makes sense to me,' he said.

'Except for the fact *you* didn't actually see *me* unless you could somehow beam vision from the centre court at Wimbledon to my house in Sydney.'

He grinned. 'Maybe. Maybe not.'

'I think we'll go with "maybe not",' she said, laughing again. 'As far as I recall, the first time you ever laid eyes on me was at the wedding rehearsal. By my count, that makes nine and a half years to go before—'

He sobered. 'Before you could trust me. Or any other man.'

'That's right,' she said, thinking she'd dug herself into a ditch. 'Though there could possibly be time reduced for good behaviour.'

He leaned closer to her, concern warming his eyes. 'Why, Nikki? Why such distrust? It's not just Alan, is it?'

'No, it's not,' she said, unable to stop a hitch in her voice. 'I had a long-time boyfriend and that didn't end well. A few other disasters when I started to date again. But I don't know that I want to talk about all that. It's a bit heavy for a first date.' She frowned. 'That is, if this is what you'd call a date?'

'It can be whatever you want it to be,' he said. 'I don't much care for labels.'

'We said one night only.' Already the hours were counting down. *One night wouldn't be enough.*

'May I remind you I still have ten more nights on the island after tonight. We could make it ten nights. I can't speak for after that—I don't know where I'll be. It wouldn't be fair to say otherwise.'

'I could be exaggerating about the ten years. But I'm not ready for a relationship. Not sure when I ever will be ready.'

'I'm not in a position to offer one. I don't even know where I might be living. Anyway, "relationship" is just another label.'

'I'm glad you said that. Tag me in a relationship and it's doomed.'

Nikki hated that she sounded down on herself. She was strong, intelligent, had everything going for her. She knew that. But she chose the wrong men. Trouble was she didn't know they were wrong for her until she was already in too deep to easily extricate herself. Perhaps it was because she didn't want to admit she'd made an error of judgement. Or perhaps she was too willing to try and see the best in people and forgive them when she shouldn't. She got that trait from her mother, who had never said a bad word about her duplicitous father, right up to the day she'd died. Given Max's reputation—perhaps he was a mistake too.

'The media, they made a big deal about you and Ellen Trantor. That you…that you cheated on her.'

Max's face set grim. 'I was never unfaithful to Ellen. Ever.'

'That photo…' Nikki hated to dig when it so obviously made him uncomfortable. But she had to know.

'That photo of me having lunch with a female friend was taken after I'd broken up with Ellen.'

'But I thought—?'

'That we were still together? The press certainly took great delight in pointing that out. Fact was we'd split weeks before. But Ellen was facing one of the most important tournaments of her career. She knew the media would make a song and dance about a break-up and asked me to keep it quiet as she didn't want to be distracted from her game.'

'Then they broke the story about your date with the other girl.'

'Which made it look like I was cheating on my girlfriend. Ellen was furious on two counts. The adverse publicity put her off her game and she lost. Then she refused to believe that I hadn't been dating the girl during our relationship. For the record, the girl I was lunching with was an account executive from the sportswear company that sponsored me. There was nothing romantic between us, and there certainly wouldn't have been after that whole thing blew up. As the so-called "other woman" she was hunted by the press everywhere she went, even had paparazzi popping out of the flower beds at her parents' house. She hated me.'

'Wow. I'm sorry. I had no idea.'

His mouth twisted into a bitter line. 'You can see why I despise press intrusion into my private life. That incident cost me several matches, too. I've never played so badly. It also lost me the friendship and respect of Ellen, a woman I had deeply cared for and a peer. Playing against her in a doubles match became a nightmare—every time a "grudge match" according to our media "friends".'

'And that other girl? The former girlfriend from your home town who gave that horrible interview in that magazine?' She shuddered at the memory of those vindictive words.

He grimaced. 'How did I get cast as the villain in that case? I was single, she told me she was single when we met up again on one of my flying visits home to see my parents.'

'You mean you had ex-sex?'

'No strings. By mutual consent. But she couldn't have been single at the time because I was definitely not the father of her child.'

'Yet you got branded as the love cheat?' she asked, puzzled. 'How did that happen?'

'Turns out the father was a guy I'd known at school. Not difficult in a small school in a small country town. The media made out I was cheating on a friend.'

'Then you were made out as doing the same thing with me—the best man betraying his friend the groom. Which was utter nonsense, of course.'

'*All* of it utter nonsense. But the gutter press breeds on creating scandal. That kind of beat-up story gives their readers and viewers a temporary "ooh-ah" kind of thrill. Makes them think they "know" a celebrity. But it changes the lives of those involved and not for the better. Mud sticks. There are people who believe there's no smoke without fire. Each time it's happened to me, people I respected thought less of me.' His eyes were clouded with disbelief that he should have been judged so unfairly for something he hadn't done.

'I think more of you for sharing that with me.' He took her hand again. She tightened her clasp on his hand when what she really wanted to do was hug him and comfort him. 'And I appreciate you want to take a chance on me, in spite of the consequences if we're discovered.'

If the press who hounded him could blow up something as innocent as a lunch date, what might they make of the best man and the runaway bride 'hiding out' on an island six months down the track?

'Why don't we take it day by day?' Max said. 'One night at a time.'

Her heart kicked up a beat. 'Are we talking a fling? A no-strings fling? If so, I've never had a fling. I don't know how—'

'Just another label,' he said.

'So a no-label fling?'

'If that's what you want to call it. But I'd rather forget about labels altogether.'

'No labels…no expectations,' she said slowly.

'Just enjoy each other's company without worrying where it's headed,' he said.

It was a refreshing thought. She'd always worried about where a relationship was headed before it had really started. Here, away from her life back home, could be the right place to take a risk on something different. With a man so very different from anyone she had ever met before.

'Yes,' she said. 'Get to know each other in the time we have.'

'The clock has already started ticking on that time,' he said. 'There's so much I want to know about you. So many questions I want to ask you.' She was surprised at how urgent he made that sound.

'Fire away,' she said. 'I'm ready to answer your questions. Like you answered mine. But there's one thing I want to get out of the way first. I… I haven't been completely honest with you about something important.'

Dread clutched Max deep in the gut. Just when he was allowing himself to relax into the real-life scenario of being with his dream girl in the blue dress. That kiss had taken his dream a whole lot of steps further from where it usually ended. Nikki. In his arms. Passionate. Exciting. *Real.*

A hundred hideous reasons for Nikki being dishonest with him churned through his brain. He had always placed great store on honesty and trust, even before he'd been played by the press. He let go of her hand, placed his on the table. Immediately felt bereft of her touch. 'What do you mean?' He braced himself for her reply.

'I said I was dreaming up ideas for a new venture. Truth is, that venture is well and truly in the development stage.'

'A business venture? And you didn't tell me that because—?'

Her eyes flickered nervously. 'It's that trust thing again.'

'So why confide in me now?'

'Because I don't think you look at me with dollar

signs flashing in your eyes.' She looked down at the table. 'Like Alan so obviously did.'

He was so relieved he nearly gagged. 'Dollar signs are not what I see when I look at you, Nikki, I can assure you.' What he saw was a woman exceptional, not just in looks, but in nature. How could any man let her go? No wonder Alan had whacked him in the nose. Nikki underestimated herself if she thought a man would only be interested in her money. Even Alan must have been hurting at her loss from his life.

'I also think you probably have enough of your own money not to be interested in mine,' she said.

'You're right there. I've been caught too often by people more interested in what I have rather than who I am.'

Nikki nodded. 'Just Max. Not Max the celebrity. Not Max the millionaire. The Max I've got to know and to…to like.'

'Exactly,' he said. 'And I like you for the you I've got to know over the last days. Not just beautiful Nikki—that's a given—but smart, clever, kind Nikki. I can assure you your personal wealth has no interest for me.'

I have more than enough for both of us. Max swatted the thought from his mind. He wasn't thinking of a future with Nikki. He couldn't. He was a single-minded kind of guy. Needed to get his life sorted before he could consider a relationship. He had to be careful he didn't raise expectations of anything he couldn't fulfil. Especially when he was beginning to realise the damage that had been done to her by unscrupulous men in her past. He didn't want to be another man who hurt her.

'So as far as wealth is concerned, we're on an even playing field,' she said.

'And perhaps I've gained a few minutes' credit in the trust department?' he said.

'Maybe even a few hours,' she said with a smile that made her eyes dance.

He wanted to kiss her, but fought the urge. Holding hands under the table was one thing in terms of possible exposure. Kissing in a crowded restaurant was another, even if most people's focus was on the last minutes of the setting sun.

'Tell me about your new venture.'

'Private swimming clubs for women back home in Australia,' she said. 'Since I've been here I've been shocked at the number of people who can't swim but want to enjoy the water or to keep their kids safe. Australian women from various backgrounds who didn't learn to swim for one reason or another but are embarrassed to admit it. I think they'd value a safe, private environment where they could be taught. Not just to swim but to snorkel and dive, even surf. Remember you said to me, "I'm an Aussie, we swim?"'

Max nodded.

'That's not always the case. The Australian statistics on non-swimmers are quite alarming for a country where death by drowning is a real issue.'

He smiled at her enthusiasm. 'Sounds like a worthy idea. But would it be profitable?'

'I'm looking into that.' Her eyes narrowed in an expression of concentration that was almost sensual in its intensity. 'The clubs would be luxurious without being intimidating. Stroke correction as well as beginners' classes for a wider customer base. A health and beauty spa. Branded swimwear. A swim travel company to take postgraduate clients to destinations like Frangipani Bay and Greece and Croatia for fabulous swimming tours.'

'You thought of all that since you've been here?'

'I would never have thought of it otherwise.'

He realised both her ideas for businesses sprang from a desire to help people, a generosity of spirit he admired in her. First her sister with her skin problems and now women who yearned to be able to swim. He could learn from her. His thoughts for his future had focussed on his needs, not the needs of others. Perhaps he needed to re-think that. Could he, after so long focussing on his need to win? Could he ever share his life with someone else?

'How far advanced are you with your plans?' he asked.

'As far as I can be from up here. I'm working through my father's property development company to search out potential sites, talk to architects.'

'You're on such good terms with your father?'

'I haven't always been. We clash. Perhaps we're too alike. But he and my mother started the company together—she was an interior designer, he a real-estate agent. They started by flipping houses and went on to apartment blocks and commercial developments. The partnership fell apart when he left her for his assistant. But the point is, my mother left me and my sister her shares. So of course I work through the company.'

'You're at a crossroads in your life,' he said.

'So are you,' she said. 'I'm interested in what path you might take after tennis.'

Work. She was talking about work. Did he have to walk that path alone?

He would usually keep such matters very close to his chest. But suddenly he wanted Nikki's opinion, her business smarts and maybe— No. He was *not* seeking her approval. That would imply something he didn't want to acknowledge.

'Okay. The options. I'm tempted by a directorship of a big sporting goods company.'

She nodded. 'Could be a plan. Keeps you in the world of sport and is prestigious. As long as the directorship would be an active role, not just there for them to have you on their masthead for prestige. I suspect you would get easily frustrated by a passive role.'

'You're right about that,' he said. She was both shrewd and perceptive. 'There's also an opportunity with an elite tennis coaching ranch in the US.'

'Might you find it too difficult to be training others when what you really still want to do is to be out there competing yourself?'

'You've nailed it,' he said, shaken at how she seemed to read his mind. It was disconcerting.

'There is another option.'

She smiled. 'Now I hear some excitement in your voice.'

'Excitement and a touch of trepidation,' he admitted.

'Spill.' She leaned a little closer to him.

'Sports commentator for one of the big cable networks. Covering the major tournaments. All around the world.'

'Wow. You've got the knowledge, the screen presence, the personality. I could really see you doing that.'

'But it would involve the kind of peripatetic lifestyle I've been living since I was a teenager. Perhaps I want to put down roots.'

'Where?'

He shrugged. 'Ideally Australia. It's home and my

parents aren't getting any younger. But I've lived in the UK and the US too.'

'It's all very exciting for you, isn't it?' she said.

Not half as exciting as being here with you.

He looked up to see a waitress heading their way bearing a tray. 'I see our starters heading our way,' he said, welcoming the opportunity to change the subject. 'I'm ready to eat.'

'Me too,' she said. 'But we can't touch a thing until I've taken shots with my phone for Maya. We mustn't forget the reason we're here. I don't want to let my friends down.'

Max pretended to grumble. Made to snatch up the little 'fusion' tacos with an Asian filling before she finished her photo. Complained he would faint of hunger if she didn't let him start on the tuna slices with a spicy soy dipping sauce and a wasabi mayo. Told her it was torture to keep him from the fritters.

But he liked her loyalty and commitment to her friends. Loyalty wasn't something he'd experienced from a female companion. But then perhaps he'd been too focussed on his game to be able to give it in return.

'Okay, we can start now,' she said. 'Sorry to have made you suffer.'

'You don't look sorry at all,' he said. 'I think you enjoyed torturing me.'

'I'm admitting to nothing,' she said with a delightful curve of a smile.

He held back on his hunger. *Ladies first* had been a strict rule at his house when he'd been growing up. He always followed it. At the table. When it came to opening doors. In bed when his lover's pleasure was as important as his own. He watched Nikki as she savoured her tuna, making little oohs and aahs of appreciation and tried not to think of how she would react if he were to make love to her. He had to suppress a groan at the thought.

'Aren't you having any?' she asked, innocent of the not so innocent thoughts that were occupying him.

'Of course,' he said. 'I was waiting for you to go first.'

'Why thank you, I appreciate that,' she said, oblivious to any play on words.

'Try the corn fritters—they're scrumptious.' She caught his eye. 'Watch out for the sambal that accompanies them, though. It's really spicy. I know you don't like it too hot.'

He might surprise her, if he ever got the chance. 'Yes, scrumptious,' he said as he sampled the food. How he wanted to sample *her*.

'What do you think about the restaurant and the menu?' she asked. 'What shall we report back to Maya?'

'I'm no foodie,' he said. 'But it's a bigger menu than at Big Blue, going by their room-service menu.'

'You haven't actually eaten in the Big Blue restaurant?'

'Privacy and anonymity, remember,' he said.

'Of course,' she said. 'Though I don't think anyone has recognised you here tonight.'

'They were too busy taking selfies in front of the sunset to notice anyone else, I think,' he said.

'I know,' she said, rolling her eyes. 'The last time I was here one girl had three changes of clothes for her photographs.'

'Now they're all heads down eating. Which is just

what I want to do too. I hope the main courses won't take too long.'

'Be patient,' she said. 'The service is very good here. Another thing to report back on.' He was good at being patient when it came to the food, impatient when it came to having her in his arms again.

The sun had finally slid into the sea and the place was lit by strings of glowing lanterns. The white foam of the surf glistened where it caught the light. Even over the chatter of guests and the clatter of dishes he could hear the water pummelling the cliffs. 'It's very atmospheric,' he said. He'd nearly said *romantic* but caught himself in time.

'It is, isn't it? I might suggest to Maya they invest in some of those lanterns. I really like the effect.'

'It's an impressive menu too,' he said. 'A good mix of Indonesian and Asian food with Western dishes too. People from all around the world come to this island. The variety is excellent. Vegetarian and vegan choices too.'

'It's impressive all right. I notice here they specialise in barbecue foods. I wonder if Big Blue should specialise to make their menu stand out.'

'Desserts,' he said immediately. 'Really fabulous desserts. That would draw the punters in, I reckon.'

Her eyes widened. 'I didn't think of you as a dessert fiend.'

'I had to suppress a lot of cravings when I was training. There's a lot you don't know about me.'

Her eyes glazed over, narrowed a little. 'And I have ten nights to discover it,' she said, her voice low and husky.

Max was too astounded to reply. He wondered if he had underestimated lovely Nikki when it came to the not so innocent thoughts.

CHAPTER NINE

WOULD MAX EXPECT her to go to bed with him tonight?
It was all Nikki could think about as she stood shoulder-
to-shoulder with him in front of the carved wooden gate
to her villa. Surely the thought must be playing on his
mind as much as it was on hers? Not to mention the urgent signals her body was sending her. *My needs, remember?*

She wanted him. She *really* wanted him. But she
still didn't know him very well and to be intimate with
someone who was still virtually a stranger had never
been part of her romantic game plan.

She'd always been a commitment type of girl. Ad-
mittedly she'd been a schoolgirl at the time but she'd
dated Ray for six months before they'd made love—
her first time.

Perhaps it was to do with her upbringing by her re-
ligious mother. One of the reasons her mother's last
years had been so miserable was because her religion
didn't recognise divorce. While in the eyes of the state
her mum had been divorced, in the eyes of her church
she wasn't. There'd been no thought of a second marriage for her, despite her father having wed his mistress
to make her wife number two. Her mum had drummed

into both the girls that sex should be part of a committed relationship. Nikki had discovered the truth in that herself. Now she wasn't so sure.

Maybe now was the time to stir up her life a little and do things differently. Take what she wanted without worrying about where it might lead. By agreeing to the no-label fling she'd taken the first step. *With Max.*

Kadek had picked her and Max up at the restaurant in the truck. He'd just said goodnight and was headed back to Maya and the baby at his house at the back of the resort. Nikki listened to her friend's footsteps on the wooden walkway until they faded into the distance then disappeared altogether.

The silence between her and Max seemed to stretch out for too long—although it was probably only seconds. She became intensely aware of the sounds of the evening on the warm, tropical night. Birds rustled in the trees above them. Some kind of insect gave an intermittent chirrup. The sea swished gently onto the sand of Frangipani Bay. There was the distant crow of a rooster—they seemed to crow without timetable at all hours of the night. And her own breathing, too rapid, making her feel faint. Perhaps from the rich fragrance of frangipani that hung in the air. Or was it because she was alone with Max for the first time since that hungry, passionate kiss had changed everything between them?

It was ridiculous to feel so nervous. She was a grown-up woman of nearly thirty. Not a starstruck adolescent. She turned towards him. His face was illuminated by the lantern above the gate. He looked very serious and impossibly handsome. She was awestruck at the thought she had him in her life, even if the time had limits on it.

'I...er...would like to ask you in for a nightcap.

But—' She stuttered away into nothing. How did she say this?

Without speaking, Max gathered her into his arms and held her close. It felt so good to be back close to him, his warmth and strength. Her dress swooped low at the back and he stroked her bare skin until she relaxed against him. 'But you're worried I might try to seduce you,' he said, his voice deep and rich and laced with humour, his breath ruffling her hair, his hands warm on her body.

She pulled back within the circle of his arms so she could look up at him. A hint of his endearing grin lingered and his eyes were warm. Her heart seemed to flip over inside her chest. 'How did you know?'

'A lucky guess,' he said. 'Or it could be that I'm learning to read you.'

'Oh,' she said, disconcerted that he could understand what she was feeling without her having to say a word. 'It's not that I'm *worried*. Just... I want to. I want *you*. But it seems too soon. I... I told you I haven't had a fling before. I don't know the rules.'

'No rules, no labels, remember?'

Wordlessly she nodded, bowed her head so she looked down at her feet, feeling awkward and more than a little foolish. If they only had the one night she would probably rush him inside to the bedroom. But it was a big turnaround for her to contemplate sex as part of a fling with no future. She would feel so much happier if she knew him a little better before she took that step. Even though it might be a kind of torture to wait. Even though he might lose interest if she put him off.

He tilted her chin with his fingers so she was forced to look up at him. His eyes searched her face. She could see an undisguised desire in them but also a warmth of understanding that surprised her. *Sexiest man alive.* This man could pick and choose from a waiting list of women who wouldn't hesitate to take their clothes off for him.

'Of course I want to take you to bed,' he said. 'You're gorgeous and sexy and I can't think of anything more wonderful than making love to you, Nikki Lucas.'

She thrilled to hear his words and an answering desire shimmied through her. 'Me too. I mean, I want to make love with you too. But—'

'When you're ready,' he said.

'It's not that I'm a prude or anything but I—'

He laid a finger on her mouth to silence her. 'You don't have to explain or make excuses.'

'It's just that I've always—'

He followed his finger with his mouth in a brief kiss that left her breathless. 'I tell you what,' he said. 'How about I leave it for *you* to seduce *me*?'

'What do you mean?'

'When you're ready, I'm sure you'll be able to find a way to let me know you want to have your way with me.' He gave an imitation of a wicked leer that made him look more handsome than devilish.

'Oh, I think I could manage that,' she said, laughing. She could already think of several ways. *When the time was right.* She felt instantly more relaxed and happier once he'd taken off the pressure. Pressure, she realised, that was self-imposed. He hadn't tried to push her into anything.

He kissed her again. She wound her arms around his neck and kissed him back—a long, slow, exploratory kiss. It was a kiss that acknowledged mutual desire, that agreed they both wanted more than kisses and—importantly—that insisted there be mutual respect.

'Are you going to invite me in?' he asked, still holding her close, his breathing not quite steady.

Nikki hesitated for only the merest fraction of a second but it was obviously enough for him to pick up on. 'I'll sit on one sofa and you can sit on the other, look don't touch,' he said.

'That's a plan,' she said, not liking it in the slightest but seeing sense in it.

He put on a woeful expression. 'It's not late and if I go next door I'll only sit out in the courtyard and think of you on the other side of the wall.'

So he did that too? 'Would you really?' she said, wondering if she should admit to doing exactly the same thing, deciding she should maintain at least a semblance of mystery. She most certainly wouldn't admit she fantasised about him soaping his magnificent body in his outdoor shower.

'Of course. Then I might dive into the pool and wonder if you might be doing the same thing.' If he did that, and she heard him splashing, she'd drive herself crazy imagining it and wondering if he swam naked. Her breath caught. *She wanted to see him naked.*

'You…you could come into my courtyard and swim. Or…or we could sit on the sofas opposite each other as you suggest.'

'Or do both?'

'What about—?'

'I can swim in my shorts,' he said.

He must think she was a real prude if he'd picked up on her thoughts about what he might wear to swim in her lap pool tonight. She wasn't ready for naked just yet. But she wasn't a prude—and she looked forward to showing him that. But not tonight.

She reached into her purse for her key. 'I'd only sit on this side of the wall and think about you if I let you go,' she said. She inserted the big, old-fashioned metal key in the door. 'So please do come in.' He followed her over the threshold.

'Ah, the bliss of the air-conditioning,' she said, holding her arms up to the chilled air. Even at night it was hot and steamy.

Max looked around him with obvious interest. 'It's just like my villa but the mirror image. Nice to see you've added some personal touches. I like the Balinese puppets on the wall and the prints you've got propped up against the desk.' He picked up one of the framed photographic prints. 'Is this the abandoned seaweed farm near here? The colours of the water are incredible.' She nodded. Tourism was beginning to overtake the traditional industry of seaweed farming. 'And this black and white view of Mount Agung is so atmospheric.'

'They're by a local photographer,' she said. 'I bought some other knick-knacks too, so I could personalise the place.'

'The more I look around, the more I see,' he said.

'I've lived here for six months. The villas had only just been finished when I arrived. It's my home. For the time being at least.' When she'd first come to the island she'd thought she'd never want to go back to Sydney.

She noticed he put the frame back in the precise spot he'd taken it from. 'How long do you think you'll stay up here?' he asked.

'Not much longer. I'll need to be in Sydney to decide on sites for my swim clubs.'

'Are you frightened of going home?' he said quietly.

She felt herself flush. 'Frightened? Of course not. All the fuss with the media will be over. Hopefully the runaway bride is yesterday's news.' But she'd go back to Sydney single. The thought of having to face the dating scene again was not an appealing one. Especially when she'd be comparing every man she met to Max.

'Are you worried about Alan?' he said.

She shrugged. 'Not really. When I first saw you here I thought he'd sent you and I felt fearful. He continued to make threats against me for months after the wedding. Scary stuff.'

Max's hands curled into fists. He cursed in extremely uncomplimentary terms about Alan.

'Don't worry,' she hastened to assure him. 'My father paid him a visit and there have been no more threats. In fact, my sister informed me just yesterday that Alan has recently been seen around town with a wealthy widow.'

'It didn't take long for him to bounce back,' he said, his distaste for his former friend evident.

'Perhaps the ex-wives will warn her off like they did me.'

Max moved towards her, his stance protective. 'Make sure you don't do the warning. I suggest you stay right out of it.'

She shuddered. 'I intend to. I want absolutely nothing to do with that man.'

'But you're worried Sydney might be too small to contain both you and him.'

Again he seemed to read her mind. 'Maybe,' she admitted. 'But I have to suffer the consequences of my own actions, don't I? I was the one who was foolish enough to be taken in by him.'

'But you were also the one who found the courage to leave Alan.'

'I keep telling myself that,' she said, but couldn't help a catch in her voice. 'And I know I have to go home soon.' She headed towards the small kitchen area. 'But here I am, offering you a nightcap and all I'm doing is talking. Beer?'

Nikki carried two local beers and a packet of spicy pretzels into the sitting area, and put them on the coffee table. She sat down on one of the sofas and Max, true to his word, sat on the other facing her. It seemed a vast distance over the low, carved wooden table.

'You look lonely over there,' he said.

'I am,' she said. 'It was you who suggested separate sofas.' She patted the cushion next to her.

He needed no further urging and came over to sit next to her. When he put his arm around her, she snuggled close with a happy sigh. 'That's better,' he said, as he pulled her closer.

'So much better than being on opposite sides of the coffee table and certainly opposite sides of the wall,' she said.

The door to the bedroom was open. The staff had been in to arrange the mosquito net canopy over the traditional carved wooden bed. It was a big, lonely bed and she wondered if she was making a mistake by not taking Max by the hand and leading him in there. 'So, do you want to watch a movie? The Wi-Fi is good here so there's a choice.'

Nikki only offered to be polite. She would so much rather talk to him.

'Why would I want to watch a movie when I can

sit here on the sofa with my arm around a beautiful woman?'

She looked up at him and was struck by the admiration in his eyes. Admiration and something more she couldn't put a word to but which might have been longing, yearning even. But she had to be careful not to read into it what she wanted to see rather than what was there. She'd been so easily fooled by Alan. For all her jokes about ten years to trust, she didn't know Max well enough to trust him.

For all his denial of any wrongdoing in those publicised cases, she couldn't be sure he was trustworthy in other ways. If she did have an affair with him—no label, no strings, whatever she might choose to call it— if the press found out and her bad choice was once again emblazoned all over the media for the world to know, she didn't think she could endure it. But she could not admit that to him, to anyone.

But right here, right now, she wanted him and she wasn't thinking past that. 'When you put it that way...' she said, letting her voice trail away.

'There's something I didn't get to ask you over dinner,' he said.

'Fire away,' she said.

'You once told me that Alan knew how to play you,' he said.

'Yes. He was a master manipulator.' And how gullible she'd been to be taken in by him. Would she ever be able to trust her judgement in men again?

'You said something like he made you believe everything you most wanted in life, he wanted as well.' Max's gaze connected with hers. 'So after everything, what is it that you most want from life now, Nikki? I'm really curious to know.'

* * *

Max was surprised at how the shutters seemed to come down over Nikki's face, blanking her expression. She edged away from him on the sofa so she was no longer touching distance.

'If I tell you, will you promise not to run screaming from the room?' she said. If she was attempting humour, it fell flat.

'I can't ever see myself running screaming from you under any circumstances,' he said.

'You might change your mind when you hear what I have to say.' Her eyebrows lifted. 'Seriously.'

'I very much doubt it. Don't keep me in suspense.'

'Okay. The truth is, I still want what I wanted then. And what I most wanted was to be married and starting a family before I was thirty,' she said.

He knew he shouldn't be surprised. She'd alluded to that a few times. But not stated so bluntly.

'No chance of it happening now as I turn thirty in September,' she continued. 'But when I met Alan it was feasible.'

'Okay,' he said cautiously, not sure where she was going with this. 'And he said he wanted that too?'

'I told him after our first few dates.' A black mood descended over Max at the thought of Nikki dating another man. He had to shake it off. He had no right to be jealous.

'That was my dating policy,' she said. 'There was no point wasting time with a man who didn't want what I wanted.'

'Like other guys you'd dated?'

'Yes. You might be surprised at the number of commitment-phobic men there are in Sydney. Maybe everywhere in the world, according to my girlfriends. An epidemic of men just wanting to have fun.'

Max hated the cynical twist to her mouth. And yet, could he not count himself among the commitment-phobes? Not for ever. One day he wanted all that. *Just not now.*

'But Alan didn't run screaming?'

'Far from it. He seemed delighted to meet a woman who wanted a family as much as he did. Reminded me of my advancing age. Suggested we get married as soon as we could, while I was still fertile. Of course, he didn't mention he'd had a vasectomy.' She twisted her face into a mock comic expression but didn't manage to disguise the hurt in her voice. *Was she completely over her former fiancé?*

'We all know what a pack of lies that was,' she continued. 'I would have had a family quickly all right—stepmother to his twins. Those poor little kids having a father like him. How I despise him.' *Guess that gave him his answer.*

'You didn't ever meet a man who shared your views?'

'I didn't actually date enough to find out,' she said. 'Between the time I broke up with the long-time boyfriend and the time I met Alan, I was working insane hours establishing my business.'

'What happened with the long-time boyfriend?' he asked. He hated the thought of lovely Nikki with some other loser who'd wounded her. But he had to know.

'We met in my last year of high school. Lasted all through uni. I actually thought he was "the one". We were unofficially engaged for years.' She paused. 'Are you sure you want to hear all this? It was years ago now.'

'Yes,' he said. He needed to know what made her

tick. He'd always made it his business to thoroughly re-search an opponent to give him any advantage. Not that Nikki was an opponent. Fact was, she fascinated him.

'Okay,' she said. 'Cracks started to show around when I started the business. He didn't like the idea I was more successful than he was, I think. I lost count of the number of times we broke up and then got back together and plastered it all over.'

'What happened in the end?' he said through grit-ted teeth.

'I was looking at engagement rings while he was cheating on me.' She said it so matter-of-factly, yet it must have hurt like hell at the time. 'I discovered she wasn't the first. He confessed his first infidelity was when I was mourning my mother. Didn't give him enough attention at the time, I suppose.' She shrugged but he could still see tension in her shoulders. 'Worse, he got the last woman pregnant and married her, not me.'

'Your first lucky escape, by the sound of it,' he said.

'I can see that now,' she said.

'And I can see where your ten-year trust again thing comes from,' he said.

'You get a few more hours' credit for recognising it,' she said, in a dismally failed attempt at humour.

'Thank you,' he said, gathering her into his arms again, breathing in her closeness, the scent of the flow-ers in her hair. 'Please note that I haven't run scream-ing from the room.'

'No need to worry with a no-label fling is there? We've both been honest about what we expect from the time we plan to spend together. Both realise it can't be more than that.' She kissed him, her mouth sweet and tender on his. 'Besides, I might have to rethink what I want from life. By the time ten years rolls around and I trust someone enough to consider marriage, I'll be heading for forty.'

'Women have babies in their forties.'

'I guess,' she said sounding doubtful. 'I think my only babies are going to be my businesses.'

He went to protest but she spoke over him. 'Look, can we not talk about this stuff any more? Now you know all about my dismal dating past and I don't particularly want to rehash it. Right now I'd rather look to the future than the past.'

'Meaning?' he asked.

'Meaning you've got Wayan and his boat on a retainer for the rest of your stay. I happen to have the day off tomorrow but I'm happy to be your guide if you'd like that.'

'I'd like that very much,' he said.

She smiled. 'Good. I thought maybe some more snorkelling and perhaps we could take a kayak out, just the two of us, currents permitting. That can be a lot of fun.'

Just him and her in a minimum of clothes alone together out on the sea? 'I can't wait,' he said.

CHAPTER TEN

THERE WAS SOMETHING very sexy about secrecy, Nikki thought as next evening she sounded the door chime to Max's villa. 'Room service,' she called in her most official voice, trying not to give the game away by laughing at the surreptitiousness of it all. Anyone passing by would see a staff member. Nothing suspicious.

The night before, she and Max had discussed how they still needed to be circumspect about being seen together. It was important to both of them to avoid any kind of adverse publicity. Behind the high walls of their villas seemed to be the best option for privacy. Hats and sunglasses when they were out in public. The pretence of her as staff and he as 'Mr James' at other times.

She was wearing the hotel's traditional style uniform and bearing a large covered tray containing dinner from the restaurant. One of the girls in the kitchen had remarked that it was a lot of *mee goreng* for one person. In response she'd laughed and said Mr James must be very hungry. After all the exercise she'd done throughout the day she was hungry and was glad he had ordered for big appetites.

Underneath her modest clothes she was wearing her favourite pink bikini. The previous night she and Max had never got around to swimming in the lap pool. In fact they had drowsed off together on the sofa. She'd awoken, startled, in his arms at the same time he had. Just as he'd done on the day of the wedding, he'd picked her up, then carried her into her room and laid her on her bed under the mosquito net. He'd kissed her and left. She'd drifted back off to sleep feeling, safe, happy and something not at all expected from a no-label fling—cherished.

Not that she read anything into that. Max was a gentleman—he'd shown that from the beginning in spite of his reputation. He liked her. He desired her. He was honest about his intentions. As far as she could ascertain, he was not pond scum. That was all there was to it.

She'd woken up alone, happy she'd made the decision not to invite him into her bed before she'd got to know him better. A perfect day had followed, snorkelling in a different spot at Crystal Bay, lunch at a quiet table in an out-of-the-way *warung* at the mangroves end of the island, followed by taking out a double kayak in the waters around Frangipani Bay and around to the next beach. She couldn't remember when she'd had more fun. She'd done all those things before. But being with Max had made them magical.

The door opened. Max stood before her, framed by the doorway, clad only in a sarong slung low on his hips and that winning smile. Nikki was struck speechless, all the breath knocked out of her body.

The sarong was in a Balinese *ikat* print in multiple shades of blue and contrasted with his smooth golden tan. Blue eyes, blue sarong and a whole lot of muscular male perfection in between. With a hungry gaze she took in the sight—broad shoulders tapering to narrow hips, his hard defined belly, the rippling muscles in his torso, the strong arms that had powered his killer tennis game, and seen them surging through the water in the kayak earlier that day.

Yes, she'd been with him all day when he'd been only wearing swim shorts. But that was for swimming. This was altogether different. This was…more naked somehow. *Was he wearing anything under that sarong?*

'What do you think of the sarong?' he said. 'I bought it from the hotel store. Kadek advised me on how to tie it.'

She swallowed hard. 'You look hot.'

He frowned. 'Do I? The idea is that a sarong is cooler than shorts or trousers in this climate.'

'I didn't mean that kind of hot.' She could feel her eyes glazing over. If she wasn't holding the tray she thought she might simply swoon and fall at his feet.

'I'm glad you think so,' he said. 'It's a guy thing in this country but not where we come from. I was concerned I might look ridiculous.'

'Not ridiculous,' she said. 'Very…very manly.' She had to clear her throat again. 'If they put a photo of you looking like that on a poster for your fans it would sell out.'

'Thank you. But I'd rather keep my new look just between us,' he said.

'Me too,' she said. A sudden possessive urge swept over her. *She wanted him all to herself.*

If she just undid that one knot at the front, would she see the sarong fall away from him? Perhaps it was as well that her hands were firmly clenched on the tray.

'Let me take that from you,' he said, taking the

meal from her. He inhaled. 'Smells good.' He carried it through to the circular dining table in the living area.

Then he turned to her again, put out his arms. 'I'm glad you're here,' he said. 'And not just because you come bearing food.'

She laughed and went willingly into his embrace. All she wanted was to be close to him, to be near to him, to be kissed by him. She couldn't let her thoughts stray further than that.

She put up her face for his kiss and a few blissful moments followed. How could she ever imagine sharing such a thing with anyone else? Excitement built as the kiss intensified. *Take what you can, while you can,* she urged herself. Spending all day together had accelerated the 'getting to know him' process. Too well. It had been a wrench when she, as guide, had said goodbye to 'Mr James' on the beach. In just the few hours since, she'd missed him with an intense sense of loss. Maybe it was time. Maybe tonight.

'Today was one of the best days of my life,' Max said, his voice deep and husky.

Nikki's heart gave a little lurch at his words. Being with him, enjoying the same experiences, laughing with him. His presence nearby had added such a wild joy to the day she'd found herself wishing it would never end. Had he felt the same about her?

'It was for me too,' she murmured. What if he didn't mean being with her at all? What if he'd been referring to the water and the weather? She stepped back from him. 'Yes, it was a perfect day,' she added hastily. 'Those beautiful fish, the coral, the lunch and—'

He reached for her, swivelled her so he could look deep into her face. He traced his finger down her cheek.

'All that. But it was the company that made the day. Being with you, Nikki. That's what was so special for me. You.'

An unreasoning hope soared to life in her heart at the expression in his eyes. 'Thank you. For me too. I mean you. Your company. I… I can't remember when I last enjoyed a day as much.' *Enjoyed a man as much.*

But she couldn't let herself think that this was any more than two people thrown together by circumstance with limited time on a beautiful holiday island. She forced her voice to sound steady. 'You're a mean hand with a kayak. All that upper body strength. You did all the work. I scarcely had to paddle.'

'We were in perfect rhythm together.'

'Yes, we were,' she said, feeling a little breathless. Within minutes on the kayak they'd found their rhythm with the double-bladed paddles, in sync with each other, propelling through the sparkling aqua water in perfect harmony. Even when they'd hit one of the notorious unpredictable currents they'd worked effortlessly together to get the kayak out of trouble. Of course her thoughts had wandered to how their rhythm might match under other circumstances. After all, she was a red-blooded female with needs clamouring to be acknowledged.

'I missed you,' he said, tracing her lips with his thumb.

'It's only been a couple of hours.' She couldn't show how affected she was by his touch, by his words. *She didn't trust this feeling.*

'Those couple of hours away from you seemed very long.' *Was this genuine or a practised seduction?*

'I missed you too.' The words blurted out despite her

best efforts to hold back. 'I... I've been counting down the minutes until I saw you again.'

'The wait seemed interminable. But I couldn't very well storm in next door and drag you in here.'

Why not? she thought. It might make it easier for her if he kissed and caressed her senseless until she thought of nothing but making love with him. But she wouldn't want to feel overwhelmed by caveman tactics. 'I... I guess not,' she said.

He looked unbearably appealing in that sarong. Sexiest man alive and then some. Because of her reluctance he was waiting for her to make the first move. *Her call.*

Was now the time? She didn't know how to deal with this. Nothing had prepared her for the way she felt about Max. Why couldn't she allow herself to look at sex simply as an appetite to slake rather than something special to share between two people who cared about each other? What had she got herself into by agreeing to the no-label fling?

She couldn't let him read those thoughts on her face. Instead she took the few steps over to the table and took the cover off the tray. 'What have we got here? *Mee goreng*—my favourite, thank you.'

He walked over so he was behind her, looking over her shoulder. Too close for her to be able to keep a clear head. All that bare skin and muscle with nothing but the light cotton of her top between them. 'I remembered you said you liked it,' he said.

'And *tom be siap*, steamed chicken wrapped in banana leaves with a lemongrass salsa. That's yummy too. So is the tuna *bakar*—it's a grilled tuna fillet with a spicy Balinese sauce. You chose well.'

'They all sounded good,' he said. 'I was hungry.

All the swimming and kayaking today. I thought the kayaking might have made my damaged arm ache but it didn't.'

'That's good news. I'm glad.'

He put his hands on her shoulders and turned her halfway towards him so there was no escaping his gaze. 'For the first time in a long time I feel relaxed. Able to think clearly about the decisions I have to make. It's like I've turned some kind of corner. Thanks to you, Nikki.'

She picked up a fork and started to pull apart the banana leaf wrapping from the chicken. Anything but look at him. 'Any good guide would have done the same,' she said, purposefully misunderstanding him. She'd felt it too out there with him. The magic. The happiness she'd felt at being with him. At playing at being a couple. Struck in unguarded moments by an inexplicable longing for it to be real.

'That's not true and you know it,' he said. 'It was more than that.'

Again her heart gave that painful lurch. It would be only too easy to develop feelings for Max. But she couldn't allow that. He'd made it very clear he wasn't looking for a relationship. She had only just recovered from the emotional fallout from her failed engagement. She couldn't let herself fall for a man who only wanted a fling.

She screwed up her eyes in a kind of despair. *Don't let yourself fall in love with him, Nikki.* She could lie to herself all she liked but she knew she was in serious danger of losing her heart to this man.

She looked up at him. 'We're away from home, in an exotic environment. Both escaping trauma of a kind. It would be easy to think there's more to some vacation fun than there really is.' She was trying to talk herself into believing that as much as she was him.

'You can say that,' he said, his voice controlled. 'That doesn't stop me from believing it was an exceptional day and that the reason it was exceptional was the company of a wonderful woman.'

Max tried to sound on top of the situation but inside he was in turmoil. Things with Nikki were not going as planned. He had intended a no-strings vacation affair. Something warm and sexy and fun that would help them both heal from the calamities that had driven them in their own separate ways to this island.

It should be something easy to walk away from at the end of his time here. He had his farewell speech prepared—something along the lines of it would be awkward to stay in touch. They both had lives to get back on track. No point in trying to prolong something that had a limited life. No need to exchange phone numbers.

Trouble was, it wasn't turning out like that. *He was falling in love with her.* Head over heels and so rapidly he could hardly keep his feet on the ground. Or that was how it seemed.

It wasn't what he wanted. Not now. Not even in the foreseeable future. Not when he was forging a new post-tennis life. When he got married, he wanted all his ducks to be in a row so he could have the kind of relationship his parents had. One that lasted. Where he would be there for his wife and children. Not absent. It hadn't just been conflicting training schedules that had ended his relationship with Ellen. It had been what she had called—what she had screamed at him when she'd ended it—his absence both physical and emotional.

Truth was, the career he'd striven for most of his life had defined him. He was used to being a champion. A winner. He needed to be back on top with whatever new path he chose before he could ask a woman to share his life.

Nikki could be the right girl at the wrong time. *Perhaps he should back off.*

Although it was hardly likely that she reciprocated any deeper feelings. In fact she'd just given him a nice little lecture about how he shouldn't mistake a vacation fling for anything more significant. He should take heed of her advice. Hope like hell she hadn't read anything deeper into his compliments about how much he'd enjoyed her company.

And stop speculating whether that was a pink bra or a pink bikini giving him tantalising glimpses of the top of her breasts through her lacy white cotton uniform top.

'This dinner will be getting cold if we don't eat it soon,' he said. 'Do you want to eat inside or out in my courtyard? There are citronella candles to keep mosquitoes at bay.'

'The courtyard, please,' she said. 'Do you mind if I change into my swimsuit first?'

No, I'd rather you stayed completely covered up so I'm not tempted by your lovely body. 'Sure,' he said. 'Whatever is most comfortable for you.'

Would she do a striptease in front of him? If so, might he offer to help her undress? First that lacy blouse slid over her shoulders and breasts, then the long skirt, sliding it down over her legs and—

'If you'll excuse me for a moment, I'll pop into the bathroom to change,' she said, heading in that direction.

He suppressed a groan of frustration, turned it into an awkward cough.

'You okay?' she said, turning back.

'Chilli fumes wafting up from the food, making me cough.' He faked another cough. 'Nothing to worry about. You just go.'

'Are you sure? I've seen how chilli can affect you.'

'I'm *okay* with the chilli,' he said, tight-lipped. Would he ever live down that earlier incident? 'You go. I'll unpack the food.'

Just minutes later she came out wearing just a pink bikini top and an orange-and-white-striped hotel towel wrapped around her waist. It stopped short of covering her legs. 'I hope you don't mind if I borrowed a towel,' she said.

Lucky towel. 'Of course not,' he said through a suddenly choked throat that had nothing to do with chilli fumes. Did she realise how artlessly sexy she looked?

'I feel much cooler now,' she said, stretching up her arms so her breasts threatened to fall out of her bikini top. 'That long-sleeved blouse is actually quite warm when it's this hot.'

She was hot. He hadn't seen her before with so little clothing—she wore a sun protective swim shirt out on Wayan's boat. In the kayak she'd worn leggings and a life jacket. Now, the triangles of the bikini top drew attention to the swell of her breasts as much as covered them, emphasised the shadow of her cleavage. Her body was lithe and strong—her slender waist, the flare of her hips, her firm, finely muscled arms in perfection proportion. The more he saw of Nikki, the more he wanted her.

But that was all it was. A healthy sexual attraction.

A friendship of sorts. Not anything more. *Of course he wasn't falling in love with her.*

She sat down in the chair opposite him at the outdoor bamboo table and served herself her favourite noodles. 'You didn't order dessert?' she asked.

'Nothing really appealed,' he said. 'I've ordered the caramelised bananas a few times already.'

'I told Maya what you suggested about spectacular desserts. She agreed. In fact she's organised a meeting with her chefs to discuss a new dessert menu. She said to say thank you for the suggestion.'

'She's so welcome,' he said. 'Can you tell her I'm volunteering to taste any new dishes?'

Nikki laughed. 'I'll pass that on.' She sobered. 'Although it's likely that will be happening after you go home.'

'Shame,' he said. Truth be told, he hadn't been thinking that far ahead. Without being consciously aware of it, he had abandoned timetables completely and given in to 'rubber time'.

'Don't worry, I'll send you photos to drool over and…' Her voice trailed away. There had been no mention of any future contact between them after the eight remaining nights. She flushed and looked embarrassed. 'Or…er…not.'

'I'd like that,' he said. But he knew his voice came out sounding half-hearted.

The sudden silence between them stretched out too long to be comfortable, even taking into account that they were eating a meal. She was the first to break it. 'I have news,' she said. 'A very good friend of mine might be coming to the island tomorrow.'

Her news came from left field. 'A friend?' *Male or female?*

'Yes. Sammie and I go way back to high school. She's friends with Maya too.'

Suddenly his wariness about being seen with Nikki returned in full flood. 'Why might she come to the island?'

'First and foremost to catch up with me and Maya. But she wants to write a profile on me. She—'

Max got up from the table, pushed his chair back so hard it fell over, clattering on the paving. 'She's a journalist? You're inviting a journalist here? After all we went through with the media?'

Nikki got up too, not one to let herself be put at a disadvantage. 'She's not *that* type of journalist. Sammie writes for one of the weekend newspaper magazines. She's in Bali for a short holiday. But Sammie being Sammie never switches off. Her boyfriend is a photographer, he's here with her and—'

'A journalist *and* a photographer? What are you thinking?'

Nikki frowned. 'Sammie is one of my oldest, dearest friends. Another of my bridesmaids. I trust her implicitly.'

'What if she sees me here? What if she puts two and two together? Is that what you intend to—?'

'No! Sammie is writing a feature about me as an Australian female entrepreneur. About how one of the biggest cosmetic conglomerates in the world purchased my company that was born as a little, underfunded start-up in Sydney. About what my next venture will be. Her boyfriend also works for the magazine. It's absolutely nothing to do with *you*.' Her eyes flared, the green flecks sparking.

'But if she sees me—'

'You could stay in your room. Or leave early and spend the afternoon elsewhere. Go way out to sea with Wayan—'

'Why should I have to hide?'

She put up her hand in a halt sign. 'I haven't finished yet. I was going to say you *could* do all that but you don't need to do anything. Because the alternative is that I go in the morning to Sanur to the hotel where she's staying, for the interview and photo shoot. Then Maya will go over in the afternoon and we'll both stay in Sanur for a girls' night out with Sammie. I really want to see my friend. I haven't seen her for more than six months. But I don't want to put you out either. So that might be the best decision all round.'

In the face of her annoyance Max felt petty and mean. And gutted he wouldn't see her for all the time she was in Sanur. But the fear of media exposure of his affair with Nikki was still very real. Not that you could call it an affair yet. And the way she was glaring at him made him doubt an affair would ever eventuate.

Perhaps this would be a good opportunity to cool things down between him and Nikki before they ever really heated up. Before anyone—he was thinking of her—got hurt.

'You go to Sanur and do what you have to do. I hope the interview goes well for you.' He sincerely meant it.

'Thank you,' she said. 'It will be good PR for my new business. And for me. A positive feature should help re-establish my image as a serious businesswoman after the "runaway bride" scandal. Sammie has promised to completely avoid that term in her profile.'

'Good,' he said. 'Let's sit down and finish our meal.'

Nikki remained standing. 'Sorry. No can do.' She stood there in a revealing pink bikini top with a hotel towel tucked around her waist, her feet bare, yet he could see her morphing into Nikki the businesswoman. Could almost see her thoughts veering away from him and towards her goals for the next day. 'I have to go,' she said, with what seemed to him to be only the merest trace of regret.

How could he have forgotten? Nikki Lucas was a high-powered businesswoman who had admitted to him she'd put dating on hold in favour of her work. She had been as driven to make her company a success as he'd been in his career as a sportsman. The odds of a young woman succeeding so spectacularly in the international market as she had were probably the same as of him winning the US Open.

'It's still early,' he said.

She shook her head. 'Not for all I have to do this evening. I have to call Sammie and tell her I've decided on the Sanur option. Let Maya know—Kadek will look after Putu for the night she's away but she might have to rearrange some staff shifts.'

'I get that, but it won't take long. Surely you don't need to go just yet.' Was he begging? Max swore under his breath. He never had, and never would, beg for a woman's company.

'Sadly I do,' she said. 'Because the shoot won't be happening here, I have to pack and take over stuff I might need in Sanur. I'll need to get an early boat, organise a hairdresser, then grab the opportunity to shop in boutiques in Sanur for a more businesslike outfit for the shoot than I brought with me when I came here. If we'd shot here, Sammie would have brought clothes with her for me but this way is better because I can choose my own outfit. I always like to have control of the image I present.'

'I was the same in my tennis career,' he said. Though in fact it had been his manager who had insisted on control over his image. Max had just wanted to play tennis. *To win.*

'Really? I suppose you would,' she said without any real interest.

The stiff set of her shoulders told him she was not happy with his reaction to her news about her friend's visit. But it wasn't just that. Her thoughts were racing away in a direction that led away from him. And Max wasn't sure he liked it.

CHAPTER ELEVEN

NIKKI HAD STRETCHED out her time in Sanur with her friends, delaying her return to Lembongan for as long as she could. Maya had left on the earliest boat in the morning. But it was late afternoon by the time the speedboat transporting Nikki back to the island was nearing the beach at Jungut Batu.

Nikki was oblivious to the beauty around her, the aquamarine waters, the tree-lined shore coming into view, the excited chatter of first-time visitors to the island. Despite the fun of seeing her friends, the challenge of the interview and photo shoot, she was too preoccupied.

She'd endured some emotional pain in her life, but few things had hurt like the shaft of pain that had stabbed her at Max's response to her thoughtless comment about sending him photos of desserts from the kitchens of Big Blue once he was back in Sydney. Of course she knew the score for a no-strings fling—don't expect anything more. Just walk away and pretend it doesn't hurt. But the obvious discomfort that had flickered across his face that she should dare to presume any ongoing contact with Max Conway, the celebrity sportsman, had made her cringe. Then his instant suspicion

of her because she was seeing a friend who was a journalist—someone she'd known since they were fourteen
years old—had driven the blade in deeper.

No more Max. She wasn't cut out for no-label flings,
one-night stands, or whatever she chose to call them. He
was a celebrity used, no doubt, to picking up and putting down women when it suited him. She, for all her
business success, was just a girl who'd been wounded
by the men she'd misjudged while looking for love and
the not unreasonable expectation of marriage and a family. She wasn't good at pretending to be something else.

She liked Max. She liked him a lot. Thought he was
the hottest man on the planet. But that closed-over look
had told her she was in way above her head when it
came to pretending she could easily cope with the aftermath of how she would feel when what Max was offering came to an end. She simply couldn't deal with it.

How could she endure these remaining nights with
him on the island? She didn't want to let Maya down
but she might have to decamp over to Sanur for the
duration.

Not that Maya had expected her to stay as long as
she had. They'd talked about that with Sammie on their
girls' night out at a restaurant in Sanur. How Nikki had
stretched her time on Lembongan for as long as she
could—or should. That an exciting new venture awaited
her, one that would continue her links with Maya and
Frangipani Bay. But her life was in Sydney, not here.
Sammie had asked her about her love life, concerned
that she might not be getting over the Alan debacle. But
Nikki had reassured her friend she was okay. Not ready
to date okay, but okay just the same.

Neither Maya nor she had breathed a word to Sammie

about Max being at Big Blue. Privately, Maya had voiced her concern that Nikki might be heading for heartbreak. Which was perceptive of her as Nikki had not even confided in her how she felt about him. She had denied that she and Max were anything other than friends. But Maya's expression told her she knew better but wasn't going to interfere with further advice.

Perhaps, when it all boiled down to it, she should be thinking of flying back home rather than skulking in Sanur until Max checked out of Big Blue. Maybe she'd needed a kick in the butt like this to get back to face her real life.

Nevertheless, as she hitched up her dress above her knees to wade through the shallow water to the shore, it was with a heavy heart. Despite it all, she missed him. Every minute she'd been away from him, she had ached for him. There was something about her connection to Max that went beyond the physical, that called not only to her heart but to her soul.

Which was why she thought she might be hallucinating when she saw him standing on the beach, in the same place he'd stood when she'd last been here. She blinked. It was Max all right. Tall, imposing. The same but different. Even more handsome, if that were possible. His beard was a proper short beard now, not the stubble of when she'd first seen him there. His shorts were grey not blue. And he was wearing the hat and sunglasses they'd agreed to wear in public.

Had he seen her? Could she turn around and take the speedboat back to the mainland? Panic tightened her throat. She wasn't ready for this. Had thought she'd have time to prepare herself before she spoke to him. *What was he doing here?*

He waved to her. There would be no escape. She would have to face him. But she wasn't going to be cowed by his presence.

'Mr James, what a coincidence,' she said lightly.

'It's no coincidence,' he said. 'Maya organised for the truck to come pick you up. I hitched a ride so I could meet you at the boat. I didn't want to hang around at the hotel waiting for you.'

She wasn't going to act all passive aggressive and angsty because he'd hurt her feelings. But she wasn't going to let the conversation get personal either. As far as she was concerned, their no-label fling had fizzled out. 'Thank you, but that wasn't necessary,' she said, forcing a polite smile. 'I trust our driver to get me back to Big Blue.' She knew she sounded stilted. But it was the best she could do. She screwed her eyes shut tight and wished he'd be gone when she opened them.

Nikki looked different, Max thought. Gone were the hippy pants, the tangle of windblown hair. Now her hair was sleek and sophisticated, falling below her shoulders; her eyes made up with some dark shadow; her mouth slicked a deep pink. Her natural-coloured linen dress looked elegant and businesslike, even with the flip-flops she'd worn for the boat. This wasn't his Nikki of the island or the Nikki of his dreams. Not that she'd ever been his, either in reality or dream.

He felt as if there were a sheet of glass between them. And it wasn't because she was wearing sunglasses and a hat and he couldn't properly see her expression.

He offered to carry her backpack for her but she demurred. 'It's nicely balanced,' she said.

'How did the interview go?' he asked as they walked

to the waiting place for the truck. The streets were much too narrow for the driver to park anywhere and they had to wait for him to come back for them.

'Very well,' she said. 'Sammie asked some interesting questions, which really made me think.' She put up her hand as if to forestall a question from him. 'Rest assured, your name wasn't mentioned at all. The wedding incident was a no-go zone so you didn't even come up in reference to your role as best man. It was strictly business.'

'Good,' he said, relieved to hear it. He still worried at the wisdom of her meeting with a journalist. Journalists went for blood at the slightest sniff of a story, the more scandalous the better. And if it wasn't a scandal, they turned it into one—as he'd learned to his peril. If the press hadn't got hold of the paternity dispute story, it wouldn't have given his opponent the fuel to goad him into the ill-timed shot that had ended his career. He was glad he hadn't had to meet Sammie. It would have been difficult to be polite to her.

While he waited with Nikki for the truck they made small talk about the hotel she had stayed at with her friends in Sanur. She was polite, pleasant, not a trace of snark in her voice or demeanour. But he realised she had not once met his gaze.

He'd blown it with her.

They sat on opposite benches on the back of the truck all the way back to the hotel. Max tried not to think of the last time they'd sat there together, Nikki with her blue dress slipping up her thighs, he trying not to stare too blatantly. Or to remember the previous night when his 'Nikki in her blue dress' dream had turned into a nightmare.

It had started as usual with her gliding up the aisle towards him, then lifting her face for his kiss. Only instead of kissing her, he'd watched as she'd turned away from him back to her groom. A groom who suddenly wasn't Alan but some anonymous dude gazing at her in adoration. The symbolism was painfully obvious—he couldn't give her what she wanted so she'd found someone else. In the dream the pain of his loss had seared through him. He'd awoken in a sweat and never returned to sleep, tossing and turning, thoughts and regrets churning through his brain.

He was beginning to realise that relationships were a fluid thing. Opportunities for something exciting and unexpected could slip away while he was trying to make everything perfect. There wasn't a perfect time for a relationship. You had to *make* the time. He might have good balance when it came to being nimble on his feet. What he didn't have was balance in his life. He *could* have both a career and a relationship. What appeared so patently obvious to others had been a revelation to him. Look how Maya and Kadek worked so harmoniously together—a business, a happy marriage, a child.

When it came to Nikki, it seemed he'd kept his eye off the ball and lost the game, forfeiting the prize that had been right under his nose.

Nikki looked unseeingly out of the truck as it bumped its way back to the hotel. Seeing Max, wanting him, was too difficult. It was impossible for her to stay in any kind of proximity to him. She would have to get right away from here, from Bali, from anywhere in Indonesia. Time to move on. Tonight she would get online and book a flight home. Many of the flights to Sydney left from the Ngurah Rai international airport in Denpasar very late in the evening so she would almost certainly be able to leave tomorrow. Maya would understand.

When they reached the hotel, Nikki accepted Max's offer of assistance with her backpack but not his hand to help her down from the truck. Not after what had happened last time. She flushed at the memory of that passionate, public kiss, furious at herself for the wave of longing for him that swept through her. Now Max kept at a polite distance but she was aware of him as if they were skin-to-skin close. His scent, his warmth, the essence of his Max-ness. It was too painful. She had to go, and go quickly.

Packing up to leave Lembongan wouldn't take long. She hadn't brought much with her when she had fled Sydney and hadn't acquired much during her stay. Just the knick-knacks she'd bought to personalise her villa, a couple of gorgeous sarongs, this dress she'd bought for the interview.

Oh, and her heart. She'd been at risk of leaving that behind with the best man. It had been a close call.

She thanked the driver. He wasn't known to her, so she was very careful to stay staff-guest distance from Max and to address him as Mr James. But when the truck drove away from the driveway nearest to their villas she was left alone with Max. Most likely for the last time.

He refused to give her back her backpack, saying he would carry it to her villa for her. She walked the short distance to her door aware every second that he was only a few steps behind her. They reached her villa. He put her backpack down.

'Thank you,' she said. 'That was kind of you.' She

went to fish in the outside pocket of it for her room key but her hands were shaking too much to make a connection. She closed her eyes in despair. This was dreadful. They'd been so at ease with each other. To be reduced to this level of awkwardness was unbearable.

'Let me,' he said, deftly retrieving her big old-fashioned key with the wooden tag and handing it to her. A gentleman to the last.

She took it, being ultra-careful their hands didn't brush in the process. 'Thank you,' she said again, in an excess of politeness to cover how she was crying in her heart that it had come to this. She feigned a yawn. 'I'm so tired, can't wait to get inside.' She'd been about to add *and out of this dress* but stopped herself in time.

'You left your uniform in my villa the other night,' he said. 'The top, the sash and the sarong.'

Nikki snatched her hand to her mouth. 'How careless of me. The housekeepers would have seen it and drawn their own conclusions.' She groaned. 'So much for being discreet.'

'They couldn't have seen it. I packed it away in my suitcase in my closet to keep it hidden until you came back.'

'Good idea,' she said. She would just leave the clothing there. Maya could retrieve it after she'd left.

'I could bring it out to you,' he said.

'That won't be necessary,' she said.

'Or you could come into my villa and get it,' he said.

'I… I don't think so.' She couldn't bear to be alone with him in the privacy of those high walls.

She looked up and finally caught his gaze, intensely blue in the fading light of the day. 'Please come in, Nikki,' he said. 'Please.'

CHAPTER TWELVE

Nikki took a deep breath to steady herself. Now would be as good a time as any to tell him she intended to fly back to Sydney tomorrow evening. After all, he hadn't actually done anything wrong. She had simply decided not to accept the terms he was offering. Her choice. They should part on civilised terms.

Mutely, she nodded.

She followed him through the courtyard and into his villa. He closed the door and stood with it behind him, facing her. 'I missed you, Nikki. Every minute you were away I missed you. This place was so empty without you. I know you were angry with me. I was—'

Her carefully rehearsed explanation of why she was going fled from her mind. 'I missed you too,' she said, something she had had no intention of admitting. 'Every second I wished you were with me. I couldn't sleep for thinking about you. Yearning for you. But I can't do a no-strings fling, Max. And I actually don't see at this stage what's stopping us from treating this like a normal boy-meets-girl scenario. Okay, so we want to avoid media intrusion, keep things private. We're on the same page there.'

'Yes,' he said vehemently with a curse that told her exactly what he thought of the media.

'But we're both single. Free to see whoever we want. We've both been burned before in other relationships. I… I'm scared of getting hurt again. I admit I have trust issues. But I also really enjoy being with you. More than any other man I've ever met. A few days here has established that. If we like each other why—?'

'Can't we just date and see where it leads to?'

'I was going to say why hedge ourselves with restrictions like one night but you said it better. I deserve better than to be seen as a no-strings fling to be picked up then discarded. And so do you.'

He looked at her quizzically. 'That's not the kind of thing a girl usually says to a guy. That he deserves more than a passing encounter.'

'I mean it. But if you still don't think you can fit a meaningful relationship into your new life after tennis, then say goodbye for good now.'

Their gazes held for a long moment. The hunger she saw in his eyes was surely reflected in hers. She swayed towards him. All thoughts fled her mind except how much she wanted him. *Max*.

'I don't want to say goodbye,' he said.

He kissed her and she kissed him back without hesitation. They skipped the tender, questing kind of warm-up kiss and went straight to demanding and urgent. He bunched her hair in his hand and tugged to tilt her face upward to deepen the kiss. The tug on her hair should have hurt but it didn't. It thrilled her. *He* thrilled her.

Pent-up desire ignited and flamed through her. He pulled away from the kiss, to say something, she thought. But there had been enough words. She pressed her mouth back against his to silence him, slipped her tongue between his lips, demanded more. She slid her arms under his shirt, around his waist to hold warm, bare skin. He slid his hands down her shoulders past the curves of her breasts to hold her bottom. Her nipples tightened and tingled and she pressed her body close to his. Close, closer, not close enough. *She wanted more.*

She murmured deep in her throat. Pleasure, want, hunger. He groaned and held her closer. She stepped back, trying to drag him in the direction of the bedroom but she met an immovable wall of muscle. Then he propelled her forward. Then they were stumbling towards his bedroom, laughing when they bumped into the wall and knocked a wooden carving askew, laughing when they got tangled up in the mosquito net, laughing when they met a recalcitrant zipper or tore off a button in their haste to strip each other of their clothes.

'This would be so much easier if we were wearing sarongs,' she murmured in mock complaint.

'Or a towel and a pink bikini,' he said.

Then their laughter slowed to murmurs and sighs and moans as they explored each other's wants and needs.

Nikki woke up and thought for a moment she was in her own bed in her own villa. The bed was identical. Same mosquito-net canopy. Same ceiling fan with cane blades flicking languorously around. What was different was the warm male body next to her, hand resting possessively on her thigh. Max. *Her lover.*

And what an awesome lover he was. Passionate, energetic, inventive. Not to mention thoughtful and considerate. They had seemed to instinctively know what pleased each other. After their first time together, they had fallen asleep in each other's arms. It was dark when they'd woken, ravenous, and ordered pizza from room service. *Nasi goreng* didn't seem quite the thing to eat in bed.

He'd then fulfilled all her built-up fantasies of him— and she his—in his open-air bathroom as they'd showered together. When they eventually fell asleep again it was the deep sleep of the totally exhausted.

Now shafts of sunlight were filtering through the blinds, picking up the gold in Max's beard, the fine hair on his chest and legs. Heaven knew what time it was.

She stretched out her satisfied, pleasurably aching body. Max lay asleep on his back beside her, his limbs sprawled across the bed in the same confident possession of space that had become so familiar. His hand stayed on her thigh and she tentatively covered it with hers.

She didn't think she had ever felt happier. She wanted this. Wanted *him*. There was no use in denying it any further. *She was falling in love with him.*

The first thing Max saw when he woke was Nikki smiling into his face. She lay next to him, her head turned to his. With her hair dishevelled and spread across the pillow, dark smudges of make-up under her eyes, her lips swollen from his kisses, she had never looked more beautiful. She was naked and unselfconscious, her lovely body gilded with sunlight.

He noted with a stab of guilt slight marks from his fingers on the smooth skin of her thighs. But he remembered when he'd given them to her and she hadn't been complaining. A fierce possessiveness surged through him. She was perfect in every way. *She was his.*

'Hey, you,' he said, dropping a kiss on her mouth.

'Hey to you too,' she said, nipping on his lower lip.

'This is nice,' he said, knowing the words were grossly inadequate to express how he felt.

'Yes,' she said, and he knew he didn't need the words. 'Do I wish we'd done this the first night we knew we wanted to do it?'

'Do you?'

'No. It wouldn't have been the same.'

'I think I could have been okay with it that first night,' he said. In fact he knew so. He had wanted her from the get-go. 'But I want more.'

'Now?' she said, wiggling closer to him.

He stroked the fine strands of her hair back from where they were falling across her face. 'Yes,' he said, immediately ready for her. 'But what I meant was I want this to continue. Us, I mean.' He laughed. 'I'm not very good at this. If I was sixteen I'd say I want you to be my girlfriend.'

'That's not a bad way of putting it even for a thirty-year-old,' she said. 'I know exactly what you mean. I'd like to be your girlfriend.' She stroked his face with delicate fingers from his cheekbone to the corner of his mouth. 'Very much so.'

'I want to enjoy all the time we can have together here and then afterwards. What are your plans? I could try to get up here as often as possible, but it would be easier if we were in the same city. Sydney, I mean. For the fore-seeable future anyway.' If he took the sports announcer job he could be based anywhere. But rather than thinking he had to make those decisions on his own, he realised with a surprising sense of relief he might make them with Nikki. Make a decision based on what she wanted as well as his own needs.

'I was talking about that with my friends last night,' she said. 'Me moving back to Sydney, I mean. Going back to my old life.' Her voice trailed away and he realised she was still nervous about going home.

'Not quite the same old life with a new boyfriend,' he said.

Her eyes brightened. The way the green seemed to appear among the brown at different times continued to fascinate him. 'What an exceedingly appealing thought,' she said, her lips curving into a luminescent smile. 'That makes me much happier about going home—sooner rather than later.'

'Good,' he said. Later he might broach the subject of her coming back on the same flight as him. That and the other vexed topic of how they would handle being seen together in the public eye. Perhaps he could talk to his publicist about making a media announcement, keeping the public perception of his relationship with Nikki under his control.

But right now she was snuggling close to him and pressing a trail of little kisses across his chest and up towards his mouth. Thoughts of an entirely different nature took over and he rolled Nikki over so he could kiss her back. She wound her arms around his neck and whispered exactly what she'd like to do to him. Who was he to resist?

CHAPTER THIRTEEN

WHEN NIKKI NEXT woke, the sun was seriously bright in Max's bedroom and her mobile phone was vibrating all over the bedside table. Blearily she reached out to get it, blinked herself awake when she noticed the number of messages, both voicemail and text, that had come in.

Alarmed, she sat up in bed, now wide awake. Was something wrong back home?

She opened the urgent text from her sister.

Nikki, you need to look at this. Then call me.

With fingers that were suddenly unsteady, Nikki clicked on the link to the website of a popular tabloid newspaper. The words screamed up at her: *'Runaway bride and traitor best man enjoy raunchy romp in tropical love nest!'*

For a shocked second she thought it was a rehash of the 'secret Fiji love nest' beat-up that had run six months ago. Then she focussed on the photos that ran below the headline. And had to swallow against the nausea that rose in her throat.

The photos had been taken here on this island. Recently. The main shot was a zoomed-in image of her and

Max kissing in the laneway outside the sunset restaurant, her blue dress rucked up and exposing an indecent amount of bare thigh as well as bare back. The kiss was hungry and passionate—as indeed it had been. But the way the image had been cropped made it look seedy.

The next one was another of her with Max, their heads very close together, smiling intimately at each other at the restaurant table. They looked like lovers. In fact it was captioned *'The Look of Love?'* Under any other circumstance Nikki would think it beautiful and want a copy.

The final shot was of her and Max, shoulders touching, wading out of the water together at Frangipani Bay, she in her high-cut red swimsuit and the tight black swim shirt that, when wet, revealed every curve and indent of her body. Max was wearing just his black swim shorts, the rest of his magnificent body bare and glistening with drops of water. She was laughing up at him as if she was besotted. That one was captioned *'Hot Stuff!'*

And of course, under those photos, there was an old one of Max running away from the church, carrying her in his arms.

Other captions referred to Max's tennis career: *'Tennis star not too injured to enjoy sexy tryst with friend's fiancée!'* was the only one she could bear to read.

She closed her eyes but it was all there in front of her when she opened them again and she was plunged back into the nightmare she'd thought she'd left behind. *Dear heaven, how had this happened?*

She scrolled down her messages. They were from other friends alerting her to the article. Reporters asking for comments. Her father demanding to know what the hell was going on.

She gagged as she forced herself to read through the rest of the story, under the byline of *'Our reporter on Lembongan Island'*. She and Max had let themselves believe they'd had privacy in this out-of-the-way place. How naive they'd been.

Beside her, Max stirred. Looking over to his side of the bed, she could see his phone was flashing with messages too.

He opened his eyes. Smiled at her as if it was the happiest thing ever for him to find her there in his bed. But her expression must have told him something was wrong. He sat up. 'You okay?' he asked, wary.

Nikki shook her head, fighting tears. She wanted to scream and cry and shout. But she managed a choked, 'Not okay.' Without another word, she handed him over her phone open at the offending article.

'Why have the bridesmaid when the best man snagged the bride?' was another headline.

Oh, it was awful. What was beautiful between them was now being made to look sleazy. But at least this time they could face the media united as a couple.

Max's face darkened as he read. He cursed. Threw her phone on the bed. Then scowled. 'Your friend Sammie.' He spat out the words. 'Some friend she is. How did you let this happen, Nikki? I thought you said you could trust her.'

'You think this is Sammie? This isn't her. She's not that type of journalist. It's some tourist with a smart-phone. Everyone is a paparazzi these days. He—the photo credit is a he, probably a fake name—most likely recognised you then realised who I must be. Then he's stalked us. Taken the opportunity to make some cash to fund his vacation by selling the photos to the trashy tabloid. They've then got some desk hack to cobble together an article.'

She picked up her phone from where Max had thrown it and scrolled through some more. 'Thank heaven he didn't get behind our courtyard walls.'

Max glared at her. 'Only because I stopped your friend from coming over here.'

'That's ridiculous,' she said.

Nikki pulled the sheet up over her breasts. Felt uncomfortable in front of him now when she'd been so uninhibited all night.

'Is it? You shouldn't have talked to a journalist, Nikki.'

She gritted her teeth. 'This has got nothing to do with me talking to Sammie.'

'She could have shared her information with a mate on the tabloid. These photos were taken with a long-distance lens. A professional camera.'

'Smartphones can have adjustable lenses. I'm telling you this is an opportunistic amateur trying to make a tidy sum from invading our privacy.'

Max swung his legs over and sat on the edge of the bed, his bare back to her. He muttered an inventive string of curses. 'You'd better get back to your own villa now this has hit the fan.'

'What? You're kicking me out?'

He turned to her. 'We don't want your "opportunistic tourist" seeing us like this.' He cursed again. 'Don't you see how bad this is? Last time, the media could lie all it liked but I knew the truth. I had behaved with honour. Now it looks like I ran away with you for a quick—'

'Don't say it. That disrespects me. And you. How do you think I feel about this? It's always worse for the woman. My father will be spitting. My sister is upset too.'

'My parents won't like it either. They wouldn't see this as honourable behaviour. Even though my father didn't particularly like Alan when we played tennis together all those years ago.'

'Actually it was an honourable thing you did by helping me escape what would almost certainly have been a disastrous marriage. This interest in us is only because you're a celebrity. You're news. I'm not. *Any* female "frolicking" with Max Conway would be news.'

'The way you look in the red swimsuit makes you news,' he said through obviously gritted teeth. 'And good publicity for your swim school.'

'Are you serious? You can't mean that?'

'Of course not,' he muttered. But she was shocked he could even think it.

'Max, can I be the voice of reason here? This is awful. I'm not saying it's anything less than despicable that these people have tried to drag our names through the mud. But we actually haven't done anything wrong. Nothing underhand or sordid. The wedding was six months ago. Alan has moved on to more profitable pastures. So we met when you helped me run away? Big deal. Isn't that what the movies call "a cute meet"?' The stubborn set of his face told her she wasn't getting through to him. 'Viewed through a different lens, I might have thought the way we met and then reconnected by accident on this beautiful island was…was romantic.'

He picked up his phone and groaned. 'There's nothing vaguely romantic about *"Tennis star not too injured to enjoy sexy tryst with friend's fiancée!"'*

With what seemed to Nikki like morbid interest, Max continued to scroll through the story. 'The comments from readers are even worse.' He cradled his head in his hands.

'Well, don't read them,' she said. 'I didn't.'

He didn't seem to notice when she tiptoed around the bed, still wrapped in the sheet, to retrieve her dress, then her panties and bra from where Max had tossed them on the floor last night.

She ran into the bathroom with her clothes clutched to her front. Quickly she slipped into her underwear, then pulled her crumpled linen dress on over her head. She wet a tissue and wiped away the worst of her mascara panda eyes. Then dragged Max's comb through her hair. Her worst fear—one she didn't dare share with Max—was that there would be photographers waiting outside Max's villa hoping to catch her leaving in a morning-after-the-night-before 'walk of shame'. As Sydney was two hours ahead of Lembongan in time difference, and the news mightn't have hit here yet, she might be lucky.

Max barred her way at the doorway from the bedroom. Standing there stark naked, he looked so magnificent she had to force herself not to stare. Not to take him by the hand and lead him back to the bed. But she was beginning to doubt whether she actually wanted to be his girlfriend. A good relationship needed more than good sex. Like trust. Particularly trust.

'Where are you going?'

'You told me to get next door and so I am.'

If he let her slink out there by herself without him by her side to support her, it was over.

'I'm not sure that's a good idea,' he said. 'There might be more of those leeches out there.'

She glared at him. 'Max, what's wrong with this picture? We should be dealing with this together. Instead you're blaming me.'

'I didn't say that.'

'You're refusing to believe I didn't slip an exclusive to my journalist friend.'

'You must admit the timing of her visit is suspicious.'

'We went to that sunset restaurant on Thursday evening. She and her boyfriend didn't fly into Bali until Friday afternoon. She, or her boyfriend, couldn't possibly have taken those photos. Besides, she writes serious stuff for quality media, not tabloid rubbish. It might have been someone in that group of people who brushed past us in the laneway. It could have been anyone with a smartphone.'

He brandished his phone. 'There's a lot of good publicity for Big Blue in this article. According to it, the resort is a perfect place for a "raunchy romp".'

'As it turned out, it actually was perfect for that purpose.' She caught his eye. If he laughed she'd give him more credit on his trust account. He didn't laugh. 'But surely you're not pinning any of this on Maya or Kadek?'

He paused for a second too long. 'Of course not.'

She screwed up her face in what she hoped he would recognise as a look of loathing. 'Not in a million years would they do this to me.' Not content with calling her, in not so many words, a liar, now he was casting slurs on the honesty of the most scrupulously honest people she knew. He was right back there with the wounding words, one stab for her and two more on behalf of her friends.

'Not them, but perhaps someone on the staff.'

'I didn't realise you were so stubborn,' she said. 'We're victims here, me as much as you.'

'Tenacious is how my game was described,' he said. 'I won't give up until I find out who did this to us.'

Did this to *you*, she thought. He didn't seem to give a damn about the effect on her. She was surprised to realise how self-centred Max was. How gutted she was to realise it. When she thought back to it, this...this *affair*—because she now realised that was all it was— had been all about him. His need for privacy, his need to re-establish himself. He hadn't uttered one word of comfort to her. All she wanted was for him to take her in his arms and tell her they were in this together and he was by her side. *Wasn't going to happen.*

'I told you trust is important to me. You don't believe I'm telling the truth. Can you imagine how painful it is for me to be considered a liar? You don't trust me. And I can't trust you to support me. You deal with this in your own way. I'll deal with it in mine.'

She marched to the door outside to the courtyard. Hoped he might follow her. Realised that would be impossible as he didn't have a stitch on. If there was indeed a photographer lurking, Max Conway naked after 'lusty night with busty blonde' would be the money shot of that photographer's career.

She couldn't look back. If she managed to get on a plane tonight that might be the last time she saw Max and she didn't want him to see the tears that she could no longer stop from cascading down her cheeks. Once again she had totally misjudged the true character of a man she had fallen for. She was disappointed in herself as much as him. She'd really thought he was everything she wanted.

CHAPTER FOURTEEN

MAX IMMEDIATELY REALISED he had made one of the worst mistakes of his life. Nikki had hit him with the news of the latest media outrage as he'd woken up from a new and improved version of the 'Nikki in the blue dress' dream. Nikki had been in the church wearing the blue dress but not for a wedding rehearsal. She'd been holding a baby in her arms and they were there for a christening. At first it was black-haired baby Putu with Nikki but then, in the way of dreams, the baby morphed into a blond-haired baby that looked just like Max's baby photos. His baby.

His and Nikki's baby.

In his dream, she'd held their baby out to him and he'd been overjoyed, which was odd as he wasn't at all comfortable with holding babies. That was probably why he woke up. But he'd been only half awake. Awake enough to register the joy of finding Nikki naked in his bed, asleep enough to be about to murmur, *Did we have a boy or a girl?* Then her real-life expression had alerted him to the fact that something was very wrong.

He'd overreacted big-time to what he'd seen on her phone. Thinking on his feet had stood him in good stead on the tennis court. But it had let him down badly here.

Worse, he'd been unable to let go of the idea that Nikki had somehow contributed to the disaster through her journalist friend, Sammie. He'd just looked Sammie up to find what Nikki had said was true. She was a serious, award-winning journalist. Not only would she be unlikely to stoop to tabloid trash, he doubted she'd betray her friend. Nikki inspired loyalty from a group of long-term friends. He, having just asked her to be his girlfriend, had been guilty of stunning disloyalty in not believing her and supporting her. He'd virtually called her a liar.

Fact was, he'd been so determined to pin down the nearest scapegoat, because he knew who was really at fault. Him. As soon as he'd seen that photo of him kissing Nikki in that laneway he'd known the whole disaster had been because of him. In spite of his past history with the tabloids he had been so enchanted with her he'd let down his guard. He had given in to the impulse to kiss her in that laneway even though there had been people about. And as such, he'd failed to protect her. It was that photo that had led to the others. To some creep stalking his lovely Nikki.

The other fact was he simply was not used to thinking as a couple. What had Ellen accused him of being? *'Max first, Max last, and Max in between.'* That might have been true then, when his entire focus had been on his game. But it shouldn't be now. He'd gone into his default protect-his-reputation-at-all-costs mode as soon as he'd seen those scurrilous headlines—so like the headlines that had plagued him before. It was like when he'd got completely immersed in 'the zone' before a game. No one could reach him once he'd reached that state.

But he wasn't playing competitive tennis any more. He'd zoned out and been impervious to the common-sense explanations that Nikki had repeatedly tried to get him to accept. Worse, he had hurt her. Hurt the woman he had realised was vital to his future happiness. Possibly scuppered his chances to make any kind of life with her.

He had to find her. Apologise. Explain. Make amends.

He quickly showered and headed next door. She wasn't there. Or was refusing to acknowledge him. He sounded the chimes. Shouted into the intercom. Even gave an impatient kick to the heavy carved wooden door. Which wasn't a good idea when he was wearing flip-flops.

Kadek approached from the boardwalk just in time to see him kick the door. 'Sorry, Kadek, I'll pay for any damage,' Max said immediately.

Kadek looked amused. 'You're more likely to damage your foot than that door,' he said. Max could hardly look the guy in the eye. Kadek had invited him to dinner at his house the night Nikki had stayed in Sanur. And in return he had included him in his list of suspects. He had a lot of amends to make.

'If you're looking for Nikki, I saw her heading down to the beach. She said she was taking a kayak out.' Thankfully Kadek didn't mention any media reports. He'd see them soon enough, if he hadn't already. Something good might come of it if it helped put Big Blue more on the map for potential guests.

Wayan was on the beach when Max got there. He confirmed Nikki had taken out a kayak. Even though he had warned her that the currents might be unpredictable today. He pointed out to Max where she'd gone.

Shading his eyes against the sun, Max could see

Nikki in her red swim shirt and yellow life jacket paddling to the headland at the south end of the beach. *What the hell was she doing?* Around that headland were wild surf beaches, including the beach at the sunset restaurant. He recalled with a shudder how those waves had pounded against the limestone cliffs. Even in a special surf kayak it would be highly dangerous.

Nikki. She seemed very small in a very big sea out there by herself. As he watched, she disappeared out of sight around the headland.

Max ran to Wayan. 'Let me have your boat,' he said.

Within minutes he was heading out after Nikki in Wayan's *jukung.* As he neared the headland the currents came at him from all directions, buffeting the boat. Nobody should be in a kayak in these waters. Fear gripped his gut.

He gunned the motor. The boat surged through the water. He had to get to her. Had to make sure she was safe. Had to tell her…had to tell her so many things. How sorry he was. How much he regretted the way he'd behaved, not just this morning, but since he'd been on the island. How he'd let his loathing of the media make him hide her, as if she were some guilty secret, instead of shouting to the world how lucky he was to have this beautiful, perfect woman in his life. How blind he'd been to place her behind his career plans instead of putting her first. First in *everything.* Most of all he had to tell her how much— Max stopped his crazy flow of thoughts as the truth hit him harder that the most powerful wave. *How much he loved her.*

Love. He'd tried to deny to himself that he had fallen in love with her. But he'd been kidding himself from the word go. He'd fallen a little in love with her as far

back as her wedding rehearsal. That was another reason
he'd overreacted to the media interest in them. Deep
down, when he'd helped her run away from her wedding, hadn't part of his heart wished he were running
away with her for himself?

That was what all the dreams had been telling him—
his subconscious shouting out to him what his conscious
mind refused to acknowledge. *He loved Nikki Lucas.*

He rounded the first headland, scanning the water
for her. Nothing. Not even other small craft. Sensible
people did not go out in this kind of current. Why had
Nikki?

The current got stronger, the water choppier; he had
to fight with the steering wheel to keep the boat on
course as he rounded the next set of jagged cliffs.

He saw the oar first. A lone paddle floating on the
surface, pulled inextricably by the water towards where
it would be smashed against the rocks. So close it wasn't
safe for him to retrieve it. In the next split second he
saw Nikki. Lying draped across the hull of her capsized
kayak. She was very, very still. Injured? Unconscious?
Worse? *No!*

He hit the gas so hard the boat reared up out of the
water. 'Nikki!' he shouted, the word reverberating
around the empty sea.

As he neared her, she lifted her head. 'Max. Thank
heaven,' she gasped. Her face was pale, which made
the blood trickling down her mouth seem shockingly
red in contrast.

He manoeuvred the boat as close as he could get to
her. Fear strangled his voice. 'I'm coming for you,' he
choked out.

'The kayak capsized. I tried to grab the hull to pull

it back over to me, like I've done a hundred times be-fore.' A choppy wave broke over the kayak, pushed it forward and splashed into her face, sending her slid-ing back into the sea. 'Aargh!' she spluttered. 'But that keeps happening.'

His first instinct was to dive overboard and get her. But that would leave them both bobbing in the ocean while Wayan's boat drifted away. 'Grab the outrigger,' he said as he manoeuvred the boat closer.

Nikki was an excellent swimmer. She was wearing a life jacket but she was bleeding. His gut roiled as he watched her wait for a lull in the choppy sea and then push herself forward until she was gripping the outrig-ger. He reached out to haul her in but she was just out of reach. He cursed. Then remembered the ladder. He quickly put it in place. 'Swim to the ladder,' he urged her.

Then he had her in his grasp as he pulled her on board. She was in his arms, wet, shaking, *alive*. He guided her onto the bench, where he sat next to her. 'You're bleed-ing,' he said, wiping the blood away from her chin.

'Am I?' she said, putting her hand up to her face. 'Oh. That. Bumped my nose. It's nothing. I'm fine.'

'Nothing!' Anger surged through his relief. 'I thought you'd drowned. What the hell were you thinking, com-ing out here by yourself? How many times did you warn me against it? Don't you ever do something so foolish again.'

Nikki stiffened and shuffled herself along the bench as far away from him as she could without toppling back into the water. As he manoeuvred the boat away from the rocks and back towards the shore, he realised with a chill that went right through to his heart that she wasn't just putting a physical distance between them.

'I'm glad you came along,' she said finally after what felt like hours of silence. They were nearly at the beach when she continued, 'Appreciate the help. But I don't owe you an explanation. Not as your ex-girlfriend of less than twenty-four hours' standing.'

'You're my ex-girlfriend before you've even had time to be my girlfriend?'

'Why would I want to be the girlfriend of a guy who calls me a liar, who refuses to listen to me, who can't act as a boyfriend-girlfriend team, who kicks me out of his room after we'd spent the night making love?'

As he hauled the boat onto the deserted beach, he moored it, finally turning to help her out of the boat. Her eyes were red-rimmed, her face splotchy. Not just with salt water. She'd been crying, crying for some time. Her words were tough but he could see the deep level of pain in her eyes. *He'd hurt her badly.* That was why she'd gone out there by herself. To get as far away from him as possible. *He'd lost her.*

But Max Conway didn't easily accept defeat. He waited until she stood beside him on the sand before finding the words he needed to say.

'Nikki, I'm sorry. You're right. I'm a rotten boyfriend who doesn't deserve you. I've been an idiot. Not just this morning but since the day I watched you step off that boat at Jungut Batu and wade back into my life. For too many stupid reasons I've handled this so badly.'

'Handled what, Max?' she said, her chin still held at a mutinous angle but her expression softened into wary anticipation.

'The fact I'm head over heels in love with you. That nothing else matters but that I'm with you. Not career, not reputation, nothing. That I fell in love with you that first night at the rehearsal of your wedding to another man. I had to deny it then. But I don't have to deny it now. I love you, Nikki.'

Nikki wondered if she'd been knocked unconscious by the edge of the kayak and was hallucinating. Perhaps she was still drifting along in that glorious sea, dreaming of what she wanted most in the world. That Max loved her.

Then she felt the touch of his hand on her arm. Saw the trepidation in his eyes as he waited for her response. *Max loved her.*

'Is there a chance you might love me too?' he said. 'Or is it only about the hot sex for you?'

Her joyous laughter pealed out across the empty beach. 'I love you too, Max.' He kissed her, warm and passionate and tender and *loving* all at the same time. 'And I love the hot sex too,' she murmured against his mouth. They kissed for a long time, each repeating those magical words 'I love you' with increasing wonderment and joy.

'When—?'

'Did I first fall in love with you?' she said. 'I realised I was attracted to you when you carried me away in your arms at the wedding. But here, on this island, on this sea, exploring the underwater paradise together, I realised it was so much more than that. When you kissed me at sunset I knew I was in love.'

'We wasted so much time,' he said.

'Only a few days, though it seems longer,' she said. 'Can we truly fall in love so quickly?'

He smiled. 'Thirty-two years ago my father spotted my mother across the hall at a country dance. He was smitten. Fortunately so was she. They married three months later and are still the happiest couple I know.'

Her breath caught. 'Do you take after your dad?'

'Definitely. I don't need more time. Will you marry me, Nikki?'

Her heart seemed to swell with her love for him. 'Yes, Max, yes.'

'I want to give you everything you want, Nikki. Marriage, children when you're ready. Most of all a husband you can trust to love you and care for you for the rest of our lives.'

'All I want is you,' she murmured through a suddenly constricted throat. 'Everything else will be a bonus.'

He kissed her again for a long time. She couldn't think of a more perfect proposal on the beautiful empty beach, with the vastness of the ocean stretched out before them, in this magical place where they'd each found their for ever love. That they were both wearing life jackets was something to tell the grandchildren.

He broke away from the kiss. 'Instead of hiding us from the media, I should have taken out an advert in that dreadful tabloid and screamed it out in tall black headlines: *"Best Man Loves Runaway Bride."* Only now I'd add, *"And Makes Her His Wife".*'

She laughed. 'Sounds like a plan,' she said, as she drew him to her for another kiss.

CHAPTER FIFTEEN

Three months later, Nusa Lembongan

THIS WEDDING WASN'T strictly their wedding. Nikki and Max had discovered it was legally more straightforward to actually get married in Australia and have the wedding blessed in Indonesia. But this was the place they'd fallen in love and the place they wanted to make a public declaration of their commitment to each other. With a big party to celebrate.

In Sydney, Nikki and Max had got married in the tiny chapel at her old school with just a handful of guests comprising family and their very closest friends, including Max's mother and father, who Nikki already adored. She'd had just her sister Kaylie as bridesmaid and Max's brother had been best man. Her father had given her away and she'd been surprised to see him shed a tear as he'd told her how much he wished her mother could have been here for her special day.

Now here she and Max were on the beach at Frangipani Bay under an arch covered with frangipani and gold-painted ceremonial flowers. She wore a long, white dress trimmed with handmade lace, her feet bare in the sand. Max wore white trousers and shirt, his feet bare too. Kaylie was bridesmaid again, along with Maya and Sammie.

The entire resort had been booked out for the guests they had flown up to the island. They included staff members from the residential tennis training college Max had started to give talented kids from underprivileged backgrounds the same opportunities to excel that he'd had. He'd told Nikki he was enjoying his involvement with it more than he could have imagined. But he got a different kind of satisfaction from his directorship of the sporting goods company. He had a team working on the swimwear for Nikki's first swim club, which was nearly ready to open its doors—already there'd been a lot of interest and advance bookings.

The wedding was being covered by the same classy magazine that had published the feature on Nikki and Max's romance to set their story straight, from the 'cute meet' as runaway bride and the best man, to the happy coincidence of their meeting again six months later on the island.

As they joyously repeated their vows, Max kept Nikki's hand firmly held in his. 'There's no way you're running away from this wedding,' he said.

'Why would I,' she said, looking up to his beloved face, 'when I'm already married to the best man?'

* * * * *

NINE MONTH COUNTDOWN

LEAH ASHTON

For Regan — who thinks all my heroes are based on him, but they're not.

You're my hero, though, baby.

I'm having so much fun sharing my happy-ever-after with you.

CHAPTER ONE

IT HAD STARTED exactly eleven steps down the aisle.

Ivy knew this, because she'd been counting.

Step, together *one*. Step, together *two*.

Generally the counting happened when she could feel the famous Molyneux temper bubbling away inside her. Or on the rare occasions she was nervous—although she couldn't remember the last time that had been. But today, it was neither of those things. The bride—her sister April—was the one who should be feeling anxious. Marriage wasn't something Ivy could see herself doing any time soon. She dated, occasionally, but never anything serious. Right now, her focus was on her work, and the family business, and everything else took a back seat. Because in Ivy's experience relationships had an irritating habit of leaching into everything. And when it came to her career, well—anything that could damage *that* was just not acceptable.

But anyway… She'd been walking down the aisle, happily aware that the crowd seated in rows of white wooden chairs were peering around her for a glimpse of the bride, when she'd *felt* it. At exactly step eleven.

Someone wasn't looking around her. Not at all. Someone was looking right at her, in a way that Ivy wouldn't have thought possible. In a way that had *weight*.

And it was so strange, and so unexpected, that Ivy even stopped counting.

But she didn't stop walking, and she didn't shift her gaze from exactly where she was heading: the celebrant, a pretty wooden trellis temporarily constructed on the exclusive Nusa Dua beach, and the cerulean blue of the Indian Ocean beyond. Because today she was April's chief bridesmaid, and she took any job that she was given seriously. Bridesmaid or Board Executive—it didn't matter. Work was work, and Ivy *always* lived by the idea that you should never do *anything* if you weren't going to do it right.

So she started counting afresh, and then made sure she completed her bridesmaid duties to the best of her ability.

But that weight didn't lift until well after April had kissed her new husband. In fact, it wasn't until April and Evan stood together to accept the hugs and well wishes of their guests that Ivy could *finally* openly search the crowd without fear of raising the ire of the videographer.

But by then it was too late. That heavy, heavy gaze was gone.

Much later—what seemed like *hours* of smiling for the photographer later—Ivy stood with her two sisters and the rest of the bridal party at the back of the enormous marquee that would host the wedding reception.

The luxury hotel their mother had booked for the occasion loomed four storeys high on three sides, hugging the marquee as it stared out to the ocean. A welcome whisper of a breeze skimmed Ivy's bare shoulders and pushed the silk of her full-length dress against her legs. It was still warm, but Bali's famous humidity appeared to have let up just a little. Regardless, a blonde make-up artist hovered amongst them, busily 'fixing' Ivy and her sisters before their big entrance. *Can't have your faces melting!*

Ivy shifted her weight rather than rolling her eyes—which reminded her once again that crazily expensive, handmade, bespoke heels did not guarantee comfort. Not even close.

The Balinese wedding planner was barking out instructions in a failed attempt at a stage whisper, but having reviewed the day's minute schedule—and provided a few useful suggestions—Ivy knew exactly where she should be. She strode over to Sean, Evan's best mate—and best man—and hooked her arm through his.

'Are we going in?' he asked. Beer in hand, he clearly wasn't taking his best-man duties as seriously as Ivy would've liked.

In fact, the music April had chosen for their entrance had started, so Ivy used her free hand to pluck the beer from Sean, and to hand it to the wedding planner.

'And we just follow them?' Sean asked as he watched Mila and Ed disappear into the marquee.

'You *were* at the rehearsal, right?' Ivy said, but she was smiling as she tugged Sean behind her.

Inside, the marquee opened up—it was only the rear wall that had, well, *a wall*. Otherwise it was edged with white fabric gathered curtain-like against each support. April's two-hundred-odd guests sat at white-draped tables topped with ivory flower arrangements amongst dozens of sparkling chandeliers—and beyond them, framed by the marquee like a postcard, was the ocean. Of course, a Molyneux wedding would never be anything less than spectacular—but even Ivy was impressed. And timing their entrance *just* as the sun began to sink beneath the darkening blue of the ocean? Perfect.

Ivy was about halfway to the bridal table when she realised she was counting her steps again.

Thirty-two. Thirty-three. Thirty-four...

But this time it annoyed her. Maybe it was the distraction of...of whatever it was she thought she'd felt during the ceremony—or maybe it was just that it kind of made sense that she'd be a bit tense while walking down the aisle, given her feelings about love and relationships. So counting her steps then had been okay.

But now? No, it wasn't acceptable. Because now she recognised why she was doing it.

She *was* nervous. The way her stomach was flip-flopping all over the place made that crystal-clear.

Why?

She was used to having so many eyes on her. How many times had she been the spokesperson for Molyneux Mining? She had years of media training behind her. She'd been interviewed on live television, and she'd been splashed all over the newspapers—accurately and otherwise—her entire life.

So, yes, nineteen-year-old Ivy counted her steps *all* the time. Twenty-seven-year-old Ivy a hell of a lot less. Now, *thirty-one*-year-old Chief Operating Officer of Molyneux Mining Ivy shouldn't need to do it at all.

Thirty-one-year-old Ivy was an accomplished, confident—*powerful*, some might say—*grown-up*. Counting steps was just…juvenile.

Fifty-seven. Fifty-eight. Fifty—

'What did I do?' Sean asked as he pulled out her spindly chair at the long bridal table.

Ivy blinked. 'Pardon?'

'You just told me to "Stop it".' He looked at her curiously. 'With some force.'

'I didn't,' she said, very quickly. Then sat down and fussed needlessly with her silverware as Sean took his own seat.

Ignoring Sean's gaze, Ivy looked up to watch April glide across the marquee, arm in arm with her new husband—and both with stars in their eyes.

Her little sister had never looked more beautiful: like a princess with her blonde hair piled up high, and the oversized skirt of her dress floating about her like a cloud.

Ivy couldn't help but smile, the ridiculous mystery of the

step counting put aside for the moment. She was so happy for April. Today was her dream come true.

Slowly she relaxed into her chair, allowing that inexplicable tension to ease from her body.

And it was right about then—right about when she decided that *yes*, it was totally fine to slide her heels off beneath the privacy of the long table cloth—that she felt it again.

That look. *That* heavy concentration of attention that made the back of her neck prickle, but other parts of her… tingle. And Ivy was not one for superfluous *tingling*.

But this time there was nothing stopping her from looking up—from searching the crowd for this person, for this…

Man.

There he was, on the opposite side of the parquet dance floor. With his close-cropped hair, and the broadest of broad shoulders, Ivy would've guessed he was in the military, even if she hadn't already known he was.

Angus. His name was Angus…Something. She remembered his name had stood out amongst April's seating plan and guest list—a name she didn't recognise, and who April also didn't know. An old school friend of Evan's: *All I know is that he's a soldier,* April had whispered with some awe, *one of those special ones. SAS.*

Amongst a million other wedding-planning things to do—and a million more work-related concerns—she hadn't given the mysterious Angus Somebody another thought.

But right now, the man had somehow taken up *all* her thoughts. And when their gazes finally connected—when she could truly *see* all that remarkable intensity—it was almost as if he'd taken over her body, too. Her skin was hot. Her mouth was dry.

And from this distance, she couldn't even see the colour of his eyes.

Oh, God. What would happen if he was close enough for her to see if they were blue, or green, or grey?

Based on her current reaction, she'd most likely burst into flames.

No.

Now she was being silly. He was just a man, just a guest at the wedding.

Just a distraction she didn't need.

She was April's chief bridesmaid. And she was Chief Operating Officer of Molyneux Mining. Neither of those things were conducive to gazing like a lust-crazed idiot across the dance floor at her sister's wedding.

Yet she was still doing exactly that.

And just as she was sternly telling herself that it really wasn't that hard to look elsewhere...*anywhere*...but at *him*...

Something happened.

He winked.

Angus Barlow always knew what he was doing. He was measured, methodical, structured. Calm. Not easily distracted, or swayed by others.

So he'd known what he'd been doing when his gaze had first collided with Ivy as she'd walked down that aisle. He'd been having a damn good look at a beautiful woman.

Her long black hair was looped and twisted up to leave her neck exposed above her bare shoulders. Her skin had glowed in the sunlight, and was still managing to do so now, even in the candlelit marquee without the help of the rapidly setting sun.

She had a great profile. A long, thin nose and a strong chin.

The sea breeze had done fabulous things to the pale purple dress she wore, plastering it hard against her curves as she'd walked. And if he'd continued to watch her rear

view, rather than turning to observe the bride's arrival—
well, Angus didn't really think anyone could blame him.

And now, hours later, he'd found himself again compelled to look at Ivy.

Angus supposed it could be argued that Ivy wasn't the
most beautiful woman at the wedding. In fact, Angus had
heard that many considered her unlucky she didn't inherit
more of her father's movie-star looks, the way her two
younger sisters had. Although Angus couldn't agree. It
was true she did take more after her unusual mother—in
both looks and personality, given the way she was following exactly in her mother's business footsteps. But he liked
the angles to Ivy's face: the sharpness of her cheekbones,
the slant to her brows.

Plus he'd *really* liked the contrasting plump of her lips.
He'd never noticed before tonight, never really even looked
at the many photos of her that could be found in the paper,
or the footage of her on TV. But right now it seemed impossible he hadn't.

So yes, he did know what he was doing.

Right on cue, he felt a twinge in his bandaged right wrist,
as if to remind him at least partly *why* he was doing this.

Not why he was looking at Ivy Molyneux. But why he
was here, at this wedding, at all.

He wasn't supposed to be here, of course. He'd declined
the original invitation, only to break his wrist during a
training exercise in Darwin a month or so later.

So rather than where he *should* be, deployed with his
squadron in Afghanistan, he was at Evan's wedding. Surrounded by people who were part of a world he'd exited
so abruptly more than fifteen years earlier, and that he'd
truly not missed at all.

This was not his thing: an opulent, diamond-drenched
evening jammed full of the superficial and the vacuous.

He was on a singles table of sorts. His fellow guests

were a mixture of the different flavours of wealth he remembered from high school: old money, new money, and used-to-have money. Then there were the people aware of their luck and good fortune—and then those that were painfully, frustratingly oblivious. In his experience, most of the wealthy fell into the second category. But even then, they generally weren't bad people. Just not his type of people.

Ivy Molyneux was certainly not his type of people either. A billionaire heiress born into obscene wealth, how could she be anything but extraordinarily ignorant of what it was like to actually exist in the real world?

And yet that was the thing. Amongst the hundreds of faces here at this wedding, amongst all this glitz and glitter, when she'd met his gaze it had felt...

Real.

That he certainly hadn't expected.

That was why he hadn't looked away, and why his interest in her had become *much* more than a simple visual appreciation of a beautiful woman.

That was why he'd winked.

And Ivy's jaw had dropped open, then almost immediately snapped shut.

Then her eyes had narrowed, just before a near imperceptible shake of her head—and she'd turned her attention to the groomsman beside her, as if Angus no longer existed.

But somehow he knew, knew deep within his bones, that this wasn't even close to over.

It had taken considerable effort, but Ivy managed to avoid looking at Angus throughout her entire maid of honour speech. Thanks to years of practising public speaking, Ivy knew how to ensure the entire crowd felt she was talking directly to them. Unfortunately tonight the block of about five tables immediately surrounding Angus's might have felt rather ignored.

But, it couldn't be helped.

Not that the not looking helped a lot. Because he'd definitely just kept on looking at her.

She knew it, because her whole body felt his concentrated attention. It had only been sheer will that had prevented the stupid racing of her heart or the odd, inexplicable nerves that churned through her belly from impacting her voice. Honestly, she felt as though, if she let herself, she'd come over all soft and breathy and...*pathetic*.

But of course she hadn't, and April had given her the tightest of hugs after her speech, so that was a relief. That was all that mattered tonight, that April was happy.

Even her mother—on the parents' table in prime position near the cake—had lifted her chin in the subtlest of actions. Ivy had learnt long ago that that was about as effusive as Irene Molyneux ever got, so she'd take it.

With her formal duties out of the way, Ivy should now be able to relax for the remainder of the speeches. But of course she couldn't.

By the time dessert was served, and Evan had delivered his—hilarious by the reaction of the guests, even if Ivy registered barely a word—speech, Ivy was about to crawl out of her skin in frustration.

Finally the dancing began—and Ivy made her escape.

With the straps of her heels tangled in her fingers, the lawn outside the marquee was cool beneath her bare feet. She had to walk some distance before she could hear the ocean above the exuberant cacophony of music and voices of the reception.

The hotel gardens stretched along the beach from either side of the main hotel building. Lights dotted pathways that led to bungalows and villas, but they were all empty, with every guest at the hotel also a guest at the wedding.

And it felt empty, which Ivy appreciated. She'd flown in from London only...yesterday? No, the day before.

Ivy smiled—it was recently enough, anyway, that jet lag still had her confusing her days.

But after a series of intense business meetings, a thirty-six-hour journey from London after delays in Dubai, the madness that was the last-minute planning for the wedding, and then that disconcerting attention from Angus Whoever—Ivy was seriously happy to finally be *alone*.

She took a long, measured breath and waited for her muscles to relax as she exhaled.

But they didn't.

'Ivy.'

She spun around to confront the reason for the tension throughout her body. Angus wore a cream linen shirt, untucked, and dark knee-length tailored shorts—a variation of what the majority of male guests were wearing. Unlike the majority of male guests, he still managed what should be impossible—to look as if he was attending a wedding, rather than a barbeque. Maybe it was his posture? The extreme straightness of how he stood, combined with the way his clothing hung so perfectly from his muscular frame? Whatever it was, Ivy suspected he looked equally gorgeous taking out his garbage.

'You followed me,' she said.

He shrugged. 'You knew I would.'

Ivy's mouth dropped open. 'Don't be absurd.'

While his shirt was clearly visible in the limited light, the rest of him blurred into the darkness behind him, his face all angles and shadows. Even so, Ivy knew, *knew*, he was looking at her in disbelief.

'Look,' she said, in her no-nonsense work voice, 'I really don't have time for this.'

'This being?'

He really did have a fantastic voice. Deep and authoritative.

Not that it made any difference.

'*This,*' she said, waving her hands to encompass them both.

'I'm still confused,' he said. 'Can you elaborate?'

Ivy gave a little huff of frustration. 'I don't have time for whatever two random strangers might do when they meet at a wedding.'

And she didn't. It had been hours since she'd checked her email.

A laugh. 'C'mon, Ivy. I'm sure you can think up a far more interesting descriptor than *whatever.*'

'I could,' she said. 'But that would take more of my precious time. So—'

She was half a step towards the path when Angus's hand wrapped around her lower arm. He wore a light bandage that encircled his palm and extended halfway to his elbow, the fabric just the tiniest bit rough against her skin.

'Honey, *everyone* has time for...' his grip loosened and his fingers briefly traced a path across her wrist '...talking.'

Ignoring her body's traitorous shivery reaction to his touch, Ivy went on the defensive. 'This isn't just talking.'

But, of course, that was a mistake.

She sensed, rather than saw, his smile.

'No,' he said. 'That's the point, isn't it?'

Ivy shook her head, as if that would somehow help her brain reorganise itself. She was just...off. Unbalanced. If she was to walk away from him now, she'd be counting her steps, definitely.

'No,' she said. 'The point is there *is* no point. That's the point.' Seriously? Could she be any more ridiculous?

She tried again. 'You're not my type, Angus.'

The shadow of his smile told her immediately that she'd made a mistake. Now he knew she knew his name.

But standing so close to him, Ivy supposed she should be relieved she could speak at all. What did this man do to her?

'I don't believe you,' he said. As if that was that.

And then he surprised her by casually sitting on the sand. He leant right back on his elbows, his legs crossed at the ankles. 'Sit.'

Logic would've had her back at the marquee by now, so it came as no surprise that she found herself seated beside him. She sat more stiffly though, her hands rested on the silk skirt that covered her knees, her gaze firmly on the black of the ocean.

A big part of her knew she really needed to get back to the marquee. What if April needed her? Plus it really had been hours since she'd checked her email—maybe she could pop by her suite on the way back?

She'd levered herself onto her knees to stand when she felt Angus's hand on her arm. Electricity shot across her skin and she found herself completely still.

'Hey,' he said. 'We're supposed to be having a conversation, remember?'

'But, my emails—'

The man's laughter was loud, and strong and totally unexpected in the darkness.

'Emails? You're on a deserted tropical beach with a guy who is seriously attracted to you—and you're thinking about email? That cuts deep.'

Ivy smiled despite herself, and rearranged her legs so she was sitting again, his hand—unfortunately—falling away.

'You're seriously attracted to me?' she said.

'I'll take smug if it means no more talk of work.'

Ivy smiled again. 'Deal,' she said. For a long minute, she studied the ocean again. Her eyes had adjusted now, and she could just make out the occasional edge of foam along the crest of a wave.

Something had changed, Ivy realised. The stiffness in her shoulders had loosened. A tightness in her jaw was gone.

She couldn't say she was relaxed, not sitting beside this

man. But the tension she felt had shifted—maybe it was that her everyday tensions had lifted? Only to be replaced by another flavour of tension, but Ivy had to admit the tension that radiated between her and Angus was vastly, vastly preferable—no matter how uncomfortable it felt.

Uncomfortable, because she didn't know what to do with it. But also…different. Unfamiliar. Exciting.

She twisted to face him.

'Hi, I'm Ivy Molyneux,' she said.

'Angus Barlow.'

And she smiled. It had been an intense few days, so frantic that she'd barely acknowledged her beautiful surroundings.

For the first time, she really felt the beach sand beneath her toes. Felt the kiss of the ocean breeze.

She deserved a break, even if she didn't have time for a holiday.

And really, what was the harm of letting her guard down with a gorgeous, charming stranger, just for a few minutes?

Then she'd go check her email, and then back to the wedding.

Simple.

CHAPTER TWO

VERY CALMLY, IVY snapped the clear lid over the end of the test, and took a long, deep soothing breath.

She was sitting on the closed lid of a toilet. A very nice toilet in a very expensive Perth skyscraper, but a toilet, none the less. A public toilet.

This had been a very stupid idea.

Buying the test itself had seemed the rational thing to do this morning. Her driver, Simon, hadn't suspected a thing when she'd asked him to stop at a pharmacy on the way to her ten a.m. meeting. And even if he had wondered why Ivy Molyneux was bothering to run into a pharmacy for whatever lady thing he thought she needed—rather than asking one of her assistants—it wasn't as if he'd ask her.

Yet she'd still fidgeted in the back seat of the car as they'd driven away, as if Simon had X-ray vision and could see through the layers of her handbag and pharmacy paper bag should he glance in his rear-view mirror.

The plan had been to wait until she was home this evening. Safely alone in the privacy of her home in Peppermint Grove, where she could pee on a stick and irrationally stress and worry *alone* for the two minutes she was supposed to wait because—come on, it was *totally normal* to be two days late, even if that had never, ever, ever happened before...

Of *course* someone else had just walked into the bathroom, and now she had to wait in this excruciating state as she listened to the other woman pee—because it now seemed beyond her to look down, to look down at the test that by now would display the result.

The reality.

All she had to do was look down and this would all be over.

This *thing*, this *day*, this *moment* that she had not expected at all. *That* night seemed a lifetime ago. April was already back from her honeymoon. Ivy's work days had been as endless as ever and her weekends had been so blurred into her weeks that she'd barely noticed them. Life had gone on. She'd gone on, just as normal. That night—that *totally out of character* night—was long behind her. She hadn't given it, or Angus, another thought.

Well, barely. Maybe, just maybe, when she'd been in that space between wake and sleep when her brain finally emptied of all things Molyneux Mining, *maybe* she'd let herself remember. Remember the way her skin had shivered when Angus had looked at her. The way her heart had zipped to a million beats a minute when he'd finally touched her. How she'd felt in his arms. How *he'd* felt beneath her fingertips.

How it had *all* felt. To do that. To do something so crazy, so uninhibited, so...

Reckless.

The toilet flushed beside her, then footsteps, and then the cubicle door closed. The basin had some silly sensor arrangement to turn on, and Ivy had to wait as the other woman tried to work it out, and then listen to her jump and giggle when the water finally gushed out.

Just go. Just go, just go, just go.

But also just stay. Stay, stay, stay for ever, so she never had to look down, never had to know.

But then she wasn't into delaying things, was she? That was why she was here, in this public toilet, holding the test.

Because she couldn't wait. Couldn't even wait until her

ten a.m. meeting was over. She'd excused herself mid meeting, and now she'd taken way, way too long.

The bathroom door clicked shut, and Ivy was finally alone amongst all this marble and the softest of background music.

And now she had to look down.

And now she couldn't lie to herself that she was just being silly, and that there was *nothing* to worry about, and that she was on the pill and even if she couldn't be sure she hadn't forgotten a pill amongst all the time zones and delays on the way to April's wedding that surely the odds were *still* in her favour. Because people tried to do this for *years* and it didn't work. People who were trying, people who wanted this, people…

Two pink lines.

She'd looked down only to confirm what she already knew. What she'd known deep down for the past two-hundred-odd minutes since the absence of her period had suddenly dawned on her.

She was pregnant.

She was pregnant.

Ivy took a deep, audible breath, and willed the tears in her eyes to go still. Then she stuffed the test back into its box, back into its pharmacy paper bag and back into her handbag.

Then she went back to the meeting with her business face on and no one—she hoped liked hell—was the wiser.

No, only one person knew that Ivy Molyneux's life had just completely fallen apart.

And unfortunately, that number would soon have to increase to two.

Angus's feet pounded on the heavy rubber of the treadmill, his breaths coming slow and regular.

Sweat had long ago soaked his grey T-shirt black, and

the muscles of his calves and thighs had given up protesting and now simply burned.

This was the bit he loved. This time after he'd conquered the arguments from both his brain and body and simply *kept on going.*

He'd been like this since his late teens, since the sudden death of his father. He'd gone for his first run immediately after his mum had told him the terrible news—an impossibly long run fuelled by intense, raging grief. And that run had triggered a near addiction that had him craving the adrenalin rush of exercise, craving the burn, and craving the pain.

He had no issue admitting that one of the reasons he'd joined the army was so he could be paid to reach this high. On some days he couldn't believe his luck that he earned his living effectively living out many a childhood fantasy—the helicopters, the firearms, the boats, the tactical training...

Angus shook his head as he ran, shifting his focus back to his body.

Running on a treadmill was not his preference. Here in the gym at the barracks, he'd much rather be lifting weights, or, even better, completing a punishing PT session with the rest of his squadron.

But when it came down to it, the method was irrelevant. Winning the battle over his body was what mattered. Especially now, especially while injured.

Technically he was on medical leave, but clearly losing physical condition wasn't an option in his job. He'd been down at the barracks daily, excluding that weekend in Bali. Even there he'd made locating the hotel gym a priority.

Except the morning after the wedding. That morning he'd slept in.

Despite the sweat and the screaming of his muscles, Angus grinned.

Ivy must have worn him out.

He reached out to slow the speed on the treadmill, reducing his pace from near sprint down to a brisk walk as he cooled down.

It wasn't the first time the beautiful billionaire had popped into his head. It surprised him. There had been no question as to what that night had been. Neither he nor Ivy wanted anything beyond those few...admittedly incredible...hours on that beach.

Angus smiled again as he remembered the way Ivy had taken charge as they'd walked back to the hotel.

If anyone asks—I was in my suite, working.

He'd grinned then, too. *And how would I know that?*

She'd just glared at him, and protested silently when he insisted on walking her to her room. He had, of course, checked that no one would see them.

He wasn't a total jerk, after all.

Although kissing her on her doorstep had not been gentlemanly—or planned.

He'd seen it in her eyes—and felt it in her body—that she'd been about to invite him in. But she hadn't.

And he would've declined, anyway. He was sure.

It was for the best.

In his experience, keeping things simple was always for the best.

Later, after his shower and as he walked across the car park, he felt his phone vibrating in the backpack slung over his shoulder. Automatically he fished it out, then, on seeing it was an unknown number, considered for a moment whether he should bother answering.

Work-related numbers weren't stored on his phone, of course—but then, no one was going to be calling him while he was on leave.

But could it be to do with his mum?

So he answered it, if a bit gruffly, and was certainly not

expecting the contradictory soft but firm—and *familiar*—female voice he heard.

'Is that Angus Barlow?'

'Ivy Molyneux,' he replied, and then smiled when she gave a little sound of surprise.

'Uh—yes,' she said. A pause. 'I asked Evan for your number.'

She was nervous, her words brisker than normal.

'That wasn't very discreet,' he said.

Hell, it didn't bother him. Ivy could've announced the fact they'd had sex on the beach to the whole wedding reception and he wouldn't have cared.

But he knew she did.

Unease prickled at the back of his neck.

'No, it wasn't discreet at all,' Ivy said, her words pancake flat.

Then there was a long, long pause.

'Why did you call me, Ivy?' He *was* gruff now.

She cleared her throat. 'Are you free tonight?' she asked, much more softly.

Relief washed over him. He'd continued walking as they'd been talking, and now he propped a shoulder against the side of his black SUV.

He smiled. He remembered that tone from that night. That soft, intimate—almost *shy*—voice. So different from the brash confidence of Ivy Molyneux, mining executive.

He was jumping at shadows. Ivy Molyneux was a woman who went after what she wanted. This phone call was nothing more. Unexpected, but also—not unwelcome.

'I'm free,' he said. 'How about we meet at Ms Black at eight?'

A wine bar in Subiaco he'd visited with the rest of his squadron after they'd returned from their latest assignment—before they'd quickly relocated to the pub next door. It was sophisticated, intimate, stunning. Very Ivy.

'Fine,' she said. 'I—uh—guess I'll see you there.'

'Ivy—' he said, before she had the chance to hang up. 'I'm still not after anything serious.'

He felt it was important he was honest.

But judging by her almost shriek of laughter before she ended the call, he had nothing to worry about on that front, regardless.

How had she let this happen?

For what felt like the hundredth time, Ivy had to stop herself fidgeting. So far she'd swivelled her bar stool, kicked her heels against the foot rest and attempted to tear a coaster into a million pieces.

She'd counted every step she'd made tonight. From her house to her car, and then from where her driver dropped her right outside this incredibly trendy bar to this seat. It was *ridiculous*.

In front of her sat an untouched glass of champagne.

She didn't even know why she'd ordered it. Out of habit? Or denial?

Ha!

As if it weren't the only thought reverberating about her head.

I'm pregnant. I'm pregnant. I'm pregnant.

How had she let this happen?

This being pregnant. *This* being dressed in a cute cocktail dress on a Thursday night to tell a man *she didn't even know* something that would change his life for ever.

The dress was new. She'd dragged one of her assistants out shopping. Ivy had made sure she'd smiled a lot and dropped hints about her 'date' tonight while still being deliberately coy.

That was all that had kept her going as the seconds and minutes had crawled along—focusing on her...*plan*.

In all honesty, it was far from her best plan. In fact, it was most likely her worst.

But she needed a plan right now. She needed a way forward, a way to fix this.

Because Ivy Molyneux didn't make mistakes.

'Ivy.'

At the sound of Angus's already familiar deep voice, Ivy channelled Julia Roberts in *Pretty Woman* as she slowly pivoted her chair to face him. What she really wanted to do was disappear between the floorboards. So, so badly.

But then she saw him.

In Bali, in his casual wedding attire, he'd been undeniably handsome. Heck, he'd be undeniably handsome *anywhere*.

But in the intimate lighting of the bar, in dark jeans, boots and a slim fitting black shirt he was…just plain gorgeous. His clothes weren't particularly formal, but he somehow managed to still look effortlessly dressed to impress. He looked darker, taller, *broader* than she remembered.

Especially now that he was standing so close to her. Close enough to touch.

And then he did touch her. Casually leaning forward to brush a kiss against her cheek and to bring his lips to her ear.

'You are stunning,' he said. His breath momentarily tickled her neck.

Ivy shivered.

He stepped back, his appreciative gaze sweeping over her.

She loved the dress she'd bought today. Teal silk with a feminine wrap bodice and a fitted skirt that hit mid-thigh, it flattered her curves and on any other day would've made her feel on top of the world.

That it didn't helped bring her back to reality.

This wasn't a date.

This *so* wasn't a date.

Ivy slid off her chair, waving away the arm he offered her. Without a word she headed to the back of the bar. It was busy, with all but the three tables along the far wall occupied.

Each was marked with a small reserved sign, and it was towards the middle table that Ivy gestured.

'I booked a table,' she said.

She'd booked three, actually, and paid for a night's worth of meals on all. It was still hardly private, but it would have to do.

'Dinner?' Angus asked.

Despite everything, Ivy managed a smile. Clearly dinner and conversation were not what Angus had planned for the night.

He was close beside her, and she could practically feel his growing tension.

Well, that situation wasn't about to improve for him.

She took her seat, and Angus took his. He must have plucked her champagne from the bar, as he placed it before her, his wrist still bandaged as it had been in Bali.

That was nice of him.

Would he be a good dad?

She gave a little shake of her head. No. This wasn't fair, that she knew and he didn't. That he thought he was here for meaningless flirtation followed by meaningless sex, when he so, so wasn't.

'Ivy, what's going on?'

She'd been staring, unseeing, down at her fingers, which she'd been wrapping and unwrapping around the stem of her champagne glass.

She took a breath. The deepest breath she could remember taking.

Then she lifted her gaze, and met his.

Even in the moody bar lighting, she now finally had enough light to see the colour of his eyes. Hazel.

They were lovely eyes, sexy eyes, but right now they were hard and unyielding.

Yes, he'd worked out that this night wasn't going to pan out the way he'd planned.

'Angus—I'm pregnant.'

CHAPTER THREE

PREGNANT?

All the stupid, obvious questions were on the tip of his tongue.

Are you sure?

How...?

Is it mine?

But he knew all the answers:

Of course she was. That she wanted to be anywhere but here was clear in everything about her. She was one hundred per cent sure or she wouldn't be putting either of them through this.

The how hardly needed explaining. He'd been there, too.

And was it his?

Well, that was only a faint hope that this was all a terrible mistake, rather than a genuine question.

And he was grateful that a small smidgen of his brain told him to swallow the words before they leapt from his mouth.

Because of course it was his. He had known what he'd been doing in Bali—known he'd pushed her out of her comfort zone, known he'd pursued the electric attraction between them to what he'd felt was the only logical conclusion...

But that she didn't normally have random sex with a practical stranger on a beach had been abundantly clear.

So yes, it was his.

With the basics covered, he dropped his head, gripping his skull with his hands.

He swore harshly.

That was about the sum of it.

'Angus?'

He kept his head down, but he nodded.

'I know this is a shock. I know this is the wrong place to tell you. When I called I hadn't planned this…but…'

It didn't matter. Who cared where she told him?

His thoughts leapt all over the place, as if his brain was incapable of being still, or of grasping onto anything at all.

He'd never felt like this.

He'd been in combat many more times than once.

He'd been in the most stressful situations that most people could imagine. Real stress. Real life-and-death stress, not running-late-for-work stress.

And yet *this* had thrown him. This had sent his ability to think, and apparently to talk, skittering off the rails.

'Um, the thing is, Angus, I have a plan.'

His gaze shot up, linking with hers in almost desperation. 'A plan?'

Ivy nodded slowly. And then she seemed to realise what he was thinking.

She looked down, studying her untouched champagne glass again.

'No,' she said, so softly he had to lean closer. 'Not that.' Her gaze darted back to his, and she looked at him steadfastly now. With that directness, that *realness* he'd liked so much in Bali. 'I'm thirty-one, and I have money and every resource I could wish for at my disposal. In every possible way this is the *last* thing I want. But a termination isn't an option for me.'

She barely blinked as she studied him. Long, long moments passed.

Angus cleared his throat. 'I'm thirty-four with a career I love that takes me away from home for months at a time and could one day kill me. I don't want this. I don't want children.' Ivy's gaze wobbled a little now as Angus swallowed. 'But for no reason I can fathom, I'm glad you've made that decision.'

Now he glanced away. He didn't know why he'd said that, or why he felt that way. The logical part of him—which was basically *all* of him—didn't understand it.

It made no sense. But it was the truth. His truth.

When he looked back at Ivy she was again studying her champagne glass.

'Well, it's good we're on the same page, then,' she said, her tone now brisk and verging on businesslike. 'So, here's my *actual* plan.' By the time she met his gaze again, she was all business. Ivy Molyneux of Molyneux Mining—not Ivy the girl from the beach. 'I'll get straight to the crux of it: I'd like us to get married.'

Straight after the pregnancy news, Angus would've thought it would take a hell of a lot to shock him.

That did it.

'What?'

She held up a hand. 'Just hear me out,' she said. 'What I'm proposing is a business arrangement.' A pause, and then a half-smile. 'And, yes, marriage.'

Ivy might find this funny, but Angus sure as hell didn't.

He remained stonily silent.

'The term of the agreement would be twelve months from today,' Ivy continued, clearly warming to her topic. 'As soon as possible we would reveal our—until now—several months' long secret relationship to family and friends, and, shortly after, our engagement. Then, of course, our—' now she stumbled a little '—our, um, *situation* would mean that we'd bring our wedding forward. I thought that we could make that work in our favour. A Christmas Eve wedding would be perfect, I felt.'

A Christmas Eve wedding would be perfect?

Angus's brain was still requiring most of its synapses

to deal with his impending parenthood. But what little remained was functioning well enough to realise that this was *completely and utterly nuts.*

'Is this a pregnancy hormone thing?' he asked, quite seriously. 'Can they send you loopy?'

Ivy's gaze hardened. 'I can assure you I am *not* crazy.'

More than anything, Angus wished he'd had time to order a drink. For want of another option, he gestured at Ivy's champagne. It wasn't as if she could have it, after all.

She nodded impatiently, and then carried on with her outrageous proposal as he downed half the drink in one gulp.

'After the wedding we'd need to continue the illusion that we're a couple, but given the nature of your work that shouldn't be too hard. My house is huge, so we could live quite separate lives when you are home. Not being seen in public together will help, anyway, for when we separate a few months after the baby is born.'

She blinked when she said *baby*, as if she couldn't quite believe it was true.

'After the separation you're free to do whatever you like, and then, as soon as legally allowable, we'll divorce, and carry on with our lives.'

'Except for the fact that we're parents of a child we had together.'

A reluctant nod. 'Well, yes.'

Angus took a second long swig to finish the champagne he'd barely tasted. He plonked the glass down with little care, and then leant forward, watching Ivy's eyes widen.

'Why?' he asked.

Ivy actually shrugged. 'Does it matter? I can assure you that the remuneration you'll receive for this will be a life-changing amount. Millions of dollars.'

Pocket change to her.

'And a house, too, if you like,' she added, as if an afterthought.

'Before tonight, Ivy, I never wanted children, and I never wanted to get married,' he said. 'Now I'm having a child, but, I can assure you, absolutely nothing has changed on the marriage front. I wouldn't have picked you to be the old-fashioned sort, Ivy, but I'm not. Even with a diamond-encrusted solid-gold carrot.'

Ivy shook her head, as if she couldn't comprehend his rapid refusal. 'I promise you that this will cause you minimal impact, I—'

'It's *marriage*, Ivy. Nothing minimal impact about that.'

She gave a little huff of frustration. 'Don't think of it like that. Think of it as signing a contract, nothing more.'

'Signing a contract of *marriage*, Ivy. And you still haven't told me why.'

Now that he had her glass, Ivy had transferred her fidgeting to her fingers—tangling and twining them together.

Had she really thought he'd agree, just like that? An offer of a crazy amount of money and all sorted? Even if her proposal made no sense on any level?

He studied her. Was she was so detached and separate from reality in her billionaire's turret that she truly believed that money *could* buy her anything? It was his immediate and rather angry conclusion.

He could feel every sinew in his body tense in frustration at the thought of the level of entitlement, of arrogance that would lead to such an assumption…

But now as he looked at Ivy, it didn't fit. He hadn't seen it in her in Bali, and he still didn't recognise it now.

Sure, she was still some distance from *normal*, but he knew it wasn't entitlement, or arrogance, that had triggered her plan.

It was something he could understand. That he could recognise.

It was desperation.

Ivy didn't know what to do now.

Maybe he was right. Maybe pregnancy hormones *had* sent her loopy, because, honestly—had she really thought he'd just agree?

In her experience some people could be bought for the right price. Actually, make that many, many people. But nothing about Angus had indicated to her that he was one of those people. In fact, if she'd spent even a minute properly considering her plan, she would've seen this fatal flaw.

Which of course was the problem. She hadn't spent any time thinking about it, at least not thinking about such pesky details like: *what if he doesn't agree?* Because she'd been clinging to this plan as if it were a rope suspended over the abyss that was her pregnancy, and she just couldn't, could *not*, let it go.

But, the thing was, if this plan had something to do with mineral exploration or extraction, she certainly wouldn't give up this early in the fight.

And that meant that she'd have to—at least partly—answer his question.

'When I turn thirty-two,' she said, looking him in the eye just as she always did during business negotiations, 'my mother will relinquish her position as Chief Executive Officer of Molyneux Mining to me. It's the same age she was when my grandfather died and left her the company, and this has been planned literally from when I was born.' She paused. 'I turn thirty-two in July next year. Based on some useful internet calculators—pending me seeing a doctor—our baby will arrive approximately one week before that date.'

Our baby. A slip of the tongue, but Angus displayed no reaction.

'Although the succession plan was determined before *my* birth, I can assure you that I want this too. I'm very different from my mother in many ways.' A huge understatement. 'But in this way, we are in sync. We both live for Molyneux Mining. This is incredibly important to me.'

It is everything to me, she almost added. But somehow she didn't think that would help.

It was near impossible to read Angus's expression, but he nodded. 'I get that you love your job. I get that you don't want to give that up. What has this got to do with marrying me?'

'About ten years ago just under half of Molyneux Mining was listed on the Australian Stock Exchange. We're still majority family owned, but I report to a board of executives, as well as to our shareholders. We also have a number of significant projects in progress, including a joint venture to mine manganese in the Pilbara, which is reaching final negotiations. It is also widely known that I will take over Molyneux Mining next year, and that we are already in a period of comprehensive change management.'

'So you're worried that a baby will impact your share price?'

Ivy's eyes narrowed. 'No, not the baby. No one had better think that a baby will impact my professional performance.'

Oh, how she *hoped* that was true. She ignored Angus's mildly incredulous raised eyebrows.

'It's all about how the baby came to be here, that's the problem. My whole career has led to my next birthday. Everything I have done, every decision I have made, has been with this succession in the front of my mind. I am known for being meticulous in my planning. For never making a snap decision, for never being reactive in my actions. Even my boyfriends have been chosen with some consideration for my career—I always do background checks. I never take anything or anyone on face value.'

Except she'd never done a background check on Angus. The only thing she'd cared about that night was how good Angus had made her feel.

'So a baby is okay. But hot, crazy sex on a beach with a stranger isn't.'

Ivy recoiled a little, and felt her cheeks grow warm.

Now her gaze dipped to her fingers. With some effort she untangled them, laying her palms flat on the table to force them still.

'I wouldn't have put it quite like that,' she said. 'But yes. Ivy Molyneux would *never* be that reckless.'

There was that word again. Reckless.

This time it triggered a remembered snatch of conversation, the echo of her mother's voice from a time for ever ago: *How could you, Ivy? How could you be so reckless?*

'But you were,' Angus said. 'We both were. I was there.'

His low words snapped Ivy's attention back from a better-forgotten memory. And something flickered in his eyes. Despite all this, despite this situation, despite this conversation, she recognised it.

Heat. Not like in Bali, but still there. Despite everything.

She knew her already warm cheeks were now scarlet, but all she could do was ignore that. And, as she should've at the wedding, ignore this *thing* between them.

Or at least try to.

'I know,' she said, very softly. 'That's what I'm trying to fix.'

The shocking warmth of his hand covering hers drew her attention downwards again, and she realised belatedly she must've been wringing her hands.

She'd trained herself out of all her fidgeting and step counting years ago, but right now this unexpected regression managed barely a blip amongst everything else that whirled inside her.

As in Bali, his touch impacted everything. She knew her heart had accelerated, and her whole body now seemed focused on where their fingers overlapped. Completely inappropriate warmth pooled low in her belly, and for long seconds Ivy wished like anything that this were a very real date.

But then Angus spoke.

'I get what you're trying to do, Ivy,' he said.

Instantly hope began to blossom inside her, delicate and beautiful. But then his fingers tightened gently on hers, and Ivy knew.

'My answer is still no.'

And for the second time today awful, unwelcome tears filled her vision.

Ivy never cried.

But then, Ivy never did a lot of things she'd been doing lately.

She snatched her hands away from beneath his, and for the briefest moment Angus reconsidered his decision.

He'd never be this close again to the fortune she'd offered him. Would he regret it some day? Was living a lie for twelve months really all that bad given such a massive payday?

And a second consideration snuck into his subconscious. *Or maybe he should just do this for Ivy?*

Angus straightened in his chair, subtly putting further distance between them.

No. He wouldn't regret passing on the money. His parents had taught him the value of hard work and, in every aspect of his life, he'd never been one to take shortcuts.

And for Ivy?

No. That was a slippery slope he did not want to get

on. When he was deployed, he never allowed himself to clutter his mind with those he left behind. It was why he would never marry, and it was why he had never meant to have children. It wasn't fair to anyone to be shoved aside in that manner. But it was what he did. It was, quite simply, who he was.

So no, he wasn't going to do this for Ivy.

'I'm sorry, I don't feel like eating,' Ivy said, breaking the silence. She pushed her chair backwards a little quickly, and steadied it with one hand as she stood.

Angus followed her lead and pulled himself to his feet, more than keen to get out of the bar. Around them, other couples and small groups appeared to be enjoying their meals. A man reached out to stroke the cheek of his date. Four well-dressed young women suddenly cackled with laughter and clinked their wine glasses together.

Everyone else's lives appeared to be carrying on beautifully, and normally, and yet Angus's life had just irrevocably changed for ever.

It still didn't seem possible. Didn't seem real.

Ivy was already negotiating all the happy diners, and Angus needed to take several large strides to catch up with her. Automatically, he reached out and rested his hand in the small of her back.

At his touch, she went still, her chin shooting up as she met his gaze.

She'd done a poor job hiding the sheen to her eyes back at the table, and she was far less successful now. Again her gaze was more than wobbly, and he was reminded that he wasn't alone in his shock and disbelief.

He felt he should say something. Something reassuring and supportive.

But he didn't have any experience in this kind of thing. Hell, his ex-girlfriends had made it clear he was a complete failure at even the most simple of relationships—let alone what to say to the woman who had just announced she was carrying his child.

So he said nothing at all, and Ivy's gaze just kept on wobbling.

'Ivy!'

Against his palm, Angus felt Ivy tense.

At the bar, only a few metres away, sat a seriously glamorous blonde. Her hair tumbled in generous waves over one shoulder, and beside her was a significantly less glamorous man.

Ivy appeared struck dumb, and didn't move a millimetre as the pair approached them.

'It's been months!' the blonde exclaimed. 'How are you?'

'I—uh—' Ivy began, and then went silent, simply sending him a panicky glance. Her body was moving now. She was trembling.

Immediately Angus slid his hand from her back to her waist, and tugged her gently against him. Even now, when he shouldn't, he noticed how naturally she fitted against him. And how soft and warm her body felt.

'I'm Angus Barlow,' he said to the couple, offering his free hand.

Then for the next three minutes he scrounged every last ounce of charm he possessed to conduct the most trivial of conversations, while Ivy managed the occasional nod and single-word response. And then he politely excused them, and escorted Ivy outside as quickly as their legs would carry them.

Outside, the night was cool against his skin. His arm was still around Ivy, and in the cold it seemed illogical to remove it, given the flimsiness of her dress.

He was still walking briskly, keen to put as much space between himself and the bar, when Ivy came to an abrupt stop and disentangled herself from him.

'Where are you going?' she said.

Angus paused. His car was parked in the opposite direction.

'I have no idea,' he said.

And amongst all that had happened tonight, those four little words were suddenly hilarious, and he burst into a harsh bark of laughter.

A moment later, Ivy joined in, and they both stood together on the footpath, cackling away just like those women having dinner.

When they both fell silent, Ivy looked up at him again. No wobbles this time, just direct, real Ivy.

'Thank you,' she said.

CHAPTER FOUR

Ivy LISTENED HALF-HEARTEDLY to her sisters' enthusiastic gossip. They sat across from her, their finished breakfast plates pushed aside. To her left sat Ivy's mother, nursing a mug full of cappuccino.

Around them, Sunday morning at the exclusive beach-side café was a buzz of activity. Ivy found herself picking up random snippets of conversation: the waiter two tables to her right repeating an order; an older man complaining at the lateness of his grandson; and from somewhere behind her a high-pitched: *Really?* followed by raucous laughter.

Their table abutted a wall of bi-fold windows, their louvred glass panes opened to welcome the salty breeze. Beneath them, keen sunbathers lay on brightly coloured towels in an irregular patchwork. It was an unusually warm October day, and Cottesloe Beach was, it seemed, the place to be.

It had worked out perfectly, really. Her family—just Mila, April and her mother—had dinner every second Sunday. But this weekend she'd suggested breakfast instead, so here they were.

The weather would be perfect for it! she'd said.

And everyone agreed.

As lies went, it was very much the whitest of them, but it still sat so uncomfortably. All to avoid refusing a glass of wine.

She was so close to her sisters, as different as they were. Mila, with her chocolate-brown curls and brilliant smile, was the baby, and the family artist. Never much interested in study, she'd barely finished high school before beginning a string of courses at TAFE—jewellery design, dress making, and a few others that Ivy had long forgotten. But then she'd started—and this time finished—a pottery course, and that was it. Mila had found her calling. Now she had her own studio, with a shop front for her work out the front, and space for her to teach out the back. Quiet, but opinionated and wise, Mila could always be counted on to see through the crap in any situation.

Then there was April. Beautiful, clever but flighty, she'd been the real rebel. She'd partied through uni, and still partied now. She'd completed her Environmental Science degree—chosen for its not so subtle dig at the way her family had made their fortune—but, apart from a few internships, hadn't settled into full-time work. April brought sunshine wherever she went—always the first to smile and the first with a kind word.

And there she was. Ivy. The eldest by three years, she'd followed the script exactly as her mother had hoped: a diligent student throughout school. A top student at university, all the way through to her masters. Then straight to work for the family company, working her way up, just as her mother had, with, of course, a healthy dose of expected nepotism.

But Ivy knew she deserved her position at Molyneux Mining. She'd worked her butt off to get there.

So, yes. In contrast to her arty sister, and her partying sister, there she was: studious, perfect daughter Ivy. Mila and April even gave her well-deserved needling for it.

But, of course, it had never been entirely true.

Ivy knew that. Her mother knew that. But no one else did.

Her mother had fixed her mistakes of more than a decade ago.

Unfortunately, Ivy was no closer to fixing her latest mistake.

She just needed time.

She *would* tell them about her pregnancy. Soon.

Just not today.

'Earth to Ivy?' April was grinning at her, fun sparkling in her gaze. 'You still with us?'

Ivy blinked, and forced a smile. 'Sorry. Just thinking about an email I have to write when I get home for the Bullah Bullah Downs project.'

In unison, her sisters groaned.

'I was just saying that I saw Holly at the shops yesterday,' April said, with a grin. 'She had some *very* interesting news.'

Ivy went perfectly still, pasting on a faux smile. She had the fleeting, horrifying thought that somehow she'd forgotten blurting out the news of her pregnancy to Holly as she'd exited the bar on Thursday night.

'*Apparently,*' April continued, 'you were with a rather hot guy?'

So Evan hadn't told April she'd asked for Angus's number. She could barely remember the vague, somehow work-related excuse she'd given her brother in law, but apparently it had been plausible.

'Oh, he was a blind date,' Ivy said, with a dismissive smile. 'He was nice enough, but it was a bit of a disaster, really.' That was true, in a way. 'No spark, you know?'

Definitely a lie.

The conversation moved on, her mum and sisters familiar enough with her occasional forays into dating to accept what she'd said.

But Ivy remained silent, quietly furious with herself.

She couldn't have news of her pregnancy leaked until she was one hundred per cent prepared, and gossipy speculation about her and Angus would not help that cause.

She needed to be more careful.

And more importantly, she really needed to fix this. Soon.

'Gus! How are you, mate?'

Angus finished the last two repetitions of the set, then swivelled on the seat of the leg press to grab his towel. Cam Dunstall wore his own towel hung over his shoulders, but he clearly hadn't begun his workout as he was the only person in the crowded barracks gym not coated in a layer of sweat.

'Good,' Angus said automatically.

Cam's attention darted to his still-bandaged right wrist. 'Going okay?'

Angus smiled at his friend's obvious concern. They both knew if his wrist was busted, so was his SAS career. He wasn't much use if he couldn't use a firearm.

'Nah, it's no big deal,' he said, truthfully. 'I met with the specialist today. He's happy with my progress. He sees no reason why I shouldn't be back on deck within the month.'

Cam's smile was broad and relieved. 'Awesome news, mate. Hey, you missed out on some fun last week—middle of the night hanging out of a Black Hawk chopper. Good times.'

Cam then went into great detail about the training exercise, while Angus mopped his face and arms of sweat. He'd finished today's workout. In fact he'd been here for the couple of hours since his doctor's appointment.

The good news about his wrist was not unexpected. To be honest, his hand felt very near to normal now—if the doctor had let him he'd already be back at work.

So his workout was supposed to be the highlight of his day. It was Monday, four days since Ivy had dropped her bombshell.

On Friday he'd gone for a run instead, needing to be outside.

Then on the weekend he'd stayed at home, deciding that

cutting back two huge branches from the towering blue gum in what was once his mother's back garden was the best use of his time. But even two days wielding a chainsaw hadn't helped.

And today hadn't helped either.

He still didn't feel normal. The exercise high he craved eluded him.

It wasn't fair.

That made him smile. Out of all that had happened, the incredible bad luck that had plonked him and Ivy in this situation—*that* was what was unfair?

'Mate?' Cam was looking at him strangely. 'I was just asking if you'd heard that Patrick has been moved. To *training*.'

Ah. A smile was certainly not appropriate here. That was no promotion.

'He's still not right, then?' Angus asked, knowing that was probably the wrong way to phrase his question, but at a loss to come up with something better.

'Yeah. That post-traumatic crap. Like Tom, I guess.'

Like Tom.

Guilt lowered Angus's gaze momentarily. How long since he'd called him? They'd come through SAS selection together seven years ago. Tom—strong, confident, supportive, *brave* Tom. His closest mate. The best soldier he knew.

Or at least, he had been.

'Some of the boys are going out for a beer tonight. Want to come?'

Cam was clearly keen to move the conversation on.

Angus got that.

But he shook his head. No. Ivy had texted him earlier, and he was meeting her for a coffee.

Not that he told Cam that, but the other man jumped to

the approximately right conclusion anyway, giving him crap about choosing a girl over his mates.

So Angus laughed and let the words roll off him, wishing like hell they were true.

'Thanks for meeting me.'

Angus raised an eyebrow as he slid into the fifties-style café booth. 'This isn't a business meeting, Ivy.'

She shook her head. 'No, of course not.'

It was just easier for her to think of it like that. She'd even prepared for this *meeting*, in a way. Mentally determining an agenda of items to cover, so that this could be over as efficiently as possible.

She was sure Angus would appreciate that, too.

Quick, efficient and over quickly. A good plan.

'So, I've got a couple of points I'd like to discuss, and I'll start with the most important. Do you intend to be a part of our child's life, and if so, to what extent?'

Angus didn't even blink at her directness. 'I intend to be the best father I can be,' he said. 'Which means I want to be a huge part of their life.'

Ivy nodded sharply. It was the answer she'd expected, although she couldn't exactly say why. She was pleased, though. She'd never been close to her own father. 'Excellent. Okay, so the next point is—'

'Hold it there.' Angus glanced at the coffee she'd downed in the few minutes she'd been waiting for him. 'Now the big question is out of the way, how about I go get us both a coffee, and some cake, and we relax a bit?'

'Relax?'

He grinned. 'Honey, the way I see it we just agreed to another eighteen-odd years to talk about this baby. Why rush things now?'

And with that he stood, and headed for the counter.

Ivy just watched him in somewhat stunned silence as he

made his order, and returned to the table with a number on a chrome stick, which he placed between them.

'I just asked for whatever you had again, plus a selection of cakes as I have no idea what you like. Okay?'

Ivy nodded numbly.

'Great!' he said. 'So, tell me something about yourself.'

'Pardon me?'

He shrugged. 'You heard me.'

Ivy bristled. 'Look, it's great that you're all so fine and relaxed and cool with this, but I don't think you understand how—'

'Ivy,' he said, so firmly that her words froze on her tongue. 'I promise you that I *understand* exactly what is going on here. It's all I've thought about for *four days*. I dreamt about it, even, although I can't say I've spent much time sleeping. I am exhausted, and stressed out of my mind. And frankly, I'm over it. I'm over feeling like that, but I can't do anything about it. Neither can you.'

Ivy's gaze travelled across his face, for the first time noticing the dark circles beneath his eyes and the spidery lines of red in his stare.

He'd just described her weekend, and beneath a thick layer of concealer she even had the matching blackened eyes.

'But we've both decided to do this, so we might as well get to know each other. So again—tell me something about yourself.'

Tell him something?

I'm scared? I don't know what I'm doing? I have *no idea* what to do with you?

'I think that Aussie Rules football is the best game in the whole entire universe.'

And then Angus smiled. A gorgeous smile, an amazing smile.

'So now we have two things in common,' he said.

* * *

A selection of cakes later, Ivy stood with Angus outside the café. It was dark between the street lights, and only the occasional car swished past.

'Where'd you park?' Angus asked.

Ivy shook her head. 'I didn't. I just need to call my driver and he'll come pick me up.'

A sudden gust of wind made her shiver, and Ivy wrapped her arms around herself tightly.

Angus took a step towards her—and for a moment Ivy thought he might put his arm around her again, as he had at the wine bar. But then he didn't, and Ivy took a little longer than she would've liked to decide she was relieved.

Tonight hadn't been as she'd planned. They'd talked about all things unimportant—the favourite football team they shared, the latest movies they'd seen, and even the weather. It *had* been kind of like a date.

Or rather exactly like one. Except it hadn't had that early-date awkwardness. The overenthusiastic laughter or the well-rehearsed anecdotes.

It had been...nice. Better than nice.

'I don't remember—did you ask me to tell you something about myself?'

'No,' Ivy said, smiling. Then added in an obedient sing-song voice: 'So, Angus, tell me something about yourself.'

'I don't leave ladies waiting on the street in the dark. Come on, I'll drive you home.'

Ivy raised her eyebrows. 'What if I live on the other side of the city?'

Angus had already walked a few steps, and looked surprised she hadn't already followed. 'Do you?'

She lived a five-minute drive away. 'No.'

He smiled. 'Well, there you go. But it wouldn't have mattered. I like driving.'

He waited another moment. 'So am I waiting here while you call your driver, or are you letting me drive you home?'

It would take longer to call Simon and wait for him than for Angus to drive her home, and she could think of no good reason to refuse. So she found herself walking beside Angus the short distance to his car, parked around the corner.

It was exactly the type of car she'd expect him to drive: big and black and foreboding. Although its vast size didn't assist with the unexpected sensation of intimacy when the doors were shut and they both sank into the lush leather seats.

Angus didn't switch the radio on, and they sat in silence after she gave him the brief directions to her house.

Now it did feel like a first date. As if they'd just been out for a romantic dinner and Angus were driving her home and they were both wondering if there'd be a kiss on her doorstep.

How sweet. How quaint. How *backwards* given how she and Angus had met.

Ivy dug her nails into her palms, needing to force herself to face reality.

She couldn't let her thoughts wander like this. She needed to focus, to remember what this *really* was.

'I have an estimated due date,' she said, the words sounding brittle in the silence. 'July the second.'

Instantly the atmosphere in the car shifted.

There. Romantic notions *gone*.

'Okay,' Angus said. And Ivy supposed he couldn't say much else.

'That was what we were supposed to talk about today,' she said. 'That's why I wanted to meet. To tell you that I had a scan today, and the baby has measured at five weeks and one day and that it's due on July the second.'

Her words were more jumbled than brittle, now.

'Thank you,' Angus said, and Ivy couldn't interpret his tone at all.

He slowed the car to turn into her driveway. The entrance was gated, but Ivy reached into her handbag for the small remote that swung the gates open.

Angus nosed the car up the long curved driveway and came to a stop before the limestone steps that led to the front door of her rambling nineteen-thirties double-storey home.

An automatic porch light flicked on, but otherwise the house was in darkness.

'No butler to meet you?' Angus asked, although his tone was not pointed, but curious.

Ivy laughed. 'Do you think I have someone feed me grapes as I bathe, too?'

He shrugged. 'You have a driver, so I assumed you had other staff.'

'No,' Ivy said. 'I mean, because of the hours I work I have a weekly cleaner and a regular gardener, but that's it. My home is my sanctuary, and I value my privacy.'

It already felt a little too private in the car, so Ivy opened her door and slid her feet out onto the driveway. She turned to thank Angus for the lift, but he'd climbed out of his seat too, and in a few strides stood beside her at the bottom of the steps.

Ivy didn't know what to do now. Why had he done that? Why hadn't he driven off and escaped while he could?

'So I'm confused. If you value your privacy, why have your driver ferry you to meet me, twice? Where did you tell him you were going?'

'Simon would never intrude on my personal life,' Ivy said.

Although it had taken considerable subterfuge to attend her dating scan today without Simon knowing. In the end, she'd had him drop her off some distance away, and she'd walked to her appointment.

He never would've commented if she'd asked him to drop her off right outside the ultrasound clinic. But really? April and Mila didn't even know yet. She couldn't have her driver find out first, no matter how discreet he might be.

'But regardless,' Angus said, 'wouldn't it just be easier to drive five minutes from your house to meet me?'

He appeared genuinely flummoxed, and Ivy couldn't help but smile. 'Easier, yes—if I had a licence.'

At this he went from flummoxed to stunned. 'How is that possible?'

'I never learnt,' Ivy said. 'Long story.'

And it was. Long and best forgotten.

Ivy turned slightly towards her house. 'So, thanks for the lift, Angus.'

She spoke a little softer than she'd planned, and his name sounded unexpectedly intimate on her lips.

'My pleasure, Ivy,' he said, but totally normally, as if he were talking to the waitress back at the café.

Ivy gave her head a little shake. She was being very, very silly with all these thoughts of dates and doorsteps and softly spoken names.

He'd already started to walk back to the driver's side of the car, so Ivy quickly raced up the steps, the heels of her boots clicking against the stone, and her hand already in her bag, searching for her keys.

But then she heard heavier footsteps on the steps behind her.

'Ivy, wait.'

So she did, key in hand. 'Yes?'

Angus took the steps two at a time and soon stood before her. The porch light's glow was soft, but the angles of his face seemed sharper in the mix of light and shadows.

'Were you okay today?' he asked. 'At the scan?'

Ivy blinked, and her throat felt suddenly tight.

'Uh, yes,' she said. 'Of course. It was fine. I was fine.'

She'd been beyond nervous. Scared and clueless, but still okay. More okay than she'd expected, actually.

'Good,' he said, with a sharp nod. And with that, he was off back down the steps.

Ivy put her key in the lock, but then found herself turning back to face him. He wasn't in his seat yet; instead he stood inside his opened door, as if he'd been watching her.

'I saw him,' she said. 'Or her. Just a spot at the moment. Or a blob. A cute blob, though.'

Angus nodded, and his lips quirked upwards.

'Goodnight, Ivy.'

'Goodnight, Angus.'

And then he climbed into his car and drove away.

CHAPTER FIVE

IVY HAD JUST broken into the secret stash of dry crackers in her desk's bottom drawer, when her phone rang.

Angus.

When he'd driven away from her place last week, they'd had no further plans to meet. So she'd decided she'd just call him occasionally with details of the baby's progress; after all, it was wise to keep her distance until she'd worked things out.

Yes, she knew at some point she'd need to organise some formal access arrangement or similar. But again, that could take place between their lawyers.

So there was definitely no real need to see him again.

Which was a relief, unquestionably.

Then why was her stomach doing all sorts of odd things?

'Hello?' she said, finally picking up the phone.

'You hungry?'

'Starving,' she said, honestly. 'I'm always starving now.'

Ah. That was what the stomach thing was. She clearly hadn't eaten enough crackers.

'Great. Meet me downstairs in five minutes. I know a great burger place we can go to.'

She had a meeting in twenty minutes, so she couldn't, even if meeting Angus in public again wasn't a terrible idea, anyway.

'Sure,' she said, instead.

Then Angus ended the call, and Ivy called her assistant into her office to rearrange her meeting. Ivy chose to ignore

Sarah's incredulous expression—people shifted meetings for frivolous reasons all the time.

Just not Ivy.

Even so, just over five minutes later her heels were clicking across the terrazzo floor of the Molyneux Tower's foyer. Angus stood against one of the mammoth round pillars that dotted the vast space, and also stopped the thirty-three-floor building from collapsing into St Georges Terrace.

Around him men and women in suits and smart coats flowed past, hurrying to lunch, or coffee or meetings. In contrast, nothing about Angus was hurried.

He'd propped his shoulder against the pillar, his arms crossed loosely before him. He wore jeans that might have once been black, but now were faded to a steel grey. His navy T-shirt fitted snugly, highlighting his width and the muscular strength of his arms, while one booted foot was crossed casually over the other. Every line of his body looked one hundred per cent comfortable. As if, despite the marked difference in his attire from every other person in the building, he fitted here perfectly.

But he didn't.

Here, in contrast to the gloss and shine that was Molyneux Mining, Angus looked *raw*. Strong, and hard and… virile.

Here, he was juxtaposed against Ivy's real life—her reality. It should have been a shock, and it certainly should've bothered her.

It definitely would've if she'd allowed herself to think about it. Or if, in fact, she'd been able to think at all.

But she couldn't. As soon as she'd heard his voice she'd apparently lost all common sense. And the instant she'd stepped out of the lift she'd known he was watching her.

Just like in Bali the weight of his attention was remarkable. Remarkable enough that she wobbled a little on her heels when her gaze met his.

He studied her as she walked towards him. She sensed, rather than saw, his gaze travel along her body, taking in her heels, her charcoal pencil skirt, and the pale pink of her silk blouse. She wore a short, three-quarter-sleeved cream wool coat, but it wasn't because of the cold that she shivered when she came to a stop.

That would be because he'd smiled.

'I have a meeting in forty-five minutes,' she said, instead of smiling back.

Her voice was more prickly than the professional she'd hoped for. An attempt to regain control, maybe.

When had she ever been in control around Angus?

He shook his head, his smile now even broader. 'Ivy, Ivy, Ivy…'

She didn't know what that meant, and her eyes narrowed.

But he didn't give her a chance to speak, instead reaching out to wrap his large hand around hers.

'Come on,' he said. 'We'd better hurry up, then.'

Angus considered letting go of Ivy's hand once they'd stepped outside onto the gusty, skyscraper-lined street.

But then he just didn't. What was the harm, really, of holding a gorgeous woman's hand for a minute?

None he could think of. At least none that bested the satisfaction he was getting from Ivy's rather stupefied, and also rather un-Ivy-like acquiescence.

As much as he liked driven, determined, controlled Ivy, there was something to be said about how she reacted to him. He hadn't forgotten a moment about what had happened between them in Bali, and certainly not the way she had responded to him. It was as if *all* her nerve endings had become focused on where he'd touched her. As if how she felt, and how he made her feel, were all that had mattered.

It had given him a sense of control—but not. Because there was no doubt that everything Ivy had done was what she'd wanted to do—it was just that instead of focusing on work or responsibilities, she'd been focusing on what felt good. What felt *really* good.

So it had felt natural to grab her hand today. To stop her beginning another unnecessarily professional and awkward conversation between them. Because he'd known his touch would shut her up.

What he'd forgotten was the impact of her touch on *him*.

Which was why he'd considered dropping her hand as they'd stepped outside.

Considered, then dismissed.

Because touching Ivy felt pretty damn good.

And triggered some pretty damn *amazing* memories. Of naked skin that glowed in the moonlight. Of the glide of her body against his. The sound she'd made when he'd finally slid inside her...

They were at the burger bar.

Angus dropped her hand, and Ivy put space between them, not meeting his gaze.

'There's a table free at the back,' he said, spotting it amongst the lunch-time rush.

With barely a nod, Ivy walked over while Angus grabbed a couple of menus.

Soon after they'd ordered, and Ivy sat with her water glass cupped in both hands, waiting.

She might just as well have spoken: *Get to the point, Angus.*

It was tempting to do the opposite, as he had in that café. To force her to slow down. To just talk without purpose for a minute or as long as they liked.

But his body was still heated from the simple touch of her hand and those not so simple memories.

And seeing Ivy today was about the future, not the past.

'Have you told anyone?' he asked.

'No,' she said, studying him almost cautiously. 'Why?'

'Because I'd like to tell someone.'

Her eyes widened. *'Why?'* And then, *'Who?'*

She looked so shocked he had to smile. 'My mother, and for the usual reason I tell her things—I'd like her to know.'

'Oh,' she said. 'I suppose I hadn't thought you'd want to tell anyone now. It's still so early.'

Yes. His late-night Googling had taught him a lot more than he'd ever thought he'd need to know about pregnancy.

Ivy's gaze had dropped to the table. She'd abandoned her water to fiddle with a napkin, weaving the paper between her fingers. 'Can you wait?' she said. 'I…' a long, long pause '…I need more time.'

Angus almost told her why it didn't really matter when he told his mother. He could've told her yesterday and it was almost impossible she'd remember today. Most weeks, he was lucky if she remembered his name, let alone that he was her son.

But then Ivy would wonder why he'd asked her permission at all.

Angus wasn't entirely sure himself, beyond a sense that it was the right thing to do.

Ivy had raised her gaze again, and she met his, waiting impatiently for his response.

'Okay,' he said, with some reluctance.

When he visited his mother—at least a couple of times a week whenever he was home—he talked. Talked more than he'd talked all week, about anything and everything.

Because that was how he remembered his mother: talking. Once she could've talked the ear off anything and anyone, revelling in her ability to draw remarkable stories out of the most random of people: the girl at the checkout, the elderly man at the park, the parking officer issuing her a ticket…

So silence in her presence made Angus excruciatingly uncomfortable. And while, like his father, he was *not* one to ever talk for the sake of it, when he visited his mother, he did.

And he told her everything. Partly because he did actually want to tell her, but mainly because he desperately needed to fill the space around them both with words.

He'd visited her yesterday, and omitting Ivy and the baby from his monologue had felt like a lie of omission.

Stupid, really, given she'd never know. Really stupid.

Lunch arrived, and for a few minutes they both ate in as much silence as was possible when eating burgers stacked high with gourmet ingredients.

Ivy had been visibly relieved when he'd agreed with her, but the atmosphere between them had changed.

'I thought that after the twelve-week scan would be a good time for us to formalise arrangements,' she said suddenly, a tomato-sauce-tipped chip in her hand. 'Then we can both be free to share the news appropriately.'

Formalise? Appropriately?

Angus gritted his teeth. *Really? This again?*

'Haven't we got beyond this, Ivy? This isn't a business deal. This is our child.'

Ivy put the chip back down on her plate, untouched.

'Of course,' she said. 'But I find it's easier if everything's in writing. Then we won't have any more misunderstandings like today.'

'I wouldn't call today a misunderstanding,' Angus said. 'I'd call it a conversation.'

Ivy raised an eyebrow. 'Hmm.'

She pushed her plate away, although it still held half her lunch.

'I thought you were starving?' he asked.

'I was wrong,' she said. 'I need to get back to that meeting.'

Angus checked his watch. 'You still have fifteen minutes.'

She hooked her handbag over her shoulder, the motions rushed and tense.

'I have to make a phone call I forgot about.' A pause while her gaze flicked out towards the busy street. 'Sorry.'

She was clearly running away, and Angus was not about to chase after her. She reached into her handbag, but Angus stopped the movement with a pointed look.

'I'll cover it,' he said.

Ivy nodded, another agitated movement.

Then she was gone, walking as fast as she could in those towering heels.

And Angus sank back in his chair, leisurely enjoyed the rest of his lunch and wondered what on earth to do with Ivy.

It's better this way.

Ivy nodded sharply to herself as she sat alone in the VIP Lounge at the Perth Airport charter terminal.

It is.

Simple. Uncomplicated. Straightforward.

Sensible.

Why she hadn't thought of it in the first place was beyond her.

Her lawyer had couriered the contract to Angus this morning. Its intent was simple: from now on, all communications between them would be via their lawyers, and they both agreed to keep the pregnancy secret until mutually agreed to in writing. Plus, of course, Angus would receive a generous lump sum on signing.

Now she really didn't need to see Angus again.

Which was *such* a relief.

And necessary.

Because what had she been thinking when he'd called a few days ago? In the same breath that she'd acknowledged to herself that meeting with him so publicly was a terrible idea, she'd cancelled a meeting to do just that.

And of *course* Angus had been noticed in the Molyneux Tower foyer, but she'd been too swept up in…in whatever stupid hormonal thing that Angus did to her that she hadn't cared.

By the time she'd returned from lunch the office had been full of gossipy murmurs. No one was silly enough to ask her about Angus directly, of course—not that that made any difference.

Why had she let him hold her hand?

And how did she fail to consider that Angus may want to tell people?

Her behaviour when it came to Angus Barlow made no sense, and more importantly—it was dangerous. She needed to protect herself, and her child. Hadn't she learnt all those years ago how foolish it was to allow how she felt to guide her decisions?

Back then, she'd lost herself amongst her silly, fanciful ideas about love, and she'd vowed never to let that happen again.

Now she dated appropriate men. Men who were a good match for her life and her career.

Certainly not men who made her skin tingle and her heart race.

If, after the tragic events of all those years ago, she needed a reminder that her decision was for the best—well, this was it.

From the moment Angus had watched her walk down that aisle, she'd got just about everything wrong.

Today, that fat contract with Angus had put things right.

Angus might not like it, but it was for the best.

Ivy stood up, walking over to the small coffee station in the corner of the room. Two walls of the lounge were almost entirely windows, offering her a floor-to-ceiling view of the runways. She was at the northern end of the airport, but the main public domestic and international terminals were close by, so large passenger jets dotted the landscape—both on the tarmac and in the cerulean sky.

The Molyneux Mining jet sat patiently in front of her, and Ivy expected one of the flight attendants would come and collect her shortly.

This trip to Bullah Bullah Downs was just what she needed. It had meant a bit of schedule reshuffling, but it would be worth it. Maybe there, amongst the million-odd acres of space the station stretched across, she'd feel more like herself again.

Her stomach growled, and Ivy glanced downwards, surprised to see her hand resting on her still-flat stomach.

'Ivy.'

Ivy spun around, recognising that deep voice instantly. 'What are you doing here?'

She'd tried to keep her voice calm, but failed miserably, her words all high pitched.

Angus stood in front of the closed door to the lounge, a backpack slung over his shoulder. He wasn't leaning against anything this time, but he still managed that lackadaisical *thing* he did, every inch of his lean frame all easy and relaxed.

Except for his jaw. That had a harder line than usual.

And his eyes.

His eyes… Ivy didn't know how to describe them, she just knew that as he walked—casually—towards her, they were all that she could look at.

Today they didn't have that sexy sparkle of green amongst the hazel…they were just…*flat*.

Even when she'd told him she was pregnant, he hadn't looked like this.

'So, where are we off to, today, Ivy?'

'Pardon me?'

Angus folded himself into the chair Ivy had been sitting in earlier, casually leaning backwards and crossing his feet at the ankles.

'You heard me,' he said. 'I made an educated guess of our destination, so I suspect I've packed appropriately regardless. But still. I'm just plain curious.'

'Packed?'

He nodded, raising his eyebrows. 'Now, this is one thing I haven't read about in early pregnancy: hearing loss. Interesting.'

Ivy's gaze narrowed, her brain rapidly recovering from the shock of Angus's sudden appearance.

'You're not coming with me,' she said.

While she might have worked that out, she had no clue why on earth he would want to. *What was going on?*

'Of course I am,' he said. 'Your very helpful assistant advised that you would be unavailable for the next three days, which is unacceptable to me. So here I am.'

'Nothing I do needs to be acceptable, or otherwise, to you,' Ivy said, with some venom.

He nodded again, the action utterly infuriating. 'Oh, yes, it does, Ivy. I think that's the bit you forgot when you spoke to your lawyer. Your disregard for our agreement *not to tell anybody* is remarkable.'

Ivy crossed her arms in front of herself. 'I had to tell my lawyer.'

'No,' Angus said, softer now. 'You didn't.'

Ivy bit her lip. He was right, and she wasn't sure the fact that she really hadn't wanted to would make Angus any happier.

'I've realised that it would be better to formalise things sooner rather than later. Neither of us meant this to happen, and although I appreciate how nice you've been so far—' Angus raised an eyebrow when she said *nice* '—there really is no need for it. I can keep you updated on the baby's progress via my lawyer, and we can organise an access arrangement for after the baby's birth.'

'Yes,' Angus said. 'I noticed that part in the contract—organised between our lawyers, of course.'

Ivy nodded. 'Yes. That way we have everything in writing. Nice and clear.'

'And you don't have to see me.'

Angus stood up, and in three large strides was right in front of her. Close enough that it took everything in Ivy not to take a step backwards.

'We don't have to see *each other*,' Ivy clarified. She held Angus's gaze as he looked at her, but it was hard. It was as if he was attempting to look beyond her eyes—to work out what she was thinking.

Unfortunately with Angus so close, what she was thinking was nothing particularly coherent at all. Which was, of course, the problem. She just couldn't allow this—this pointless, hormone-triggered *reaction* to him.

'But what if I like seeing you, Ivy?' he said. Deliberately he swept his gaze along her body, from her hair to her toes, and slowly back up again. She was dressed for the flight in skinny jeans and a fine wool long-line jumper. Hardly her most glamorous outfit, and yet she still felt the appreciation in his gaze. Felt that *weight*.

'I—' Ivy began, but really had no idea what she was trying to say.

'Ms Molyneux?'

The voice came from the doorway. A male flight attendant in his perfectly ironed uniform waited patiently, his expression curious.

'We'll just be a minute,' said Angus, and Ivy glared at him.

'We?' the attendant asked. 'Ms Molyneux, should we have the paperwork for your guest?'

Ivy shook her head, but said nothing.

Angus leaned close, so only Ivy could hear him. 'I am going to be a part of this child's life, Ivy, and that means being a part of yours—and *not* through a lawyer. This is the second time this week you've run away from me, Ivy, and I don't like it.'

'I don't run away from things,' Ivy said, low but firm.

'Don't you?' he said, taking a step back. 'What would you call this?'

'Work,' she said. 'Besides, how would I explain who you are?'

Angus's lips quirked into a smile of triumph.

Ivy closed her eyes and counted to ten. Slowly. More than once.

'Fine,' she said, when she looked at him again. She turned to the still-waiting attendant. 'Louis—please organise the appropriate paperwork with Mr Barlow.'

Then, with a resigned sigh, she went to collect her laptop and handbag from the coffee table as Angus left the room.

Alone again, Ivy looked back out to the runway. Her plane still waited patiently for her, but the sky beyond had turned from a perfect blue to an ominous grey. Appropriate.

Her stomach growled, but the platter of plastic-wrapped cookies at the tea and coffee station suddenly held no appeal. Instead she watched the trajectory of a passenger jet across the gloomy sky as she struggled to get her thoughts back in order and work out what on earth she was going to do next.

But it was a pretty impossible task.

As with everything that had happened with Angus until now, Ivy had absolutely no idea what she was doing.

CHAPTER SIX

TWO HOURS LATER the plane touched down at Paraburdoo airport.

For the entire flight, Ivy had sat stiffly across from Angus, appearing remarkably uncomfortable despite her luxurious leather seat. She'd spent much of her time busily typing away on her laptop, only occasionally taking a break to stare out of the window.

It was quite a view, too. In Perth, the landscape had been in shades of green, but as they'd travelled north it had transformed into a world of browns and ochres, patterned with deep cuts and ridges—some the ancient gorges of Karijini National Park and others the brutal gash of an iron ore mine.

Unlike Ivy, Angus had enjoyed his time aboard the Cessna. He'd chosen a European beer from the extensive bar, and worked his way through a good portion of the cheese platter placed before them.

The silence hadn't bothered him; he knew—with the pilot and Louis nearby—it had not been the time to talk.

At the airport, the heat buffeted them the moment they exited the jet. Perth in October was quite mild, still a good few months from summer. But here in the Pilbara it never really got cold—at least not during the day—and today the temperature was well into the thirties.

The airport was busy—a hub for all of the iron-ore companies ferrying their fly-in/fly-out workers from the city. Even with only a single runway, it had a decent terminal, today filled with men and women in high-visibility clothing and steel-capped work boots.

Outside, a car waited for them. A hulking white four-wheel drive with a substantial bull bar, an oversized aerial and an air snorkel, it was far from a limousine—and yet there he was, the driver, waiting beside the front wheel for them.

'Do you know how to get where we're going?' Angus asked Ivy as they walked to the car.

'Of course,' she said. 'I've been coming here my whole life.'

'Then tell him he's not needed.'

Ivy stopped dead. 'Pardon me?'

'There it is again, that early pregnancy hearing loss.'

Ivy's lush lips formed into a very thin line.

Angus sighed. 'We don't need a driver. I can drive.'

Her mouth opened and closed a few times, as if she was searching for the perfect argument.

'If he drives, I'll talk about the baby all the way there.'

Ivy's eyes widened. 'That's blackmail.'

Angus shrugged. But then, Ivy had stopped playing nice when she'd had that contract couriered to him.

He wasn't surprised when Ivy walked ahead to speak to the driver. Minutes later, the other man was gone, and Angus was in the driver's seat, Ivy belted in beside him.

She tapped away at the GPS embedded in the dashboard.

'There,' she said. 'Follow this. I'm going to take a nap.'

Then she turned slightly away from him in her seat, and firmly closed her eyes.

Angus didn't believe for a second that she was actually going to sleep, but he didn't argue.

They had two days ahead of them to talk, if necessary. He was in no hurry.

* * *

'Ivy?'

Ivy blinked sleepily. A large hand cupped her shoulder, shaking her gently.

'We're here. But it doesn't look much like an iron-ore mine.'

Slowly her eyes focused. The car's windows were coated in a thin layer of red dust, thanks to the kilometres of unsealed roads they'd travelled along to arrive at their destination. Fifty-seven kilometres north east of Paraburdoo, Bullah Bullah Downs homestead sat silently against a backdrop of yellow-flowering cassias and acacia trees and amongst a tufty carpet of spinifex in greens and blueish grey. The building was old, originally built in the early nineteen-twenties, but renovated extensively on the inside by Ivy's mother multiple times over the past thirty years.

The homestead's red tin roof was exactly the same shade as the soil it was built upon, reaching out to create a veranda to encircle itself. The walls were solid stone, the mortar rough and ready.

It was remote, it was arid, and it was *home*. In many ways more like home than the mansion in Dalkeith where Ivy had grown up.

Ivy loved it here. Despite everything, and despite having Angus Barlow beside her, she smiled.

She'd slumped against the side of the car as she'd slept, and Ivy now straightened up, stretching out her legs.

The road out here was mostly dirt and studded with pot holes. How she'd slept was beyond her, and it hadn't been intentional. She'd planned to just close her eyes and buy some time before she and Angus spoke.

Buy some time to do what, she wasn't exactly sure.

'Where are we?' Angus asked.

'The homestead,' Ivy said as she opened her door and

pivoted in her seat to climb out. 'Come on, I'll give you a tour.'

Keen to get inside, Ivy jumped from the car, but the instant her feet touched red dirt she knew something was very, very wrong.

Patches of white flashed into her vision, blocking the homestead, and blocking Angus when she instinctively turned to him.

'Angus?' she began, but that was all she could manage before everything went black.

'Ivy?'

Everything was still black. Something coated her lips, so Ivy took an experimental lick.

Dirt.

Yuk.

Her eyes sprung open. Immediately in front of her was the deeply corrugated tread of a four-wheel drive tyre. She was on her side, her legs bent, her arms laid out in front of her.

Ivy knew enough from basic first-aid training to know she was in the recovery position.

'I fainted,' she said.

'Just for a few seconds,' Angus said from where he knelt behind her. 'Enough time to freak me out.'

The remnants of that sudden dizziness remained, so for now Ivy didn't move.

'Freak you out?' Ivy said. 'Surely a simple faint isn't going to ruffle a soldier?'

Angus's laugh was low. 'I suppose you'd expect a soldier to catch you, too.'

'You didn't?' she asked, surprised, although now she registered a dull ache in her hip and she could see a few grazes on her arms, tiny pinpricks of blood decorating her skin. 'You're right,' she said with a smile, 'I am disappointed.'

'One moment you were there, then I heard the thud as you hit the ground. Thank God you didn't hit the car or a rock.' He paused. 'Has this happened before?'

'No,' she said. 'Although I have felt a bit nauseous if I don't eat regularly.'

'You didn't eat on the plane,' Angus said. 'So it's been at least three hours.'

'Yeah,' Ivy said. 'I was too grumpy during the flight to eat.'

She must still be dizzy; it wasn't like her to be quite so candid.

Angus laughed out loud. 'Grumpy with me or not, promise me you won't go so long between eating again.'

Ivy's automatic reaction was to tell Angus she was a grown woman perfectly capable of feeding herself. In fact, she rolled onto her back to tell him exactly that—but then met his gaze.

And it wasn't flat any more. It wasn't anything like it had been back in the VIP Lounge, or on the plane, and definitely not the ruthless stare he'd maintained when he had demanded she send her driver away.

The flecks of green were back in his eyes, and all she could see was concern.

Big, bad, brave soldier or not, she had scared him.

So those sharp words stuck in her throat.

'When we get inside, I want you to call your doctor.'

Ivy nodded obediently.

'Feeling faint is common in early pregnancy, but even so I'd feel better if you discussed this with a professional.'

She nodded again. 'You've done more research than me,' Ivy said.

He shrugged. 'I believe in being prepared.'

'Except when making love on the beach,' she teased.

Ivy had absolutely no idea where that came from, and instantly her cheeks went scalding hot.

But Angus laughed again. 'Maybe a bit too early for that joke, Ivy?'

'Probably,' she agreed, but her blush was fading.

Fainting was almost worth it to hear him laugh. To see that sparkle back in his gaze.

'How you doing now?' Angus said. 'Do you think you'll be able to walk to the house?'

'Of course,' she said, levering her upper body off the ground.

'Not so fast,' he said, and then in a smooth, effortless motion, he scooped her up. With a powerful, warm arm beneath her knees, and another encircling her back, it was momentarily impossible to talk. He held her close, her head nestled against his shoulder. He smelt fantastic: clean and strong. Instinctively she curled closer, wanting to be as close as possible to all that heat and strength.

In the shade of the veranda, finally Ivy's voice returned.

'Why did you ask if I could walk if you were always going to carry me?'

'Because I like it when things don't go the way you expect.'

She had a feeling she should be offended, but a combination of sun, dizziness and Angus's befuddling proximity meant she was in no position to mount a defence.

And with that, he carefully placed her back on her feet, a supportive arm remaining around her waist.

With his free arm he gave Ivy her handbag, liberally covered in dust.

In silence she found the key, unlocked the front door, and, with Angus's arm still close around her, led them inside.

The homestead's lounge room was something else. Angus couldn't imagine the room had even a passing resemblance to the decorating of the early nineteen-hundreds, but it was certainly beautiful. The floors were polished jarrah, the leather couches oversized and comfortable. Above the cast-iron fireplace a huge mirror reflected the view—although now it was dusk the undulating landscape's shades of red and splashes of green were muted. Elaborately patterned curtains edged the windows, and a thick-pile rug lay beneath their feet.

Air conditioning ensured the temperature inside was perfect, which Angus was grateful for as he studied Ivy.

She lay stretched out on the couch, her gaze trained at the ceiling. She'd had a shower to wash away all that red dust, and now she wore a loose singlet and yoga pants, her wet hair looped into a ponytail.

She insisted she was fine, but still—he worried.

He didn't think he'd ever forget the sound of Ivy's body thudding against the red earth.

Amongst so many—objectively far worse—memories that crammed his head, it was strange that he was so sure of that fact. But he was.

And he couldn't even say it was just about their baby. In fact, it wasn't until she finally opened her eyes—and it had felt like hours, not seconds—that he even thought about him or her.

Was that bad?

He propped his elbows on his knees, rubbing his hand against his forehead.

Probably.

Slowly, Ivy pulled herself to a seated position.

'Careful!' he said, automatically.

She responded with a glare. 'I am not an invalid. Even my doctor gave me the all-clear.'

'As long as it doesn't happen again.'

She sighed. 'It won't.' She gestured at the half-eaten box

of crackers and the remaining wedge of Cheddar cheese on the coffee table. 'I am suitably fortified, I promise.'

But still, he watched warily as she crossed the room to the adjacent kitchen. She walked slowly—he suspected mostly for his benefit—and made it to the fridge in one piece.

On cue, she threw her arms out with a flourish, and took a theatrical bow in his direction. 'Waa-*lah*! Behold! The amazing walking woman!'

Angus didn't even bother to raise an eyebrow, although he couldn't help his halfway smile.

Somehow they had fallen into a truce. A demilitarised zone of sorts.

But this wasn't what he had planned—this rather cosy scene in such a luxurious setting.

But then, he'd expected they would talk in a meeting room at a mine site. As it turned out, the three Bullah Bullah Downs mines were located many, many kilometres away from the homestead, and when he'd asked Ivy said she'd had no plans to visit them.

So he had been right. Ivy had run away to Bullah Bullah Downs. She'd quite literally sent the contract, and run.

And while a big portion of him was incredibly angry at her behaviour, all he saw as Ivy walked towards him with an overflowing platter in her arms was how she'd looked, crumpled on the ground beside the car.

Fragile. Vulnerable.

Not that she'd appreciate him thinking that. And Angus didn't really think it was true. Ivy was strong, Ivy was independent.

But she was also pregnant, and for reasons he didn't fully comprehend—she was scared.

'I may have gone overboard in my attempt to divert any hint of a rumour,' Ivy said, putting the platter down on the coffee table. 'So please enjoy your sushi and selection of soft cheeses. There's also a *lot* of wine in the fridge.'

Angus leant forward to study the feast. 'And I see you aren't about to starve, though.'

'No,' Ivy said with a smile. 'Hard cheeses, bread and nuts seem to be my thing at the moment. And apples. And cake. There are actually quite a few cakes in the fridge. I may have been a little overenthusiastic when I made my catering order, too.' She paused. 'I suspect any rumours will instead be in relation to my new-found gluttony.'

For a while they both ate quietly, picking at the decadent food before them.

Tension still simmered between them, but now it wasn't tinged with anger.

Pity he'd have to change that.

'Why did you send me that contract, Ivy?'

Ivy's head jerked up. She put her plate back on the coffee table, and then rearranged her legs from underneath her so she sat primly on the edge of the sofa, rather than comfortably cross-legged amongst the pillows.

'I should've done it to start with.'

'That doesn't answer my question.'

She looked away, staring out through the now darkened window at nothing.

'I felt it was my only option.'

'That doesn't answer it either. Why?'

Her gaze snapped back to meet his, and it was immediately obvious that their truce was over. 'You just don't get it, do you?' she said, jumping to her feet. 'This is so easy for you, while *everything* in my life has to change. It's not fair.'

Just like that, Angus was angry, too.

'This is life-changing for me too, Ivy.'

But she shook her head. 'Don't be ridiculous. I told you what's at stake here. My entire professional career hangs in the balance. Nothing has to change for you.'

Nothing had to change for him?

But before he had a chance to set her straight, Ivy continued, oblivious to his clenched jaw and the frustration running through his veins. 'I don't think you understand that I *have* to fix this. I can't just carry on like it's all okay, and that we'll work it out, because we *won't*. We can't have coffee and lunch and talk about football and cancel meetings and just hope that magically it will all work out. Because it *won't*.'

She was pacing the room, crossing from the couch to the kitchen and back. Her arms were wrapped tight around her, and she didn't look at Angus at all.

He stood up, deliberately blocking her path, needing her to look at him.

Needing the Ivy he knew to be looking him straight in the eye when she spoke.

But she instead stared at a spot somewhere on his chest, her jaw in a stubborn line.

'How does not seeing me at all fix anything, Ivy? That was all I saw in the contract, nothing about your career. Or about how you'll erase what happened between us in Bali.'

Her gaze shot upwards to cling with his. 'I don't want to erase what happened in Bali,' she said softly, then shook her head as if she'd only just realised what she'd said, her cheeks a deep pink. 'I mean, just the bit where I forgot to take my pill that day.' Then her gaze dropped down to her belly, which she covered with her hands. 'Oh, I don't think I meant that either, which makes no sense at all.'

Her fingers rubbed at her eyes, smudging make-up he hadn't even realised she'd put on after her shower.

'Ivy, tell me how the contract fixes anything.'

Her hands fell away. 'It doesn't fix everything,' she said. 'But it fixes *you*.'

'What does that even mean?'

She threw her arms in the air, taking a step backwards

so she could gesture between them. 'It fixes *this*. It fixes me having to see you, having to deal with you being all strong and nice and sexy and *confusing*. I'm not myself when I'm with you. I make poor decisions; I don't think straight; I don't do *anything* right. I can't control anything right now. I can't stop my stupid body fainting. I can't stop eating crackers. I can't stop the fact that my whole world is going to collapse around me once I finally get the guts to *tell* anyone but my lawyer that I'm pregnant.' She took a step towards him, tilting her chin upwards to meet his gaze. 'But I can control *this*. I can stop *this*. It's a start, anyway.'

Then her shoulders slumped, and she went to walk away.

But Angus's hand shot out, wrapping around her upper arm.

'You can't control me, Ivy. You can't control everything, no matter how badly you want to.'

He stepped even closer. Ivy's chest was moving up and down as she took deep breaths, as if trying to pull herself together.

Angus loosened his grip on her arm, letting his hand run down past her elbow to her wrist. Beneath his fingertips, she shivered.

'Are you okay?' he said, suddenly worried. 'Are you cold?'

She laughed, but without humour. 'No, Angus. That's just yet another thing I apparently can't control.'

Ivy's heart felt as if it were beating a billion miles an hour. That seemed to be what it did when Angus was so close to her, doing that strong and sexy thing he did so well.

And her skin shivered too, of course, when he touched her.

He'd gone completely still, which was good. It gave Ivy some chance of pulling herself together. Mortification was attempting to distract her from the immediate sensation of

Angus's touch. Because mortified she should be, for pacing around the homestead, ranting to Angus about things he certainly didn't need to know.

But then his fingers began to move again, and the only thing Ivy could possibly think about was the man standing right in front of her.

'I didn't need to carry you inside today,' he said, his voice low and like velvet.

'You were making a point,' she said. 'About expectations.'

She'd barely needed the prompt. Today had confirmed that Angus Barlow was never going to behave the way she expected—or wanted.

But he shook his head. 'No,' he said. 'At least that was a far secondary consideration. Mostly I just wanted to touch you.'

Ivy closed her eyes as warmth pooled low in her belly.

He was still touching her, his fingers having traced their way back up along her arm, across her shoulder to lightly brush against her exposed collarbone.

His touch was so light Ivy found herself swaying towards him, wanting him to be firmer, wanting to feel more than a hint of his strength and his heat.

She jumped at the sudden weight of his other hand on her hip, and his hand went still, as if allowing her a moment to adjust.

And then that hand was moving too, his thumb exploring the shape of her hipbone, his fingers flaring out to caress the upper slope of her backside.

Then the hand curled around further, to splay across the small of her back. Firm. Hard.

Her eyes still closed, she could suddenly feel his breath against her cheek, then her ear.

'You lose control when you're near me,' he said, so softly.

It was pointless to argue, even if she was capable of it. Instead she simply sighed.

'Ivy, I don't want to be in control around you.'

Her eyes snapped open at the feel of those words against her lips. If she moved even a centimetre, their mouths would touch.

But she didn't have to. The hand on her back pulled her firmly against him, his other hand sliding up to tangle in her still-damp hair.

And then his mouth took hers, and he was kissing her.

Hard and hot and all-consuming.

Out of control. But then, that was hardly unexpected.

Her own arms had managed to make their way to his shoulders, to cling and to wrap behind his neck. He didn't really need her to pull him closer, but she gave it a go, wanting to feel every inch of him plastered against her body.

She kissed him back without restraint, far more so than in Bali. She tasted his tongue, explored his mouth, licked and sucked his lips.

And, *God*, how he kissed her back. He was right, she was never in control around him, but as they kissed he gave her the illusion of control, letting her take the lead, letting her press smaller kisses along his jaw, or break away to change the angle of their lips or choose to take things slow or fast.

But it wasn't real. The moment Angus lost patience with her playfulness she found herself in the air for the second time today, being carried to the couch, and pushed deep into the pillows beneath his delicious weight.

And he kissed her then with intent, his hands inching beneath her singlet, her skin aching for his touch.

Her fingers slid along his spine, digging into the heavy muscles as they explored his breadth and shape. But then they found what they were really after—the hem of his T-shirt—and she got to work pulling the fabric upwards, desperate to feel his naked skin against hers.

She cradled him between her thighs, and it was impossible not to rub her body against that hardness.

Then his fingers made it to her bra, cupping her through the satin and lace, his thumb perfectly rough against her nipple.

But then he went still. Completely still.

'Is it okay for the baby for me to be on top of you? Should we swap?'

He might as well have thrown a bucket of water over them both.

Ivy had frozen when Angus went still, but now she felt as cold as ice, the mention of their baby plunging her back into reality.

How had she let this happen?

She pulled his shirt back down, and shoved both her hands against his shoulders.

'Get off me.'

Instantly he was on his feet. 'Are you okay?'

There they were again, those lovely concerned eyes.

Ivy sat up, pulling her bra and singlet back to where they were supposed to be. She knew she was blushing, could feel it covering pretty much every square inch of her skin.

'I'm going to bed,' she said. 'Take any of the other rooms. They all have fresh linen.'

Then she noticed all the food still out. She grabbed at a random serving platter. 'I'll just put this away first. You can go to bed, though.'

She just wanted him away from her.

'Ivy,' he said. 'What just happened?'

She shook her head. 'I think it's better if we both agree nothing happened, don't you?' She remembered his words from that first coffee. 'You know, we've got eighteen years ahead of us and all that?'

Eighteen years with yet another meaningless night of

sex to try not to think about…which of course, would be all this would've been. No, not a good idea.

Finally she managed to look at him.

He nodded sharply. 'You're right,' he said. 'I'll help you tidy up.'

Then together they put the food away and cleaned up the kitchen.

Very politely, very awkwardly.

Then, just as Ivy began walking up the hallway to her room, Angus spoke.

'I'm not going to sign that contract, Ivy. I'm going to be part of our baby's life, and that means I'm going to be a part of yours. Like it or not.'

She didn't bother turning around. 'I know.'

CHAPTER SEVEN

ANGUS LAY IN his incredibly comfortable king-size bed and stared up at the elaborate ceiling rose above the guest room's elegant chandelier without really seeing it.

He'd had a really good night's sleep.

He'd always been good at sleeping anywhere, and at any time—an essential skill in his career. And he certainly didn't need air conditioning, a fluffy doona and fancy sheets.

There were only two times in his life he remembered being unable to sleep: a couple of weeks ago, when Ivy told him she was pregnant. And the night his father died.

That was it.

He also didn't really dream. He just lay his head on the pillow—or in his swag, or on the ground—and slept. *Boom.* And he slept for however long, and woke up. That was it.

Tom had asked him once if he had bad dreams.

Bad dreams about what they'd seen. What they'd done. What had happened to them. What could've happened to them. What could still happen to them.

Because it turned out Tom had really bad dreams. The type of bad dreams where he woke up soaked in sweat, or where his wife needed to shake him awake.

The type of dreams where sometimes he didn't want to go to sleep.

Sometimes, Angus had said. *Sometimes I have bad dreams.*

And Tom had nodded, and swallowed, and looked so

damn relieved that his mate understood what he was going through that Angus had been glad he'd lied.

But it had been a lie.

Because he didn't have those dreams.

He didn't come home from combat and then feel unsafe in his own home. He wasn't alert to every sound, to every movement.

He didn't sometimes sleep in his lounge room with all the lights on. Or drive all night so he didn't have to sleep at all.

He didn't gamble or drink or do drugs to dull painful memories.

He debriefed, he came home, and he was fine.

But not everyone came home fine. Tom hadn't come home fine. The guy that Cam had told him about—Patrick—he was messed up too.

And Angus knew some of the guys saw psychs at times. It made sense. Most guys seemed to work their way through it, and they'd all been told enough times about normal reactions to trauma that he knew it was just that: *normal*.

Although some guys didn't work through it. Tom hadn't.

But how about him? How about Angus?

How could he be so unaffected? How could he blissfully sleep like a log when he'd experienced so much, *knew* so much?

When your work dealt directly with life and death—and the pendulum could so easily swing one way or the other—*of course* that would mess you up, at least a little?

At some point—before Tom's diagnosis with posttraumatic stress disorder—Angus had been quietly rather proud of his resilience.

He'd thought he was particularly tough. Thought he was particularly strong.

But Tom had been tough, as tough as Angus. Tougher. Stronger.

So now…now he didn't think he should be proud.

Now he wondered what it was he lacked.

Of course it wasn't the same, but wasn't it at least a little unusual that he could have the most explosive kiss of his life with a woman who'd literally turned his life upside down, and then sleep in a strange bed for—he rolled over to check his phone—almost eight hours straight?

Shouldn't he have tossed and turned, just a little?

Yesterday Ivy had tried so desperately to control him—to pack him away into a neat little lawyer-lined box. She didn't like the undeniable pull of attraction between them, that was clear. To be honest, Angus wasn't a big fan, either.

It *did* complicate things.

Last night Ivy had told him she lost control around him, and he'd openly told her that he found it pretty hard to stay in control around her, too.

And that did surprise him. He'd followed Ivy up here because that contract had made him so damn angry—and because he wasn't going to let Ivy manipulate him.

He certainly hadn't intended to kiss her.

He wanted a relationship with his child, and he wanted a cordial relationship with Ivy. Nothing more.

There was a reason he was single now, and his previous girlfriends had all eventually become fed up with him.

He'd begun to join the dots years ago, beginning to see the similarities between his ability to process and shrug off the impacts of war and his ability to distance himself so effortlessly within a relationship.

The thing was, in his job, it was a good thing. In day-to-day life, not so much.

So it was better, he'd decided, simply not to have relationships. That way he didn't hurt anyone. And he certainly didn't want to hurt Ivy.

Angus levered himself up and swung his legs off the

bed. He'd slept in only his boxers, and the air conditioning was cool against his skin.

Last night, when Ivy had yanked up his T-shirt, the air conditioning had been shockingly cold against his heated body—for a moment. But he'd immediately forgotten that when he'd been so absorbed in Ivy and the soft skin of her hips, and belly and breasts...

Angus smiled.

So no, he might not have dreamed of Ivy, or tossed and turned all night.

But it couldn't hurt to think about her now: how she felt, how she'd looked.

The flush to her cheeks, the pink of her lips, how she'd felt so perfect beneath him, even if separated by too many layers of clothes...

The house was silent as Angus walked to the en-suite bathroom for a shower.

He wasn't usually one to daydream, either.

But for Ivy, it would seem he'd made an exception.

Ivy woke up to the smell of cooking bacon.

Mmm. Bacon.

Bacon?

Ivy's eyes popped open. Sun was streaming in through the curtains she'd left open all night, and it was clearly a long time past dawn.

Angus.

She squeezed her eyes shut again.

Angus.

He'd filled her dreams—not for the first time—and he was still here now that she'd woken up.

Not that he could've left. It wasn't as if he could easily flag down a taxi.

But that would've been nice, though. To wake up, and for Angus to have magically disappeared.

That way this weekend could've been what it was supposed to be. A break. A *proper* break, not like every other holiday she could remember.

No work. No nothing. Just—herself, and Bullah Bullah Downs.

Perfect.

But that really wasn't working out, was it?

Nothing was working out right now. *Nothing.*

Not her supposed holiday, not the contract, and not that kiss.

How had she let that happen?

Ivy noticed she'd brought her fingers to her lips and snatched them away. Why had she done that? To test if they felt different? Bruised? Ravished? Special?

They didn't, of course. Because nothing had changed, not really.

What was yet another awkward memory between them?

She climbed out of bed and got dressed. It would be hot today—it always was this time of year. She'd planned to head out to one of the gorges at Karijini today, but without a driver that wouldn't happen. She'd had Martin booked all weekend to come collect her as needed, but she'd been too flustered at the airport to think of only cancelling his initial task of driving her to the homestead.

Instead, she'd organise for the Molyneux jet to fly both Angus and herself home today. It wasn't as if she'd be able to relax this weekend, even once Angus left.

Besides, it would also give her all of Sunday to work.

Dressed in tailored navy-blue shorts and a cream linen tank-top, she headed for the kitchen.

Angus sat on one of the tall stools at the breakfast bar, a full plate of bacon and eggs piled up in front of him.

'I hope you don't mind,' he said, his back to her. 'I may have already started.'

He twisted on his seat, and then paused as he ran his gaze along her body.

'You have great legs,' he said, so matter-of-fact that Ivy blinked. 'I haven't seen that much of them before in daylight.'

At this, she blushed.

He grinned, and left his plate to walk to the other side of the bench. The gas cooktop sat in the middle of all that white-speckled granite, a couple of fry pans already in place.

'How do you like your eggs?'

Ivy still stood, frozen, in the door way. This wasn't what she had expected. She'd expected silence. Possibly antagonism.

Not this. Not a sexy smile, complete with matching sexy stubble.

He stood comfortably in her kitchen. As if he belonged, and as if he had nowhere else to be.

'Scrambled,' she said, eventually, then left the relative safety of the hall to slide onto the stool beside his.

She ate her breakfast almost warily, not at all sure what was going on.

'What are we doing today?' he asked, laying his knife and fork together on his now empty plate.

'I'll phone my office after breakfast and organise for the jet to come pick us up. With any luck we'll be home by late afternoon.'

'Why would you do that?'

Ivy looked up from her eggs, surprised. 'Because you want to go home, and I can't justify the cost of the jet flying up tomorrow as well.'

Angus leant against the low backrest of his stool, and crossed his arms. 'I never said that. I'm happy to stay.'

'You're happy to stay?' Ivy repeated. 'You mean, you're

happy to remain uninvited in my home with me—a woman you don't like very much?'

His lips quirked upwards. 'Oh, I think we both know that isn't true, Ivy.'

Ivy shook her head as her cheeks heated, ignoring him. 'No,' she said, 'I think it's best if we both go home. I was silly to fly up anyway. I have so much work to do—'

'Ivy,' he said firmly. 'I meant it last night. I'm going to be a part of our baby's life, and that does mean being part of yours. Given that, doesn't it make sense we get to know each other better?'

'Didn't we try this before, at the café?' she said. 'Besides, we can talk on the plane if you want. Play twenty questions with each other or something.'

'I'm not getting on a plane today, Ivy. I'm going to drive out to Karijini and explore. I've never been to the national park before—it would be crazy not to go this weekend when we're so close. And I was hoping you'd be my guide.'

His plans were so similar to what Ivy had originally intended, it would've been uncanny—if visiting Karijini and mining iron ore weren't basically the only two things you *could* do in the Pilbara.

Even so, it was tempting.

A big part of her—the stubborn part—wanted to stick to her guns, and insist she absolutely must fly home to work.

But another part of her—the bit that was tired of arguing, and also just plain *tired*—couldn't do it.

She could think of a lot worse things to do today than go swimming in a secluded waterhole amongst plunging gorges two and a half billion years old. And working all afternoon was certainly one of them.

Plus, reluctantly, she had to acknowledge that Angus had a point. If she was stuck dealing with Angus—and she was, now that he wouldn't sign her contract—maybe it would help to spend more—platonic—time together. Maybe familiarity would even dilute the attraction between them.

She could hope, anyway.

'We'll go to Fern Pool,' she said, 'but we need to get moving. It's a decent drive.'

Angus studied her for a long moment, and Ivy liked that she'd clearly surprised him.

Then he smiled, and Ivy found she liked that even better—and couldn't bring herself to care that that probably wasn't a good thing.

'Sounds like a plan,' Angus said. 'Let's go.'

Angus drove them out to Fortescue Falls. The forty-minute drive took them from red gravel to smooth bitumen and back to red gravel again as they approached the car park. October wasn't the best time of year to come to Karijini, with the unrelenting, impossible heat of summer only weeks away, but it did mean far fewer tourists, with only two other cars parked amongst the dirt and the surrounding scrub-tufted hills.

But they were lucky—today was perfect: low thirties with a glorious, cloudless blue sky. At a little hut, Ivy paid the small entry fee, then smiled at Angus over her shoulder as she pointed towards the deep red sand track ahead of them. He wore a black T-shirt, knee-length shorts, leather work boots and a backpack slung over his shoulders—and he looked one hundred per cent like the soldier he was, complete with bulging biceps and muscular calves. Ivy didn't think she'd ever admired a man's calves before. In fact, until today, she wouldn't even have thought it possible that they could be attractive.

But, it turned out, they could. Hair and everything.

It wasn't a long walk to Dales Gorge, less than half a kilometre. Here it was perfectly flat and easy—a stark contrast to the descent ahead of them. Ivy enjoyed the silence as they walked, after Angus had taken her twenty questions dig to heart and they'd talked most of the way here. About nothing particularly important, mostly about the Pilbara and the sights of Karijini Park—which Ivy had appreciated, still feeling a little raw from the night before.

There was just something about this man that had her revealing more than she ever intended.

In more ways than one, actually.

That thought made her smile, and she must have giggled, as Angus went still beside her.

'What's the joke?' he asked.

Ivy forced her lips into a horizontal line, and shook her head. 'I don't know what you're talking about.'

Which was completely the wrong thing to say, as now she'd intrigued him.

'Oh, really?' he said, 'Because—'

'Why don't you have a girlfriend?' Ivy blurted out, cutting him off.

Slightly horrified and with no clue where the question had come from, Ivy charged on ahead, although, given they were almost at the start of the walk down to Fortescue Falls, she really didn't have very far to go. At the lookout she pointed down into the abrupt one-hundred-metre-deep gash in the landscape.

'This is Dale Gorge,' she said. 'You can see the falls all the way down there.'

Angus, who had easily kept pace beside her, laughed. 'Yes, I got that.'

Ivy nodded. 'Of course. Right—so—this way!'

She knew he was still smiling, but decided not to pay any attention. Instead, she thought it was better to focus on her surroundings. It had been a couple of years since she'd been into Karijini. As she took in the vivid red of the ruthless, tiered red-brown cliffs and the rumbling sound of the falls beneath them, it seemed impossible she'd left it so long.

'I don't have a girlfriend because of my job,' Angus said.

Ivy tensed at the words, wanting to wish back her question. She had to walk slowly now. The path was narrow and twisting.

Angus was directly behind her, his boots crunching far more loudly than her sneakers.

'I'm not a fan of emotional farewells.'

She'd meant to remain silent, hopeful the subject would change, but once again she'd lost control of her mouth. 'But wouldn't that be worth it for the equally emotional welcome home?'

'I'm told I'm not much good at those either,' Angus said. Ivy sensed his shrug, even though she couldn't see him. 'Besides, that's only if I do come home.'

Ivy slipped on some gravel, and threw her hands out for balance. Instantly Angus's hands were on her, catching her at the waist before she could fall.

He quickly righted her, but slid his hands away just a little more slowly than was necessary.

'Thank you,' Ivy said softly, but was quick to start walking again.

Stupidly, she hadn't really put a lot of thought into Angus's career. She'd been caught up in the sexiness of it—the idea of a soldier: the uniform, the weapons, the courage. Not the reality, and certainly not the brutality of war and of death.

Her stomach had plummeted at his casual words: *only if I do come home.*

For their child, of course. She'd lost her father—not through death but through distance and lack of interest—and that had been difficult enough.

And maybe it had plummeted just a tiny bit for her.

'How do you do it?' she asked. 'How can you risk so much?'

They were about halfway into the gorge now, and the

colours of the rocks led the way—changing from orange to red to purple as they descended. To their left, the falls, which had seemed barely more than a trickle from a distance, now revealed their true size. A tourist, clambering along the adjacent rocks, gave some scale to the sprawling, towering year-round falls.

'Because I love it. The teamwork, the tactics, the challenge. It's what I've wanted to do since I was seventeen, and I'll do it for as long as I can.'

'But what about—?' Ivy began, but didn't really know how to continue.

'The bad stuff? You mean like death and destruction? Living under constant threat? Killing people?' He rattled off his terrible list roughly, and didn't wait for her to clarify. 'Of course that isn't fun. At times it's awful, actually. Indescribably awful. But then I get to come home.'

If he came home.

'And then a few months later, go and do it again.'

That was what Ivy couldn't wrap her head around. To survive war, and then risk it all again.

'Yeah,' he said. 'Sometimes—' he began, then stopped.

'Sometimes what?'

They were deep within the gorge now. Down here they walked amongst greenery and paperbarks—an incredible contrast to the parched landscape above.

'Sometimes I wonder if maybe it should be harder for me to go back.'

There was enough space for Angus to walk beside her, and she looked up at him.

'What do you mean?'

But he wasn't looking at her. Instead he lengthened his stride, then looked back over his shoulder. 'Come on, I'm keen to get to this Fern Pool you were talking about.'

He clearly wasn't going to answer her question, but still

Ivy very nearly repeated it. Besides, wasn't she just trying to get to know him better? Just as she was supposed to?

But it was something she'd glimpsed, however briefly, that meant she kept on walking in silence. For the first time since she'd met him he'd looked…

Ivy wouldn't have said *vulnerable*, because that wasn't even close to true. But something like that, something she'd never expected to see in Angus Barlow.

Angus had made it to the top of the falls, and he stood there, waiting for her.

He studied her as she approached, his gaze sweeping over her, the motion not all that dissimilar to the water as it rushed across the ancient, angular, straight-edged rocks, tracing the shape and lines of her.

But Ivy forgot to be annoyed or embarrassed by his attention, because she'd just worked it out—worked out what she'd seen.

Just for a moment, the shortest of moments, Angus had looked *exposed.*

Fortescue Falls was unusual. When Angus thought of waterfalls, he thought of a sheer pane of water, tumbling from a cliff. But here, the falls surged along a gradual series of steps and benches—like an elegantly curved stairway from amongst the trees down to the clear green pool below.

Ivy was playing tour guide, telling him that the waterfall flowed—miraculously—year round. She pointed out some of the vegetation and talked of local birds and bats. She was nervous, although Angus wasn't entirely sure why.

One moment she was so, so self-assured, the next self-conscious and talking too quickly, her gaze skittering away.

He didn't know what to make of her questioning his single status. Part of him liked it—liked that she'd wondered, liked that she'd been so appalled that she'd actually voiced the question. But another part of him—a big part—shied away from even such an oblique reference to a relationship between them. Ivy had been absolutely right to stop them both last night. Another night in bed together was not going to aid the relaxed, shared—and lawyer-free—parenting arrangement he kept telling Ivy he wanted.

Although of course it didn't mean he had to stop checking her out. She'd stepped away from him now to head down the track to Fern Pool, their true destination today. So of course he took the opportunity to have a good old look at her very nice view from behind.

It wasn't as if he hadn't noticed Ivy have a pretty thorough look at him at times.

Sex might be unwise. But looking didn't hurt anyone.

CHAPTER EIGHT

EXACTLY WHAT A terrible idea this had been only became clear to Ivy when she stepped onto the man-made wooden boardwalk that provided the only access to Fern Pool.

No one else was here, of course. Ivy had been here dozens of time with her family over the years, and *not once* had they had the pool to themselves. Even out here, more than a five-hour drive from the nearest major regional centre, tourists made sure they got to the Karijini. And they certainly made sure they got to Fern Pool.

Just not today.

Angus dumped his backpack onto the wooden boards, and Ivy looked determinedly across the crystal-clear water as he tugged off his T-shirt. Above them stretched a remarkable fig tree, and, of course, ferns were everywhere. It was lush, it was green, it was *wet*—everything that the desert-like Pilbara shouldn't be.

But it was also supposed to be full of tourists—a handful of lily-white British backpackers, a posse of raucous kids up here camping with their parents, or at least a pair of retired grey nomads.

Someone. *Anyone.*

Because without them, this place—this place with its mirror-flat water; its pair of tumbling waterfalls; its surrounding, towering layers and slabs of rock in reds and browns and purples was just…was just…

Undeniably, terribly and completely…romantic.

Dammit.

'You coming in?'

Angus stood directly in front of her, so of course she had to look at him. She made an attempt to stare only at his face, but almost immediately failed, her attention sliding rapidly downwards.

She'd felt that chest beneath her fingertips, felt it pressed hard against her.

But she hadn't had a chance to look at it—the moonlight in Bali had certainly not been as generous as the Karijini sun.

So she'd known he was broad, and hard, and ridiculously strong. But seeing him made it all new again. He was muscular, of course, but not in a stupid, body-builder way. There was still a leanness to him, a practicality—this man didn't just lift weights, he was fit, agile, supple.

He had a smattering of black hairs along his chest, but otherwise his skin was smooth. The occasional freckle dotted his lovely olive skin. His nipples were somehow darker than she expected. The ridges of his abdominal muscles deeper.

His board shorts sat low on his hips. He had that muscular V thing going on, and her eyes followed in the direction it was pointing...

Before she finally came to her senses and snapped her gaze back to his.

His grin was broad, and his eyes sparkled.

'So, Ivy—are you coming in?'

It was the same question, but also different. Was his voice lower? More intimate?

She took a deliberate step backwards, and promptly stepped onto his backpack, and the beach towels that Angus had pulled out for them.

It was the pool. The damned pool's fault for being so intimate and dreamily secluded.

Still grinning, Angus walked to the metal ladder that

provided access to the pool, although Ivy finally managed to drag her gaze away as he climbed in.

Instead she turned her back, as pointless as that was, to pull off her top and shorts. She liked that Angus had bothered to read the sign beside the pool, and he hadn't jumped in, as many others did. Ivy hadn't read it today, but she knew what the first line said: *Fern Pool is a special place.*

A place where you didn't make loud noises or jump off the waterfalls. Where you respected your surroundings and the traditional owners of the land.

It certainly shouldn't be a place where she ogled a half-naked man.

Her clothes neatly folded on top of Angus's backpack, Ivy rolled her shoulders back, and took a handful of long, deep breaths.

She told herself not to be self-conscious, although of course that was pointless. She could've been underwear-model thin and she *still* would've felt insecure around all of Angus's bronzed perfection.

And she certainly wasn't underwear-model thin. But she *was* in her favourite black and white striped bikini, and if she breathed in her stomach was almost flat.

Her hand rested on her still-normal-sized tummy.

She'd forgotten again.

Although this time, remembering that she was pregnant didn't trigger a spiralling panic, or make her want to squeeze her eyes shut and wish just about *everything* away if she could just find a way to fix what she'd done.

In fact, all it did was cause her to turn around, and to search for Angus in the water.

The pool wasn't large, but Ivy didn't have to search far anyway. His forearms rested on the edge of the boardwalk as he floated in the water, watching her.

'How long until the baby starts to move?' he asked.

'Ages,' Ivy said. 'Eighteen to twenty weeks, I think?'

Her lips quirked upwards. 'I thought you were full bottle on all this pregnancy stuff?'

He pushed away from the boardwalk, his eyes still on her. 'Haven't got to that chapter yet,' he said. He flicked his hand through the water, sending a light spray of water in her direction. 'I've noticed you're still not swimming.'

The drops of water that now decorated her feet were surprisingly cool, given the heat of the day. But then, down here, beneath the shade of the great fig, the light was diluted.

'Although I'm not really complaining,' Angus continued. He was treading water only metres from the ladder. Close enough that Ivy knew he was—and had been—checking her out.

She blushed, which was just about her default reaction to Angus it seemed, but also found herself smiling. Almost as if she was enjoying his attention.

Fern Pool romanticism *was* getting to her.

That was enough to get her into the water quick smart.

And it *was* cold. Cold enough that she gasped.

But just as she had as a kid, she immediately ducked beneath the water to soak her hair.

Better to get it over with quickly.

Ivy and Mila had always agreed on that approach. While April had swum around shrieking about not getting her hair wet *yet*, which had been pretty much an engraved invitation for her sisters to splash her with as much water as possible.

'What are you smiling about?' Angus asked, treading water beside her as she tucked her hair behind her ears.

'A nice memory,' she said, and then filled him in.

Angus rolled onto his back as she spoke, so he floated, staring up at the sky. 'It doesn't surprise me at all that you've always got straight to the point,' he said.

Except around Angus. Somehow, and sometimes, around

Angus, being direct seemed impossible. Her words escaped her. Her *brain* seemed to escape her.

'Do you have any brothers or sisters?' Ivy asked.

'No,' Angus said. 'Just Dad, and Mum, and me. We didn't really travel as a family all that much. You're lucky.'

Ivy laughed. 'We didn't always think that coming up here was all that great. But Mum was all for multitasking on a holiday—coming up here meant a business trip *and* a family getaway. Although my sisters and I did go to the US a few times to visit my dad.'

'The actor?'

'Yeah,' Ivy said, not surprised Angus knew that detail. Most people in Western Australia did—but then, a mining heiress didn't elope with a handsome, if small-time, Hollywood actor and have nobody notice. 'He left when I was pretty young, and we've never been close. He calls me on my birthday.'

She followed Angus's lead and stuck her legs and arms out so she could float on her back. Water lapped against her ears and she closed her eyes, enjoying the sensation of weightlessness.

'Are you close to your parents?' Ivy asked.

'Yes,' Angus said. 'And no. I mean—'

Ivy tilted her head so she could see him. He floated so close to her that if she reached out just a little bit further, their fingers would touch.

'I was very close to my father, but he…died. And my mother has early-onset dementia, which is pretty awful really.'

'Oh, that *is* awful,' Ivy said, jackknifing from her back to swim to him. 'I'm so sorry.'

He'd done the same thing, but he didn't wait for Ivy. Instead he swam away, in big, generous breast strokes, to the pair of tumbling waterfalls.

But he stopped just short of where the falls hit the pool,

and turned as he treaded water. 'I wish we had travelled together as a family more. But my dad worked too hard. Every weekend he was at the shop. He *had* to be at the shop—at the furniture shop we owned. Even when he didn't really need to be, he still thought he had to.'

Angus wasn't looking at her. His chin was tilted upwards, as if he was examining the thick, ropey branches of the fig tree that stretched towards the sky.

'My mum's like that,' Ivy said.

Now he looked at her. '*You're* like that,' he said.

'I am not!'

He simply raised an eyebrow.

Ivy opened her mouth to argue, but realised it was pointless. The fact was she wasn't very good at holidays. When she did go away, she kept one eye on her smartphone, and made damn sure she always had access to a Wi-Fi network.

But she'd hated how her mother had never truly been present on family holidays. She couldn't do that to her own child.

'I'd like to take our baby on holidays when he or she is older,' Angus said.

'Me too,' Ivy said. Then quickly added, 'Not with you, of course.'

'Of course,' he said, glancing at her with a smile. But there was a sadness to it, as if he was thinking of the family holidays he never had. Or the father he had lost.

'How old were you?' Ivy asked, 'I mean, when your dad died?'

'Seventeen,' he said. 'It was very sudden. I'd always thought I'd follow in his footsteps, continuing to run the family business or something. Although to be honest I hadn't worried too much about it. I was at an age where all I cared about was playing footy on the weekend. Or hanging out with my mates. I'd never had to deal with the future before.'

'So the army wasn't a lifelong dream?'

Another smile, but still without humour. 'No,' he said. 'Part of it was the physical aspect of the job. When dad died, I started to really get into my weights, and fitness. It was a distraction, I guess. A focus. As mum started to get unwell not long after. So the sense of achievement from lifting heavier weights or running further, or faster…it was… I don't know. Something. Something that wasn't thinking about what I'd lost, and what I was losing.' Angus wasn't looking at Ivy now, his gaze again focused somewhere in the giant fig's branches. 'But now I think it was a lot about the structure. The formality. With my dad gone and mum not really my mum any more—it was kind of a relief to have a schedule and orders to work to. Later, I fell in love with the job, with the mateship, the teamwork, the tactics. But early on the job was like an anchor for me, something I could rely on.'

'That's a heck of a lot for a young man to deal with,' Ivy said, her heart aching for a lost and grieving teenage Angus.

He nodded. 'Yeah,' he agreed. 'It was. Sometimes I wonder if—' But his words trailed off, and he turned back to the cascading water. 'Did you ever climb up behind the waterfall?'

Ivy blinked at the abrupt change of subject, but didn't push. Somehow she knew that Angus didn't share that story easily. If at all. 'All the time,' Ivy said, her tone consciously upbeat. 'It's slippery, though.'

He threw her an amused look, that sadness erased from his gaze.

'Oh, I'm sorry,' Ivy said, deadpan, as she swam up to the rocks. 'I should've realised you did slippery-rock training in the SAS.'

'Honey, you'd be amazed at what I can do,' he replied, and then, right on cue, slipped a little as he hoisted his legs onto the lowest, moss-slick rocks.

Ivy giggled, and Angus glared—but couldn't hide his grin.

The falls here were delicate in comparison to Fortescue, falling gently only about three metres from the protruding ledge of red rock above where they swam. Beyond the curtain of water, slabs of rock provided tiered seating of sorts, decorated with clumps of ferns.

It had been a while, but Ivy remembered which rocks provided the best grip, and it only took her a few seconds to clamber past Angus and to settle into her favourite spot—directly behind the waterfall, the tumbling water blurring and distorting the world around her into indistinct reds, blues and greens.

It didn't take long for Angus to join her, seated to her right. He stretched his longer legs out in front of him, just as Ivy had, although his toes also touched the falls. The sound of the water echoed back here, but it would still be easy to hold a conversation.

But they didn't say a word.

Instead, they both just sat silently together, not quite touching, looking through the waterfall.

At first, Ivy itched to speak. To say something. Anything.

But she couldn't.

Back here, on the other side of a blurry world, Ivy somehow knew that to talk would break this. Would break this moment, would destroy this unexpected sanctuary.

So while at first she'd wanted to shatter the silence, to pop the bubble of this special place, in the end she couldn't.

All she could do was sit here, and breathe in the scent of ferns and moss, and lick drops of water from her lips.

She'd propped her hands behind her, to balance herself on the rocks. Angus had done the same, but now he twisted slightly. Ivy turned to look at him, and his gaze locked with hers.

The light was different back here, and his eyes seemed different too. The flecks of green more emerald, the hazel base more gold.

As he looked at her he reached across his body, and skimmed the side of her thigh with his fingertips. His touch was impossibly, tinglingly light—and then it was gone.

There wasn't so much a question in his gaze. It was more he was simply waiting.

Because he knew, as she knew, where this was going to end.

But he needed to wait, because Ivy needed to wait.

Ivy needed to hold onto whatever tatty remnants of control she might still have when it came to Angus for as long as possible. He'd said, last night, that she couldn't control him.

Well, she couldn't control anything around Angus.

And now, just like last night, she really didn't want to. Despite everything.

She let go of a breath she'd been unaware she was holding, and something in Angus's expression shifted.

His gaze dropped to her lips, and his hand went back to her thigh.

But again, his touch was light.

Ivy didn't move. She couldn't really, without the possibility of sliding back into the pool. But again, she really didn't want to.

Her gaze followed the trail of his fingers.

Along the outside edge of her thigh, leaving a smattering of goose bumps.

Up, over her hip, and around the knot on the side of her bikini bottoms.

She was leaning back against her hands, so she was looking down her own body as his hand slid from her hip to lie, momentarily, flat against her belly.

Her gaze darted to his face, but his attention remained on her stomach, his expression unreadable.

Then he was on the move again, moving even more slowly now, tracing loops and circles along her ribs, beneath her breasts.

Her breath was coming more quickly now; she could see her chest rising up and down as warmth and need swirled within her.

Then, too quickly, his fingers moved up and over her bikini top, only brushing the swell of her breasts with the most frustratingly light movement.

But she couldn't protest, because words would end this.

Ivy didn't ever want this to end.

Everything she had was focused on his touch. Her eyes fluttered shut.

Over her collarbone. Across her shoulders. Up against the delicate, shivery cords of her neck.

Along her jaw, tilting her chin. Slowly, slowly, upwards.

His breath against her mouth. His hand sliding backwards and amongst her tangled hair.

Then, finally, his lips on her lips. His mouth on her mouth.

Cool, and firm, and tasting of the waterfall. Fresh, and perfect, and magical.

It was the most tantalising of any of their kisses. The most delicate, the most careful, the least carnal.

But it fitted this place.

And Ivy was lost amongst their kiss. She touched him only with her mouth but it was more than enough. She kissed him slowly, he kissed her leisurely, as if they had for ever.

Here, it felt as if they did.

Then a splash tore them apart.

A blokey laugh and then a yell: *'Cannonball!'*

Through the waterfall heads bobbed in the water, and then a shape flew through the air.

Another splash. More laughter.

They had company.

Angus was already on the move, and he turned to offer her his hand.

She shook her head, and smiled. 'No, I've got this.'

As she swam towards the boardwalk, Ivy knew that now was about when she should be feeling that familiar cloak of regret.

But she didn't.

She couldn't.

Angus did help her climb up the ladder, and gave her hand a little tug when she stood on the boardwalk, to pull her close so he could kiss her quickly—but firmly—on the lips.

Ivy knew what that was.

A promise.

And she shivered, despite the heat of the sun.

CHAPTER NINE

IVY FELL ASLEEP on the drive back to the homestead.

A combination of hours in the sun and early pregnancy fatigue.

And also, probably, that delicious lethargy from being so very thoroughly kissed.

She dreamed of that kiss, and of that place behind the waterfall.

When Angus shook her gently awake after he'd brought the car to a stop, it felt only natural to reach for him. To curl her hands behind his neck and to pull his lips down to hers.

But this was a totally different kiss from before.

This kiss wasn't slow, or gentle or restrained.

And neither was Angus.

There was a *click* as he released her seat belt, and then he was pulling her towards him, and then on top of him as he leant back in the driver's seat. Ivy smiled as she straddled him, rising up on her knees so she could reach his mouth.

His hands slid up to grip her butt, and then one slid upwards to reach beneath her top.

She still wore her bikini, dry now after the walk back from Fern Pool. It only took one tug on the string at the back to loosen the top half, and Angus just shoved the fabric away as he filled his hands with her breasts.

Ivy sighed into his mouth.

Their kiss before had been unforgettable, but this—this rawness, this lack of restraint—she *needed*.

And that need superseded any other emotion that did

its best to wave manically at Ivy from somewhere within her subconscious.

Because frankly Ivy knew that this was a bad idea.

The same way it had been a bad idea in Bali, and it had been a bad idea last night.

But that hadn't been enough to stop her then, and it certainly wasn't going to stop her now.

She needed this. Her structured, controlled, *planned* life had plummeted into a chaos that she had no idea how to fix. Maybe she couldn't fix it, and if she thought about that too long it terrified her.

But *this* felt good. *This,* at this moment, felt right.

Even if it wouldn't feel right tomorrow.

It didn't matter.

Angus's lips coasted along her jaw, pressing hard kisses along her neck.

'You good?' he said, deep and low, against her ear.

She nodded firmly *yes.* And as if that might not be clear enough, she said it aloud, too.

She felt his smile against her skin.

Ivy's hands had shoved his T-shirt up as much as was possible, her fingernails grazing his chest and those lovely muscles of his stomach, before she explored lower, sliding just beneath the top of his shorts.

Then Angus pushed her top up, and his mouth quickly covered her nipple, and Ivy went perfectly still.

His tongue was hot, gentle, rough, all at once. He took his time, licking, kissing—waiting for her reaction before doing again what made her sigh.

His big hands were flat on her back, holding her still. She sank down onto him as her head fell backwards, loving the feel of his hardness beneath her.

She impatiently shifted her hips, and Angus used his teeth, so, so gently, against her breast. *Later.*

But it already felt as if she'd been waiting far too long.

Since the waterfall. Since Bali.

Her hands had lain, useless and forgotten, on her lap, but now she put them to use, feeling for the snap closure on his shorts, as his head and shoulders blocked her view.

For a moment, she did go still, though. To watch him kiss her breasts. She had the same realisation every time she was close to him: he was *so* big, *so* broad, *so* overwhelming.

But right now, so careful. So focused.

On her.

It was a heady sensation. Sexy.

And she didn't just get to look at him, she got to feel him. Got to explore his strength, and experience how incredible all that controlled, amazing, coiled strength made her feel.

Finally she pulled the snap open, and it was easy to rip apart the Velcro fly on the board shorts.

He wore nothing beneath, and she shimmied backwards on his thighs so she could see what she'd just revealed.

Angus leaned back against the chair, and then, with a cheeky grin, reached down to adjust the chair so he reclined back further.

He looked so pleased with himself, Ivy grinned back, but then he reached for the button of her own shorts, and she formed her lips into a stern line.

Later.

She gripped his length in her hand, running her fingers from base to tip.

His breath had quickened, and he studied her from beneath half-lidded eyes.

She moved her hand again, enjoying the feel of him, the warmth and the sensation that he was growing even harder as she touched him.

'*Ivy.*'

The roughly spoken word dragged her attention back to his lips. She rose to her knees, desperately needing to kiss him again.

And when they did kiss, it was rough and messy and desperate.

Between them they unzipped her shorts, and somehow she managed to wiggle her way out of them, along with her bikini bottoms, twisting this way and that on Angus's lap.

'You're killing me here, Ivy.'

But finally she was free to straddle him again, and his hands cupped bare skin, gliding around to slide through her wetness, and to circle her where she needed it most.

She groaned, and kissed him again. Hard.

She reached for him, but then his lips were at her ear.

'I'm clean. There's been no one else since Bali.'

It shouldn't have been the perfect thing to say, but somehow it was. 'Me too,' she whispered.

And then she couldn't wait even a moment longer.

She wrapped her hand around him again, then slid, not slowly at all, downwards.

She sucked in a breath, the sensation of having him inside her, stretching her, filling her, almost *too* good.

But then she moved, and that was even better.

His fingers gripped her bottom, but she didn't need him to guide her. They fell instantly into the perfect rhythm, and his mouth found hers, kissing her again and again.

And the tension built inside her, growing and tightening low in her belly with every stroke and slide and sigh.

Then his clever fingers touched her where they were joined, and that was all it took to push her over an edge she'd felt she'd been teetering on for ever.

And fall she did, into wave after wave of sensation.

Then Angus was moving her hips harder, and faster, and the waves just kept on coming, overwhelming her in a way she'd never, ever experienced.

Then he was groaning into her ear, and finally, finally Ivy began to float back down to earth.

She lay there, sprawled on top of him, the four-wheel drive loud with their heavy, laboured breathing.

'Would it be wrong if I asked you to carry me inside again?' Ivy asked.

Her legs felt as substantial as fairy floss.

She sensed his smile, even though her face was pressed against his chest. 'No problem, just give me a minute. Right now, I just about need someone to carry me.'

And Ivy just smiled against his still-heated skin.

'So I have a theory,' Ivy said, a few hours later.

On Ivy's king-size bed, Angus rolled onto his side to face her. She stood in the en-suite doorway, wrapped in a pure white bathrobe, and with a towel twisted around her hair.

'Yeah?'

She nodded. 'A theory that makes this weekend okay.'

'This weekend is better than okay, Ivy.'

She narrowed her cool blue eyes. 'You know what I mean.'

She crossed the wide floorboards to perch primly on the edge of the bed. Angus sat up, the sheet puddled around his waist.

'Well, my theory is that you'd already seen me naked in Bali, so it isn't like this weekend makes any difference.'

'Because I would've been thinking of you naked whenever I saw you to pick up or drop off our kid, anyway.'

'No!' she said, swatting at his legs beneath the sheets. Then, 'Really?'

He shrugged. 'Of course. On the plus side, now I can imagine you in daylight.'

Ivy flopped onto her back on the bed and stared up at the ceiling. 'Oh, no.'

Angus grinned. 'Look, we both knew in Bali that we were just having fun. We both know now that we're just having fun. I'm sure we're both mature enough to behave like grown-ups in the future.'

'Except for the imagining me naked bit.'

'If it makes you feel better, I don't mind if you imagine me naked, too.'

Ivy tilted her head to glare at him.

'Do you want to hear my theory?' Angus said.

'Only if it doesn't involve nudity.'

'Done,' he said. He reached for the tie of Ivy's bathrobe, and tugged it open, just because he could. Ivy watched him, but didn't move, the hint of a smile on her lips. The terry towelling of the robe didn't move a lot, but it did reveal a lovely slither of skin. Not enough, though. 'Okay, so my theory is that this weekend is a great idea because clearly we needed more than Bali to get this thing out of our systems. If we *hadn't* slept together again, we would've had all this unresolved tension between us. This way we clear the air.'

'So having sex now will be good for our parenting in the future.'

'Exactly.'

'You should be in the Molyneux Mining marketing department,' Ivy commented.

'*You* shouldn't be wearing so many clothes.'

He moved so he was leaning across her, one hand on either side of her face.

'Well,' she said, very softly, 'technically I'm not wearing any clothes.'

Angus reached between them, pulling her robe completely open. He levered himself upwards, to survey what he'd revealed.

'You know what?' he said, after a very long while. 'I think you're right.'

He leant down, kissing her gently before pulling away to look at her again.

'Although, maybe I'll just check one more time.'

Ivy laughed, then tugged him down for another kiss.

Angus made breakfast again the next morning.

He'd woken beside Ivy after—as standard—another excellent night's sleep.

It had been a very long time since he'd last woken up in a woman's bed. A year, at least. Maybe two.

It was a slightly uncomfortable realisation.

He'd had girlfriends, of course. Nothing too long-term—a few months, maybe.

What he'd told Ivy yesterday had been partially true. He didn't like emotional farewells.

But not because *he* found them emotional.

It was stupid really, that the tears always surprised him. There he was, thinking everything was fine, that both he and the woman he was seeing were happy casually dating. And then the tears came. The earnest requests to keep in touch whenever he could.

Yet he never felt that way. He had no problem at all leaving. And if he was honest, it was more that he didn't make time—rather than that he forgot—to reply to emails or to video call home when he could.

So those farewells simply exposed a disconnect. Between the type of relationship he wanted—with no tears and no expectations—and the starkly, starkly different relationship his girlfriends had expected.

Eventually a pattern even he couldn't fail to miss had arisen amongst his ex-girlfriends' angry, parting words.

Thoughtless. Selfish. Cold. Distant.

And he'd realised, maybe around the time that Tom had left the regiment, that it was better if he didn't do relationships at all—even the most casual. So he might go out on the occasional date. But he'd never stay the night.

No expectations. No hurt feelings. No confusion.

He'd determined he simply wasn't wired for long-term relationships. For marriage. For commitment.

But everything had changed with Ivy's pregnancy. Now he, like it or not, had a permanent commitment—to his child. He'd have a child who might, once old enough, want to come and wave goodbye. Who would expect him to email or video call and would maybe even make one of those welcome home signs to hold on his return.

He hadn't planned this, but it was his new reality.

But what if he fell into his old habits? He'd been no good at maintaining a romantic relationship—what if the same applied to his child?

He remembered how much it had hurt when his dad had chosen hours in his office over his son. He'd adored his father, and deep down he'd known he was loved. But sometimes he had felt like an afterthought. Forgotten amongst the importance of work.

He didn't want to be that type of father. It was why he'd never intended to have children, to avoid the risk altogether.

So he needed to do everything he could to prevent that happening. To prevent his child being hurt.

It was why he was so persistent that he would be part of Ivy's life. They hadn't yet talked about how they would manage their co-parenting, how they would share custody—how they'd do anything. He knew, instinctively, that Ivy wasn't ready for that discussion yet.

But what he *did* know was that he needed to do this right.

Lawyers, obviously, wouldn't work. Neither would unresolved tension with Ivy.

'Morning.'

Ivy padded into the kitchen, rubbing her eyes. She wore a pale pink singlet and neat white underwear, and Angus honestly didn't think she'd ever looked more beautiful.

She hardly looked at him as she climbed onto the bar

stool. A hand reached up to pat ineffectually at her less than sleek hair.

'I couldn't bear to look in the mirror,' she said, looking at him with a half-lidded sleepy gaze. 'But I still suspect I should apologise for the state of my hair.'

No, last night she'd been a bit too distracted after her shower to think about drying it.

'You look stunning,' he said, meaning it.

She stuck out her tongue. 'Ha-ha.' Then she grinned. 'But I forgive you, because you've made me breakfast again.'

'Pancakes, bacon, bananas and maple syrup,' he said.

'Bacon?'

'It's a taste sensation,' he said. 'Trust me.'

She raised a sceptical eyebrow, but tucked into her breakfast, none the less.

Later, she helped him load the dishwasher.

'I wouldn't have picked you as a cook,' she said.

'Don't get too excited—breakfast is my speciality.' He could've left it at that, but then found himself still talking. 'My mum was an incredible cook. I guess I picked up a few things from her. I do a mean lasagne.'

'I'd love to try it one—' Ivy began, then stopped abruptly.

She took an already clean plate to the stainless-steel bin, and scraped at it with a knife to remove non-existent scraps.

I'd love to try it one day.

The atmosphere in the kitchen had shifted.

Before it had been all light, and flirtatious, with everything they said and did touched by the afterglow of the night they'd shared.

But with that one short sentence, this wasn't the casual, one-off weekend they'd agreed to last night.

Sun still streamed through the huge sliding doors, but now it seemed *too* bright. As if it were shining a light on all that was wrong with this image, rather than all that was superficially right.

He should have returned to his own bed last night.

Maybe it was just a slip of the tongue. Maybe Ivy wanted nothing more, either.

But it had been unwise to persist with this faux cosiness, this illusion of a sexy weekend away between a loved-up couple—complete with a home-cooked breakfast.

He didn't want this.

He didn't want any of this.

But more importantly, he wasn't capable of it, either.

CHAPTER TEN

THE DRIVE TO Paraburdoo could only be described as awkward.

As was the flight home.

They spoke, but it was terribly, terribly polite.

Everything had changed so quickly. One moment all was well, and Angus had been all warm and sexy; the next it was clear—*so clear*—that it was over.

But what was *it*?

It was dangerous. As dangerous as how she'd felt when she'd woken to the smell of pancakes, or when Angus had kept touching her so subtly as they'd cleaned the kitchen. A hand on her hip, here. A deliberate brush of her fingers, there.

So, so dangerous.

She should be grateful she'd made that silly comment. And logically, she was.

She'd known that it would end, and soon. Was it wrong that she'd hoped it to last even a few hours longer? Could it really hurt if they'd pretended until they arrived back in Perth?

Or at least until they'd left the homestead?

Well, of course it could. Because what would it have achieved? Really?

A few more kisses. Maybe more, if they'd been quick.

No. Stop it.

Ivy had her hands rested neatly on her lap as she sat in the back seat of her car. It took everything she had not to twist them into knots. Because Angus sat beside her.

That had been another brilliantly awkward conversation:
'*I'll get a taxi home.*'
'*Don't be stupid. I insist.*'
'*Ivy—*'
'*Please just let me drive you home.*'

And however she'd said that last bit had finally convinced him. That bothered her, too.

What had she revealed for him suddenly to agree? Why had she even cared?

Why couldn't he have just signed the bloody contract?
Why? Why? Why?

The car rolled to a stop on a quiet, tree-lined street in Swanbourne. Ivy didn't know what she'd expected, but the lovely federation cottage with its neat box hedges and generous sprays of lavender was definitely not it.

'It was my mum's,' Angus said, reading her mind. 'But I like it.'

She liked that he did, not that it mattered.

'I'd imagined something more…macho,' she said.

'And what does that mean?'

Something modern and concrete and angular?

No. That didn't fit Angus.

'I don't know,' she said. 'Maybe a log hut where you drag the food you've hunted with your bare hands?'

Angus barked a surprised laugh, the sharp sound unexpected amongst the still-simmering tension. 'You're unique, Ivy,' he said.

She liked that he'd said that too.

He grabbed his backpack, and climbed out of the car.

He didn't say goodbye. He didn't look back, either; he just walked up the recycled brick path to his front door.

'We going straight to your place, Ms Molyneux?' her driver asked, looking in his rear-view mirror.

Ivy realised she was staring at the now-closed cottage door.

She gave her head a little shake.

'Yes,' she said. 'Thank you.'

The weekend was over.

'Ivy? Are you listening?'

Ivy blinked. She was at April's place, a lovely house perched on the beach in North Cottesloe. She held a mug of hot chocolate in her hands, and she'd been watching April as she'd talked, but, as hard as she tried, she hadn't really been listening.

It was three days since she'd arrived back from Bullah Bullah Downs, and yet Angus still crowded her thoughts.

She tried to tell herself that was normal; after all, she'd never had such a casual—uh—*relationship* before, so it probably made sense that the experience would linger.

It was just that the lingering had been at *the* most inappropriate times. Like during an important conference call today when she'd completely lost her train of thought, or now—when clearly April had just told her something important.

'I'm sorry. Something's on my mind.'

'I know, I know,' April said, with the air of the long suffering, '*work*.'

Ivy opened her mouth to correct her sister, but then snapped it shut. No. It was impossible to tell April only part of the story, and she still wasn't ready.

'Well,' April said, dragging out the word theatrically, 'I know it's a bit earlier than I've always said, but Evan and I have decided to try for a baby!'

Ivy went completely still.

April was beaming. 'I know it's kind of weird to tell you—I mean, basically I'm telling you that Evan and I are having lots of unprotected sex—but, you know, I just *had* to tell somebody.'

It took some effort, but Ivy arranged her lips into a smile. 'That's brilliant, April, how exciting.'

April tilted her head, studying Ivy. 'You okay?'

Ivy nodded vigorously. 'I'm fine. And I'm *thrilled* for you.'

And she was. Just the secret that she was keeping from everyone now felt a million times larger.

'I'm going to tell Mila too. *Not* Mum though.' Her sister paused. 'I'd rather keep it a big surprise for her and tell her when we fall pregnant. She'll be over the moon!'

'You think?' Ivy asked, surprised. 'She wasn't all that maternal with us.'

They'd had a team of wonderful nannies to look after them while their mother worked her incredibly long hours. She still worked those hours, now.

'Of course. Who wouldn't want to be a grandmother?'

'I suppose,' Ivy said, but didn't really agree.

But then, her relationship with her mother had always been different from that of Mila and April. Her mother had always been tougher on her, always held her to a higher standard of achievement, always pushed her harder. Because—her mother said—*you're just like me*.

Now would be the perfect time to tell April of her pregnancy.

Right *now*.

Because now she didn't just feel as if she were omitting something, she felt as if she was outright lying.

But April would shriek with excitement and ask a million questions and be all joyful and just plain *happy*, and she wouldn't understand when Ivy tried to explain why she was so damn terrified about it all. So. Now wasn't the right time.

But she did have to tell her. And Mila, and her mother.

Soon. Very soon, because she couldn't keep hoping she'd miraculously come up with a better plan.

It wasn't going to happen.

And as nice as it would be to tell only April and Mila, and to bask in their excitement before they started to connect the dots and work out what it actually meant for Molyneux Mining, the better way was to tell them all together.

Because her mother would connect the dots immediately. She'd leap right to the point, because that was what she did. As in business, it would be better that way.

April had left the room, and came back now with a small pile of pregnancy magazines, which she placed carefully on the coffee table in front of Ivy.

'Look, I know this is totally jumping the gun, but honestly, I don't know *anything*, and none of my friends have had kids yet, and...'

Yes. She'd tell them all at dinner on Sunday.

That evening, Angus pushed the buzzer on the stainless-steel panel bolted to Ivy's limestone fence, and waited.

After a minute, Ivy's voice came through the speaker. 'Yes?'

'It's Angus,' he said.

He'd then fully expected to have to explain why he was here, but instead the gate immediately began to open.

Surprised, he climbed back into his car, and drove up the neat driveway.

Ivy stood with her arms folded at the base of the steps that led to her front door, dressed in jeans and a loose T-shirt, waiting for him.

He jumped out of his car, and slammed the door behind him. 'I expected that to be more difficult.'

'I expect that people call before visiting,' Ivy said, one eyebrow raised. Her hair was loose, and a few tendrils blew across her cheeks in the evening breeze.

He shrugged. 'I was concerned that warning you may have resulted in another contract on arrival.'

'I let you in because I didn't want you to pull another stunt like at the airport.'

Angus grinned. 'I like that. Now I'm a stuntman, *and* a soldier.'

Ivy rolled her eyes, but his comment had the desired effect as she couldn't hide a subtle smile. 'I suppose you want to come in?'

'Up to you,' he said. 'I'm mainly here for a delivery.'

He held out a small brown paper bag.

Now he'd intrigued her. 'For me?'

'Don't get too excited.'

She took the bag, and he could see her warring with her inherent politeness.

'It's dark,' she said, eventually. 'Come inside, I'll open it in there.'

He followed her into the house. They walked past a broad, curving staircase and elaborate leadlight doors to the open-plan kitchen and living area.

While the kitchen was modern, the house seemed to have retained most of its original features—with detailed ceiling mouldings, a high plate rail on the walls and wide polished jarrah floorboards. The furniture was a mix of old and new, and it felt as if Ivy had decorated it, rather than some fancy interior designer.

He liked it, and he told her so.

Ivy smiled. 'Thanks. I used to walk past this house on the way to school. I always wanted to live here when I was a kid. I thought it was magical with all its arches and curves, and the Juliet balcony upstairs. My mum bought it for me after...' Her words trailed off as she walked over to the fridge. 'Would you like a drink?'

'That's quite a gift.'

'Well,' Ivy said, 'at the time my mum wanted to make quite the gesture.'

'About what?'

Ivy held open the fridge door and pointed at the shelves. 'Juice? Wine? Beer? Water?'

'Beer,' he said. He hadn't planned to stay, but now he couldn't remember why.

He watched her as she carried the beer to the bench, and then located a bottle opener in her cutlery draw.

Her jeans were faded and loose, as if they were her old favourites—and he imagined her taking off her tailored work clothes to slide into them.

Which wasn't the greatest idea.

He immediately wondered if she'd worn the same style of underwear today as she'd worn in the Pilbara: plain and simple but incredibly—incredibly—sexy. Or if she'd worn a skirt to work today like the one she'd worn when they'd had lunch. Prim, and fitted and—yep—incredibly sexy as well.

'Let's just say,' Ivy said, 'that my mother was keen to end what she considered my *rebellious* phase.'

It took him a moment to remember what they'd been talking about.

'Aren't you going to ask me when *I* was ever rebellious?' she prompted.

He shook his head. 'It doesn't surprise me at all.'

Ivy pushed the now-opened bottle across the kitchen bench towards him. She leant one hip against the granite, a glass of juice in her hand.

'Really?' she said, and seemed pleased. 'I don't think anyone has ever thought me capable of being a rebel.'

'But you just said you were.'

This wasn't making a lot of sense.

Her gaze darted downwards, as if she now found her juice endlessly fascinating. 'I wasn't, not really.'

'Just enough for your mum to buy you a house so you'd stop being one.'

'No, it wasn't like that,' Ivy said to the flecks of stone in the bench top. 'I mean, yes, I did say that, but...' Then she looked up and caught Angus's gaze. 'Really, it doesn't matter, does it? My mum bought me a house, which probably fits every spoilt-little-rich-girl stereotype ever, and that's the end of it.'

She'd left the bag he'd handed her on the corner of the bench, near where Angus stood, and now she strode over to pick it up, clearly hoping to change the subject.

Her movements were rushed and awkward, and it took some effort for Angus not to reach out for her—but to do what, he wasn't sure.

'Ivy, you go after what you want, and what you think is right,' Angus said, deciding if he couldn't reassure with his touch, he'd try something else. 'I might not always agree with you, but I can still respect your drive, your focus. So yes, if what you wanted wasn't the "right" thing to do, I have no trouble imagining you rebelling.'

Ivy studied him for a moment, with wariness in her eyes—as if waiting for a punchline.

But after a while, her lips curved into half a smile. 'Thank you,' she said. 'That was a nice thing to say.'

'And for what it's worth,' he added, 'I don't think anything about you is stereotypical. Of anything, or anyone.'

Her smile broadened. 'Are you saying I'm a bit weird?'

He grinned, too. 'You know I'm not.'

Her gaze dropped again.

He tapped at the bag she was still holding. 'Can you hurry up and have a look?'

When she looked up her gaze was teasing again. 'Goodness, you're pushy!'

'You're surprised?'

Then she laughed, and it was as if all that awkwardness—and whatever it was she'd almost told him—had never happened.

She dumped the contents of the bag onto the bench.

A couple of thick, glossy booklets; an application form; and a few other bits and pieces he'd printed off the Internet.

'A learner's permit application?' Ivy asked, picking up the offending piece of paper as if it had a disease. 'Why would you think I'd want this?'

'Because I think it's crazy that a woman your age, in a city like Perth with less than stellar public transport, *doesn't* have a licence.'

Ivy shrugged. 'I'm not going to get a licence just to make you feel better.'

'No, although I'm surprised you'd be comfortable being the only mum in your mothers' group being dropped off with bub in a limo. Now, *then* you'd be fitting every spoilt-little-rich-girl stereotype in the book.'

Her eyes narrowed. 'Did you come across mothers' groups in all your researching?'

No, actually. Tom had told him, years ago, after a 'swarm of babies' had descended on his home a few months after he'd had his first.

'I can come up with other similarly awkward scenarios, especially as our baby grows up. I don't know about you, but I would've hated being dropped off at footy training in the family Rolls Royce with a driver in a silly hat in the front seat.'

'I don't own a Rolls, or a silly hat for my driver to wear,' Ivy said, but the bite had gone from her words.

'I've hit a nerve?'

Ivy ran her hands through her hair, absently piling it up on top of her head before letting it tumble back down to her shoulders. 'You can be very annoying, you know that?' she said, then sighed. 'I used to get crap at school because I had a driver drop me off, not my mum. Everyone thought I was a snob—which is saying something given I went to a very posh school. My sisters were good at dealing with that sort of teasing, but I was just rubbish at it. I tend to think of clever things to say half an hour after it would've been useful.' She looked down at her tummy. 'What if this little bub takes after me in that way, and not you?'

'True,' he said, with a completely straight face, 'that would be tragic.'

Ivy reached out to gently shove him on the shoulder. 'Ha-ha. Let me guess—you were the most popular boy in school?'

'Close,' he said. 'Maybe third most popular is more accurate.'

He was only partly teasing. School had been a lot of fun for him—until his father's sudden death had ripped it all away.

Ivy was looking at him curiously. 'You okay?'

Angus deliberately smiled, annoyed that he'd revealed something in his expression.

'Of course. So—you're going to get your licence, then?'

Slowly, Ivy nodded. 'Yeah,' she said. 'It would seem so.'

'Great!' he said, with a little more enthusiasm than was necessary. 'I'll come over on Sunday for your first lesson.'

'Pardon me?'

Angus took a long sip of his beer. 'I'll teach you,' he said. 'We still have a lot to work out before the baby arrives—and we'll need to come to some sort of parenting arrangement so access, financial issues and so on are clear between us. And I still think it's important we continue to get to know each other better.' He paused, then added, 'Clothed.'

As he'd intended, Ivy blushed a deep scarlet.

'Are you sure that's the best idea?' she asked. 'We can have those discussions in a meeting room at the Molyneux Tower. Or my lawyer's office. Keep it more formal. And surely they can wait a few months, anyway?'

'I can't see any benefit in a delay,' Angus said. 'Especially as I could be deployed at any time once I return to work.' He raised an eyebrow. 'But what are you worried about? Am I that irresistible?'

Ivy glared at him. 'I know that *I'm* clear that we can't… um—'

'Have sex?' he prompted helpfully.

'Yes,' she said. 'We can't do that again. It's too complicated.'

'Agreed,' he said.

But still it took some effort to leave his half-drunk beer with a comment that he needed to drive home, and to make his exit only a few minutes later.

It would've been far too easy to stay.

CHAPTER ELEVEN

'YOU BOUGHT A new car?'

Angus stood in front of Ivy on her driveway, dressed in faded jeans and a T-shirt, squinting—somehow attractively—just a little in the bright early afternoon sun.

Ivy smiled, running a hand along the neat Volkswagen hatchback's glossy silver hood. 'Yes. I thought it was better to learn in a smaller car, rather than your giant four-wheel drive. Also, apparently it's better to learn to drive a manual.'

'So you bought a new car,' Angus repeated, shaking his head.

She shrugged. 'I don't think it's that big a deal.'

Ivy had embraced this 'learn to drive' project a little more zealously than was necessary, she knew. She'd read the books Angus had left her, done a couple of online mock learner's quizzes, then gone in to sit her learner's test at the local licensing centre during her lunch break the very next day.

Buying the car had been surprisingly fun. She'd never really given any car a second thought, but suddenly she was reading motoring reviews, going out for test drives with her assistant, and picking out her favourite colour.

She was enjoying the distraction; it meant she had something else to think about whenever her day wasn't wall-to-wall Molyneux Mining that wasn't her pregnancy, or Angus.

And cars were a lot less scary to think about than what on earth she was going to tell her mother and sisters that night at dinner.

Or so she'd thought.

It was one thing to agree with Angus's irritatingly accurate logic and to get her learner's permit. But quite another to actually, physically drive.

Angus theatrically opened the driver's door for her. 'After you, m'lady.'

With a deep breath, Ivy slid into her seat. Once seated and strapped in, she focused on her breathing.

One in, two out, three in, four out, five in, six out...

It was the first time in weeks she'd counted anything, although it wasn't all that surprising.

The breathing had helped when she'd first got in a car again when she was nineteen. So had the counting.

In fact, that was when the counting had started. All those years ago, as she shook with nerves in the passenger seat of her mother's car.

Seven in, eight out, nine in...

Angus was explaining something. 'So from left to right it goes clutch, brake, accelerator,' Angus said, pointing at the pedals at her feet. 'Remember it's just ABC, in reverse.'

Ivy nodded, although it was a bit difficult to focus on what he was saying beyond her mental counting.

He then talked her through how to use her mirrors, and Ivy managed to follow his instructions well enough to adjust both the rear-view and side mirrors sufficiently.

Then she fussed around quite a bit adjusting her seat.

Too far forwards. Too far back. Too far forwards again.

Seat-back was too upright. Too reclined.

Then she found she could lift the seat up and down. So she did that a bit too, the little motor whirring away as she pushed the up and down buttons.

But eventually she'd adjusted as much as was possible, so had to sit still.

'Don't be nervous,' Angus said. 'You'll be fine.'

It was lucky Ivy was wearing sunglasses, because otherwise Angus wouldn't be so sure. She'd tried this once before, years ago.

She remembered how she'd looked then, in that mirror behind the sun visor. She'd flipped it down and stared into her own eyes as she'd given herself a little lecture:

You can do this, Ivy. Everyone learns how to drive. Don't be so pathetic.

It hadn't worked then, but surely now—twelve years later—she would've got over it all?

Surely?

'Ivy?' Angus asked gently. 'Can you start the car? Foot on clutch, gear in first. The handbrake is still on, so we won't go anywhere.'

Ivy guessed he'd given her these instructions more than once, but they might as well have been gobbledegook.

Regardless, she put her left hand on the gear stick, and shoved her left foot down hard on the clutch. With a wiggle that was probably too rough, she put the car into first gear.

There.

A ghost of a smile curved her lips. *Maybe she would do it this time?*

Hand back on the wheel, she reached with her right hand for the keys.

All she had to do was twist the key forward and...

She couldn't do it.

She snatched her hand away—why she wasn't sure—and the key dropped to the ground, landing with a thud on the soft carpeted floor.

'Ivy?'

But she didn't wait; instead Ivy threw open her door and leapt from the car, running up her front steps two at a time.

At her door she realised she'd left her handbag—and house keys—in the back seat of her new car.

When she pivoted back to the car, Angus was right

there—only a metre or two away. He'd taken his sunglasses off, and concern was obvious in his gaze.

Ivy kept hers on, despite the shade of the veranda.

'You're not just nervous,' Angus said.

'No,' she said.

'And the reason you don't have a licence is nothing to do with being a spoilt little rich girl who couldn't be bothered.'

'No.'

'Can you tell me the real reason?'

No.

'I was in a car accident when I was nineteen.'

That was more than she'd told anyone, ever. More than anyone else, but her mother, knew.

Oddly, even though she hadn't meant to say the words, it felt good to say them.

'Were you hurt?'

Ivy shook her head. She didn't want to say this bit. This bit wouldn't feel good to say.

'A few bruises, a big one from the seat belt,' she said. 'But nothing, not really.'

She'd often felt it would've been better if she had been injured. A gash to her face that everyone noticed. A scar on her skin, and not just on her insides.

'You were the passenger?'

Angus had stepped closer. His hand moved, and for a second Ivy thought he was reaching for her, but then the moment was gone.

'My boyfriend was driving us home. He'd taken me to this club, a pretty seedy private one, upstairs somewhere in Northbridge. He'd been drinking, a lot, but he insisted on driving home.' Now she'd started talking, the words wouldn't stop. 'I'd only been seeing him for a few weeks. He was really tall, with overlong brown hair and an eyebrow ring. He had tattoo sleeves up both arms, but one was only half inked in. I thought it *so* cool. I thought he was *so* cool. He wasn't like any guy I'd met before. He wasn't rich. He wasn't poor, either, but I kind of pretended he was—like he was the kid from the wrong side of the tracks and I was the sweet rich girl he was going to corrupt.'

'He was your rebellious phase,' Angus said.

'Oh, yes,' Ivy said. 'I wanted to rebel so badly that I grabbed the first vaguely disreputable guy I could find and held on tight. We barely knew each other, really. All we did was go out drinking and clubbing. But I thought I was in love, you know? I'd spent my whole life being the perfect firstborn daughter, and now I wasn't. Although I wasn't all that brave. I told my family I was with girlfriends. So I was kind of rebelling on the sly.'

Ivy smiled without humour. She knew she was saying too much, and all jumbled in the incorrect order—but she couldn't stop.

'So Toby drove me home. I knew he'd had too much to drink, and I told him I'd call one of the family drivers to come pick us up. Or I'd pay for a taxi. And honestly, he looked at me like I'd just suggested we take ballroom-dancing classes.' She shook her head. 'I knew he shouldn't drive. I mean, I didn't even have a *sip* of alcohol until I turned eighteen. I'm that person. I'm the annoyingly sensible one. But that night I decided I wasn't. That I was cool and relaxed. But I wasn't. I couldn't relax. I basically held onto my seat for dear life, and Toby noticed, and got angry, and told me I had to trust him.' Ivy kept entwining and untwining her fingers, again and again. 'And he drove faster. And faster. And I told him not to, at first I tried to sound relaxed but then I was literally screaming at him as he thundered down the street.' A long pause. 'Then he lost control, hit a tree, and was killed instantly.'

The simple words, in a way, reflected that night. In the end, it was so simple. One moment Toby was there, beside her: loud and arrogant and drunk. Then—gone. Just like that.

'What an idiot,' Angus said.

'He paid a high price for his mistake,' Ivy pointed out.

'But he almost took you with him.'

Ivy couldn't argue with that. 'The whole driver's side of the car caved in. I had to be cut out of the wreckage, but I was okay. Totally okay. I walked away.'

That night was still mostly a blur. She'd had a few drinks herself, although she'd been far from drunk.

Her memories were more little snapshots from the night: Toby's smile when she'd walked into the bar and he'd checked out her too-short skirt; putting her mobile phone back into her bag, without making that call for a driver; the click of her seat belt when she strapped herself in; Toby's frenzied, ugly, manic expression when she'd pleaded with him to slow down, to stop, to let her out…

Then the impossible arrangement of Toby's seat and the steering wheel after impact. The feel of his pulseless wrist beneath her fingertips.

Ivy hadn't realised she'd closed her eyes until she felt her sunglasses being lifted from her face.

She blinked up at Angus. He was very close, but not touching her.

'But you weren't okay,' Angus said. 'No one is okay after something like that.'

Ivy bit her lip, and ignored him. 'When the police arrived, they found drugs in the car. I was so stupid and naïve I'd had no idea. I didn't even know what drugs they were. I still don't. And the worst bit is that even if I had known, I was so caught up in Toby and his tattoos and being an edgier version of myself it probably would've only added to Toby's mystique. The police questioned me at the hospital, but then my mum arrived, and it all went away.'

'What does that mean?' he asked. He still stood close. Too close, probably, but Ivy didn't mind. It helped, actually.

'It means what I said. My mum made it all go away. I don't know what she did. I didn't ask. Maybe I wouldn't have been in trouble, anyway? Who knows? All I know is that when I went home, my sisters didn't know I'd been in a car accident. When I read about the crash in the papers the next day, there was no mention of me. It's like I was erased from the whole incident.' She paused, thinking. 'It wouldn't be all that hard. I know the right people to call, now, should I want a story pulled. For Molyneux Mining, it's important to have a close relationship with the media. Bad publicity can be so damaging.'

'But what about the damage to a teenager?' Angus asked, his words harsh.

Ivy had been staring at the print on the front of his T-shirt, but now her gaze shot up to meet with his. 'I would've been a lot more damaged if the story had got out,' she said. 'It would've followed me for ever. It was difficult at the time, but I'm grateful for what my mum did. It turned me around, set me back on track.'

'On track to take over Molyneux Mining next year.'

Ivy nodded sharply. 'Yes.'

'And you never made another mistake again.'

'Yes,' Ivy said, automatically. 'I mean, no, of course I've made mistakes. I make mistakes all the time.'

'But nothing big. Nothing that would ever have anyone question Ivy Molyneux's competence, or business sense, or suitability to take over the company.'

'No one would *dare* do that,' Ivy said, getting annoyed. 'I would never do *anything* to jeopardise Molyneux Mining. I learnt my lesson.'

Angus studied her, his gaze tracing her eyes, nose and lips, then returning to meet her gaze. 'I get it now,' he said.

'The marriage proposal, the contract. Your rabid need to fix everything, to control everything.'

Ivy bristled, but he didn't let her speak.

'It's because you actually think it's possible, don't you? That you can do what your mother did all those years ago, and sweep it up—make everything uncomfortable, messy and awkward just disappear. Just go away without any consequences.'

'It is possible,' Ivy said, stubborn enough to argue. 'And there are *always* consequences. Like how I can't drive.'

That poor attempt at a joke received only a look of derision.

'It's about minimising damage,' she continued. 'About controlling the…'

But she heard what she was saying and knew she was going around in circles.

Suddenly she *was* standing too close to Angus. She stepped around him, intended to go and get her bag out of the car. There wasn't going to be a driving lesson today.

She should get inside. Get some work done.

But Angus grabbed her hand.

Ivy spun around to face him, snatching her hand away. 'But *you* won't go away, will you?' she said. 'No matter how I ask you, or what I say, or what I offer…'

'No,' he said.

One simple word, but it made her want to scream.

But scream at what?

That, as he'd told her before, she couldn't control him?

Or scream at the fact that she didn't really want him to go away at all?

Ivy's shoulders slumped.

She couldn't pretend any more. She wasn't miraculously going to come up with a plan. She wasn't going to fix this. This wasn't going to go away.

'I'm telling my family tonight,' she said, very quietly.

'I'll come with you.'

'I didn't ask you to come,' she said.

'You never would,' he said, stepping closer to her again. 'But I'd like to be there. Maybe it would help.'

Ivy was absolutely sure it wouldn't. He would only complicate the most complicated of situations.

And yet...

'Okay,' she said.

She'd told herself she didn't want him to come, but couldn't quite make herself believe it.

He took another step closer, and she tilted her chin upwards. Then, before she really knew what was happening, he kissed her.

A soft kiss, a gentle kiss.

'It'll be okay,' he said, against her lips.

She stood stock-still as he skirted around her and walked to his car.

'What time should I pick you up?' he asked.

'Six-thirty,' she said.

And then he was gone.

Of course, it wasn't a surprise that Ivy's mother lived in a palatial mansion. Angus had expected nothing less.

The dining room was very grand. The table was long enough to allow space for two chandeliers above it, and the table was set like something from a magazine, with white flowers everywhere.

Ivy's sisters sat at the table. The pair had been chattering loudly as they'd walked into the room, but when they saw him they instantly fell silent.

Through another door, Ivy's mother entered the room with a bottle of champagne.

'Oh,' she said, her gaze flicking over him. 'I'd better get another table setting.'

Then she turned on her heel, and walked out.

Ivy was incredibly tense beside him. Very, very softly, she was counting under her breath.

His instinct was to put his arm around her, but he knew that wouldn't help.

Although, in fact, his true instinct was not to be here at all.

He hadn't done this before—this 'meeting the family' thing. So far, he wasn't much of a fan.

'Thirty-seven…thirty-eight…'

He reached out and wrapped his hand around Ivy's.

Maybe it wouldn't help, but maybe it would.

Ivy glanced up at him, and attempted a smile.

There was a clink and clatter at the table as Ivy's mum returned and set a place for Angus.

She walked to him, holding out her hand. 'I'm Irene.'

He needed to drop Ivy's hand to shake Irene's, and instantly Ivy stepped away. She rushed to the table, and dropped into her seat as if they'd been playing musical chairs.

'Angus Barlow,' he said.

Irene's handshake was firm, but that was no surprise. She studied him with care, distrust flickering in her blue eyes.

This also was no surprise. He'd bet his house that Ivy hadn't brought another man to Sunday dinner before.

A minute later they were all seated. Irene's personal chef came out to talk them through the upcoming courses, and shortly afterwards their entrées arrived. A tiny stack of vegetables and salmon, with a sauce smeared theatrically across the plate.

April and Mila remained silent, seated across from them, as if waiting for Ivy to speak. They snuck curious glances in his direction, and the tiniest of encouraging smiles.

Irene sat at the head of the table, to Angus's right. Her lips were formed into a perfectly flat line.

But she was waiting, too.

No one touched their cutlery. No one picked up their glass of champagne.

And the tension just continued, and continued to build.

Ivy took a long, deep breath.

Then she shifted in her chair so that she faced her mother.

Another long, deep breath.

'I'm pregnant,' she said.

Silence.

'I'm the father,' Angus said, because he couldn't let Ivy do this alone.

But Irene didn't pay any attention to him. Instead she surged from her seat and went to one of the room's huge windows, staring out into the night.

'Oh, my *God*!' April shrieked, clapping her hands together. 'Ivy! That's amazing! Congratulations!'

Ivy picked up her water glass, then put it back down again, untouched.

Mila's reaction was more subdued. Her gaze flicked between Angus and Ivy. 'Was this planned?'

Ivy shook her head, but didn't seem capable of speech.

'No,' Angus said, unnecessarily, but needing to say something.

'You kept *this* on the down low, Ivy,' April said, indicating the two of them—and seemingly oblivious to Ivy's discomfort. 'When did you start going out?' She paused, then laughed. 'Goodness, I was so distracted at the wedding I didn't notice *anything* between you. Can you believe it?'

April turned to her younger sister, but Mila was watching Ivy.

'We're not—' Ivy began.

'Going to bore you all with how we met,' Angus finished for her.

Ivy's eyes widened in surprise, but she didn't correct him.

'What will you do next year?' Mila asked, and at her question Irene turned from the window, crossing her arms in front of her chest.

'Yes,' the older woman said, her gaze steely. 'What are we going to do?'

Not 'you', but 'we'.

'Well,' Ivy said, 'around about July, *I'll* be having a baby.'

There. There was a bit of the bite and sass he was used to.

'Don't be facetious, Ivy,' Irene said. 'I think you understand what is at stake here.'

'Of course I understand what's at stake here, Mum,' Ivy said. She pushed back her chair, and stood up, gripping the edge of the table. 'I'd like to negotiate a period of maternity leave, and a delay to me taking over your position. I do apologise for that, but it's unavoidable.'

'Unavoidable?' Irene zeroed in on Angus now. 'I have no idea who you are, but I'm sure you've heard of condoms?'

April and Mila both looked mildly scandalised that their mother had said *condoms*.

Angus leant back in his chair, deliberately relaxing his body, knowing that would infuriate Irene. He shrugged. 'Accidents happen.'

'They do,' Ivy said. 'Everyone makes mistakes sometimes.'

She glanced down at him, her lips shaping into the tiniest hint of a smile.

'This isn't just a *mistake*, Ivy! Your *recklessness* has ramifications for the entire company. I don't think you do fully understand the gravity of the situation, and frankly I'm disappointed that you don't. I—'

'Mum,' Ivy said, cutting her off. 'I think you need time

to digest this news. I think we should go. I'll see you at the office, tomorrow.'

This was Angus's cue. He casually rose to his feet, then took his time saying goodbye to Ivy's sisters.

They didn't rush as they left the house. Ivy just walked with purpose, without saying a word, until they stepped out onto the terraced entrance to the Molyneux mansion.

The heavy door clicked shut behind them.

'Ivy—'

But then Ivy halted his words with her lips.

She kissed him as she hadn't kissed him before. It was more intense, more thorough—more *confident*.

She wrapped her hands behind his neck, tugging him as close as possible. Her body was plastered against his, chest to breast, hip to hip.

She kissed him, and he kissed her, until they were both breathing heavily, until Angus *needed* to drag her to the car, and then home, as quickly as possible.

But then Ivy took a step back, and ran her hands through her hair.

'Wow,' she said. 'I haven't pashed a boy on my mum's front doorstep before.'

Angus laughed. 'I always knew you were a rebel.'

CHAPTER TWELVE

IVY WASN'T SURE how she felt.

She wasn't sure how she was supposed to feel.

She hadn't expected to feel like this.

She felt…

Okay, mostly.

Not great. But okay. She'd spent so much time imagining what it would be like to tell her mother about her pregnancy that she hadn't really thought about what would happen *after*.

But she'd known it would be bad.

But it wasn't. It was…okay.

Ivy leant back against the headrest as Angus drove her home.

'I'm starving,' she said. 'I can order some takeaway when we get home if you like?'

The question sounded like something she'd say if she and Angus were the couple he'd implied they were, and inwardly Ivy cringed a little.

But although Angus slanted a look in her direction, he nodded.

'You're not going to faint on me before then?' he asked.

She smiled. 'No. I had a pretty good idea we wouldn't be eating dinner at my mum's, so I had a snack before we left.'

A fortifying most of a block of chocolate, actually.

But by the time Angus stopped the car at her place, the atmosphere between them had shifted.

At her mother's house, it had seemed almost like they

were a team—banded together against anything her mum could throw at them.

Afterwards, she hadn't thought twice when she'd flung herself into Angus's arms. It had just been the right thing to do, her way of releasing some of that tension. And, *wow*, it had felt good.

But really, her pregnancy announcement hadn't solved anything. She was over the first hurdle, but there were a whole crap load of hurdles still to come.

It had felt like a victory, but really it wasn't. Her bravado had been false.

Kind of like she and Angus were a team—but really, they weren't.

At the front door, in the pool of porch light, she paused as she fished for her keys in her bag.

'Why did you let my family think we were a couple?' she asked. She sounded more defensive than she'd intended.

'I figured it was one less thing you had to deal with tonight,' he said.

'Okay,' she said. 'But what happens now?'

'Nothing happens,' he said. 'One day you'll just tell them we've broken up.'

He made it sound so easy.

She'd found her keys, and stabbed at the lock, taking a couple of goes before the key slid in.

Then she shoved the door open, her movements stiff.

'Isn't that what you wanted?' Angus said, remaining on the porch while she stepped inside. 'Even right at the beginning? A fake boyfriend, to avoid the so-called scandal?'

Ivy wasn't sure why she was angry, but she definitely was.

'A fake boyfriend who kisses me sometimes,' she said.

'You kissed me, tonight.'

'I know,' she said, with a sigh. 'This is confusing.'

'Ivy, I can't offer you any more than—'

She held up her hands, her cheeks turning pink. '*No.* Stop. I don't want this either, so no need to let me down gently.'

No. She'd made this mistake before, with Toby—getting caught up in attraction and hormones. Letting her emotions lead her, rather than logic and common sense. A relationship with Angus was not a good idea. The way she lost control around him… No. She couldn't risk losing herself in some crazy idea about love, again.

But still…even if allowing anything serious—if allowing the hint of love—was not acceptable, maybe there was still an alternative?

'Maybe what I want,' Ivy began, searching for what she was trying to say, 'is a fake boyfriend, with benefits.'

A way to, once and for all, sate this *thing* between them. To get it over with. But with no false expectations. No risk.

There was a long, long pause.

'A fake girlfriend, with benefits,' Angus said, as if testing the concept out on his tongue. His grin was wicked. 'I think I can work with that.'

This time, Angus kissed her.

And Ivy kissed him right back.

For the first time in as long as she could remember, Ivy was late to work on Monday. She'd had no excuse—Angus had left before dawn for the barracks as he was back at work now that his wrist was fully healed. He'd woken her when he'd left, and kissed her gently on the forehead.

Not long after, her alarm had gone off.

But she hadn't been ready to get up yet, so she simply hadn't. She'd curled up beneath her doona and fallen asleep to the vague idea that she should probably reset her alarm— and fortunately the arrival of her driver at seven-thirty had later served as a sufficient alarm replacement.

In the end, she wasn't that late, not really. It wasn't even nine a.m., but even so her staff seemed not quite to know what to do with her.

Ivy didn't know quite what to do, either.

She wasn't as bothered by her lateness as she would've liked, which concerned her a little.

But then, today she was doing all sorts of unfamiliar things—confronting her mother being number one on that list. So yes, maybe tardiness was the least of her worries.

Later that morning, Ivy took the lift to her mother's office.

It was on the very top floor, a floor above Ivy's offices, and was a hive of activity. Ivy weaved her way past the network of open-plan workstations and glass-walled meeting rooms to reach Irene's suite, separated from the rest of the floor by heavy, jarrah doors.

But her mother's assistant looked confused by Ivy's appearance.

'I have a meeting booked with Irene,' Ivy said.

Theresa shook her head. 'No,' she said, 'Irene has cancelled all her meetings for the rest of the week. She's flown to a conference in Berlin.'

'Oh,' said Ivy. 'Of course!' She shook her head, as if she'd just made a silly mistake.

But this had never happened before.

Ivy would never have described her relationship with her mother as perfect.

For all they were the same, they were also very different—despite her mother's insistence that Ivy was just like her.

But in business, they *were* in sync. Together they'd run Molyneux Mining for nearly a decade, with Ivy's role growing year by year.

The conference in Berlin did exist, but they'd decided, together, that another senior executive could attend in their place.

Irene's sudden change of mind was not a business decision.

It was extremely personal.

For all her bravado last night in the face of her mother's disappointment, it had been incredibly hard for Ivy.

But, she realised now, some part of her had hoped for something different today. That after a night to sleep on Ivy's revelation, Irene's reaction would be different.

After all, Irene had three children—*surely* she should understand?

Surely some part of her would be excited to meet her first grandchild? Just as April had said?

But no.

Ivy had, for the first time in her life, put her own needs ahead of Molyneux Mining.

Her mother didn't like it. She would never like it.

And that hurt.

'You're counting again,' Angus said.

Ivy's gaze shot up to tangle with his, her lips now pressed firmly together.

Then she sighed. 'I do that sometimes. Despite my best efforts.'

They walked together from the car park to the front of the nursing home.

'Nerves,' she continued. 'Stupid nerves. I used to do it all the time, and I thought I'd grown out of it, but apparently not.' A pause, then a pointed look. 'I blame you.'

'Me?' he asked, innocently. 'I don't make you nervous. Hot and bothered, maybe?'

She glared at him.

'But you don't need to be nervous tonight. My mum will love you.'

'And that's the problem,' she said. 'I always *know* I shouldn't be nervous. That's the frustrating thing.'

They stood outside the glass door of Reception. Ivy rolled her shoulders a few times, and took a deep breath.

She was still dressed for work, in fitted trousers and a spotted silky blouse.

Angus leant close. 'You look gorgeous. You won't say the wrong thing. And if you do, don't worry—she probably won't remember anyway.'

Ivy's jaw dropped open. 'Isn't that in terribly bad taste?'

Angus grinned. 'Trust me, my mum would've been the first to make that joke. Come on, let's do this. I *promise* my mum won't bite.'

The nursing home was a small, boutique facility, made up of a collection of detached villas and a larger single-level building for the high-dependency patients, like his mum. Once through Reception, Angus led Ivy through the communal living and dining rooms to his mum's room. It was spacious, like a generous hotel room, with a bed, a small seating area, and a separate en-suite bathroom.

His mum sat on the couch, watching the ABC news.

'Angus!' she said, smiling at him as they entered the room.

This was a good start. On the very worst days—for both of them—Angus needed to remind her who he was.

'Mum,' he said, 'this is my friend, Ivy Molyneux. Ivy, this is my mum, Hillary.'

'Nice to meet you,' Ivy said. She held out her hand, which Hillary shook firmly.

Hillary glanced between the two of them. 'And?'

'We have some news,' Angus said. 'Can we grab a drink, first?'

Soon they were all settled with cups of tea, seated around the small coffee table.

Ivy was fidgeting. Subtly—by twisting her fingers in her lap—but fidgeting none the less. It made Angus smile.

Such a powerful, polished, woman.

Yet so...*Ivy.*

'So, Mum,' Angus said. 'Ivy and I are having a baby.'

Ivy's eyes widened, as did Hillary's.

Then his mum's eyes squeezed shut. The older woman twisted to face Ivy. 'I've forgotten you, haven't I?' she said. 'I'm so sorry. I do that a lot, now.'

'Oh, no!' Ivy said. 'You haven't met me before.' When Hillary raised an eyebrow, she added, 'I promise.'

Hillary's gaze zipped back to Angus. 'I feel I've missed something here.'

Angus smiled, and then—briefly, and significantly censored—told his mother how he and Ivy had met.

She smiled, and nodded, as he spoke.

Angus was relieved. He'd asked Ivy to come tonight because when he'd called the nursing home earlier, he'd been told his mum was having a good day. But that was never a guarantee.

And it was important to him that Ivy met his mum. Stupid really, but somehow, given he was beside her when she told her family, he felt it should be the same with his.

His mum would never be as she had been—the woman who would've put Ivy instantly at ease and talked her ear off about all manner of random things.

But at least tonight she was a reasonable-strength version of his mum—not a version so diluted by dementia that he felt as if he was interacting with the disease, and not the mother he loved.

Now Hillary asked Ivy a bit about herself, but Ivy was talking too much, and over-explaining. Not Ivy's fault—he should've warned her—but he saw Hillary's eyes lose focus as all the words began to overwhelm her.

Ivy noticed too, and her sentence trickled out to nothing.

She looked stricken, and Angus reached out to squeeze her hand briefly. 'You're doing good,' he said, softly.

Then he asked his mum about her day. Hillary launched

into a detailed explanation, which might have been a true reflection of today, or an amalgamation of the last week or month—or have never happened at all—but regardless, his mum was animated again, her eyes full of life.

Ivy slowly began to relax back into her chair, her tea cradled in her hands.

'How is Scott?' Hillary asked Ivy, suddenly.

Ivy's body instantly stiffened, and her gaze flicked to Angus.

'Pardon me?'

'Scott is Carise and Tom's son,' Angus said. 'This is Ivy.'

But his mum shook her head firmly. 'No, no. I remember her. Long brown hair. Pretty blue eyes. Baby boy with a pink blanket because she believed in gender neutrality in colour schemes.'

This was the frustrating, awful bit. That a snippet of conversation from years ago could be remembered, but not the person his mother was talking to right now.

Ivy leant forward, placing her teacup carefully back in its saucer. 'My name's Ivy,' she said. 'I don't have a baby yet. But when I do, we'll bring him or her to visit you.'

Another agitated shake of the head. '*No*,' Hillary said. 'I haven't forgotten. I saw the wedding photos. Your husband is very, very handsome. Almost as handsome as my son.' She paused, looking thoughtful. 'But he got sick, didn't he?' Hillary balled up her fists, rubbing them into her eyes. 'Why can't I remember?'

'Mum,' Angus said gently, 'it doesn't matter.'

His mum turned back to Ivy. 'So, Carise, how is Scott?'

Ivy sent Angus another panicked glance. 'I'm not—'

'Scott is well,' Angus interrupted. 'He's walking now! Getting into everything. Tom is having to baby proof everything.' He forced a laugh. 'I guess I'll find out all about that soon enough.'

Hillary blinked. 'What do you mean?'

Hell.

It *still* hurt, every time.

'I'm going over to help Tom out with installing latches,' Angus said, improvising.

He had, actually. Three years ago, when Scott had started walking.

His mum seemed happy with that.

She also looked tired. Impossibly tired.

For the next few minutes he filled the silence, just as he always did. With bits and pieces about work, about things that happened years ago, things that happened today.

Hillary soon finished her tea, and Angus called a nurse to help her get ready for bed.

He kissed her on the cheek, and her hand reached up to curl into his hair and pull him close, just as she always had.

'I love you,' she said into his ear, as clearly and as firmly as ever.

A few minutes later, as they stepped outside the building, Ivy once again threw herself into his arms.

But this time it wasn't a kiss. There was nothing frantic or desperate in her action.

She simply hugged him. And held him.

'Who is Scott?' Ivy asked. 'And Carise and her husband?'

She'd propped herself up against her pillows, the sheet pulled up over her legs. She wore a faded navy singlet and her underwear, while Angus wore only boxers. Tonight was the first night they'd climbed into bed even partially dressed.

It was dark in Ivy's room, the only light glowing from a bedside lamp.

'Carise is the wife of an old friend, Tom,' Angus said. 'Scott is their eldest son, although they have a daughter now, too. Maybe more.'

It had been too long since he'd been in touch. Appallingly long.

'Were they close to your mum?'

Angus shook his head. 'No. They visited once to support me. I needed someone else who'd experienced my mum like that, you know? I had no family to come with me. To talk to about how I felt. I thought maybe if...' Another shake of his head. 'A stupid idea. It didn't help.'

'What happened to Tom?' she said gently. 'Your mum said he was sick?'

There was sympathy in her eyes, and Angus realised what that meant.

'He's not dead,' he said, very quickly. 'He wasn't that type of sick. I mean, he isn't that type of sick—cancer type of sick. He had PTSD.'

'Post-traumatic stress disorder.'

'Yeah. We worked together.'

Ivy nodded her head, as if that explained everything. 'Ah. That doesn't surprise me. You must deal with such awful, awful things.'

This bothered Angus.

'Why shouldn't it surprise you?' Angus said. 'It's what we train for. It's what we're *built* for. It's what we do. Why should it be such a shock that we manage to deal with it okay?'

His words were harsh, and far louder than he'd intended.

'I didn't say that,' she said. 'I just said I'm not surprised that some soldiers are impacted by PTSD.'

'And what does that make the rest of us? Robots?'

Ivy looked taken aback. She reached out for him, but he shifted a little so her hand fell to the sheet without touching him.

He knew he was being unfair. This wasn't about Ivy and what she'd said.

It was about his guilt. For a lot of things.

He slid from the bed, the thick rug beneath Ivy's bed soft under his bare feet. Despite how little he wore, Ivy's state-of-the-art climate-control system meant he wasn't at all cold.

Even that irritated him for some reason.

'It doesn't make you a robot,' Ivy said, very softly.

He had his back to her, but he could see her in the reflection of her ornate dresser mirror. She'd pushed herself up from the pillows, as if she'd been about to follow him, but had changed her mind.

'This is what you meant,' she said, after a while. 'At the gorge. You said that maybe it should be harder for you to go back. To go to war, to leave your loved ones behind. I didn't understand at the time.'

He shook his head. 'You wouldn't understand now.'

Why had he done this? He'd only needed to tell her enough to explain who his mum had been asking about. Ivy didn't need to hear any of this. He didn't need to answer any questions to do with this.

'No,' Ivy said. 'I'd never truly understand. But I can listen to you.'

Angus still watched her in the mirror. She hadn't moved. She looked beautiful, her hair loose, her face freshly scrubbed of make-up.

And she carried his child.

The scene was so domestic. They could be a married couple, thrilled at the impending birth of their first child.

Was this what had happened to Tom? Had he started to realise how much he had, and how much he had to lose?

Angus wanted to leave. He wanted out of this room and this domesticity.

But what would that achieve? If he went home, Ivy would still be pregnant. They were tied together for ever.

'When I go away,' Angus said, 'I won't be able to tell you where I'm going. Or what I'll be doing, or when I'll be back. Sometimes I'll get no warning at all, so neither will you. Sometimes I might be able to contact you when I'm away, sometimes I won't.'

Ivy's reflection nodded.

'I'll probably miss some special occasions,' he continued. 'Like birthdays. School assemblies, that type of thing.'

'How do you feel about that?' she asked.

'Not good,' he said. 'But not bad enough to quit my job.'

Ivy's eyes widened. 'It never occurred to me that you would.'

'Really?' he said. He turned to face her now. 'You think it's normal to still want to risk my life and to want to be away from home for indefinite periods of time now that I'm going to be a father?'

'I don't think what you do is normal,' Ivy said carefully. 'But that's why people like me do jobs like mine, and people like you are in the SAS. We're lucky there are incredibly brave, strong people like you. Australia is lucky.'

'How patriotic,' Angus said, his tone completely flat.

'Hey,' Ivy said. She pushed herself onto her knees, crawling to the edge of the bed so she was close to him. 'Don't dismiss what you do. What you do is important.'

'What a lucky kid we'll have,' Angus said. 'A mum who works seventy-hour weeks and a dad disappearing for months overseas.'

'I won't be like my mum,' Ivy said. 'I *won't*.'

'I know. You'll hire the very best nannies. And I'm hardly in a position to expect you to stay at home. I—'

She'd jumped to her feet, and laid her hand flat against his chest—although her push didn't move him an inch.

'Yes, I *will* hire a nanny, but not the way you think. I've already had preliminary designs drawn up for a nursery and play room on my floor at the Molyneux Tower. That way I can spend all my breaks, and lunch, with the baby. Plus I've been reading about breastfeeding, so this way I'll be able to continue after I return to work after six months.' She sighed, rubbing her forehead. 'I know it's not perfect. I've thought about maybe working part time, but I just can't, not right now. Maybe in a few years, once the company is more established under my leadership. So you're right, I won't win any mum of the year awards…but it's all I can do for now. I can't give up all I've worked for—' she snapped her fingers '—just like that.'

Her hand still rested on his chest, but it was gentle.

'I can't understand what you do,' Ivy said, 'but I *do* understand loving what you do. My sisters honestly believe I've been somehow forced into my role at Molyneux Mining, as if Mum managed to indoctrinate me into her mining executive regime, but it's not true. I love it. I love the challenge, the pressure, the responsibility. And maybe it makes me selfish not to give it all up, given I don't need to work at all. I could be a lady of leisure for every day of my life, and still have more money than I know what to do with.'

Now she took her hand away, so she could wring her fingers together.

'I don't think you're selfish for wanting to do what makes you happy,' Angus said.

'Ditto,' Ivy said.

But it wasn't the same.

'Tom used to be like me,' Angus said, unsure why he was trying to explain. 'We even look kind of the same, about the same height, weight, brown hair—that kind of thing. We did the selection course together and then the eighteen-month reinforcement cycle. We were even assigned to the same squadron and deployed together. Tom was great. I thought I was an insane trainer, but Tom sometimes out-did me. We pushed each other, we competed against each other—we were both just so proud to have made it. We loved the training—honestly, when you get paid to jump out of a helicopter, to storm a passenger ferry or to abseil down a skyscraper, you can't really believe it. We couldn't wait for our first mission.'

He paused, rubbing absently at his bare belly.

'He was fine, at first. Or I thought he was. He asked me, once, whether I ever had bad dreams about what we'd done, and seen, but I hadn't. I lied though, told him I had. Then he got married, had Scott. Maybe that made it worse? I don't know. He started seeing one of the psychs at work. He never told me—he never told any of us. But I started hearing rumours, you know?'

'Did you talk to him about it?'

Angus shook his head. 'No. I didn't really want to know. To believe it.' Which made him a pretty rubbish friend. 'Shortly after, he was seconded to a non-combat role. And we gradually drifted apart.'

'Why?'

'I don't know,' he said.

But that wasn't true. He just hadn't let himself think about it. So he tried again.

'I think,' he said, 'that it made me look at what I do, at what soldiers do, differently. It made me start to think that if someone as strong, as brave and as elite as Tom could be affected in that way, that maybe it might happen to me. At first, it was almost like I thought it could be contagious or something.'

He laughed without humour.

'But really, it wasn't that. I wasn't worried about it happening to me, because I know it wouldn't. It's been years now. I've been on many more missions. I've seen a hell of a lot. And I'm exactly the same. *Exactly.* I come back home, I debrief, and I carry on with my life. There's this other guy at work, now, who has just been diagnosed with PTSD. There has been at least one other I know of, too. I've read a bit about it. About guys who can't switch it off when they come home. Who patrol their home, who drive all night, who jump at every little unexpected sound. Yet I'm completely, completely fine.'

'So you think there's something wrong with you.'

'No,' he said. 'I know there are crazies in the army. People who get a kick out of death and destruction. But that's not me. For me it's a job. It's about doing what I've been trained to do: protecting my mates and achieving the mission.'

Ivy touched him again, and he realised he'd turned from her, and was staring at the bedspread.

Her fingers brushed his arm, then fell away.

'You think there is something wrong with you because you're not Tom. Because you are capable of doing your job, and also living your life.'

He rubbed at his eyes. He knew she was right; he'd had the same thoughts himself, many times.

But to agree, to voice it…

'I'm lacking something,' he said. 'I shouldn't be able to leave so easily—to walk away from my mum, my girl-friends and now from my child, and risk everything…for what? At the end of the day it's a job. A pay packet, no matter how anyone wraps it up in patriotic propaganda.'

'I think you're wrong,' Ivy said.

He faced her. She was wrong.

She'd asked why he didn't have a girlfriend at Karijini. He knew why—he didn't want a wife, a family that he'd leave again and again without issue. It wasn't fair to them.

It couldn't be normal to be like he was, to be so intrinsi-cally a soldier that nothing seemed to impact him.

Maybe he was a robot. A machine.

Ivy was looking at him with so much emotion in her eyes. She wanted to help him, he knew. But he couldn't be helped.

This was who he was.

And right now, he didn't want any help. He didn't want

words, or reassurances, or all those things that he supposed a wife or partner would offer.

But he still wanted Ivy.

So he reached for her, pulling her roughly against him.

Her eyes widened, but then her hands crept up to his shoulders.

He kissed her, and he wanted it to *just* be a kiss. A physical thing, a carnal thing.

So he wasn't gentle with her.

He held her hard against him, but she just gripped him harder back, kissing him with lips and teeth and tongue.

His hands gripped her bottom, and she wrapped her legs around his waist, rubbing herself against him.

'Angus,' she breathed against his lips.

But he didn't want that, he didn't want any more talking, any more words.

He turned, practically tossing her on the bed, then following her immediately, covering her with his body.

He kept half expecting her to push him away, to say this was too fast, too much…

But she didn't. Her hands were everywhere. Skimming the muscles of his chest. Her nails scraping far from gently down his back.

Somehow he got her singlet off over her head, and she helped him push down her underwear and throw it somewhere over his shoulders.

In between crazy, passionate kisses he tugged off his boxers. Immediately her fingers wrapped around his hardness, and he sucked in a breath, going still. Her mouth was at his shoulders, and she bit him gently.

He knew what that meant: *Don't stop.*

So he didn't. She was wet, hot, perfect.

And then he was inside her, and it was *more* perfect, more intense, more everything.

It was hard, it was fast, and all it took was Ivy moaning in his ear to push him over the edge.

He groaned, and he was gone.

For long minutes he lay collapsed partly on top of her, their heavy breathing gradually, gradually slowing.

But still, neither of them spoke.

For the second time tonight, Angus considered leaving.

But this time, because he couldn't see any point in staying.

And yet, when Ivy slid out of bed to go to the bathroom, he didn't move.

He saw the questions in her eyes when she returned. She'd expected a rapid escape as well.

But she didn't ask him to leave.

Instead, still without a word, she climbed back into bed. He reached for her, pulling her against him, her back to his chest.

And like that, they fell asleep.

CHAPTER THIRTEEN

'YOU'RE SURE YOU want to do this?' Angus asked on Saturday morning.

'One hundred per cent,' Ivy said, her attention on her feet as she pushed down the clutch.

She sat in the driver's seat of her little silver hatchback. Not relaxed, of course, but surprisingly okay.

And *very* determined.

She wasn't going to let a mistake from her past have such an impact on her present, or her child's future, any more. She *needed* to do this.

'So I put the car into gear,' she said, moving the gear stick into first, 'then I turn on the ignition…'

This was the bit that had derailed her last time, and she tensed as she twisted the key.

But…*there*. The engine came to life. Not as loud and scary as she'd imagined.

But still. It wasn't exactly reassuring, either.

'Good job,' Angus said. 'Now—'

'I've got this,' Ivy interrupted. She had to do this herself. 'I release the handbrake, but my foot is still on the brake pedal, so I'm not going anywhere.'

Why did this have to be so complicated?

'And now I just need to gently press on the accelerator, while releasing the clutch…'

Hmm. This part was most definitely easier said than done.

'All I need to do is take my foot *off* the brake pedal, and put it *on* the accelerator, and the car will move forward.

And I have heaps of space ahead of me, so I needn't worry about flying into my front fence.'

Beside her, she knew Angus was smiling.

'So yes, start to release clutch, foot *off* the brake and *on...*'

The car moved.

At about two kilometres an hour, but it had most definitely moved.

'Oh, my God, I'm actually *driving*!'

'You're driving, Ivy!'

They were approaching her front gate at a snail's pace, but the road beyond it was still far too close.

'Turn left at the gate, Ivy. There's a school car park you can practise in only a short distance away.'

Very firmly Ivy pressed on the brake, and as she forgot all about the clutch the poor little Volkswagen jerked to an inelegant halt.

She patted the leather steering wheel in apology.

'Nope,' Ivy said. 'No roads today. How about you show me how to reverse back the way I've come, and we call it a day?'

'This will be the shortest driving lesson in history,' Angus commented.

'Or the longest, if you count the twelve years it took to get to this point.'

He nodded. 'Understood. Great job, Ivy.'

She grinned at him across the centre console. 'I know,' she said. 'Thank you.'

The next day, Angus drove her to that school car park.

It wasn't exactly vast, but the stretch of bitumen still gave Ivy a relatively reassuring margin of error.

He'd even brought along a couple of traffic cones, which he set up as a mock intersection.

Slowly—too slowly, according to Angus—Ivy practised starting, and stopping, and turning, and parking.

And after a lot of encouragement, going fast enough to make it into second gear.

That was met with raucous applause from the passenger seat.

When safely stopped, Ivy glared at him.

'You're not being particularly sensitive.' She sniffed. 'This is very difficult for me.'

Angus clearly knew she was being—maybe—just the slightest bit dramatic, and laughed rather dismissively.

'There isn't a lot of use in learning how to drive if you never go fast enough to actually *get* anywhere.'

Ivy glared at him. But this time, when they did a lap of the car park, she made it into third.

That afternoon, Ivy drove Angus, very cautiously, to the café where she'd met him for coffee. It felt as if it had been for ever ago, but it had only been a few weeks.

She was doing well. Really well.

A yellow square with a big black *L* on both the front and rear windscreen of the little Volkswagen proclaimed to all around them that Ivy was a learner driver. Although the way she crept along the street made that pretty clear, anyway.

He'd kept her on side streets, not wanting to frustrate other drivers, but now, at the café, there was only one parking space left, between two of the mammoth, European-badged SUVs that were standard for this area.

When Ivy realised this, she slowed so much that the car stalled, jolting them both forward in their seats.

'Dammit!' she said, smacking the steering wheel. 'I haven't stalled all day.' She glanced at Angus. 'Maybe you should park the car this time. That looks a bit tight.'

He raised an eyebrow. 'Ivy Molyneux is backing down from a challenge?'

Her gaze narrowed. 'Of course not. It's just…' A long pause. 'Of course not,' she repeated. And then restarted the car.

Just to increase the degree of difficulty, another car had driven up behind them. Unfortunately it was impossible for the driver to pass until Ivy had parked, with a concrete median strip keeping the other car immediately behind them.

Ivy had noticed, but she said nothing, her jaw clenched in concentration. The car rolled slowly forward, the indicator ticking loudly.

'Don't cut the corner,' Angus said. 'Remember to follow a wide arc, like we practised, so you are driving into the space straight.'

She nodded tightly.

She turned, but too abruptly. 'Too close,' Angus said, 'reverse a bit and try again.'

Second attempt was closer, but still not quite right.

With a sigh, Ivy reversed yet again.

The other driver was losing patience, and revved his engine.

Ivy was tense. Her gaze kept flicking to her rear-view mirror.

'Don't worry about him,' Angus said. 'You're doing fine.'

She bit down on her lip as she tried for a third time.

'That's it,' he said. 'Now straighten up.'

And that was it. She was parked.

The impatient driver sped off behind them, wheels squealing.

Ivy calmly clicked the handbrake into place, and turned off the ignition.

'I don't think that guy realised what he just witnessed,' she said.

'Or what a momentous occasion this is.'

'Exactly,' she said, with a wide smile. 'That was awesome. Let's go have a celebratory latte.'

Ivy practically bounced out of the car.

On the footpath, she turned to face him. 'I just *drove somewhere*, and *parked*,' she breathed.

She stood on her tiptoes, brushing her lips against his.

'I think that deserves a celebratory kiss, too,' she whispered.

Because he agreed—but that didn't meet Angus's definition of a kiss—he reached for Ivy again.

But he'd barely kissed her, when they were interrupted.

'*Eeeeeuuuuwwwwwwww!* Kissing!'

They broke apart. A small boy, maybe four, stood at their feet, pointing at Angus.

'That's gross.'

Angus grinned.

'Sorry, mate, but one day—'

'Scott!'

Both Angus and the boy turned at the deep male voice.

The man, the boy's father he assumed, was shadowed by the café awning. But he was tall, and familiar.

Angus froze.

Tom?

Then the man stepped out of the shadows, crossing the short distance to retrieve his son.

He had blond hair, like his son. It wasn't Tom.

'Sorry, guys,' he said. He nodded at Scott. 'He's got some pretty strong opinions at the moment.'

Then they were gone, continuing their walk down the street.

'Angus?' Ivy asked, curiosity in her eyes.

He gave a little shake of his head, needing to refocus.

'Do you know them?'

'No,' he said, his voice cracking slightly. He cleared his throat. 'Let's get that coffee.'

But something had shifted.

After coffee, Ivy drove them cautiously home, but for the first night that week he didn't stay.

When he walked in his front door, before it had even slammed shut behind him, he had his phone in his hand, scrolling down his list of contacts.

If Ivy could work past her fear of driving, he could do this.

But he still paused before dialling the familiar number. *For heaven's sake.*

He could go to war without even a single bad dream, and he couldn't make a damn phone call?

Angrily, he stabbed at the green dial icon, and pressed the phone too firmly against his ear.

It rang.

Almost immediately, it was answered.

'Angus?'

He needed to clear his throat.

'Tom,' he said. 'I'm sorry.'

Irene Molyneux was back.

Ivy stood alone in the elevator as she travelled from the ground floor of the tower direct to her mum's offices. No mucking around today—her first order of business was to talk to her mother.

The elevator walls were mirrored, and she stared at her own reflection.

Did she look different?

She knew about the whole pregnancy glow thing, but did it happen this early?

She was seven weeks now. Seven weeks and…two days?

Her tummy looked the same, anyway. Although that would change soon, if her appetite carried on as it had been.

She smiled. On Saturday night, she'd eaten almost an entire pizza.

Angus had seemed rather impressed. Ivy had been mildly horrified.

It had been fun, though, sitting cross-legged in front of some random Saturday night movie, eating pizza out of cardboard boxes, and garlic bread from amongst infinite layers of aluminium foil.

Ivy didn't remember ever feeling so relaxed with her other boyfriends. Angus made her laugh so easily, and he was quick to laugh himself. He...

He's not my boyfriend.

She dug her nails into the palms of her hands.

And, after last night's abrupt disappearance after she'd driven them home from the café, that *he's not my boyfriend* reality had only been underlined.

The elevator dinged as it came to a stop.

This wasn't the time to be worrying about glowing, or pizza, or non-boyfriends, anyway.

The doors slid open, revealing the organised chaos of Irene's floor.

Ivy wore her favourite suit today. A charcoal-grey pencil skirt and a short fitted matching jacket.

Her hair was up, looped into a neat bun, and she wore the pearl stud earrings her mother had given her the day she started work at the family business.

She wore them to work every day, but today—as she'd pressed the backs of the earrings into place—they had felt significant.

Silly, really.

She hadn't booked a meeting, but when her mother's assistant immediately ushered her into her office it was clear Irene had been expecting her.

Of course she had.

In so many ways, they were *so* similar.

'Ivy.'

Her mum pushed back her high-backed leather chair, stood and stepped around her desk.

Good. She hadn't wanted to talk across that wide expanse of marri.

Because this *wasn't* business. Whatever her mother might think.

'Mum,' she began, ignoring her mother's gesture to take a seat. This wouldn't take long. 'I'm not going to apologise for being pregnant. I'm sincerely sorry for the inconvenience this will cause the company, but I'm not sorry I've decided to proceed with this pregnancy.'

Irene remained silent.

'All senior executive appointments at Molyneux Mining offer three months' full maternity pay, with the opportunity to take up to nine months' subsequent unpaid leave with your position held for you. I see no reason why this would not apply to me.'

Still complete, unreadable silence.

Her mother's gaze was steady, revealing nothing.

'Given the unfortunate timing,' Ivy continued, 'I'd like to take only six months' total leave. I know you only took six weeks with each of us, but I just don't think I can do that—'

Irene's gaze had dropped, and Ivy realised she'd laid her hands on her stomach.

Despite everything, Ivy's mouth curved into a smile.

She always smiled, now, when she thought of her baby.

She met her mum's gaze, trying to remember where she'd got to in her well-practised speech. But she couldn't find those words, when she realised her mother was smiling, too.

'I think that's a good idea,' Irene said. 'Six weeks wasn't long enough with any of you.'

Ivy blinked. 'Pardon me?'

'I'm comfortable maintaining my position throughout the period of your leave,' Irene said. 'Although I assume you will be returning full-time after that?'

The pointed question was almost reassuring—Irene was still very much her mother, not some strange transplanted alien.

Ivy nodded. 'Yes.'

A sharp nod. 'Good. I have heard about your plans for a nursery downstairs.' She sniffed. 'Such options weren't considered thirty years ago. I'm sure you'll find it incredibly distracting.'

Ivy opened her mouth—but was stopped with a glare.

'Although I'm sure if anyone can juggle such an arrangement, you can.'

Ivy was so stunned, that she simply mutely nodded.

'It occurred to me,' Irene said, 'on the flight home from Europe, that things have changed considerably in the past three decades. A woman in my role was unusual back then. I couldn't afford to be the mother I wanted to be, *and* the businesswoman I knew I could be.' She shrugged. 'Life is all about choices.'

And for the first time, ever, Ivy wondered if her mother questioned hers.

'Thank you,' Ivy said, because it seemed like the only appropriate thing to say.

'However,' Irene said, marching back behind her desk. She slid open a drawer on silent runners, and emerged with a thick white envelope. 'The circumstances of your pregnancy are less than ideal.'

She remained on the far side of the desk. The softness that had intermittently lightened her gaze had gone.

Right now, Irene Molyneux was all business.

'I've had our lawyers draft a contract for your...' she waved her hands in a dismissive gesture '...*boyfriend*.'

'He's not my boyfriend,' Ivy said. She wasn't interested in pretending any more.

But Irene barely blinked.

'Regardless, you're not married, or known by the public or our shareholders to be in a long-term relationship. When announced, particularly given the timing, it will be clear that this pregnancy is unplanned. Which is not what the public expects of *Ivy Molyneux*.'

Her mum made her name sound like a brand.

'However I feel it is somewhat realistic that you would keep a long-term relationship secretive. Hence I'd like our story to be that—'

'*No,*' Ivy said, as firmly as she'd ever said the word.

'Pardon me?' Irene said, her eyes narrowing.

'There will be no contract,' Ivy said. 'I'm embarrassed to say that I had exactly the same plan, myself.' She laughed dryly.

'Mr Barlow wouldn't sign?'

'He never will, no matter what we offer him,' Ivy said, 'but that's not the point.'

'Don't be ridiculous,' Irene said. 'Everyone has a price.'

Ivy actually snorted. 'Angus doesn't.'

Using his first name was a mistake.

Irene's expression became probing.

'You love him,' she said, dismissively.

'I *don't,*' Ivy said, but not quite immediately.

Love wasn't something you were allowed to consider when your relationship was based around sex and an accidental pregnancy, was it?

She squeezed her eyes shut for a long second.

'This isn't about Angus,' she said, deliberately saying his name again. 'This is about *me*. I'm not prepared to lie about this, to anyone.' She shrugged. 'I thought like you, a few weeks ago. A few days ago, even. That this was a disaster. That this could ruin my reputation. People would lose faith in me. Our stock price would crash. Our new magnesium deal would be in jeopardy. The world would end.'

It sounded ridiculous now. Yet she'd been so earnest when she'd said it all to Angus.

'I'm allowed to make a mistake, Mum,' she said. '*We're* allowed to make mistakes. Even someone like you, who never, ever does. It's not healthy to cover everything up. To pretend we're always perfect.'

'Mila said you're learning to drive,' Irene said abruptly.

'Yes,' Ivy said.

'I suppose you think I was wrong to do that.'

She meant what she'd done that night Toby had died. She didn't need to elaborate.

'I was protecting you,' Irene said. 'I knew what you were capable of. I couldn't let you destroy your future.'

'But I don't think I would've,' Ivy said. 'That night changed my life. But I never got to process it like a normal person. To deal with it. I should've learnt that I needed to trust my instincts, to be strong, to do what I knew was right. But do you know what I learnt instead? That it's not okay to make mistakes. *Ever.*'

'I've never said that,' Irene said. 'I would never tell you that.'

Ivy shook her head sadly. 'You didn't have to.'

She walked towards her mother. The room was absolutely silent now, and her heels echoed loudly on the polished wooden floor.

She reached for the large white envelope, tugging it from Irene's hands. Then turned, and dropped it into the recycling bin beside the desk.

'Mum,' she said. 'I love you. Thank you for delaying the handover of Molyneux Mining to me, and for understanding my need to take maternity leave. I love Molyneux Mining, and I'm incredibly proud that you have entrusted me with it. But I need you to also trust that it's okay that

I made a mistake and I can't fix it, or control it. That it's okay I had a one-night stand and ended up with a baby.'

At this, Irene sucked in a sharp breath.

Ivy smiled.

Irene didn't. But she did speak.

'I do trust you,' she said. 'I wouldn't be handing you the company, otherwise.' Then she reached out, grabbing Ivy's hand. 'But please be careful.' She met her gaze, and now it was her mum looking at her, not a powerful mining magnate. 'I don't know this Mr Barlow, or what type of man he is. But I do know it can be very, very difficult falling in love with the wrong man.'

'I'm not—' she began.

But Irene simply shook her head.

'I need to get back to work,' her mother said, all brisk and businesslike. 'So do you.'

'Of course,' Ivy replied.

And left.

CHAPTER FOURTEEN

THIS HAD BEEN a mistake.

Angus had an inkling as he opened his front door to let Ivy in.

And was absolutely sure by the time she stood in his kitchen and took in the two neat table settings at his dining table.

No, it was hardly white linen and candles—but it *was* a bit of an effort. Matching place mats. A jug of water. Cutlery in all the correct places.

It looked…romantic.

Which wasn't what he'd meant.

'Don't freak out,' he said, attempting to explain. 'This is supposed to be an apology for being a bit weird yesterday after we bumped into that guy and his son. Nothing more.'

Ivy's expression gave away little. 'Nothing more,' she repeated.

Great, so she understood.

Maybe.

He invited her to take a seat, anyway. She ignored the table, and slid onto one of the tall stools at the breakfast bar.

'Is that—' she asked, peering behind him and through the oven window '—*lasagne*?'

Angus shrugged. 'Possibly a bad joke,' he said. The awkwardness back at the homestead that day hadn't been all that dissimilar to right now.

But Ivy smiled. 'I like bad jokes,' she said. 'Besides, I genuinely want to try your mum's famous lasagne.'

He grinned. As Ivy relaxed, so did the tense atmosphere.

Mostly.

As they talked about favourite meals Ivy still wasn't quite *right*. She was fidgeting, for one thing.

She'd put her hands on her lap to hide that familiar twisting and untangling of her fingers, but he knew she was doing it.

Her attention was also erratic. She seemed reluctant to meet his gaze, her own flittering off in random directions.

Yes. This was stupid.

Had she even cared that he'd rushed off last night?

Maybe she'd been relieved. They'd been spending so much time together.

More time than he could remember spending with any other woman.

That realisation made him a little uncomfortable, too.

'I called Tom last night,' he said, abruptly, keen to take his thoughts in a different direction.

'Really?' Ivy smiled. 'That's brilliant. Did you talk long?'

'No,' he said. Ivy's face fell. Angus smiled. 'But that's normal. I don't think I've ever had a long conversation on the phone with a mate. I rang him, I apologised for being a useless friend and asked if he'd like to catch up for a drink. He said yes.'

'That's good,' Ivy said. 'It was pretty obvious what happened yesterday. I'm glad you did something about it.'

He wasn't sure what would happen when he saw Tom, but at least he'd tried. If it was too little, too late, then he'd just have to deal with it.

'I should've said something last night,' he said. 'Rather than rushing off.'

Ivy nodded, but then stilled that subtle movement. 'Why?' she said. She wasn't looking at him; instead she appeared to be studying the bubbling lasagne. 'It wasn't any of my business.'

Angus walked to the fridge, grabbing the salad he'd made earlier.

He walked over to the dining table, plonking the bowl down between his two neat place settings.

He knew what Ivy was doing.

Hadn't he done this himself, many, many times?

When physical intimacy had begun to merge into even a hint of more?

It was just different with Ivy, of course.

Her pregnancy had added a complexity, a depth to their relationship that wouldn't have existed, otherwise.

Wouldn't it?

No.

'I told my sisters today that we weren't really a couple,' Ivy said, twisting on the stool to face him. 'I'm not much good at subterfuge, I've decided.' She paused. 'And I hated lying to them. I spoke to my mum, too. She's approved my six-month maternity leave.'

'That's good,' he said.

Their conversation was almost formal, now. It reminded Angus of that very first coffee, which Ivy had attempted to run like a business meeting.

It remained that way when they took their seats at the table and as Angus served the lasagne; their knives and forks scraping noisily against their plates.

Ivy discussed the obstetrician she'd selected, but didn't invite him to her first appointment in a few weeks' time. She'd keep him informed, of course.

Of course.

He was relieved. This *thing* had always had an end date.

He'd known, hadn't he, that tonight was a mistake? That he'd inadvertently set up a scene that could be misinterpreted? That Ivy might think meant more?

So it was good that Ivy had come to her own conclusion. That together they could end this amicably.

If part of him was disappointed, it was because he was still just as attracted to Ivy as he'd been when he'd seen her walk down that aisle in Bali. Even tonight, dressed in jeans, a T-shirt and an oversized cardigan, she was beautiful.

Of course he'd regret that he wouldn't get to touch her again. Kiss her again.

He'd thought he'd have longer.

But not too long. Too long would just confuse an already overcomplicated situation.

'Angus?'

He blinked. Clearly Ivy had been talking to him, but he had no idea what about.

But he smiled, and she repeated her question, and their formal, just slightly uncomfortable conversation continued.

At least the lasagne was delicious.

You love him.

Her mother's words still bounced about in her brain. It had been almost twelve hours since their meeting, and yet she still couldn't shake her mother's erroneous assumption.

Telling her sisters had helped.

It was good to lay it out so brutally: we met for the first time at April's wedding. We had sex. Now we're having a baby. The End.

April had been her usual starry-eyed self: *'Are you sure there's not something between you both? You seemed so natural together. So right.'*

But Ivy had laughed, and made absolutely no mention of their…affair? Fling? Thing?

It was irrelevant, anyway. Something short term based purely on physical attraction. No more substantial than what had happened on the beach in Nusa Dua.

Except for what you've told him. What he's shared with you.

Mila had been pragmatic. *'Maybe it's good you're not*

in a relationship. At least that way you don't need to worry about what happens when you break up.'

Ivy stared at her dinner.

True to form, she'd made her way through a mammoth slice of lasagne. Remnants of white sauce and a lone champignon were all that remained on her plate.

Conversation had spluttered out, although they'd both made a good go at it.

But the atmosphere was just *wrong*. None of the ease and the fun of before.

Which made sense, of course.

When she'd walked into Angus's kitchen and seen all the effort he'd put in—and *then* the abject horror on his face when he seemed to realise what all of that could imply...

Well, it had made a decision she'd already made just that much easier.

This had to end. But now it would end, tonight.

She didn't want this, this faux intimacy, this illusion of something more.

Angus *clearly* didn't.

She offered to help him tidy up, but she knew he'd refuse. It was best she left as soon as possible.

At the open door, Ivy's hand stilled before pushing open the flyscreen.

She turned to face Angus.

He was close, very close. She needed to tilt her chin upwards to meet his gaze.

His front room was dark, and the light that spilled from the kitchen threw Angus's face into shadows.

'It was fun while it lasted,' Ivy said, then cringed. 'Oh, God, that sounded lame.'

Angus laughed, his teeth bright in the darkness.

Ivy rushed to make her exit, yanking hard on the flyscreen handle.

But Angus reached out, pressing his hand against the small of her back and turning her to face him.

How many times had he done that? Touched her there? Both firm and gentle?

He stepped even closer.

'This is probably not the done thing,' he said, 'but how do you feel about one last goodbye kiss?'

She should feel it was pointless. A stupid idea.

Instead, she stood on tiptoes, reaching for him.

His kiss was gentle. Without demand.

And still not familiar. Even now, when they'd kissed so many times, it was *still* exciting, *still* different. Still special.

Her fingers curled up into his close-cropped hair, pulling him closer, inviting him to deepen their kiss.

And he did, but she felt the shape of his smile the second before his tongue brushed against hers.

Oh, God.

He was so good at this. Maybe she was good at this too, because his hands were now firmer at her back, drawing her closer.

She smiled now as her body pressed against his. So strong, and tall, and broad.

The tone of the kiss was now far from gentle.

But it wasn't desperate, either. This might be their last kiss, but there was no need to rush.

Then he lifted her just off her feet, moving her to her left until her back was flat against the wall.

His hands slid around to sit at her waist.

His mouth broke from hers to trail along her jaw. His breath was hot against her ear.

'I know technically I said a goodbye kiss, but how would you feel about...?'

And Ivy giggled, and nodded her head, and pulled his mouth back to hers as his warm hands slid beneath her T-shirt.

There was no question this was unwise, and unnecessary—but then, couldn't the same be said for nearly everything that had happened between them?

And she just *couldn't* regret any of it. Any of it.

She knew she wouldn't regret tonight.

Soon Angus led her down the hall to his bedroom. He flicked on the light, and she was glad; she needed to see him.

She'd never been inside his house before tonight, but she barely glanced at anything but the bed.

She just wanted to get there as soon as possible. Wanted to feel Angus against her as soon as possible.

But then he was on top of her as she sank into the mattress, and that was all that mattered.

How he felt, how he made her feel.

So good.

Somehow their clothes were gone, and her fingers drew patterns on Angus's gorgeous bare skin.

She felt the need to remember this. To savour this.

Angus had slowed too. His hands traced her curves, sliding from thigh, to hip, to waist, to breast.

She'd thought before that every kiss they'd had was different.

But *this* was different again. *This* was almost reverent, as if the two of them were etching this moment in their memories.

As if it were special.

Angus kissed the hollow beneath her hip. Then her belly, working upwards.

She shivered, her hands now still on his shoulders. Enjoying this.

It wasn't *as if* this were special. *It was* special.

Or at least, it was special to her.

I love him.

Her hands gripped his shoulders as she finally admitted the truth to herself.

That truth was why she'd needed to end this tonight, why she'd decided she no longer had time for pretending and fake anything. Not because it was dangerous, and because she needed to protect herself—but because it was already too late.

She had a choice now. To push him away. To tell him this was a mistake and escape into the night.

That would've been the right choice. The smart choice. A last-gasp attempt at protecting herself. Protecting her heart.

He lifted his head, questions in his gaze.

But she didn't shove him away. Instead she slid her hands to his arms, as if she were capable of tugging him back up to her.

Although he still understood what she wanted, and slid his body upwards.

And he kissed her again. Again, and again, and it was exactly what Ivy wanted.

She wanted all of this; she wanted him here, close against her, inside her.

Afterwards, she knew she'd been right.

She wouldn't regret this. This last time together.

But she could certainly regret loving him.

Angus considered leaving a note.

Ivy was still asleep, curled on her side in his bed.

He was showered and dressed, and he'd packed yesterday before she'd arrived. He was flying out today—on a mission that he couldn't tell her about.

So yes, a note would be easier.

Instead, he sat on the bed beside her, and reached for her—shaking her shoulder gently.

It was still dark outside, and Ivy blinked as her eyes adjusted to the glow of his bedside lamp.

She stretched, reaching her hands above her head so they bumped against the headboard.

'Hey,' she said, all sleepy.

'Good morning,' he said. 'I'm off to work.'

'What time is it?'

'Early,' he said. 'Sleep some more. There's no rush to leave. I just wanted to let you know I'll be gone for a while.'

'How long?' she asked, suddenly appearing more awake.

His lips quirked. 'I can't tell you that. Or where I'm going.'

She nodded in understanding. 'Okay. But I'm not going to see you any time soon.'

He didn't quite know what to make of her expression, but he felt he needed to say something more.

'Last night was fun…' he began. Then realised what he'd said.

'Hey, that's my lame line,' she said. Then her gaze fell downwards. Her fingers tangled in the white bed sheet. 'But yes, it was fun.'

He went to stand, needing to go.

But she laid her hand on his thigh, and he went still.

'Angus—' she said. Then sighed. She lifted her gaze, meeting his head-on. 'Look,' she said, 'I know what we said. About this being the last time. I know what I said, about that stuff with Tom not being any of my business.' She paused, but her gaze didn't waver. 'But honestly, I did care. I did want to know. And last night I wanted to tell you all about what happened when I spoke to my mum yesterday. But I didn't, because I'd decided that this had to end.'

'Why?' he asked.

'Because if I didn't end it now, I was worried I'd never be able to end it.'

Angus remained silent.

'I know this isn't what we planned. I know this isn't what either of us wanted. And it's endlessly, impossibly complicated. We need to work together for another eighteen years at least, and we need to be civil. So ending it now *is* smarter. While we can walk away without hurt feelings and anger and disappointment.' For a moment, she looked down at her fingers, but only to pull them free of the fabric and lay them flat against her stomach. 'But what if I don't want to be smart? What if I'm not quite so scared of making mistakes any more?'

Not quite so scared.

But she *was* still scared. He knew what she was offering him. What she was revealing to him.

Her gaze was raw. Open. Emotional.

It was…

Overwhelming.

He didn't know what to think.

Last night he'd been so worried about her feelings that he'd made her dinner.

And that *had* been a mistake.

That was something he'd do for his partner. His wife.

That was why it had felt wrong. Because Ivy wasn't those things.

No one would ever be those things.

She was a woman who, through circumstance, he was having a baby with.

She was smart, and brilliant and beautiful—but that didn't matter.

He wasn't built for more than what they'd had.

He just wasn't wired that way.

Ivy had pulled back subtly, her body no longer leaning towards him.

'I can't,' he said, finally.

For a long while, there was silence.

'You're wrong,' Ivy said, eventually. 'You *can*. I know you think you're missing something. I know you think of yourself as some flawed, fighting machine.'

He wanted to argue, but he met her strong, determined gaze and knew he needed to let her speak.

Besides—hadn't he used the same words? To her, that one time, and to himself, many more?

'But, Angus,' she said, softly, 'you *do* care. You *do* feel. And you do those things so, so deeply.' She sighed, her lips curving into a sad smile. 'When I told you my plan, all those weeks ago, I'd been so sure you'd accept. I mean, who would pass up the chance to be an instant millionaire? But now I know exactly who can't be bought with money. The type of person who believes in honesty, and hard work, and doing things the right way, regardless of the cost.' She paused. 'A *good* man. A very good man. A man who wants to know the mother of his child, who insists on being a part of her life for the sake of his child—because he wants the very, very best for his son or daughter. A man who loves his mum, loves his friends, and—yes, I know you'll roll your eyes when I say this—loves the country he fights for.'

Her hand was still on his thigh, and she pressed her weight against him, as if to punctuate her point. 'You don't lack *anything*, Angus. You're capable of anything you want. Even love.'

It was only now Ivy's gaze wobbled, and then eventually drifted downwards.

He didn't know what to say. He hadn't expected this.

But then, he hadn't expected any of what he'd experienced with Ivy.

Her words continued to reverberate around his head, but they were too unfamiliar and too new for him to grab onto.

He'd taken far, far too long to say anything.

'I can't,' he said again. It was all he could say.

'Okay,' she said, and her hand fell away.

CHAPTER FIFTEEN

Five weeks later

APRIL WAS A *lot* more excited than Ivy was.

Her sister had grabbed a brochure from the ultrasound clinic's reception desk, and opened it up on Ivy's lap. They sat together in the waiting room, one other couple also waiting patiently in the corner.

'*See,*' she said. 'You can have your 3D scan etched into a *glass cube.*'

Ivy raised an eyebrow. 'How about we wait until we know that I have a healthy baby before we start ordering keepsakes?'

April bumped her shoulder against Ivy's. 'You'll be fine,' she said. 'I know it.'

It probably wasn't fair to think that April was more excited than Ivy was. Of course Ivy was excited. After all, today she'd get to *really* see her baby for the first time. It was just she was also nervous.

So nervous.

Silly, really. She'd visited her obstetrician only a few weeks earlier, and everything had been fine. Her baby's heartbeat was strong.

She'd tried to explain how she was feeling to her sisters, and they'd said the right things, but…

The thing was, it wasn't the same for them. It wasn't *their* baby.

Angus would understand.

Ivy tilted her head backwards until it bumped against the wall, staring up at the ceiling.

He'd emailed her a couple of times while he'd been gone, when he'd been at camp. She hadn't really expected that, although she supposed she should've. He'd never just disappeared, even when she'd wanted him to.

He'd been polite, asked how she was going, how the baby was. That was it—nothing else. Certainly no mention of their last conversation.

Despite everything, she hoped he'd be home soon.

Yes, a huge part of her cringed at what she'd said when she'd last seen him. When she'd so haphazardly laid her heart on the line.

It was *embarrassing*.

Mortifying. And a lot of other things.

But—she couldn't regret it.

She looked down at her tummy, at where the best mistake of her life was growing.

No. She had no regrets.

And so she did wish he were here. So he could tell her his latest titbit of baby development he'd gleaned from his research. So she could voice her concerns time and time again and not feel as if she were being a crazy person, because Angus would *get* it. He'd understand. He'd be all strong and reassuring and he would probably even hold her hand—just because she needed him to.

Of course even if that morning all those weeks ago had ended differently, he still wouldn't be here.

He'd warned her of the realities of his work, and she'd understood—but it was still hard.

She didn't have any right to miss him, not really. But their baby would.

She laid her hand on her stomach.

But she reckoned this baby would be pretty tough. This

would be their reality—Daddy away for weeks or months at a time. But back for long stretches, also.

And this baby would be *loved*. So loved. Angus would love this baby with all he had. He already did, Ivy was sure.

And wasn't that what mattered, really? Love?

The sonographer walked into the reception room, and called out Ivy's name.

April grinned, immediately jumping to her feet, and Ivy followed behind her.

Minutes later she lay on her back, her still-pretty-flat tummy exposed and smeared in gel.

The sonographer explained what she was doing, and directed Ivy's gaze to a screen mounted above her and to the right. 'You'll be able to see everything there.'

And then she could see everything.

A baby. An actual tiny baby with arms and legs and a fluttering, healthy heart.

Tears stung her eyes and crept their way down her cheeks.

April gripped her hand, and smiled, with tears making her own eyes glisten.

Ivy loved this baby with absolutely everything she had. With an intensity she hadn't thought possible.

Her whole life had been about her career. Every day she'd woken up to thoughts about work and gone to sleep after checking her email. Her weekends had simply interrupted her business hours—and, while she'd had some vague, future plan of maybe, maybe one day getting married, it was always to the most sensible, the most appropriate of men. Certainly not men that made her skin tingle or who took her breath away.

She used to think she was being wise in her dating choices. That she'd learnt from the mistakes of her past, and was ensuring that she'd never again fall in love as recklessly as she had with Toby. She'd believed she needed to protect herself from the loss of control that love seemed inevitably to bring.

But now, now that all these years later she'd fallen in love again, she knew how wrong she'd been.

She hadn't put up barriers to protect her career, or to retain control—not really. She'd put up barriers because Toby had been her first love—and, however misguided, losing him had *hurt*.

She hadn't wanted to feel that way again.

But despite her best efforts, here she was.

Desperately in love with a man who didn't love her.

And it hurt. So much.

She knew what she'd told Angus had been right—that he was capable of loving her.

The problem was, he didn't.

But this baby in front of her, wide awake and rolling unhelpfully for the smiling sonographer, he or she *would* love her.

And, for now, that would be enough.

The Friday he arrived home, after just over five weeks away, Angus visited Tom.

The days were getting longer now, and Tom and Angus sat on the edge of Tom's timber decking as Tom's two kids ran about the backyard in the fading sunlight.

Carise had hugged him, hard, when he'd arrived, but said barely a word.

She was clearly glad he was here, which surprised him.

Being invited here had surprised him, too.

Surely deserting your friend in his time of need nixed any future dinner invitations? It would seem not.

Although Tom was, understandably, cautious, and far from the jovial, loud man that Angus remembered. Was that the PTSD? Maybe. But Angus guessed that, tonight, it was mostly his fault.

Tom didn't know what to expect of his supposed mate who'd just so randomly dropped back into his world.

Angus didn't blame him.

For a while, they both quietly sipped their beers as they watched the kids.

'Scott is getting tall,' Angus said, just to say something.

'Yeah. Amber will be tall, too, I reckon,' Tom replied.

Then that was that.

'Mate,' Angus said, trying again. 'I'm so sorry for—'

'Yeah,' Tom said, cutting him off. 'That was pretty low.'

'I'm sorry,' he repeated, because—if nothing else—he could at least just keep saying that again and again.

His friend sighed. 'I know,' he said. 'I know it wasn't like I told you what was going on, not really, but I'd kind of hoped you'd ask. You know?'

Angus nodded. Yes, he knew.

'I was—' he began, but that wasn't right. 'I thought—' But that wasn't right either. 'I didn't understand,' he went with, eventually. 'I didn't understand at all.'

Tom smiled, squinting a little now that the sun was low, peeking between the trees along his back fence.

'You still don't understand,' he said.

'No,' he agreed. 'I'm sorry, I don't.'

Tom slanted him a pointed look. 'Stop apologising or I'll have to ask you to leave.'

And that comment was *so* much like the Tom that Angus remembered that Angus grinned, holding his glass and spare hand up in mock defence. 'Okay, you get that I'm sorry.'

Tom nodded.

'It was hard for me to tell you,' Tom said. 'Especially you. We'd been along this SAS journey together, and I'd just seriously derailed. You were still strong, and I was weak. A failure.'

'No, Tom—'

Now his friend held up his hand. 'Nah, I know. I'm not a failure for having a mental-health issue—and I have a se-

riously brilliant therapist who has helped me realise that.'
He paused. 'She's helped me with a lot of things, actually.
Reprogramming my thoughts and reactions in certain situations, that type of thing. I still have the occasional bad
dream, but mostly I'm all good.'

Angus smiled. 'I can see that.' And he could. There was
an ease to Tom that was new, and a calmness. 'But do you
ever miss it?'

The challenge of what they did. The adrenalin rush.

Tom smiled. 'I knew you'd ask. But the answer is simple:
no. I have a new career now. I've just got my builder's ticket,
and my business is going well. I choose my own hours, I get
to spend more time with my kids…it's great.' He downed
the last of his beer. 'But then, it was always different for you,
wasn't it? The regiment is more than a career for you. It's your
life. It's who you are.'

It's who you are.

But was it?

He thought of the past five weeks, and the complex international training exercise with a close Australian ally
he'd just completed. It had been tough, it had been challenging, and he'd learnt a hell of a lot.

And he'd loved it. Loved every last second of it.

So yes, the SAS was who he was. Since his father's death
it had been all that he'd wanted, and now he'd made it, it
was all he ever wanted to do.

But for the first time maybe he needed to ask a different
question. Was the regiment *all* he was? Was it *all* he wanted?

A familiar musical jingle jolted Ivy out of her lovely deep
sleep.

She blinked, staring up at her ceiling. Light streamed
in through her lounge-room window—but then, that was
to be expected in the middle of an almost summer Sunday afternoon.

Ivy swung her legs off her couch, and padded on bare feet down the hall to the intercom panel near her front door.

'Hello?'

'It's Angus.' His voice was just as delicious as she remembered. 'Are you okay?'

'Of course,' she said, surprised. 'Why wouldn't I be?'

'You didn't answer your phone,' he said. 'Can I come in for a bit?'

She pushed the button that would let him in, then unlocked and opened her front door, before heading into the kitchen.

She grabbed the CD she'd had copied for Angus at the ultrasound clinic, and checked her phone. Three missed calls from Angus while her phone had been on silent during her nap.

For some reason that made her smile.

Angus's heavy footsteps approached down the hallway.

When he stepped into the room, he seemed bigger than she'd remembered. Even taller.

He was dressed casually, a white T-shirt, dark shorts and flip-flops. It had become warm while he'd been gone, and today it really did feel like summer. Especially for Ivy, given her body's thermostat seemed permanently set about five degrees hotter than before she was pregnant.

As always, the weight of Angus's attention did all sorts of things to Ivy's tummy. She'd need to work on that reaction; it was hardly helpful.

She was dressed in the girly version of his outfit—white shorts, red singlet, no shoes. She hadn't expected any visitors today, and she knew she was all creased from her nap, but Angus *still* made her feel as if she were the most stunning woman he'd ever seen.

Maybe that was just how he looked at all women? Regardless, it wasn't helpful, either.

'Any bump yet?' he asked.

He crossed the room, but he seemed...different. He always seemed so relaxed, so confident, so comfortable—but not today.

She shook her head. 'Not yet. A few extra kilos, but I can't blame the bub for that.' Ivy held out the CD. 'Here, so your visit to make sure I'm still breathing isn't wasted. I'm not sure if you saw that photo I emailed you, but here are the rest. Personally, I think the 3D images are a little creepy.'

'Thanks,' he said. He rotated the CD case in his hands a few times. 'I didn't just come to check on you. I called because I wanted to talk to you.'

'Okay,' Ivy said. She gestured vaguely at the couch, and then her bar stools. 'Take a seat?'

He shook his head. 'No, I—' He flipped the CD case a few more times. 'Ivy,' he said. 'I want to talk to you about my dad.'

That was about the last thing she'd expected him to say, but she simply nodded.

'I told you that my dad died when I was seventeen,' Angus said. 'But I didn't tell you what happened.'

'You said it was sudden,' Ivy said, remembering.

'Yeah. Although it wasn't an accident, or an illness—he stepped in front of a train the day he realised he'd lost the family business.'

'Oh, Angus—' Ivy began, instinctively stepping towards him.

But he shook his head. 'I used to be so proud of him. He started with only one furniture shop, and ended up with thirty. He took us from a ramshackle house to a mansion. But that was the problem, in the end—he overexpanded. Took one too many risks.' Angus shrugged. 'That's what I don't get though. I *know* he could've started again. He'd had nothing before, and Mum and I didn't care about the flash house, school and car. I'm still angry at him about that.' He paused for a long time.

He took a step towards her now, but then seemed to change his mind, and remained where he was. 'Anyway—

the point of all this, and I promise there is one, is that when my dad died, I couldn't sleep.'

'That makes sense,' Ivy said, but she was completely confused.

Angus's lips curved upwards without humour. 'I'm not very good at this. Maybe we should sit down.'

He led her to her couch, and they sat, side by side—but with a good-sized polite gap between them.

'I've always been a great sleeper,' Angus said. 'But when dad died, I just couldn't. Which I'm sure is normal. It went on for months—months of tossing and turning and snatches of sleep, and it certainly didn't get any better as Mum started to get sick. Then one night, I slept, and I was back to normal. And that only happened once I'd finished school and joined the army. It was like my subconscious could finally rest again amongst the rigidity and structure the armed forces gave me.'

He leant forward, putting the CD on her coffee table with a clatter. He remained leaning forward, his elbows resting on his knees as he looked at Ivy.

'The night you told me you were pregnant, I couldn't sleep,' he said. 'That was the first time since Dad died that's happened. But then, once I got my head around the idea and even feeling good about it—everything went back to normal.'

He sat up properly now, turning slightly so he faced her.

'Until two days ago. I had an awful night's sleep on Friday. And an even worse one last night.'

Ivy had no idea where this was going. 'I'm sorry?'

His smile was subtle. 'You should be, given it's your fault.'

'I'm lost,' she said. She'd never seen Angus like this. There was an uncertainty in his gaze she was completely unfamiliar with.

'I used to think there was something wrong with me because I didn't have Tom's nightmares, or that I was some robot because I enjoy the challenge of combat. I thought because I could walk away so easily from my girlfriends to go to war, because I never missed them—and because I was never that excited to see them when I returned—that I had to be lacking something. As if when my dad died and my mum got sick that my ability to love had gone with them. I thought that all I was was my job, and that, yes—maybe I was just a fighting machine incapable of emotion.'

Had he shifted on the couch? Or maybe she had, because now their knees were almost touching.

'But I worked out that I'm not sleeping because my life has been knocked off kilter, and until I set it right again it's not going to get any better. And the reason I'm floundering so badly—both right now and when I try to get some sleep—is because of you, Ivy. Meeting you has changed everything.'

'So you want me back in your life so you can get some sleep?' she asked, only half joking.

'No, I want you back in my life because I love you.'

And Ivy was so stunned she said absolutely nothing at all.

'I've realised I was wrong. It isn't that I'm not capable of emotion, or of falling in love—I just wasn't prepared to take that risk. And before you, I certainly hadn't met someone where that risk even seemed an option. I know how devastating it is to lose the people you love, and for the past fifteen or so years it's been a hell of a lot easier just to distance myself from all of that. If I don't love someone, it's easy when I'm deployed. It's easy to walk away.' He caught her gaze. 'You were right the other night, you know, but I wasn't ready to hear it. I had too many years of believing what I'd been telling myself, that I couldn't comprehend anything different.'

They'd both moved closer now, their knees bumping together.

'I used to think...*love* was dangerous,' Ivy said. The word was still hard to say, even if the echoes of Angus's declaration still rang in her ears. 'I thought love would cause me to lose control. To make poor decisions. To lose myself.' Her lips quirked. 'And, well—I was right about the control bit. I'm not quite myself when I'm with you, and that scared me. But the thing is, I've realised I'm *not* nineteen any more. I'm an adult, and my own person, and I'm not about to get swept up in silly delusions and daydreams. And yes—maybe it doesn't hurt if I lose control, now and again. You've even helped me learn that it's okay if I make mistakes.'

Angus reached out to still the hands that she barely realised she was twisting and untwisting together. He held them between his, his touch warm and reassuring—but, even now, shooting shivers along her skin.

'You're amazing, Ivy Molyneux,' he said. 'Amazing, and strong, and smart, and beautiful. I made the worst mistake of my life that morning, but I hope like hell I'm not too late to fix it now.'

Ivy looked down at their hands. At first she'd kept her hands still, but slowly she shifted her fingers, until their hands were linked together.

She leant closer, then lifted her gaze until it tangled with his.

'I love you,' she whispered against his mouth. 'You and our baby weren't part of any of my plans, but you've turned everything upside down in the most wonderful, perfect way. I guess that's how love is supposed to work? Without any plans.'

'Yeah,' Angus agreed, his breath warm against her skin. 'No plans. But lots of risks and probably more mistakes along the way. Are you okay with that?'

Ivy nodded as she smiled. 'Oh, yes,' she said.

She closed the infinitesimal gap between their mouths with a soft kiss.

'We all make mistakes, Angus,' she said, 'but I know I'm not making one now.'

EPILOGUE

IT WAS A beautiful day for a wedding.

Once again, an aisle stretched before Ivy. Once again, guests twisted on their white wooden chairs to look in her direction.

But today, it wasn't beach sand that she walked upon.

Instead, her path was a dusty red, her destination the dappled shade of a boab tree.

It was late October in the Pilbara, the sun warm—but not harsh—against her skin. Ivy walked to the gentle sounds of an acoustic guitar duo, the only sound amongst the surrounding silent landscape of Bullah Bullah Downs.

Until Nate began to cry.

Instantly, every guest's attention shifted to the pram that Irene Molyneux pushed back and forth, just to the left of the rest of the bridal party. Ivy's sisters, in their emerald-green dresses, abandoned their posts beside the swollen trunk of the Boab to coo somewhat helpfully—but it was Angus, in tailored shorts and an untucked white shirt, that immediately took action.

By the time Ivy stood beside him, her son was cradled against Angus's shoulder, and his cries had quietened to a half-hearted whine before spluttering out to a contented sigh. Angus smiled at Ivy, then kissed Nate's dark head.

Irene gestured to take Nate back, but Ivy shook her head.

Nate was happiest in his dad's arms, anyway.

A moment later Mila, April and Tom were all back in place, and Ivy, Angus and Nate stood before the celebrant.

A year ago, in Nusa Dua, Ivy never would've imagined any of this. A son, a soon-to-be-husband, a wedding.

Her whole life had been her career, her entire focus on Molyneux Mining.

But now—everything had changed.

Her career was still important, but it could wait a few more months.

Since Nate's birth, life had been a blur—but a different type of blur from before. Rather than meetings and emails and negotiations it was all about feeding, and nappies and—if she was lucky—sleep.

She couldn't say she loved every aspect of motherhood so far—especially not those three a.m. feeds—but she definitely, definitely loved Nate.

'You okay?' Angus asked, softly, as the celebrant introduced herself to the guests.

He was so handsome in the dappled light. His hazel eyes were gorgeous, and even now they made her heart leap whenever he looked in her direction. And he was a wonderful father. He'd been home for Nate's birth, and then gone for eight weeks. It had been hard, for both of them, but now he was back for a few months and was making every moment with his son count.

Yes, she definitely, definitely loved Angus, too.

Ivy nodded.

'No step counting?'

Ivy shook her head, surprised at the question. 'No, not in months.'

Angus's gaze had knocked Ivy off her axis all those months ago, but her world had realigned now. Different, but better than she ever could've imagined.

'I did,' Angus whispered.

'Really?'

'I counted your steps,' he said, with a smile. 'As you walked down that aisle.'

'Why? Do I make you nervous?' she teased.

'No,' he said. 'I was counting backwards, counting down until you become my wife.'

'That's very romantic,' Ivy said, with a smile. Angus's gaze traced every line of her face, as if she were the most beautiful thing he'd ever seen. She'd never felt more loved. More happy.

He shrugged. 'Seemed the time for it.'

Ivy laughed. 'But—how did you know what number to start counting at?'

'Would you believe I had special SAS training?'

'I'd believe you got it totally wrong and ran out of numbers too early.'

Angus grinned as their son burrowed tighter against his shoulder. 'If I did, it was only because Nate distracted me.'

He leant closer, to whisper against her ear. 'I love you.'

'I love you too.'

Together, smiling, they finally turned towards the celebrant, and the ceremony began.

And as the words washed over Ivy she wasn't worried about counting her steps, or work, or what anyone thought—or expected—of Ivy Molyneux.

As she stood here beneath the Pilbara sun, surrounded by the people she loved, all that mattered was *this* moment, *this* man, and this amazing baby they'd made together.

She'd wasted so much time terrified she'd made the worst mistake of her life that night in Nusa Dua.

But instead she'd got everything—absolutely everything—spectacularly right.

* * * * *

LET'S TALK
Romance

For exclusive extracts, competitions
and special offers, find us online:

f   facebook.com/millsandboon

🐦 @MillsandBoon

📷 @MillsandBoonUK

Get in touch on 01413 063232

For all the latest titles coming soon, visit
millsandboon.co.uk/nextmonth